THE
FLY

'Lasciate ogni
speranza voi
ch'entrate

THE
FLY

Richard Chopping

FARRAR, STRAUS & GIROUX
NEW YORK

Characters in order of Appearance

THE FLY

JENNIFER, aged eleven ⎫
LESLIE, aged eight ⎬ children of Mrs. Macklin,
BRENDA, aged two ⎭ caretaker at the Office

WENDY, aged fourteen, a friend of Jennifer's

MISS BETTY LYNCH ⎫ sisters, stenographers employed
MISS GLADYS LYNCH ⎭ at the Office

MR. GENDER, an Office executive

MISS JEACOCK, another Office executive

DR. BOOKER, Head of the Office staff

HIS ASSISTANT

O'FLATTERY, the Irishman, a clerk in the Office

MRS. DYMARK, a charwoman

MR. NALE, the proprietor of a Pet Shop

MRS. MACKLIN, a widow, caretaker at the Office

MISS SEAL, an Office executive

THE POSTAGE CLERK

ARTHUR, Mrs. Macklin's handyman

EDNA, a prostitute

ROY, a homosexual

DETECTIVE INSPECTOR LITOVER

1

THE PERPETUAL silent witness of the events in this un-pleasant narrative is a common house fly.

A fly with nacreous glistening body, mobile on three pairs of sharply black legs, airborne on veined transparent wings, armed with a vicious soft proboscis and vigilant with two intent revolving eyes. These many faceted globes observe everything; what unknown power of comprehension does this malevolent intruder possess? Its exits and entrances reveal an uncanny sense of timing, giving its dirty presence a significance far exceeding its size. For it is the servant of the Eumenides, those never sleeping witnesses who watch over us from the cradle to the grave; it is there, missing nothing, constantly punctuating the action. The spy sent to creep here and there, to fly round about, to go to and fro; collecting information it reports back to its mistresses, returning again refreshed with new vestiges of their power, to poison the blood-stream of our characters, to soil the atmosphere around them, to befoul their deeds. It is the miniature personification of evil, neat, fast, deadly; the flaw in the jewel, the stone in the shoe, the ever-present irritant; indeed, the very fly in the ointment.

Paradoxically, it makes itself simultaneously both the conductor and the conducted, the notes of music and the tune; it adds another dimension to the flat printed page becoming as it were the ticker-tape of the story.

To begin with it is a hungry fly searching for an appetising meal. It is a fly which has recently awakened on a warm,

7

light-aired morning and now buzzes fitfully over the gutter outside the Office building.

The gutter is puddled with the drizzle of the previous night. The puddles are speckled with dust and islanded with dead leaves. In one of them, breaking the surface scum, lies a used condom. The rolled rubber rim lies below the water, the milky teat-end rests on the edge of the curb, flattened where it was flung. The fly settles upon it. Performing its reconnaissance dance, impotently it extends and retracts its proboscis upon the resistant teat. Unable to perforate the rubber, it swivels, altering its position. As if to gain strength for a renewed attack it goes through the complexities of its toilet. First the front pair of legs lace and interlace in furious mimicry of human hands being washed, then the second pair are threaded back and forth across the front pair. Finally, with weight tilted forward, the back pair are drawn up and scraped against its wing brushes. Refreshed, it once more attacks its lifeless quarry.

Close by, in an urban garden, grows a rare shrub which carries a faultless offering of white flowers. They exude a heavy scent which penetrates the nostrils of those who approach the Office. One of these flowers hangs near the puddle spilling, from the white cup of its petals, a drift of curiously shaped anthers into the dirty water beneath.

The fly has been poised upon this elegant whiteness in order to gain height for the next sortie upon its breakfast; its tiny weight is enough to dislodge one of the waxy petals which swings slowly down to lie beside the condom below.

Two children, a boy and a girl, approach. The girl is wheeling an object in a push-chair. She disturbs the acrobatics of the fly by lifting the condom out of the gutter on the genteel end of a twig. The petal settles more securely into the water. The child holds the twig close to her face, regarding the sheath artfully; as she does so she deliberately crushes the petal with her toe. She knows what this

8

rubber object is, but is going to pretend to her companion that she does not. With slanting eyes, she peers at her brother.

"'Ere, Leslie, look at this."

Leslie who is several years her junior, drags himself away from a beetle which he has been tormenting quietly in a corner by the telephone box and scampers towards her.

"Wot! Wot cher got?" he shouts excitedly, recognising in his sister's voice a note of commanding importance.

"Yer needn't shout," she snaps testily, looking from side to side while brandishing her trophy.

"Look," she continues teasingly, thrusting it nearer his goggling eyes, "can't 'cher see? Look!"

"Wot is it then?" says Leslie in awed tones, for by a furtive gesture of his sister's he knows it to be something secret between the two of them. Another of his sister Jennifer's secrets.

"Don't cher know?" she whispers derisively, "garn yer, baby; 'e don't know."

"Yes I do," says Leslie, furious at unwittingly showing his ignorance. "Yes I do; it's a balloon, give us it."

Instantly, he snatches it with his fingers from the twig and starts to convey it to his mouth, intent upon inflating it. But Jennifer is too quick for him. Horrified by her brother's sudden action, forgetting all secrecy and her previous plan to tease, she screams out a warning.

"Aouw, put it down, put it down, don't blow it, something dirty's been in there." Already regretting her volte-face, she cracks his fingers spitefully with her little stick, venting her anger at having spoilt her own game by this sub-conscious remnant of prudery. But his sister's panic action has inflamed Leslie's curiosity. He starts to cavort round her whining in a shrill sing-song voice calculated to attract the attention of every passer-by, for he has realised by Jennifer's confusion that he, in his turn, now has the

9

upper hand; he sings:

"Wot is it, wot is it? Tell me, tell me!"

However, fundamentally Jennifer is already a woman with nerves of reinforced concrete. She has conceived a better plan.

"Shut up, kid," she says with sly scorn. "I don't know wot it is. 'Ere comes a man, let's 'arst 'im." Leslie, completely taken aback by his sister's quixotic mood, hardly has time to assume a pallid look of injured naïveté before the stranger is upon them. He is a tall old-young man with thinning hair and a melancholy expression. He trails behind him a dejected looking boxer bitch puppy, which drags on the lead, sniffing persistently to right and left.

Leslie and Jennifer, at the sight of the puppy, forget their question about the condom and both let out a prolonged high-pitched noise, which is intended to convey that they are attracted by the smallness of the animal, its youth, and apparent defencelessness. But such a shrill nasal wail terrifies the dog, which shoots forward between its master's legs, showing the whites of its blood-shot eyes. The man smiles, taken in by the assumed innocence of these two small human animals. From his expression he obviously feels that they have an unexplainable affinity with his pet, because of the compatibility of their extreme youth. He has no sooner gone smiling benevolently on his way than Leslie, in an ear splitting undertone, squeals out his comment on the dog.

"I think it's more like a pig," shattering with one blow the man's harmless sentimental picture of the kinship of young animals. He hesitates, half turning, indecisive whether or not he should go back but continues with his walk; the puppy drags behind, looking over its shoulder at Leslie and Jennifer who are once more engrossed in the problem of the condom, already having forgotten the dog.

Again they have driven away the fly which had renewed

the attack upon its objective, while their attention was taken up elsewhere.

"You never 'arst 'im, twit," says Jennifer, who knows she is as much to blame as Leslie, but to defend herself gets her thrust in first.

During the preceding pantomime Jennifer has ignored completely the push-chair which she drags behind her. This unwelcome appendage contains a living effigy of a human infant. Half lying, half sitting it gazes fixedly out at the world through still eyes, squinting and protuberant. It has been so battered into obedience by Jennifer that it knows better than to utter a sound. Its bloated appearance and its immobility are further accentuated by the lower half of its body being encased in faded blue woollen rompers, bulbously overstuffed with nappies. Its arms stick out straight in front of it as if they were articulated together on a wire through the upper part of its doll's body. The hands are swollen, mottled blue and scarlet from bad circulation. Its head is concealed in, and its face framed by, a soiled white pixie cap. From this push-chair there arises a soursweet odour of stale urine and old milk. This object is called Brenda—Leslie and Jennifer's baby sister.

Neglected and forgotten, supine, she exists, for the moment staring without any show of feeling, into the sky. A piercing shriek suddenly brings the two elder children back to their charge. The fly, disturbed from its earlier quarry, has settled upon the waxen occupant of the push-chair, thus galvanising it into life. Brenda's nose is now its airfield, and it does not zoom off until Jennifer swipes at her sister's face with one of her gloves. She continues to shriek. The flick with the glove has upset her, far more than her foraging assailant at whom it was aimed. Her yells are tempestuous.

To calm her, Jennifer dangles her twig with its appendage before her purpling face. She stops as suddenly as she had begun. Choking gulps wobble the peak of the pixie cap, convulsive tremors shake the whole unsightly bundle. Tears squeeze out of the eyes and return as quickly to the system by way of dirty runnels down the cheeks into the gasping mouth. The hands move together, jerkily, as the twig with its pendant sheath is titillated before her.

Jennifer is pleased with her handiwork and by means of it continues to quieten her sister. Leslie watches overtly, wondering what the curious thing really is. Brenda's eyes are empty now of tears and are very bright. Beneath her jellied appearance, but swamped by her sister's overbearing disposition, Brenda has still a spark of determination. She has resolved to catch this pendulous bait. Her arms thrash up and down, her hands clasp and unclasp, but Jennifer outwits her. Suddenly she has whisked the twig well out of reach, for Leslie has again started to shout, "Wot is it? Wot is it?" and it infuriates her. Poor Brenda has been foiled. With a final slap, to finish off her quietening process, Jennifer has retreated a step or two from the push chair. Temporarily, at a loss for what to do next, she makes faces at Leslie. But her indecision is soon at an end; indecision is not one of Jennifer's failings.

A figure in loose garments, with scarecrow hair, mounted precariously on the curving bar of a woman's bicycle, has stopped beside them. This is Wendy, Jennifer's friend. Wendy is what is called backward, or as the women in the fish queue say behind their hands as she rides past, "she's got all her buttons but some of them haven't been shanked." As far as Jennifer is concerned she is ideal as a friend. Usually tractable and fearless she is very useful to Jennifer. Her round pasty cheeks move continually up and down, revealing four square rabbit teeth. She is amiable and gentle but her appearance is against her. She regards the now silent trio intently. She peers into the push-chair.

"Shit 'em," she says confidentially. Wendy's conversa-

12

tion is limited and not often explicable. Leslie and Jennifer prefer to ignore her for the moment in unspoken conspiracy. Brenda seems to brighten.

Jennifer runs off brandishing her twig with Leslie in pursuit. His cry of "Wot is it? wot is it?" trails off into the distance; Jennifer taking advantage of Wendy's presence thinks to distract him by exercise.

"Shit 'em," says Wendy vaguely and starts to rock the push-chair aimlessly with one hand, while she supports the towering bicycle with the other. Her knees knock together with the effort and her already flat feet, in their plastic sandals, spread themselves on the pavement to brace herself against the double weight. Brenda sleeps.

From the opposite direction to that taken by Leslie and Jennifer come the various members of the Office staff on their way to work. Fresh from their breakfasts, adorned with early morning smiles. Detached still, for a few moments longer, from the cares of their day's toil; refreshed, it is hoped, by a night of relaxation.

First come the Misses Lynch. Two of them. They are always first. As always, they are engrossed in animated conversation. It is extraordinary how they find so much to say to one another for they are scarcely ever apart. They live together, work together, sleep together, even visit the ladies' lavatory together. They are no longer girls and it would seem after so many years of sodality that a contempt might have sprung up between them. There are those of their colleagues who claim that it has and that the reason for their clutching one another, in an opossum's hug of sisterhood, is lest one should trap a husband, leaving the remaining sister in a vacuum of profound loneliness. Be that as it may, here they come to work, chattering parakeet trivialities, intent on nothing but themselves.

Jennifer has espied them and is doubling back on her tracks, her twig aloft, its flag bravely fluttering in the

13

breeze. Brenda still sleeps. Wendy mumbles uncomplainingly to herself, shifting the weight of herself and the bicycle first to one foot, then to the other.

The fly, nestling among Wendy's greasy hair, breakfasts unmolested from her insensitive scalp. Wendy turns towards Brenda, who has done nothing more than breathe heavily, and in malignant tones yells:

"I shall smack you . . . now then . . . devil."

At which Brenda lets out an apprehensive squeal. Whereupon Wendy, true to her threat, gives her a resounding smack, making her shrieks worse instead of better.

Meanwhile, Jennifer brandishing her trophy has come level with the Lynch sisters, turns about and gangling along beside, keeps pace with them. Until at last they are forced to pay attention to this wild waving figure forgetting for a moment the fascinating, all-enthralling subject of themselves.

"Betty, what on earth has that child got?"

"What child, Gladys?"

"Why, dear, Jennifer Macklin. Look!"

"My dear, whatever is it? She's waving something at us on a stick."

Jennifer is still hopping beside them, one foot in the gutter, one on the pavement, a grimacing gargoyle.

"What is it? What is it?" she starts to chant, swishing the stick before Betty Lynch's face.

"I can't see, dear. You are wobbling it so much, keep it still."

"Looks like an old balloon to me," said Gladys, "but it's the wrong colour."

Whereupon Jennifer stops hopping and approaches nearer with her stick, swooshing it to a standstill three inches from their faces, her own face smooth with innocence.

"Get away, you horrid fly," said Gladys flapping a

14

petulant hand.

"What's that knot in it?" says Betty.

"Can't be a balloon, whoever would tie a knot at that end of a balloon?" says Gladys.

Both stare uncomprehendingly at it, their plucked eyebrows arched questioningly. Jennifer regards them in doubt; do they *really* not know what it is, or are they dissembling? Are they just being grown-ups trying to pretend to her, or are they truly more innocent than she?

"Where did you get it, Jennifer dear?" says Betty at last. But Jennifer has espied another arrival and finding that she is not making the impression she expects, darts off to try her tricks on the unsuspecting person of Mr. Gender, who is advancing towards the Office with springing strides.

The Misses Lynch turn away shaking their heads, unaware of the elemental scene in which they have just participated. Their interest, such as it is, soon flags, for they are deep in their egocentric confidences before they have taken ten steps towards the Office doorway.

Mr. Gender draws nearer. He has a boil among the short grey hairs of his neck and a hole in one shoe, through which he can feel every pebble. But this morning he rises above such things. With head held high he snuffs at the city air and behind his thick glasses his eyes peer with pleasure at the sparrows balancing on the fruit of the plane trees.

Each morning as he approaches his work he knows this moment of elation. For each morning he knows there lies before him afresh the unique joy of once more encountering Miss Jeacock.

In the last months Miss Jeacock has become to him the still-centre, the goal, the reason. Miss Jeacock the fair, Miss Jeacock the noble, Miss Jeacock the woman of his choice. Alas, how curiously short-sighted he has become since falling in love. For in reality his adored is Miss

15

Jeacock the plain, Miss Jeacock the petty, Miss Jeacock the huntress. What a wealth of detail in his beloved he fails to see. For him she exists solely as a paragon. Other people might see her, as she herself must do when she looks into the looking glass, but the mote of love is in his eyes. Both her physical image and the reflection of her personality have become refracted and disturbed. Both would have been unrecognisable to a third person, had they the ability to see through two pairs of eyes and think with tandem brains. That miracle, which to creatures well favoured by nature is so difficult to appreciate, happened several weeks previously. Mr. Gender, a plain middle-aged man, fell hook, line and sinker in love with Miss Jeacock, a plain, not even very pleasant, middle-aged woman.

In the morning, he sees her in the dawn light when he awakes; he sees her in the faces of all the women in the street going to work; he sees her in the landscape walking towards him, breaking into a run with arms outstretched to meet him; he sees her in the evening, sitting quietly sewing on the other side of his fire-place. Above all he feels her beside him in bed at night when he tries to sleep. He dreams about her when once he achieves this recalcitrant state. In fact he is obsessed.

So far, unfortunately, the miracle has only operated in one direction; his adoration is not returned. Miss Jeacock's feelings towards Mr. Gender are to him one big mark of interrogation; however clear they may be to herself. But at all events this morning he walks with confidence, despite his boil and the hole in his shoe. He approaches work pleased with himself that he has at last found a love-object; unconcerned by doubt or troublesome introspective imps. For a brief spell he is a happy extrovert striding along towards his morning duties.

How long is this to last?

A grinning goblin stands motionless in front of him, her

16

legs wide apart, her hands behind her back, her face smeared with breakfast stains. Jennifer retreats backwards before him.

"Well, Jennifer, and how are we this morning? Isn't it our birthday?" Mr. Gender has a card index memory for this sort of useless fact and remembers dates of this kind, however trivial they are personally to him.

Beaming with pleasure he seeks also to bestow pleasure by giving this unresponsive child his good wishes. But birthdays in the Macklin household are irregularly celebrated according to the mood of the Mother. Except for having the "Predictions" read out over their hurried breakfast, no celebration has so far taken place or even been planned.

Jennifer rudely ignores Mr. Gender's question and makes no answer, merely treats him to a wider, even toothier, grin.

"And how's Leslie this morning then?" he goes on, determined that the vision of these unsavoury children shall not mar his optimistic mood. Not gifted with knowing the right approach to children, usually he makes no attempt to communicate, but this morning he feels different.

Leslie gives him a look which would have withered anyone with more perception, and makes a noise of the utmost vulgarity by blowing through his mouth with his tongue protruding. Mr. Gender appears not to notice and continues to beam at Jennifer, whose face is now splitting in two like an over-ripe melon. Stealthily she draws nearer.

"Little sweets, aren't they?" drools on Mr. Gender, still looking up at the birds. Jennifer is within spitting distance and does so unobtrusively, while at the same time suddenly drawing forth her twig with its noxious emblem. Flourishing it before Mr. Gender she whirls round and round like a teetotum, screeching "Wot is it, wot is it?"

17

A blush of such disillusion sweeps down Mr. Gender's face, as if a roller blind has been drawn to shut out a previously welcoming light. Looking from Jennifer's purple face of triumph to Leslie's guilt-ridden cheesy countenance, he stammers as the fly zig-zags wildly in the air between them:

"Really I . . . perhaps . . . may be . . . I don't . . .," retreating rapidly from these two dervishes who gloat over his embarrassment. They have shattered the delicate tracery of his mood. They have deceived him in a way which has added one more brick to the wall of his misanthropy, a wall which is already too high.

Backwards he reaches the Office doors, red with embarrassed disappointment. Tears sting the ducts of his eyes, unshed. His last glimpse of the two children, before he enters the no-man's-land of the Office, is as they turn away emboldened from their last victory, ready for their next victim.

With his passion for detail Mr. Gender has also observed in the short time he saw the long limp object, that it has a knot tied in it. Like the sand in the oyster which causes the pearl's formation, a horrid question has been introduced into his mind to devastate the order therein, dispelling all idyllic thoughts of Miss Jeacock.

"Why the knot, why the knot?" the question recurs again and again. Was it some primitive desire to protect the spilled seed? Was it hygiene, simply? He did not know. Probably would never know. The query with fly-like persistence returns to haunt him throughout the day.

Wendy has ignored the capers of her friends and is performing a complicated ritual dance with Brenda and the push-chair. Brenda appears to enjoy it. Wendy, with vacant eyes and tongue lolling, pushes the chair in front of her stepping forwards for three paces with the left foot, then the same with the right. She turns and repeats the

18

measure, introducing Brenda to a novel sea-sick motion which will surely make her puke.

Leslie has now spied Miss Jeacock who is walking slowly and flatly towards the Office.

"'Ere, look Jennifer, 'ere comes Miss Jeacock, try 'er."

Delighted, Jennifer swoops down upon her new prey. Miss Jeacock sees her coming. At all times disliking children, she feels this morning an ill-concealed hatred of them, particularly these two and more especially the puppet figures of Wendy and Brenda, whom she can see oscillating in the distance.

"Damn the little beasts," she mutters between closed teeth, and quickens her pace.

"Morning Miss Jeacock, nice morning Miss Jeacock," pipe Leslie and Jennifer in affected polite unison, for they too have no liking for the florid Miss Jeacock.

"Morning," Miss Jeacock manages to squeeze out reluctantly.

"We want to know something, please Miss Jeacock," continues Jennifer with exaggerated mock politeness.

"Yes please, Miss Jeacock," says Leslie, catching on to his sister's game.

"Can you tell us, please, what this is?"

"What?" snaps Miss Jeacock as they produce nothing.

"This 'ere," says Jennifer, dramatically revealing from behind her back the horrid object once more, this time not on the stick but between her finger and thumb.

Miss Jeacock's complexion takes on the hue of rich tawny port. She is beside herself. The fly dances ecstatically from Jennifer to Leslie, back and forth, back and forth.

"Ugh!" she explodes with disgust and raises her umbrella as if to ward off an evil spirit. But Leslie and Jennifer are too quick for her and flee in laughing rout towards Wendy and Brenda, who are still going through their idiotic ballet practice.

19

Miss Jeacock stumps off towards the Office, mottled with anger and indignation.

Dr. Booker, the Head of the Office, and his Assistant are the next victims to approach. Learned gentlemen both, they proceed in step with measured tread, heads bowed down with their sense of responsibility and importance. Leslie and Jennifer dance round them, yelling their obscene question, displaying their prize once more on its twig. But neither gentleman has a moment for such unimportant vermin as children; their thoughts and time appear to be taken up entirely with considerations of the day's work. They pass by, oblivious of the saturnalian revel which is going on around them. Somewhat damped by being so completely ignored the two children return to Wendy and Brenda by the telephone box, accompanied by the fly.

Brenda has begun to howl. Jennifer recognises the danger signals. Wrenching her from the push-chair she fumbles with the bundles of underclothing, finally denuding a pair of scarlet-shrimp hindquarters, which she "holds out" professionally in the dank dead-leaf corner made by the Office wall and the telephone box, where now stands Wendy's skeleton bicycle. The yellow pool quickly spreads across the pavement; entranced Leslie rummages up his trouser leg. Standing on tip-toe, one leg bent, both legs bowed, he adds to its size.

The fly settles at its edge, testing it hesitantly, then instantly flies through a broken pane to the mouth piece of the telephone, to repeat its maniac toilette. Wendy once more in charge of the now somnolent rebundled Brenda, propels the push-chair to and fro in the lake, admiring the double track of wheel marks which she is forming into a meaningless pattern. She pursues this occupation with profound concentration as Leslie and Jennifer slip off to meet the Irishman, O'Flattery, whom they see hurrying towards them.

O'Flattery, the youngest member of the Office staff, comes to work smiling and wishing that he had the day off. His youthful half-formed face is as bland as a corn-flour blancmange, his eyes as dark as two prunes set in it. This morning his demeanour has the vacuity of utterly childlike inexperience set upon the shoulders of a grown man. He carries rather gingerly a brown paper carrier-bag. He is nearly six-foot tall and not entirely ill-favoured.

Actually his thoughts are not far removed from the subject concerned with the dread object of Jennifer's inquisition. Sex troubles him, for it is, as yet, for him an untilled field but by no means a barren one. Jennifer and Leslie catch up with him, but in their mad rush they have no time to ask their lewd question. As they reveal the twig and its burden the face of O'Flattery is already crinkled with smiles. Peals of conspiratorial laughter ripple from him as he disappears from the children's vision into the Office building.

Leslie and Jennifer look at each other in amazement. The Irishman has both spoilt and fulfilled their game. It no longer has any point. Ignoring the other members of the Office staff who arrive late and hurrying, they give up their interrogation. Jennifer flicks her twig viciously so that the condom hurtles into the lower branches of the nearest plane tree, where caught it will hang suspended as an obscene reminder of its purpose, until the weather perishes the rubber and the wind dislodges it, to fall once more back into its native gutter.

Jennifer smooths back the hair under her headgear, with an ageless gesture inherited from her whole line of female ancestors; runs a forefinger round the elastic of her knicker leg adjusting their fit to suit her fancy; then with whispered imprecations, the meaning of which are known only to herself, she performs a strange dance with the ends of her

21

fingers round the cavern of her silent mouth. Leslie watches admiringly. Brenda is asleep. Wendy has scooted off on her overgrown bicycle about some nameless mission. With a yell of 'Come on Les, maike 'aiste," Jennifer grabs the push-chair and with a howl of frightened surprise from Brenda, the two children drag her backwards from the Office doorway in search of new worlds to violate.

Their uncontrolled laughter and Brenda's cries fade away into the distance. The fly leaves the telephone's vulcanite mouth and flies back to its original quarry. Once more it settles, swivels, performs its reconnaissance dance. But the efficient rubber wall still withstands its onslaughts. Defeated, it flies towards the Office building following the late comers through its doorway, leaving the condom swinging gently in the breeze, the marvel and the mystery of the busy sparrows.

2

MR. GENDER had received a shock. He stood by the green baize letter board studying the brass-headed nails at its edge. His chubby irresolute face bore the expression of a doubtful infant. His drawn-down lower lip and his indecisive chin indicated a soured procrastinator. When he moved he revealed the flat stumbling gait of a man pledged to appeasement. Compromise and militance waged a continual war beneath his grey exterior. He had a meticulous grasp of detail, he was more thorough than most of the Office staff, but he was not a success there. Why?

His weak eyes and half finished gestures betrayed his entire lack of confident action outside the discipline imposed by his customary office routine. Like many another ant-hill worker he bore the instantly discernible stamp of the matriarchy. Although a bachelor, without the ever-present demands of a flesh and blood wife, his slavery to the gentler sex was as complete as that of the hen-pecked husband. To 'woman' he was already enslaved by his adoration of Miss Jeacock. Indeed the cloven hoof of womanhood had marked him down early in life; as the conscientious only son of an early widowed mother, he had scarcely had the chance, nor the spirit, to begin to assert himself. In adolescence he was already a grey man in embryo. Now on this particular morning he was an excessively grey adult.

His letters on the board were uninteresting. As he turned them over unopened, questioning from whom they came by the writing or the post-mark, Miss Jeacock burst through the swing doors. Her turkey-red face glared at him without recognition as she stormed past him, looking as if she considered everyone, and particularly he, was in conspiracy with the two unmentionable children. Bewilderment added to his greyness and disappointment at not receiving the customary half-smile of salutation, which Miss Jeacock usually succeeded in squeezing out for him.

Miss Jeacock was closely followed by Dr. Booker and his Assistant, still earnestly engaged in conversation as they drew off their outer coats and hung up their hats. They disappeared down different corridors without a smile of greeting to him, or a word of recognition.

Mr. Gender was a lonely man. He found it difficult to commit himself so far as to make lasting relationships with other human beings. He wanted to correct this flaw in his character but found it excruciatingly difficult. This small piece of self-knowledge only added to his loneliness. He did not make intimate friends among his colleagues, he was perfectly civil to everyone with whom he worked but he did not get near anybody. The possibility of declaring his love for Miss Jeacock seemed therefore terribly remote. He could not believe that she could even take it seriously. It was with thoughts such as these that he had entered the Office. He felt very much alone. The solitude of unhappiness weighed upon him.

He was about to follow Dr. Booker to his office on some pretext or other, when the laughing face of O'Flattery thrust itself through the door. Borne down by his loneliness and his inability to communicate with his fellows, Mr. Gender was amazed to perceive O'Flattery smiling and even giving him a knowing wink, inclined towards the ample back view of Miss Jeacock, who still stood by the letter-board. In some curious way he realised, with a creeping horror, that a hideous bond had been forged between

24

these three. He and Miss Jeacock and the Irishman were all in it together, what it was he was not quite sure but it was as if the Irishman's wink had been as eloquent as the loud crash of a hammer upon an anvil. Whether these three liked it or not, the Macklin children's droll pantomime had drawn them together into one envelope, upon which the seal of complicity had been placed by O'Flattery's conspiratorial wink. O'Flattery's young laughter followed Mr. Gender as he fled towards his day's work, his mind anywhere but upon the problems presented by his office tasks.

Once in the sanctuary of his own room he felt less disorientated. A vase of violets, bought from a stall the day before, stood beside his arid papers. Their oasis of sweetness caught at his senses; their mourning purples stood out brightly against crisp green leaves and the white of his official papers. They gave him, if momentarily, an island of grace to which he could cling, enabling him to tread water before recommencing his swim against the current of his emotions. The fly, which had made its way into Mr. Gender's room, avoided the aura of the flowers, as if they had been specifically placed there as an antidote to the plague.

He began his work by dictating letters to the eaglet face of Miss Gladys Lynch, until he was quite hoarse. Dismissing her with an off-hand smile he drifted over to the window. Unseen from this vantage point he watched two youths, on brightly painted bicycles, tantalising two half-grown girls, who had taken refuge in the telephone box. The whole quartet munched bubble gum aimlessly. The boys had lank brilliantined hair and the sleeves of their jackets were too short. They had an uneasy air of self-assurance in their half-tasted manhood. One of them was as tall and graceful as the other was short. He had a Greek god's rare purity of features but they were overlaid

25

by an awkward brutality; he sat sideways on his saddle staring at the swelling musculation of his own thighs, his right leg swinging indolently, his left supporting the weight of himself and the bicycle. The other boy, sitting astride the crossbar, had a sickly unhealthy face, peppered with pimples round his over-red lips; he was circling on the pivot of one leg, scooting his bicycle round and round with the other. The movement of the leg and the bicycle suggested other more complex rhythms, a general sexual latency which seemed to inspire the actions of the whole group.

One girl was short and square, the other tall and uncouth; unlike the boys neither of them was good-looking. Both had early-budding breasts. They shrieked and giggled at the boys from the safety of the telephone box. Their every action was over emphasised, their voices over loud as if to cover up their lack of confidence. The short one, who was obviously wearing a coat of her mother's, was more strident than the other. More forward too, for she ventured out of her refuge, shouting something and looking from side to side under her hair. She stood within touching distance of the two boys, from time to time blowing a monstrous bubble of gum from between her lips. She stood first on one leg and then on the other, bumping her haunches provocatively against the framework of the telephone box.

As he observed these wretched adolescents, already stale and bored by their existence, he noticed Wendy in the distance speeding down upon the group, hair flying, clothes flapping, maniacally scooting her bicycle along as fast as she could go. He saw her stop within hailing distance and then stand, like a wide-eyed calf outside the herd, gently watching with great moon eyes and open drooling mouth. His window was shut, so that he was unable to hear what was said. None of the four by the telephone box acknowledged Wendy. It was not until Mr. Gender saw O'Flattery with his carrier bag unexpectedly appear from the Office doorway and walk towards the group, that he opened this glass barricade and strained forward in order to overhear anything spoken, which might or might not concern him.

O'Flattery advanced, ignoring the gum-chewing ephebes, vaguely waving one hand in the direction of Wendy who was quite oblivious of his approach. It was only when he stood right in front of her, and the gum-chewers had stopped their provocative display and had also turned towards the Irishman, that she moved her attention from them to him, concentrating instantly on the carrier-bag. What did he want? thought Mr. Gender, leaning as far out of the window as he could without being seen as a listener.

Wendy was bobbing her head up and down like a wooden monkey on a stick getting more and more excited as O'Flattery talked to her while showing her what he had in the carrier-bag. The chewers became bored and sidled off; the girls first, pursued in an off-hand manner by the boys who kept stopping and fiddling with their bicycles, trying to give the impression that they were not being drawn by the bait of the budding girls.

When they had gone, taking the racket of their ribaldry with them, everything was quieter and Mr. Gender could then hear some of what O'Flattery was saying to Wendy. It became apparent from a word here and a phrase there that O'Flattery had also remembered it was Jennifer's birthday, that he had brought her a present; it was just the kind of silly thing he would do, reflected Mr. Gender, annoyed with himself for not thinking of doing so too; and whatever the present was, he had characteristically forgotten to give it to Jennifer when he arrived for work; no doubt all such thoughts having been expelled from his mind by Jennifer's grotesque charade. He was now, Mr.

27

Gender gathered, enlisting Wendy's help in the handing over of whatever the carrier-bag contained. Wendy now stood transfixed, her arms enfolding the brown bag as if it was a rare cruse of myrrh, while O'Flattery walked back to the Office, grinning and waving his hand to Wendy as he went.

As he watched her, Mr. Gender caught himself going back to a childhood habit, he was feeding himself with the pickings from his nose with the eager rapacity of a hungry fanatic. Hastily he checked himself as the fly settled on the smudgy lenses of his spectacles. Behind the thick glass, pale blue irides swam in hard-boiled egg white. The eyelashes were going grey, so were the eyebrows. A piece of cotton was bound tightly round the bridge of his horn-rimmed spectacles to conceal and strengthen an old crack. It was very greasy. A long finger with a dirty, blunt, but well-shaped nail came up to drive the intruder away. Audaciously, before retreating, the fly crawled to the full extent of the nail, to where it was bitten to the quick. Having escaped, it was able to continue its survey of Mr. Gender from the shade of the electric light bulb.

It saw damp thinning strands of hair, carefully trained across a putty-coloured skull; oiled fronds of seaweed across a dead fish's belly. Ears close to the head, shoulders somewhat round, elbows rather shiny, feet a shade too flat. It made a dart at the left eyebrow, swivelled and was once more repulsed. It swooped twice spirally past Mr. Gender's spectacles and heroically settled again, this time on the back of his neck, among the short hairs where nestled, already, the boil. Mr. Gender flicked and stung his own boil with muttered annoyance at his clumsiness. Deflected from its purpose, the fly temporarily gave up and went to the wooden acorn on the bottom of the blind cord, where it demonstrated a complicated aeronautic circus.

Mr. Gender returned to his work. He sorted out papers

for a full half hour, until his eye caught the name of a Mr. Nott, which appeared several times over in a certain lengthy correspondence. Nott . . . Knott . . . Knot. His mind had clicked back to the earlier events of the morning; the knot, what did it mean? Why was it so disturbing? Such a curious thing to notice. Was it hygiene? Or a primitive fear of spilling the seed? Both questions returned to plague him. Why tie a knot? Why tie a knot? As the thought rolled to and fro in his head like the brass marble in a penny-in-the-slot machine, he found he was watching the gyrations of the fly round the blind cord, moving his head in time with the swoops back and forth which it made. Annoyed with himself and the fly he rose and once more went to the window, driving the intruder back to the electric light bulb, with an impatient gesture.

From the window he could see that Leslie and Jennifer had reappeared carrying Brenda, no push-chair this time. They had put her down on a seat and were treating her with the roughness meted out to a favourite doll. Brenda grasped an ice-cream cornet with both fists, her face plastered from eyes to chin with melted ice-cream, as if she had just withdrawn it from a huge pot of ointment. Jennifer was carrying on a high-pitched tirade against her. Mr. Gender could catch the general trend of it, recognising words and phrases lifted from Mrs. Macklin's vocabulary.

"Look at 'cher, what a bloody mess y'erve got 'cher self into. Come 'ere. (Smack) you wait till I get you 'ome. (Another smack). I'll show yer; now then!"

Then he saw Jennifer snatch the cornet away from her sister and heard Brenda's wail of tragedy. Tempting her with it by holding it within arms' reach and then suddenly withdrawing it, Jennifer ridiculed Brenda with the fast liquefying sweet, slapping her now and again as if the child was doing something naughty in trying to snatch what remained of her own ice-cream. All the time Brenda

29

whined and Jennifer jeered up and down the scale, in her high-pitched nasal gibe. Leslie looked on delighted, occasionally prodding Brenda or giving her a surreptitious smack between those of his sister. The thin sound of the child's crying and the strident buzz of the fly joined one another in a neuralgic pin point of strain at the base of Mr. Gender's skull. He stared up into the sky as if to soar thither to escape the realities of life. Like the washed-out blue uniform of a housemaid, the sky was covered with a soiled torn apron of cloud, through the rents of which the blue showed clear and patchy. The clouds fleeced open and shut, torn by the breeze and scattered into alternate white and muddy patterns.

Tiring of tormenting their baby sister they were delighted when with shrill cries of "Shit 'em, shit 'em," Wendy came rushing at them on her bicycle with the Irishman's carrier-bag carefully hooked over the handle-bars. Unhooking it with exaggerated gentleness she flung her bicycle away and with wild gesticulations buried her nose in the bag, jabbering in a tornado of excitement. Leslie and Jennifer bent their heads with hers and all three began giggling and gobbling like geese round bran-mash.

What were they up to now? How very trivial but how annoying not to know.

Life seemed, in that moment, so utterly pointless. The sadistic children marred the beauty of the natural scene without, and the framework of the Office discipline cramped any spontaneous happiness within. The fly added its provoking music to twang on his already overstrung nerves. The electric clock clacked round with loud insistent tread. The morning dribbled away while throughout the labyrinth of the Office, routine labours were performed with practiced clockwork skill.

Over and over again Mr. Gender found his brain returning to the knot in the condom. Why tie a knot?

30

"The Knot in the Sheath." It sounded to him like the title of some clever modern novel. One of those titles which all the way through seems to have nothing to do with the subject of the book, then at the end turns out to refer to some complicated personal tick in the author's mind, obscure to the reader.

What was in that carrier bag? What was it that O'Flattery had given those terrible children? What ever could it have been? He was seriously troubled, too, by the look of collusion he thought he had read on the Irishman's laughing countenance. He had been hurt by the red hostility of Miss Jeacock's stare and was convinced that, together, they made up the incompatible pieces of a jig-saw puzzle, which none of them had the power to put together. The puzzle's leaden pieces would be moved and solved by some outside influence, the Eumenides no doubt, who would hammer them relentlessly home to fit, come what may. Square pegs in round holes notwithstanding. He did not pay much attention, as a rule, to omens and inexplicable psychic phenomena, but this one was so stubborn that it forced itself to the forefront of his mind, time and time again. As fast as he fought back the conflagration of his misgivings, they burst out afresh to scorch him more painfully than before.

Miss Jeacock could surely not have thought that *he* had suggested the dreadful game to the Macklin children? Perhaps she had considered that he should have been able to reprimand them into stopping their pranks, and not run away in embarrassment leaving them to widen their sordid field of activity. Perhaps too, the Irishman, who must have realised that both he and Miss Jeacock had run the Macklin gauntlet, thought that it was an intentional plot on his part to excite Miss Jeacock's imagination. Perhaps the children had said some suggestive thing which implicated him in their game. He couldn't know without asking them,

31

which he would never do for fear of carrying the drama a stage further and being accused by Mrs. Macklin of corrupting the children. He certainly couldn't ask Miss Jeacock. He shrank, even, from the thought of the brotherhood which must afterwards exist between him and O'Flattery, should he be forced to question his colleague. Yet did it not already exist; for had he not read it in the laughing Irishman's eyes? Why the knot? Why the knot? There it went again. He had enough to bother him already with the complexities of the human relationships flowering beneath the Office roof, without the return of that trifling question.

He could both see and hear a commotion among the lower branches of the plane tree by the Office doorway. Straining his eyes, he could just make out the elongated shape of the noxious object which was the cause of all his tribulation, mocking in its flaccid emptiness. At least, he thought, it had somehow got out of reach of the children. If not out of sight, nor out of mind, they could hardly continue their game with it now.

Although, he reflected, nothing was impossible; for they might start the old joke of staring upwards at a non-existent aeroplane, to attract a group of the staff as they left for lunch and thus exploit a more potent mass effect. He wouldn't put anything past them. But why, why, why did this stupid thing return to bother him, as the pea beneath the mattresses of the over-sensitive princess. He had not the strength to dismiss it nor the elusive key to its explanation. His powers of reasoning, and his reserves of self-control, had been weakened by the debilitating obsession over Miss Jeacock which he nurtured.

"Buzz," went the fly, higher and higher, louder and louder until he welcomed from time to time the interruptions of his colleagues as they looked in to consult him on casual matters. With none of them did he feel at ease or able to exchange any conversation to relieve the tedium of

32

his own fixated thoughts.

Suddenly Miss Jeacock put her head round the door and was about to say something, when the resonant voice of Dr. Booker summoning her to his aid caused her to withdraw her head as unexpectedly as it had appeared; leaving behind her an equivocal impression, puzzling and disconcerting to Mr. Gender who was not expecting to see her, anyhow until the eleven o'clock tea break. She too, he thought, had that air of conspiracy, which Mr. Gender had noticed like a veil over the features of the Irishman.

He felt more disturbed than ever. The commotion of his feelings was once more encouraged to break out and disorganise his already failing powers of concentration. It was therefore with the profoundest relief that he saw the hands of the electric clock do a jerky leap to numbers eleven and twelve, startling the fly from the clock face and shattering the whole peace of the building, as the clamour of its electric bell called the office termites to their tea.

3

O'FLATTERY, THE Irishman, was a young man who remained as yet undeveloped. He still retained the simple sincerity of adolescence combined with a cynicism which was unusual for one of his age. Whereas he was intensely thoughtful, too often he was over introspective; this led him to periods of depression and what appeared to outsiders to be boredom. But more often, in fact, it was not boredom he felt but dissatisfaction with himself and his surroundings, frustration at his inability to escape from them. Sensitive and highly strung, with only a small reserve of strength, he wore himself out with trying to concentrate on the ordinary routine of life, when by nature he was a dreamer who did not take kindly to office rules and regulations.

He showed sometimes uncommon shafts of clear adult intelligence; but these were counterbalanced by his often childishly playful behaviour at the most inappropriate times. At school he had shown a certain talent for literary composition, but his imagination always far outran his skill.

Being of an affectionate, sociable nature he naturally formed attachments for other boys but these failed to satisfy him, and inevitably he turned to older and more sophisticated people from whom he hoped to learn the solution to some of the mysteries of life which tormented him rather more than his contemporaries.

Born of middle-class parents, in Ireland, he received the

education fitting to the son of people in his parents' position, at a Catholic seminary on the outskirts of Dublin. Here at the hands of the Jesuit fathers he had imbibed all the bigotry of the provincial Catholic mind; but his own latent intelligence tempered it with a tolerance and a desire to understand other people's points of view. This made him into an unsettled individual, rather than one with an ordered outlook firmly based on convention and tradition.

His education and family background had produced somewhat of a paradox. His will was ground away by the friction of two millstones: conformity and an urgent desire to rebel. At the same time he was very aware that his imperfect reasoning power kept him in a weak state of emotional indecision, making it difficult for him to achieve more than second rate accomplishments. In fact his ambition pushed him on, but a natural indolence and sensuality pulled him back.

He still had the gawky unmanageable movements of a young colt, both mentally and physically. When excited, his brogue became very pronounced, but at other times it was merely a soft burr in the background of his speech. His eagerness gave away his age and inexperience.

The restrictions of his education had produced in him a disproportionate interest in sex. His practical knowledge on the subject being limited, his fantasies were correspondingly exaggerated. His appetite was thus unrelieved. He had known neither man nor woman, but indulged all too frequently in the unsatisfactory pleasures of his right hand.

His lack of sexual experience was not due to any insufficiency of desire, but rather to his inborn fear of carnal matters which had been nurtured in him by his upbringing. Within him continual war was waged between concupiscence and guilt, the former being more frequently the victor. He was prey to the most persistent fantasies; but as yet none of these had so far exteriorized themselves

35

to become a reality. He was now at a stage in his life when the very force of the changing turmoil within him was so strong that of necessity something must happen to him. Something, almost certainly of a violent nature; something to push him over the threshold, to launch him at last towards manhood and away from the childhood memories which held him back.

In matters of the heart he was as trusting as a baby; for he loved without reason and quite indiscriminately. The liaisons he had formed at school had been disastrous, for inevitably his physical partiality interfered with his feelings of platonic friendship, only adding in his mind to his already heavy load of natural sin.

Without knowing why, and indeed without much cause, he was vain about his personal appearance. His deeply expressive brown eyes were in fact his only really outstanding feature. These gave his face the look of an unprotected hare, which had given rise to his school nick-name of "the milk-white leveret".

Since leaving school he had led a lonely life, withdrawn from contact with other people because of his shyness, and except for his colleagues at the Office, he had no friends close enough for any kind of intimacy to develop. He had romantic dreams about stalwart friends and stimulating sexual partners, but never got beyond thinking and planning how these could be achieved.

On the morning of the condom incident he had nearly been late in arriving at the Office, for he had lain too long admiring himself in his bath. Recumbent, he had looked along his shining wet limbs, considering that they were perhaps not so bad after all. His legs were a bit thin but his hips he found satisfactory, slender and rounded like a young girl's. Nevertheless, elsewhere he was unmistakably male and proud of it. If only he could hold in his stomach with its delicate feathering of hair, he felt that his figure

36

would not be unattractive. But his normal posture was lazy and relaxed so that his bent shoulders gave him an enervated appearance. His flesh glowed white and silvery under the harsh electric light of the bathroom as he lay idly rippling the surface of the bathwater; he watched the hair between his legs floating and was reminded of sea-weed gently moving in the current made by the tide above half submerged sea creatures. The film of soap, stretched across the surface of the soft water, made a ring of dirt round the edge of the bath and with his slow underwater movements he made it caress his sides with velvet scum.

He was thinking about love as he lay luxuriating in the arms of the hot water. The more passionate aspects of his fancy aroused his senses, spoiling the purity of his marine landscape.

A fly swung, like the tip of a conductor's baton, round and round the electric light bulb. He lay lifting his chest out of the water, until it dried in the warm air and then gradually sank back into the warmth of the bath's embrace; watching his dry flesh being consumed by the water, until all that was left was a little island of pink in the middle of his chest, the size of a half crown, all round which the water was held back by the skin of its surface tension. With a sigh of contentment he sank further under, contemplating this last island being flooded over, admiring again the twin black roses of his pubic hair.

He held the hard tablet of soap in his hands, soaping his limbs, dreamily thinking of Miss Jeacock. Lately, he had become increasingly sure that she was in love with him. He was also sure that Mr. Gender loved her, but that she did not love him in return. The situation both amused and alarmed him. Because of the duality of his nature, he was at a loss as to how to conduct himself towards Miss Jeacock. In his way he was fond of Mr. Gender, but he was fascinated to learn about love, even at the red hands of

37

Miss Jeacock. As the tide sweeps up the beach covering and uncovering the sand, so his decisions fluctuated between action and inaction. Slowly he rubbed his slender hands together, then in the middle of his reverie he lost the soap in the clouded depths of the bath. He was losing himself in a delicious, all pervading ecstasy; the warmth of the bath both exaggerating and encouraging it.

But he was getting too hot and his good sense told him that the minutes were ticking away, that his breakfast egg would be congealed, that he would be late for work. With a last admiring glance at his prostrate body he raised himself feebly from the bath, relinquishing his dreams as the water poured in rivulets down him. He stood on the brown checkered linoleum, trying to dry himself on a damp towel, without stepping into the puddles left by the other lodgers. As the water gurgled away, the transparent soap was left, eroded by its long immersion, in a nest of bubbles and loose hairs over the plug hole. Sleepily, in need of fresh air, he climbed onto a wooden chair by the window and laboriously lowered the sash an inch or two. The bathroom window was close up against the neighbouring fence; someone had ripped off two pieces of wood from this black tarred barrier. Through this hole was revealed a dismal glimpse of the blind empty house next door. Dead, rotten wood flaking into shreds hung round the hole festooned with cobwebs. The cold air enveloped his neck and shoulders like a throttling scarf, chilling the warm damp in his armpits and finally awakening him to the day's reality.

As he stood there he saw Mrs. Dymark, his landlady's charwoman, skuttle out to the dustbin; wiping her face on her apron she hurled a shovelful of ashes from her and was darting back when she caught sight of the Irishman milkily pink against the steamy window.

38

"Oh, Mr. O'Flattery, you did give me a turn, whatever are you thinking of?" she shrieked. "You'll catch your death you will, straight up." Scarcely had he time to dry his legs than she was up the stairs and hammering on the bathroom door.

"Mr. O'Flattery, are you in there still? Buck up do yer'heg's 'ad it," she admonished, rattling off down the passage with her dustpan and bucket.

When he returned to his room, wrapped in his dressing gown and clutching his sodden towel, he found the attentive Mrs. Dymark making his bed. Without looking up she launched herself into a conversation as if they had only recently been interrupted and was continuing from where she had left off.

"I don't know what we are going to do about our Betty. She's the one what's got this child with the water on its brain. Poor little mite, it's fourteen months and it can't only just wave its 'and. It's been under the same specialist as my neighbour; 'ad this operation to take the water away, but we think it's 'ead's gettin' bigger agin. She 'as one every year, there's another on the way now. It ain't as if there was an 'usband. I wouldn't mind so much if there was."

O'Flattery had been standing shyly by, doing nothing as she talked. Without looking up or hesitating she went on:

"Do 'urry Mr. O. you'll be late. Don't mind me, I'm a Mother, I shan't look." Whereupon she put the finishing touches to the bed and dived beneath it with her dustpan and brush. Muffled now with her lips close together so as not to get blanket fluff in her mouth, she gabbled on. The Irishman, ill at ease despite her promise, got himself behind his wardrobe door and the open door of the room so that in conditions of great discomfort, but comparative privacy, he contrived to huddle on his clothes. He couldn't attend

39

to what Mrs. Dymark was saying until suddenly he was astonished to hear her say:

"No one will get a penny out of me, not even if they give me £10 and the banner!" Which statement she delivered with great vehemence as he came out of his hidey-hole, at the same time as she came out from under the bed.

Hurriedly fixing his tie he flew down the stairs two at a time, to the dining room, closely followed by Mrs. Dymark, who seemed determined to chivvy him. He gobbled his cold egg while Mrs. Dymark poured him his tea, tepid, from a pot in the shape of a thatched cottage. As he drank it he looked up and said to his willing attendant:

"Mrs. Dymark, if you had to give a little girl a birthday present what would you give her?"

"Ow old?"

"Eleven today."

"Oh, a tortoise," said Mrs. Dymark without a moment's hesitation, as if it was the most obvious present for a girl of that age.

"Whenever I see one I feel so sorry for 'em, they look so sad," she went on with a far away look, as she began clattering the breakfast things together.

The Irishman looked at her, nonplussed by the alacrity of her reply, and saw as he had not done before that she closely resembled a tortoise herself. Her movements were of course faster but she had their strangely forlorn look and a curiously wide beak of a mouth dominating her dusty yellowish face. He was so struck by this coincidence that he decided to take her advice and with hurried thanks set off for the Office.

His way to the bus took him beside the river. The path followed a built up causeway between the actual river and an artificial lake, which had been constructed between grass banks to keep the flood water from the low-lying housing estates beyond. On the opposite bank were shipyards, noisy with the resonance of riveting. The river made a curve here, forming shallow mud banks which at low-water lay like the backs of a pair of scrofulous whales, upon which the river spewed up the sordid flotsam from up and down stream.

The bric-à-brac of an urban river does not present a pretty picture. A living bed of ochre-coloured reeds hid the aquatic graves of many animal corpses. Unwillingly, the Irishman had one morning begun a visual inventory of these unburied remains, and now found himself checking over his morbid list. Caught among some low growing thorn bushes was the long drowned cadaver of a dog. Its legs were drawn up as if it had died in the act of jumping. It lay thus, grotesque in suspended motion.

A fly now hovered over its swollen parchment belly, which had become as tight as a drum; one gaping sightless eye gazed skywards. Its decayed lips were washed away leaving its fangs bared in an endless ghastly snarl. But most macabre was its collar still fastened round the wasted neck; man's prisoner even in death.

Seeing this melancholy dog sent O'Flattery's mood rocketing towards depression. Each day he tried not to look and each day his eye was drawn to that of the dog as his gorge rose and his mouth filled with saliva. Daily he hoped that the tide would have carried it away but it stayed in the same position for weeks, left where the highest tide had stranded it.

This morning as he passed this canine harbinger of death the reeds about it were rippled by the wind. The sun played upon their light feathery tops fluttering ragged banners in the gentle air, their lance-sharp leaves changed and interchanged from deep yellow to dark green, flickering back and forth through all the kaleidoscopic subtleties of changing light and movement. His mood altered with them, as fickle and changeable as the elements.

As he walked, he trod mechanically on the halves of walnut shells which for some reason here littered the path. Their explosive cracks beneath the ball of each foot sent a flock of ill-assorted gulls and jackdaws flapping from the spattered grass which covered the causeway. Lazily they swept into the air, mingling and intermingling like black and white notes of music; caught up in a current of wind they were composed and transcribed into aerial chords of harmony and discord. Suddenly the mineral blue dart of a kingfisher shot out of some overhanging bushes and was gone again, so quickly that he thought he must have imagined so exotic a bird. Any lift given to his feeling by these quick shafts of beauty was as speedily shattered by the sight of more dead animals which lay for the last time in this watery morgue.

A cat sprawled, red-smeared with diesel oil; further on, a crow upon its back, hard black legs clutching at a perch in the empty air. A welter of sodden straw and chips of wood, broken bottles, condoms in every stage of disintegration, large seeds from handsome river plants all lay scummed together along the river's verge. An unsightly garland of putrid red cabbage leaves, dark purple and decaying, brussels sprout stalks still sporting small sprouts, these ringed the roots of what living vegetation there was upon the tide mark. Blue-mouldy oranges and squashed tomatoes fringed the artificial lake side. Upon the path there had been thrown up an old mattress, ruptured and torn to pieces by dogs or children, so that its sooty flock scarred the short grass speckled with stumpy thistle plants. These had no stalks, but were simply green rosettes of prickly leaves caught up with gossamer and spangled with sparkling drops of moisture, transforming them into shining crystal stars among the grimey entrails of the mattress.

The latest casualty was the nakedly blue carcase of a chicken, its tea-cosy feathers lay stripped off complete like a garment, a foot or so away. Then beneath the Irishman's foot, making him recoil suddenly, was the fresh-eyed red-wattled, dismembered head of this accusing fowl.

He left the path by the river at a point where it joined the main road, with the metronome of his feelings swinging towards gaiety. Caught by the thorns of some wild rose bushes were the festive souvenirs of passing revellers; rags of crêpe paper decorations streamed in a brave magenta flow.

Close by, near to where he caught his bus, there stood in the summer a large clump of a mysterious wild flower which always delighted him, swinging him finally away from the objects of death, the gauntlet of which he ran each morning, towards something more beautiful though transitory. The flowers were bright tiger orange with fulvous spots and were shaped like antique oriental helmets. They balanced on translucent pink stalks which looked brittle and as if when broken they would exude a clear stream of sap. Their long oval leaves were slightly toothed, now rich dark green, now presenting silvery undersides to the gusts of wind which shook them. The whole clump rattled its tall stalks together, while ripe seed pods, pointed like rockets, exploded, shooting their seeds in confusion, to spread the crop further from the parent plants.

At the bus stop there was the usual long queue of people so that O'Flattery had to wait, watching two buses pass. As he waited he amused himself by observing the other human beings who passed backwards and forwards before him on the limited stage within his field of vision. One of them was particularly arresting, an old woman, accompanied by her dog, both of whom moved painfully past him, unaware of his eyes upon them. The dog was very vulpine, yet at the same time so mild that it was difficult to imagine it ever living up to its fierce appearance. Its unnaturally thin legs supported a shapeless body, tousled

43

with steel-fuzz hair which gave it a sinister unkempt look. It had the vicious mien of a wild animal which, bored by captivity, practised in secret curious anthropomorphic vices. It sidled on its small feet as if they were blistered, moving at one time the hind and fore leg of the left side, then the hind and fore leg of the right side, so that its body with each step went through an ungainly undulation. Its coat was grizzled black and grey, its ears pricked up and its long thin muzzle pointed now this way, now that way, towards its mistress, away from her, and back again. Beads of gummy liquid coursed from its damson eyes down the length of its stained old muzzle. Its feathery tail, like a frond of grey bracken, wagged to and fro to counterbalance its curious undulating walk. Its mistress, drawn along behind by its lead, bore a look of expressionless stupefaction. She was the human personification of her dog and together they made the most singular pair. She wore a high crowned black hat cloven in the middle, which gave it the appearance of two ears. Her sharp yellow face was drawn forward, all nose and cut-away mouth. Her hair was worn in tarnished plaits coiled into earphones over her ears. Her lean body was encased in a shabby, dusty black garment, half coat, half cassock. Her stick legs were thrust into a pair of the longest most broken down black shoes ever seen outside an old clothes shop. These two edged along the pavement among the hurrying crowd, haltingly; the old woman very bad on her feet, the old dog walking on tender pads. O'Flattery thought that if he shut his eyes they would be gone when he opened them; disappeared perhaps in a puff of sulphur. He did so; but when he opened them again they were still there, though a few steps further up the street. He watched them intently as they threaded through the crowd until the bus came and he was able to board it. He scrutinized them as the bus drew level and swung past, then still transfixed he turned to gaze back until they were lost from view.

He fell then to thinking, first about his work; then bored by this about his own body as it sat within his clothes; of Miss Jeacock, Mr. Gender, the dead dog on the river bank, the live dog with the old woman, and the knotted condoms caught among the twigs of the flotsam and jetsam. His ruminations were not deep and his attention was soon taken by the conversation of two women who were sitting behind him. From their voices he judged them both to be young. He would not allow himself the luxury of looking round, but simply indulged in the anonymous amusement given him by these two speakers.

"Them was nice lodgin's, them was. You could do as you liked there."

"Don't you believe it."

"What duck?"

"You don't understand, I wasn't keen on staying there. That woman upstairs. Coo!"

"What 'appened to 'er dog?"

"I dunno, it always 'ad sore ears or suthink."

"Ought to 'a been done away wiv long ago."

"Ye-es, fair made me sick it did."

"Round's the Bakers, look. I used to go wiv 'im. So did Alice."

"Did you, dear?"

"Ye-es. I 'ad 'im."

Here there followed a break in their conversation, possibly, O'Flattery thought, a break of disapproval on the part of one of the speakers, but he was not sure. He looked out of the bus and saw a small baker's shop, its windows crammed with bread and vividly artificial cakes. A fly, temporarily trapped, explored delicately the edges of the bus window which bounded his vision. Three women with their arms akimbo and their loaves hanging in string bags, stood talking in front of the shop window, too far away to be audible. They all dipped their heads simultaneously, laughed and raised them together again. The Irishman remembered the articulated chickens of a wooden toy which he had treasured as a child . . . A circle of birds was made to pick up imaginary corn, by the swinging rotation of a weight which hung from their necks, through a hole in the platform on which they stood.

The disapproving woman behind him could not keep from talking and had started again.

"That's where 'er Mother live."

"Do she dear?"

"'Ad all 'er 'ome burnt down yer know."

"Did she reely? Shame."

The one who had been disapproved of was being a little frigid and refused to play conversational ball. The other one persisted and started on what was evidently some well-tried gambit.

"Fancy talkin' about a woman like that, with all them kids too."

"Oh, 'e tells me everythink. They've only been friendly again this last fortnight, she sent 'im a postcard to meet 'er or suthink."

She was beginning to thaw out her friend again, so continued speaking very fast and confidentially.

"I shan't go to the pictures tomorrow, Blondie, see. I shall go to the 'ospital to see me sister's boy, see. Little kid 'e is. In the 'ospital, see, with a bad leg, see."

The friend, at last completely thawed by the mention of hospitals and a child in pain, began speaking afresh, with all her previous warmth, in that mawkish tone reserved for kittens and children on glossy birthday cards.

"What, not that little kid?"

"Ye-es, 'es got footballer's knee, strained they say."

"Aouwoo, what a shime."

Here the conductor came along collecting fares and

46

several people got up to push their way off. But when O'Flattery could hear them talking again it was in low voices as if great secrets were under discussion.

"I wouldn't of believed it till I'd seen it with me own eyes."

"Yer do know, don't 'cher?"

"Ye-es!!"

"In 'is cigarette case."

"Because of 'er?"

"'E's got another fortnight 'asn't 'e?"

"Ye-es!"

"'E's done what, nearly six month?"

"Ye-es!"

"What'd 'e do 'xactly?"

"I dunno. We reckon 'e was put up to it. Oh 'is Mother, she's a cow."

"Went with you the night before didn't 'e?"

"Ye-es."

"Oh they're nice. 'E altered the door. Now 'e'll open it anytime of the night."

With these apparently unconnected sentences both women rose and left the bus without the Irishman ever seeing what they were like. He fell once more to thinking about the river and its bed of reeds, the flowers with their untouched grace despite the used and drying sheathes at their feet. It was with his head full of pictures like these that he left the bus and walked towards the Office through a street of small shops. One of these was a pet shop, in the window of which a great blue and gold macaw was ensnared upon a perch where it constantly broke its tail feathers in an incessant attempt to manoeuvre in so confined a space; a pen of tortoises stood beneath it in chelonian squalor, heaped up one upon another, littered with pieces of wilted greenstuff and black seeds from their neighbour above. As he saw them he remembered again

47

his breakfast conversation with Mrs. Dymark and the reason for it; consulting his watch and finding that he still had a little time he entered the shop. As he did so the bell above the door made the loudest ping he had ever heard a bell of that description make, very high-pitched and painful to the ear. At the same time a bead curtain at the back of the shop writhed and wriggled as if a person had gone through it where no person existed. This he soon realised was because a door at the back of the premises was open and a strong draught had blown through as he entered. Through this open door he could hear the pro-prietor speaking to some kind of animal in a harsh pene-trating voice to the accompaniment of yelps, whines and rattling chains. The shop around him was bright and clean, smelling of disinfectant with fresh sawdust on the floor; 'everything for the doggie', from beds to tinned food crowded the shelves on one side, balanced by a rival collection of 'everything for the birdies', on the other. Hand printed, home designed notices announced these facts from the walls. The rest of the shop was taken up with every conceivable kind of pet, an inventory of which O'Flattery had no time to make, for he was already getting impatient at the disregard the owner was paying to his embarrassed cries of "Anybody there?"

Eventually, his patience exhausted he parted the bead curtain and bellowed, not without embarrassment: "Can I have a tortoise, please?"

Slowly the owner got to his feet from a crouching position in front of a large hutch in which his head had been concealed, revealing himself as a small bactrian man with big leathery lips and a pink hearing aid.

"Sorry to keep yer waiting sir. Bin there long? Ever so sorry, deaf yer see," he shouted, fiddling with the mechan-ism of the hearing aid which seemed large considering its obvious inefficiency, "this bloody thing ain't 'ner good."

"It's alright," yelled O'Flattery in return, "but I am in rather a hurry now. Could I have a tortoise please?'

"A what, sir?" said the man whose name was Mr. Nale. "A what?" he repeated in a voice of complete amazement.

"Tortoise!" roared O'Flattery making his face and lips follow the syllables of the word and pointing towards the reptiles themselves, who lifted their heads and craned their necks, inquisitive about what was going on.

"Oh yes sir, a tortoise, course yer can sir. 'Ave a dozen if yer like sir, as many as yer like."

"I think one will be enough at the moment," said O'Flattery feeling rather an ass.

"Male or female, sir, have yer thought of that now?"

"No. As a matter of fact I hadn't. Does it matter?"

"Well," said Mr. Nale thoughtfully, "that do depend on what yer want it for."

"I want it for a birthday present," said O'Flattery beginning to lose patience. "What else would you think I wanted it for?"

"Why ter breed sir, ter breed."

This seemed so ridiculous to the Irishman that he forgot his momentary impatience and regardless of the delay proceeded with their conversation, shouting:

"How do you tell the difference then, they all look alike except some are larger than others?"

"Well, sir, there's more in it than that," said Mr. Nale, bending down and grasping one of the tortoises in his calloused hand. Holding it upside down in the palm of one hand he revealed a honey-coloured, sepia patterned shell slightly concave which he indicated with his forefinger.

"Now this here is a female yer see and this here," he grabbed another from the pen like Gulliver among the Lilliputians up-ending it as the first, "is a male; see the difference, sir, one shell is convex and the other concave?"

"Very instructive," hollered O'Flattery. "I think I'll

take a male one. Is that a male?" he said, pointing to a fair sized creature whose head had stayed out bravely despite the incursions of Mr. Nale's hands into its domain.

"It had better be as tame as possible as these are not the most fastidious of children to whom it is going," he concluded ruefully.

"Tis a tame male yer afther wanting," said Mr. Nale unaccountably adopting an Irish brogue only to irritate O'Flattery even more.

"Yes it is, do make haste," he said petulantly, "I am going to be late if we go on like this."

"To be sure and I'm sorry, no offence meant," said Mr. Nale looking far more apologetic than was necessary, making the Irishman feel ashamed of his outburst.

"And none taken," he heard himself saying as he grasped the handles of a brown paper carrier bag into which Mr. Nale had thrust the unresistant body of the chosen tortoise which, on inspection, had turned out to be of the desired sex.

With outstretched hand and holding the door open, Mr. Nale received the 5s for which he asked and which to O'Flattery seemed a modest enough sum for transporting this alien creature from its distant shores. Shouting his thanks and ignoring Mr. Nale's proffered dietary advice O'Flattery left the shop and pelted up the road towards the Office quickly forgetting what he carried, in his anxiety not to be late.

Jennifer and Leslie with their squalid harlequinade did not even remind him to present the birthday girl with her gift but instead seemed only to implement the waywardness of his thought.

He entered the Office doors laughing, not at the red bewildered face of Mr. Gender, but at the incongruity of his own thoughts about Miss Jeacock, and himself; thoughts which had presented themselves at the sight of these odd children waving their emblem of sexuality before him, that emblem which he had already seen so many times as he walked beside the river.

When the Irishman got to his room he put down the carrier-bag beside the radiator and started at once to work with unusual concentration. He worked diligently for some time until he was distracted by a crackling noise and looking up he saw the paper bag rocking in an uncanny manner. Remembering at once what was inside it, he got up and brought the tortoise over to his desk carrying it gingerly in one hand with the palm of the other across its back. As he lifted it, out came all four of its baggy old legs hanging helplessly down treading the air, while at the same time its leathery neck arched upwards like a sleepy mandarin. As soon as he put it down on his desk it set off on a ponderous voyage of exploration. The claws of its feet scraped across the papers as it made its way towards the edge of the desk. O'Flattery held his breath, ready to grab it, but it seemed to sense the yawning hazard and that to go forward meant a dangerous plunge; very delicately it advanced and retracted its head spooning away with its front legs, it paddled the air, the coarse scales of its leg joints moving with its muscles. Off it went again changing direction, steeple-chasing over pencils and rulers to the next edge of the desk.

The Irishman watched intrigued by this solemn lump of living tissue which at one moment could look so lifeless and at the next was scrabbling aimlessly over his papers. It kept trying to heave itself up onto the books with one front leg, the other flailing the air, then it would lose its grip and bang down again onto the desk. O'Flattery found that the noise he made by tapping on the desk top with a ruler did not bother it. Only when it caught a glimpse of any movement, the change of light the Irishman made when he moved or the sudden alighting of a fly, did it disappear

51

inside its shell. O'Flattery peered round it, fascinated by the way the plates of its shell fitted over the domed shape of its back, then from behind splayed out into a type of fringe over the hole from which issued its back legs, reminding him of the trappings of a horse caparisoned for a mediaeval joust. As he looked closer he noticed that these back legs had on them, situated on each side of the tail, nipple-like, hard, warty protuberances, the use of which was unknown to him. If he tapped on the creature's shell its legs and head retracted even further until the legs were quite off the surface of the desk and he could turn the beast around on its shell. When he desisted there emerged, gently, very gently, first the front legs and then the head. One front leg levered the shell round as it started to pivot itself into a turn, out came the back legs, and pulling with the front legs and pushing with the back ones it was off again, undeterred by the Irishman's idle experiments. It even heaved itself up onto O'Flattery's coat sleeve and scrabbled at his hand, quite oblivious of what it walked over, only retracting once more when he moved away. It floundered on undauntable, over ash-trays, past ink bottles, pencils, and boxes of paper clips, finally getting hopelessly stuck in its unpartnered obstacle race when it succeeded in struggling onto a flat box where it remained suspended, its back legs hanging helplessly, like empty pyjama legs on a linen line. Philosophically accepting its trapped condition and perhaps affected also by the shaft of sunlight in which it found itself, the tortoise relaxed, allowing its legs to splay out, its head to droop, its eyes to close.

After a considerable part of the morning had been occupied with these testudinate studies O'Flattery decided that he had better deliver the present or else no work would get done at all. Accordingly he left his room and went in search of Jennifer, carrying the tortoise once more, carefully, in its paper travelling receptacle.

4

WHEN MR. GENDER entered the tea-room most of the staff were already assembled there.

"I like a nice strong cup of tea, don't you dear?" said Miss Gladys Lynch, beaming innocently at her sister.

"Tea do you call it?" snapped Miss Betty spitefully, darting a sly look at Mrs. Macklin who brewed the pot which they all shared each morning.

"There are those whose principles do not allow them to take eleven o'clock tea," hissed Miss Jeacock.

"Like the senior clerk," laughed one of the typists unkindly; getting down to personalities immediately, with the cunning malice of the partially educated.

"Mentioning no names," reproved Mrs. Macklin severely in an undertone, as she wielded the tea pot for this curious collection of individuals for whom she worked, giving the last speaker an ill-natured glance.

"Some do not have it because it is bad tea," said sensible Miss Seal, also *sotto voce*; returning once more to the quality of the tea with fly-like persistence.

But she was overheard.

"Some do not know a good cup of tea when they taste one," snapped Mrs. Macklin's ally, one of the less important members of the Office staff.

"And some can't make a good pot even out of the best tea," added Miss Gladys Lynch bitterly.

"Oh but to drink even the best tea during the morning is inclined to take the edge off one's appetite, don't you

53

think?" Mr. Gender hazarded shyly, tactfully smiling at the sensitive Postage Clerk who collected the tea money, lest her feelings should be hurt by the trend the conversation was taking.

"I find it helps my neuralgia," said the girl, who uncharacteristically was ungracious enough to ignore Mr. Gender's efforts to ease an increasingly awkward situation.

"I have no appetite," said one computer programmer.

"Oh, surely sometimes," said another.

"No, never," replied the first.

"It clears away the dust," growled Dr. Booker, returning doggedly to the tea.

"Tea. We drink a lot of tea in Ireland," ruminated O'Flattery as if soliloquising.

Miss Betty and Miss Gladys Lynch clattered their tea spoons in their saucers. Everyone seemed very tiresome to everyone else this morning.

Once-pretty Betty Lynch, a blonde, with rose-bud stencilled mouth drawn upwards in the middle and downwards at the sides, tight over equine teeth, was deaf. Slightly deaf only, but it was an affliction she attempted to conceal. However, all that was in fact concealed was the knowledge, from her, that the whole staff were aware of her disability. It caused great confusion, rendering her a very difficult stenographer to employ; as no one ever knew whether or not she had heard what was said, for no change of expression sullied her inane countenance.

She and her sister belonged to that increasing army of demurely ageing spinsters. Never casting out their nets efficiently enough to catch and hold a man, but always ready to smile in a certain way at any male in long or even short trousers. They had been employed for so long now at the Office, that they had become permanent institutions. Even the handicap of Miss Betty's deafness was not enough to unseat them. Their personalities were hardly more interesting than the machines they typed upon. In fact the staccato giggles and sharp remarks which they shot at one another, were very like the clacking keys which stamped out their indelible letters.

It was difficult to estimate the age of either of the sisters, or indeed to say which was the elder. For they both affected a mode of dress which was intended to lead one to believe them still in their twenties, and a short hair style more suited to girls in their teens. However, sly little creases radiating from the corners of their eyes and a certain pink artificiality about their gums, revealed the fact that they were probably nearer to their forties.

"Hardy perennials," Miss Jeacock called them; she seemed to think that in saying this she would appear to be younger than the Misses Lynch but was in fact more or less their contemporary.

The fly had travelled to the tea-room unseen and un-molested on the greasy collar of Mr. Gender's office jacket. It was now turning its talents towards devouring the sugar from a white china bowl in the centre of the table. From time to time a member of the staff raked the table with his or her spoon, spattering droplets of tea on the cloth, but it had the usual obstinacy of its kind and returned to the fray again and again.

From the familiar heights of the electric light bulb it was able to see all. It went on pillaging exploits round the person of Miss Jeacock, for this morning she exuded an attractive aroma, but it found nothing edible.

She was, taken all in all, a disaster of a woman and yet the kaleidoscope of her appearance had only to be turned slightly and all was changed. In short, to the discriminating there were aspects of her physical appearance which could be discerned if they had eyes to see them, but in general she was seen as a calamity from her splay feet to her diadem of fiercely metallic hair. She tried too hard, that was partly her trouble. If she had not been so desperately conscious of trying to improve her appearance the whole effect would probably have been less noticeable, more relaxed.

Her spongy rubber soles squeaked against the parquet, heralding her approach long before her arrival; her thick straight legs were stuck into her shoes like stakes into the ground; the short skirts which she unaccountably affected revealed knees which were too close together for grace and the necklines of her dresses were always too low for elegance. Her face had the unfortunate appearance of being constantly chapped and was in no way assisted by her inflexible hair. Her rag-bag clothes were reminiscent of handicraft exhibitions: crocheted jumpers, tweed skirts, *boutonnières* of gaudy woollen flowers. Of such was her wardrobe.

Unsuitably and unexpectedly she used a strong and expensive scent. This, combined with an over-matt maquillage and pale nail varnish, were the sum total of the artificial aids which she employed.

One sartorial feature which she sported with almost every jumper was a wide leather belt like a railway carriage window strap. This when lashed round her waist prevented the over-flowing of her breasts, for these were in constant conflict with the loose neckline of her upper garment and appeared to be in frequent danger of being the victors of the struggle to escape. It was this exuberance of her bust, this overflowing femininity which counteracted the discouraging aspects of her appearance and gave her an indefinable shred of attraction. The older men on the Office staff, with one exception, simply thought of her as a thoroughly good sort, who did her work expertly; if they considered her appearance at all it would have been to see her as deplorable, but she had long since ceased to be a woman to them in that sense and was merely an efficient sexless colleague. But to the younger men whose sexual

56

appraisal was perhaps less sophisticated or severe, she possessed a certain maternal appeal which when seen with a characteristically girlish toss of her hair made one of them discern in her a female worthy of pursuit, especially when she wore a clean white dust-coat to preserve but fortunately obscure the horrors of her customary clothes.

But such an estimation of Miss Jeacock remains inadequate; she was in many ways incomprehensible. Her value to the male staff lay, undeniably, in her business efficiency and not in her physical attraction; the women thought her a tyrant and her appearance a disgrace, facts which they hardly ever ceased to discuss among themselves. Her ill-assorted garments were always targets for scorn; her dishevelled hair was thought to be dirty and her personal habits, it had been unanimously decided among those who were inquisitive enough to concern themselves with such matters, were practically unmentionable. She was disliked with ill-concealed fervour by all the women except her friend Miss Seal.

Betty and Gladys Lynch thought her an affront to their sex. The other female executives were jealous of the respect she received from the older men for her efficiency. The Postage Clerk harboured an old and private grudge against her, involving the supply of tea and sugar for the staff's elevenses. This otherwise friendly woman was controlled in her whole attitude towards Miss Jeacock by such petty concerns as these. The Postage Clerk had an ally in the battle of the tea supply. This was Mrs. Macklin, the tea dispenser and Office caretaker. But this last female's universal hatred of womankind was not especially increased in the case of Miss Jeacock.

Miss Jeacock herself was not aware of her curious lack of attraction, but found it galling that her efforts to be seductive met with so little response, while her work always gained her admiration.

Mrs. Macklin stood at the end of a long deal table covered by a once white cloth, now splashed with tea stains. Before her, on a tray, stood a brown enamel tea pot of large dimensions, a sugar bowl and several white china mugs, some cracked and all stained with tannin. Those which were filled with tea went from table to mouth in irregular jerks as those present drank, while the fly cleaned its legs by a puddle of tea on the tray near Miss Jeacock's empty cup.

Without warning, the door at the end of the room, which led to Mrs. Macklin's quarters, burst open as a dishevelled Leslie put his head round the door and shouted in a loud stage whisper.

"Mum, I want cher, Mum."

Mrs. Macklin scowled towards him. Dr. Booker unexpectedly turned to the assembled company and relieved himself of a devastating statement on the subject of the three Macklin children.

"To me those children represent a trio of crepuscular troglodytes, I shrink with horror from them. Why only this morning they pursued me with some curious emblem upon a stick—"

Here the consternation of the staff, particularly of Mr. Gender, Miss Jeacock and the Irishman was made manifest by such a clatter of cups that he broke off in the middle of his sentence discouraged. Everyone who had not followed the gist of the whole remark, at least had understood enough to fear a scene from Mrs. Macklin brought on by her disapproval of the use of such long words and her maternal pride; but no, her stony expression had not altered. She still stood like an inscrutable figure from Easter Island; ignoring everyone, her hand firmly on the teapot, as if to prevent anyone from the impertinence of helping themselves. A welcome interruption was caused by the fly falling plop, plummet into Miss Seal's cup, only to fly off again unharmed when mercifully rescued by her spoon.

Mrs. Macklin was a big overflowing woman, with masculine tendencies towards a moustache and a deep voice. She was the widow of Sergeant Macklin, who had been caretaker at the Office since his early retirement from the services, in which he had been the best turned out soldier in the whole British Army. He also had been built on a large scale and had died as the result of a fall down one of the iron staircases which connected the Office floors. His wife had taken over his job and with it some of the brutality of his army status, but alas without any of the qualifying efficiency for which he had been famous.

She drilled her children into a state of subservience, which no doubt accounted for why they behaved so badly as soon as they were out of her sight. She had a curious cast in one eye which added to her commanding presence, imparting as it did an intimidating look from which it was difficult to escape. One eye looked at you and the other behind you in a way that made you feel surrounded.

She made and poured out the eleven o'clock tea and washed up the cups each day, but only changed the table cloth once a month. She locked the Office up at night, put up the shutters, took them down in the morning and opened up the whole place. She saw that all the lights were out, rang the electric dismissal bell, and, when necessary, saw to it that the central heating plant was kept stoked.

This function was performed for her by a curious minion who lived, ate and slept in the coal hole. No one knew who he was or where he had come from when he appeared shortly after Sergeant Macklin's demise. He did not know his own name, how old he was or where he had been born. He could neither read nor write; but on official occasions managed, with great ceremony, to make his mark. He was of a mongolian caste of feature with slanting eyes and a Caucasian moustache. He was of heavy build and walked with a roll as if he had been often on shipboard, although actually he had never even seen the sea.

His relations with Mrs. Macklin were most singular. Some people even had the temerity to question Brenda's parentage, while casting insinuating glances in the direction of the stoke-hole. Indeed, grounds were not altogether lacking, for there had been a noticeable discrepancy in the timing of Sergeant Macklin's death and Brenda's birth. The child's appearance did nothing to put the lie to the tale, for her disastrous countenance bore strong evidence of a suspicion of oriental blood. Arthur alone was unfathomed mystery enough, a problem which the members of the Office staff had long since given up trying to solve. Mrs. Macklin had first called him Arthur and everyone else did likewise. He was an unattractive Caliban who only occasionally issued forth from his stoke-hole lair. Mrs. Macklin paid him no money for his labours, in fact she implored people never to do anything so rash as to give Arthur money. For if anyone did so, he immediately repaired to the nearest public house, where he swallowed as much alcohol as the money would purchase, only to return much later roaring drunk when his money had gone, to the cold embers of his furnace. He was rewarded for his work by plates of hot food taken down by the children, which he ate with his fingers while sitting on a soap box by the furnace.

The use of a spoon and fork was entirely outside his ken. A knife he did possess, which was always much in evidence with a blade whittled away by constant sharpening. This he used to pare his long black nails, cut off hunks of bread and rings of raw onion, and to pick at the rotting hulks of teeth which lay wrecked in his mouth.

His worldly possessions consisted of this knife and what he stood up in, as well as a curious collection of objects which he kept always beside him in a cigar box. These were a piece of foxed and broken looking-glass, in which he attempted to shave with his Tartar's knife; a filthy length

60

of medal ribbon from some long forgotten war, the colours of which had faded and become so soiled that they were hardly recognisable; and a very early photograph, peeling and dim, of a woman. It was printed on a metal plate and was framed in a small cardboard frame ornamented with a pattern of gilt stars and violets. This, Arthur insisted, was his Mother. He would whimper pathetically if she was admired, although the photograph had to be held at an angle to catch the light if one was to descry anything at all from it. Arthur's clothes were of an ancient cut and of an indescribable greasiness. He wore his trousers caught in at the knee, in the manner of old-fashioned labourers and a flattened apology for a cap served him as headgear.

Leslie and Jennifer stood in great awe of Arthur. They had been forbidden by their Mother to enter the furnace hole, as she said Arthur was 'peculiar', so naturally they were fascinated, as a rat by a cobra, to do so. They spent hours wheeling Brenda back and forth in front of the man's doorway, craning their necks to see what queer thing he was doing in the darkness. Wendy had never been told not to go in, but nevertheless something kept her on the threshold, from which vantage point she and Arthur conducted a friendship which was the only affection the man ever knew. Blinking with delight he would bring his treasures to the doorway and expose them to her with pride. They had a form of language consisting of grunts and half constructed words with which they communicated. There was between these two a feeling not of comprehension but of tenderness. They knew a greater fraternity of mind than many more normal people; their relationship was based on the loneliness of their feeblemindedness. He was the only person at whom Wendy did not hurl her vilification of "Shit 'em." She shared with him the slices of bread covered with a brown layer of pickles, which Jennifer's mother sometimes gave her when she thought she looked more than usually hungry.

61

It was as ambassador from Arthur that Leslie had made his way into the staff tea-room. For Arthur had made it clear, through Wendy, that he had some kind of urgent information to impart to Mrs. Macklin. However, she took no notice of her son and heir and continued to pour tea in weakening spurts into the staff mugs, as with decreasing insistence he called her from the doorway. Finally, as no-one took any notice of him, he came right into the room and took up his station by the door waiting to catch his Mother's attention.

The staff were once more discussing the advisability of mid-morning tea, at a desperate rate, in the hope that Dr. Booker would not start off again on his tactless controversial topic.

"Of course I like sugar in mine," shrieked Betty Lynch in a voice like a pea-hen.

"Ye-es," echoed her sister drawing out the word like elastic.

"Can't touch the stuff. Mustn't have anything sweet. Sends my blood pressure up. No sweet stuff at all," said Miss Seal, like a running commentary.

"Don't know what you do eat then," said a junior typist acidly.

"Savoury stuff. Love a drop of vinegar on things," went on Miss Seal with no one paying her the slightest attention.

"I like three spoonfuls in mine," simpered the Postage Clerk, looking coying at Mrs. Macklin, who cast a double warning glance, half at the sugar bowl with one eye and at the Irishman with the other, as if to say "you dare".

O'Flattery, suddenly aware that one of Mrs. Macklin's eyes was upon him, laughed too loudly; everyone turned round and looked at him expecting an explanation. Miss Jeacock blushed and buried her nose in her tea cup. Mr. Gender saw, to his consternation, that the Irishman was staring candidly into his face and ignoring the questioning glances of the rest of the staff.

"I think maybe, perhaps," stammered Mr. Gender, quite unaware of how he was going to finish what he had started.

"Perhaps, maybe it would be better to take coffee." This had really nothing much to do with the preceding conversation and Mrs. Macklin, sensing a change of habit at this suggestion and the consequent possibility of more work, glared round so hard at everybody that they all stopped talking.

Dr. Booker undaunted by the interrupting trivialities of the tea conversation and espying Leslie, suddenly called out:

"Leslie Macklin, come here, boy."

Mrs. Macklin's face assumed the look of a militant amazon and darted a glance of malevolent hatred at her employer, as her son crept stupefied across the room towards his interlocutor.

"Leslie," began Dr. Booker kindly, "what was that . . ." he got no further, a loud crash interrupted him, followed by a squeal. Miss Jeacock had dropped her mug sending a shoot of hot tea all over the knees of the woman seated beside her. All the women in the room, except Mrs. Macklin who sneered sarcastically, rushed to her aid dabbing ineffectually with pocket handkerchiefs and letting out little whinnies of soothing words. The drenched typist was speechless, Miss Jeacock fulsome with apology. Mr. Gender had gone scarlet and kept on repeating, "Oh I say look here," with genuine distress, over and over again until he caught O'Flattery's eye bent upon him insidiously. Whereupon he turned tail and fled back into the Office; Leslie had taken the same opportunity and had disappeared into the caretaker's quarters, as soon as the commotion over the spilled tea had started, his mission forgotten.

This timely smash broke up the eleven o'clock tea break. The Misses Lynch accompanied their damp colleague to the Ladies' Cloakroom with much clicking of tongues. Dr.

Booker and his Assistant went back to their offices once more talking, with puzzled looks, about the work which was to occupy them until they met again for lunch. Miss Seal went off with one of the younger girls saying things like, "Well I say," "I do declare," and "Fancy that now," until they were out of hearing, their heads together like Siamese twins. The Postage Clerk hurried off alone shaking her head sorrowfully. Mrs. Macklin crashed and banged the china together as she stacked it on the tray, deciding as she did so that whatever it was Leslie wanted he shouldn't be allowed to have it.

The Irishman joined Miss Jeacock on his knees on the floor, where she was slowly gathering together the broken pieces of her tea mug. They knelt together ignoring Mrs. Macklin's complaining grumbles of "I don't know what that'll cost you I'm sure." His eyes were moist with laughter and the corners of his mouth flickered, so that Miss Jeacock found it difficult to suppress an answering smile. His hands brushed against hers as they fumbled with the wet china and her hair stroked his cheek.

Outside the furnace room, he in and she out, Arthur and Wendy were communing silently together over slices of bread and pickles, sent out to them before Mrs. Macklin had started the tea break. Arthur, in the presence of food, had soon forgotten the urgent business that should have occupied him and Mrs. Macklin. Leslie had returned to Jennifer who was throwing sticks trying to dislodge the rubber object from the plane tree. Brenda slept. The Senior Clerk worked, undisturbed and unmissed, at the top of the Office building.

While the fly, unobserved by anybody, feasted upon the remains of the tea and sugar spilt upon the cloth. Moistening the granules of sugar with its saliva and sucking up the dissolved mess through its proboscis, rubbing its legs together every so often with feverish delight, greedily it fed unmolested and secure.

64

5

MR. GENDER fled back to his office much disturbed. He had not seen the look of complicity which passed between Miss Jeacock and O'Flattery, but he had been in her company without managing to speak to her alone and he felt unnerved. Her presence by him was enough to set a whirligig going in the pit of his stomach, to turn his insides to water and to dry up his powers of speech. His passionate desire to appear before her in his best light so consumed him, that he always seemed gauche while wanting to be suave, cloddish when trying to be amusing and stupid when he wished, at all costs, to shine. At such moments he hated himself and at the same time came near to hating her also. At such moments of uncontrollable despair as these, when Impatience, Desire, Envy, Greed and Ignorance contested against each other like so many physical beings for the task of driving out successfully Peace, Thought, Love and Contentment, the warm feelings within him were quenched by gusts of icy disappointment, frustration and above all fear. Fear of being for ever alone; alone to face himself.

Taking his pen he determined to write to Miss Jeacock. It was a mode of procedure which he had frequently followed. In the past it had been efficacious. He simply wrote to her from his heart, a direct flow of feeling, which usually had the effect of relieving him. As he never sent the letters, he was spared the embarrassment of having to face Miss Jeacock after she had read one of them. A virgin sheet of paper waiting to be ravished, lay prostrate before him. His pen began to whip across it and in a moment he was lost in the throes of describing his love for this *cygne noir*, who alas, existed only in his imagination.

"Darling," he began; he found it difficult to begin his love letters; the English language did not contain words to describe the feeling he wanted to express as the prefix to a letter; anyway, off he went.

"Darling,

It is three minutes since I saw you, twenty-four hours since I spoke to you. Waiting for the odd chance of seeing you is sometimes unbearable. This afternoon is one of those times. Writing to you seems to bring you a little nearer; although it is a nearness which exists only in my imagination. I do not know at this moment where you are, the precise spot I mean. If I allowed my inventiveness to run away with me and think of the various situations in which you could be, with any of my rivals in this building, my feeling of despair becomes well nigh frantic. I wonder if you will ever understand what it feels like to love someone, and to know that one is not loved in return. It is a hopeless situation which one can do nothing to alter. One is utterly powerless. I feel so terribly unhappy, darling. You don't understand, do you, how anyone can allow himself to be depressed? Sometimes I believe you do understand, or could understand, what being in love with someone, other than oneself, really feels like. Sometimes it is the most wonderful feeling. But you don't feel it? I wonder? I believe, that is when I am not watching the controls carefully enough, that you do know what it feels like to be in love; that you are in love with me; but that you are so afraid of being hurt, that you will not allow yourself to admit love into your heart. It seems to me that, helped by your business efficiency, you are deliberately erecting a kind of cortex to cover your feelings. If you succeed, you will succeed only in making yourself disliked and unhappy and the other people

66

who come in contact with you unhappy also. You yourself will become so hard that if the day comes when someone does get through your barricades you will have such a monumental revelation of unhappiness that it will be unendurable.

But perhaps this is all nonsense. I fear that it is. I try so hard, darling, to fall out of love with you. I try to cultivate indifference to you, even try to hate you. It is quite hopeless. When I look into your eyes, all my carefully prepared defences are gone in a moment. Your eyes look back into mine and there is an understanding of something between us written there, I am sure of it. They say that insanity is an inability to adapt oneself to circumstances; if this is so . . . then I am mad . . . God, all this must sound so silly. I am floundering about for words in an attempt to say something and all I really want to say is, 'I love you.' Please, please love me in return.

It is not only sexual attraction. Although I admit it is a great part of it. I have never loved anyone else before except my Mother. But that love was different. I am inexperienced, but I know enough to know that sex alone is not love . . ."

Here he threw down his pen in disgust. He had dispelled a part of his feeling but in doing so he felt exhausted, sucked dry like an orange squeezed of its juice. He raised his hands to his face in shame but they smelled of ink and he thrust them away, hating himself, hating everything, the Office, the tea break and the tap of iron shod boots on iron as messengers went up and down between the floors. Methodically he tore his letter into four, screwed up the pieces into a tight ball and hurled it into the waste-paper basket.

Work in the Office ebbed and flowed sluggishly, reaching this afternoon point when more than one person's spirits were at the lowest ebb. There was a tendency for people to get up from their desks on some pretext or other, to move about their rooms, to pick up objects and idly put them down again, to sigh and look searchingly out of windows expecting some answer, some solution; it was the

67

time of day when regret and depression nudged at the heart. If anyone had looked up at the façade of the Office building they would have seen indistinct shapes passing and repassing, white faces bobbing guiltily behind glazed windows, their outlines blurred until they came near enough to the glass for their owners to see out. It was one of those moments which come particularly at sunset and sometimes in the middle of a wakeful night, from which one has no protection even when such a feeling comes in bright sunshine, bringing a realization of the horrible, unendurable loneliness of death. One is caught defenceless and is overwhelmed.

Mr. Gender got up once more and went to the window, disturbing the fly which dithered on the slats of the venetian blind. It changed from being an obscure blob in the shadows to a vividly sharp articulate living insect in the sunlight; it had found its way undaunted through corridor and staircase to the comparative privacy of his room. As he approached, it changed its area of operations from the blind acorn to the light bulb which was already mottled with its spoor. He could see Arthur, slowly crossing a strip of sun-coated lawn, dragging a barrow of dead leaves . . . Time stood hesitant.

The morning had gone, he had eaten his mid-day meal in a dream, before it he had written this letter and now most of the afternoon had gone by without him really noticing it.

Arthur still walked on the grass with a jerky movement of his hips. The sun glanced across the metal hub of the wheelbarrow and the breeze caught the leaves, tossing them from the barrow, so that unknowingly, Arthur left behind him a copper trail burnished upon the sunny green lawn. The barrow ran smoothly. The man walked jerkily. A few battered flowers clung to the earth silently gazing at the sodden ground which had given them birth. A toy train

68

chugged across the distance making no sound, drawing out a skein of grey smoke in its wake. The clouds were plushy like feather beds slowly riding the sky. The sun had started to go down in a riot of saffron, cherry and gold; the grey, grey clouds hung in a sky faintly tinged with green. Mr. Gender could see the dim shapes of Leslie and Jennifer, watching someone by the gate, but could not see what or who it was. He saw but could not hear a figure leave the group and stamp off towards the city with a gesture of annoyance.

Leslie, Jennifer and Wendy had been playing their favourite game. Tired of aggravating Arthur, they had dragged Wendy away to look for "lovers" at whom they could stare. They had leered at a shamefaced pair, sitting holding hands on a bench, until the couple fled to the music of Wendy's yells of "Shit 'em." They had goggled at another pair who, glued mouth to mouth, took no notice of them or Wendy's remarks, but swayed drunkenly, abandoned in their own delirium.

At last, when tired of this pastime, they caught sight of the gypsy; she had just nailed a notice to a tree and now hesitated a moment in the scanty protection of its shadow. She was like a print from a child's picture book, belonging to another century, out of context and strange. This swarthy woman, as she stood, set the baby she was carrying to her breast; over her hair she wore a yellow handkerchief, an old flowered bodice and a tartan skirt covered her lissome body, a black and white plaid shawl was flung over one shoulder wrapping round the baby. Brass earrings jingled from her ears and she carried, on her disengaged arm a wicker basket of clothes pegs, among which lay the hammer she had been using to fix up the notice. One side of her bodice was unlaced to feed the baby. Her great swelling breast hung out over the front of her dress, while the helpless infant mouthed and slavered round her nipple as it sucked, slobbering milk down the shawl. O'Flattery, too, from the vantage point of his window saw her and strained forward, his temples flattened against the cold pane, in order to see more clearly this unusual Romany nomad.

Jennifer and Leslie were transported as they stood watching her.

"Know what that lump is, ape?" said Jennifer grossly.

"Yers 'a course," parried Leslie, wondering what it could be; vaguely connecting it with the cows he had seen on a rare visit to the country.

"That's a bossum," went on Jennifer, "I shall 'ave a couple of tits like that one day," she added proudly. "But I won't 'ave no kids to mess 'em about," she spat out viciously, rattling Brenda in the push-chair. Wendy had both of her thumbs wedged into her great mouth, drooling, standing first on one leg then on the other, jiggling up and down.

"Go on, if yer want to be excused. Or else keep still, for Chrise sake," snorted Jennifer; afraid that any commotion might make the gypsy woman conceal this rare treat. As the wind flapped the loose tags of the shawl over her slack white bosom, the children stared and stared, three practised voyeurs. Short black hairs ringed her pap, like a pig's bristles, as it lay first covered and then uncovered by the vagaries of the breeze.

With a hitch of her baby and stamping her feet the woman turned suddenly, as Mr. Gender had seen from the window, leaving the wondering group of children, and Arthur still leering from a distance, half comprehending. They stood for some minutes as the daylight dwindled, reading the notice which advertised a circus, a savage aboriginal frieze contemplating the distance, hardly moving; then Jennifer had one of her diabolical ideas. Dragging Leslie by one hand and Brenda's push-chair with

70

the other, she shouted, "Come on, let's go and play in the furnace 'ole now Arthur's out." Off they went with Wendy bringing up the rear bawling like a maenad.

When they arrived at the furnace hole, with its black heaps of loosely piled coke and the huge sizzling boiler, they were all afraid to go in.

"Go on Les," whispered Jennifer, "I dare yer!"

"Naouw, I don't want to. You go in, it was your idea," he whined.

"Shit 'em," said Wendy.

"Garn yer, yer dusn't."

"No, nor dusn't you. Mum said we wasn't to."

"Go on then Wendy, you go in," cooed Jennifer encouragingly. Brenda was pushed against the door, forgotten.

"Shit 'em," Wendy said again, as if it were an incantation to exorcise any evil spirits which might dwell therein. She took a step into the darkness and then stood rooted, giggling feebly, to the spot.

"Go on," forced Jennifer, "further, go on. Wos in that sack?"

"Shit 'em," replied Wendy, as with a stygian leer she dived her arm into a sack which stood on the floor.

"Aing," she yelped as she withdrew her hand more quickly than it had gone in, bringing with it a shower of brown feathers and the naked severed legs of a cockerel. Screaming, she rushed with horror from the place, pursued by Jennifer and Leslie who, as she dropped the chicken's legs, snatched them up and tore after her, pulling at the hanging sinews, making the dead claws flex and reflex as if they had come alive again.

As Mr. Gender watched the disappearing sun he beheld the figure of Wendy in full flight, chased by her two friends brandishing their sinister toys. Arthur and his barrow had gone, the world outside looked lonesome and uninviting. Inside was warmth and light at least, even if he was

71

closeted alone with his misery. He pulled down the blind and turned to his desk. He felt numbed with boredom and at a loss to know how to rid himself, even temporarily, of his obsession about Miss Jeacock. His reverie was disturbed by a knock at the door. Before he was able to say "come in", he found himself confronted by the vision of Miss Jeacock herself, drawn there as if by his will, resplendent in one of her white working coats. The superficially neat surgical appearance of her body, reminiscent of an operating theatre, was a strange contrast to the untidiness of her hair and make-up. To Mr. Gender she looked like the seraph in a blaze of light; he waited for her to say something, to break the silence and give him back his tongue. She was carrying an armful of files, which she laid upon his desk, taking from it a pile of old ones.

"I am sorry not to have given you these earlier," she said with an apologetic smile, "but Mr. O'Flattery had not finished with them until now; would you please be kind enough to pass them on to Dr. Booker, as I shan't be in tomorrow?"

He could say nothing, all he could think was, "Tomorrow I shan't see her all day. I shan't know what she is doing, where she is going, to whom she is speaking. It will be an eternity until the day after tomorrow. But she is here now. I must speak to her. I must tell her what I feel. She will understand. She must understand. Perhaps she would lunch with me tomorrow if I take the day off."

Already in his head they were alone together, their knees close beneath a long white table cloth, wine sparkled in tall glasses, pink delicate slices of ham glowed on blue and gold plates. She was raising her glass to his, over the top her eyes spoke to him, telling him clearly that she loved him as he loved her. But suddenly he realised that she wasn't speaking, they were not close together, they were separated by a desk and the length of his office, she was just standing gazing at him in surprise. He still couldn't speak, the moment of silence seemed to have lasted for a century. His stomach felt light and fluttery, his legs were weak and he clutched the desk for support until his knuckles went white.

"Thank you. Yes, thank you, I will. I hope you have a pleasant day tomorrow." Then, just as he managed to uncork the bottled up channels of his speech, the fly swooped from where it had been circling between them and fell sizzling onto the white blotting paper, struggling and fighting in frightful mockery of an old lady stranded on her back, waving black stockinged legs in the air. Mr. Gender, embarrassed by his own thoughts, felt panic blushes crimsoning his cheeks. Miss Jeacock, with a toss of her brittle hair and a wry smile, turned one crêpe rubber sole on the parquet with a shrill squeak and rustled from the room.

Alone again, he felt as if his whole strength had been drawn out of him. He had had his chance and lost it. She was gone, gone for a whole day. What did she think of him? What can she have thought of his school-boy embarrassment? What did she mean by her reference to O'Flattery? Mr. Gender with a tiger-lover's jealousy read into it an innuendo which had never been consciously intended.

This unexpected vision of his beloved had helped him to make up his mind. He must make a definite statement of his feelings, he must come out in the open, he could bear this secrecy no longer. Feverishly he opened his typewriter and inserted a sheet of paper. With a speed which surprised him he composed five lines of free verse. They welled up out of him as if they had been boiling beneath the surface like larva urgent to erupt. Eagerly he extruded this pent up expression, inept no doubt but burning with the intention to disclose the state of his heart. With trembling fingers he inserted this missive into an envelope

73

on which he had already typed his loved one's name.

Switching off the light and leaving the metronomic fly swinging to and fro in the darkness, he hurried down the corridor to the vestibule. No one was about, Mrs. Macklin must be at the switchboard in the basement waiting to pull the control switch of the electric bell which in a moment would send the Office staff back to their homes.

Furtively, he pushed the envelope through the black tapes of the letter board; grabbing his macintosh and hat from a line of pegs by the door he darted out into the open air, as the dismissal bell broke out in uncontrolled metallic peals. Half running, half walking, like a murderer flying from the scene of his crime, he saw Wendy, Jennifer and Leslie silhouetted against the warm glow of the open stoke hole. Their pinched bodies, always muffled in too many clothes, looked like mocking gnomes from a bizarre underworld. The clanging of an iron shovel against the furnace, to the music of a high-pitched maniacal song of Arthur's, made him shudder as he hurried, snatching his coat collar tight about his neck, away from the office. Already regret was gnawing at him.

To his surprise he saw in front of him the figure of Miss Jeacock, also hurrying away to catch her bus. Reprieve; he could return and get back his incriminating poem, of which he was already ashamed and the consequences of which he was already afraid. In any case, he thought, lying to himself, trying to keep his self-respect, "it is not worthy of her."

Turning hurriedly he almost collided with the other members of the staff, who were already pouring out homewards from the brightly lit vestibule. Too late, it would have been seen. Mrs. Macklin would now be stationed by the board, seeing everyone out and checking up on the late workers. Moreover, he would be forced to leave it there all day tomorrow as everyone who had seen it would know

74

that Miss Jeacock was away for the day. It must mock him until the morning after. Defeated, he turned back joining the throng of Office-workers, answering their "good nights" with a heavy heart. Miss Seal passed him with a cheerful, "Good night, Mr. Gender. Nice evening. See you tomorrow, don't be late in the morning." Her cheery well-intentioned optimism sending his already unbalanced spirits rocketing to the depths.

6

MISS JEACOCK had left a few minutes earlier than usual as she had to buy seed for her "budgie" at Mr. Nale's pet shop; she knew this would take time as he was always so long-winded and she wanted if possible to get home early enough to see her favourite television programme.

Miss Seal who could see her friend's head bobbing along ahead was curious to know why she was going so fast and was more than usually irritated by the passers-by who impeded her attempts to catch up. Shiny-rumped school-boys were lounging home, intermittently lit by the knife-sharp bars of light from shop windows. Several schools must have disgorged their contents at the same hour, for green girls, uniform grass green from hats to stockings hurried in pairs past the loose-tongued boys, while among them care-worn spinster teachers conspicuous in their mistakenly short skirts and still carrying satchels, mooched homeward gazing about them with tired unseeing eyes, exhausted by pouring their life's blood of knowledge into the unyielding sponges of their pupils' minds. Despising them, Miss Seal jostled by, finally catching up with Miss Jeacock on the threshold of Mr. Nale's shop.

Now that she knew where her friend was going and guessing why, she lost interest in her pursuit, hardly stopping therefore she called out:

"All right for tomorrow dear!" and as soon as she had heard Miss Jeacock reply in the affirmative she hurried on waving one hand in pleased farewell.

76

Miss Jeacock entered the shop where she found Mr. Nale talking to a woman customer, who in her turn was talking to an evil-looking black and red haired monkey. This creature wore a collar and chain around its waist and had yellow fur on the insides of its legs so that it had the appearance of wearing jodhpurs. The woman had got herself into its cage and in tones of the utmost intimacy was saying: "Hullo my mon, how's my mon?" over and over again. It seemed to make no difference to her that she received not the slightest encouragement from her supposed monkey friend or that she was in danger of being struck by the swinging chain as the monkey leapt restlessly about the cage. Miss Jeacock could see that its interests were entirely taken up in either biting the bark from its tree branch perch or intently watching a fly which circled outside the cage between Mr. Nale and the wire netting, its bullet head and yellow eyes circling continually with the fly.

"It used to love chasing the dogs round the garden so. Didn't you my mon?" said the idiotic woman. Then, turning to Mr. Nale, she shouted: "Have you had an offer for him yet?" Without waiting for a reply she began climbing out of the cage shouting: "I must go, I have to go out to dinner."

All very silly, thought Miss Jeacock, delaying me and how could she think that Mr. Nale, and least of all the monkey, could possibly be interested in her ridiculous life.

As the woman left the shop, Mr. Gender slunk past the open door and could hear Miss Jeacock asking Mr. Nale for a packet of budgerigar seed.

O'Flattery as he left the Office went over to the tree where he had seen the gypsy fixing her poster. In old-fashioned playbill letters it proclaimed the advent to the district of "THE WORLD FAMOUS LOTHARIO'S FAMILY CIRCUS . . . a family circus offering entertainment for the family."

His curiosity satisfied he turned away from the tree at the precise moment that Jennifer and her cronies turned from the bright doorway of the stoke-hole. Seeing him they bent their heads together over Brenda's push-chair and then in a paroxysm of shy giggling flew over towards him like an assemblage of noisy starlings. Their weedy bodies and pale faces were accentuated by the half light. The young Irishman felt sorry for them, and decided that he would both satisfy a sneaking desire to return to a childhood pleasure and at the same time, give them an unexpected treat by taking them to the circus.

"Mr. O'Flattery, Mr. O'Flattery," screeched Jennifer when she was still outside ordinary speaking distance but because of the rapidity of their approach sounding much too loud, "Ta ever so for that tortoise what Wend give me," she panted out as she almost collided with the Irishman, then stood blushing with embarrassment at her own words.

"That's all right Jennifer, glad you liked it," smiled O'Flattery, "where is it now?"

"'Ere," said Leslie indicating Brenda's push-chair, "our Brend 'as took a fancy to it."

O'Flattery looked towards where he was pointing and to his surprise saw the tortoise reclining among the grubby folds of Brenda's lap, with all its legs stretched out and its head propped up on a ridge of blanket. It rested like an abandoned odalisque, its elderberry eyes alertly watching what was going on around it. Brenda's pudgy hand had escaped from the covers and lay, an indeterminate blob on the brown and yellow speckled plates of its shell.

"It seems to have taken a fancy to her too," replied O'Flattery. "It wasn't nearly as tame as that when I had it in my office this morning."

Wendy was making wider and wider circles on her bicycle outside the perimeter of the little group, so that

78

they were ringed round by her Red Indian yells of: "Shit 'em, shit 'em," now loud, now soft.

"Oh yes, it likes our Brend," said Jennifer proudly, "but it won't eat when she feeds it."

"Oh dear, what did she give it?" said O'Flattery.

"Pudding and gravy, this dinner time," said Leslie.

"Oh no," said the Irishman aghast, "it wouldn't like that, green stuff is what it likes."

"Wouldn't eat that neither," grumbled Jennifer.

"I give it some of my greens too and that wouldn't touch it," she went on obviously disappointed.

"Cooked or raw?" asked O'Flattery.

"Cooked a corse," said Jennifer scathingly, "we don't 'ave no rabbit food in our 'ouse."

"I'm afraid it won't eat anything cooked," he went on, "I think you had better come down to Mr. Nale's shop where I bought it, he'll be able to tell you all about how to look after it."

By this time Wendy was also listening and when she heard this shouted: "Cor, old Naley, goin' to see old Naley."

As she did so the Irishman's heart failed him and he said, thinking of his embarrassment in the shop, "I think perhaps Jennifer and I had better go alone, there's not much room in the shop," he added lamely. But when he saw Leslie and Wendy's disappointed faces he relented and said:

"But I tell you what, I'll take you all to Lothario's circus when it comes, what about that?"

Leslie and Wendy jumped up and down with excitement, their hands clasped between their knees, while Brenda lay impassive, her hand still protectively spread on the tortoise's back.

Jennifer looked sour: "You look arter 'Orny when I'm gorn," she said to Leslie menacingly, "don't you let 'er drop 'im."

Leslie trundled off back to the Office pushing Brenda before him. Wendy went screeching off into the night while diminishing cries of "Shit 'em," could be heard like the steam whistle of a railway engine gradually fading away.

The Irishman and Jennifer turned towards the brightly lit shops. Jennifer ran ahead, eager now that she had got rid of the others to get to the Pet Shop which she never dared enter alone. O'Flattery hurried to catch her up and walk with her. Laying his hand on her shoulder he said:

"What did I hear you had called your tortoise?"

"'Orny," said Jennifer shyly looking up at him and pushing her head back against his arm.

"Orny, what a funny name," said O'Flattery questioningly.

"No," said Jennifer impatiently, "not Orny, *Horny*," this time over carefully aspirating the H.

"Oh, I see," he said weakly, "because of his shell I suppose?"

"Yeah a course," shouted Jennifer breaking away and approaching a group of schoolboys who because of her impunity as O'Flattery's companion failed to strike her when she rudely chanted:

"Grammar bugs eat slugs, dirty little humbugs," and then rushed to the added protection of Mr. Nale's shop which the Irishman had reached and was now entering.

Miss Jeacock was at that very moment asking for her "budgie" seed. Not even Jennifer had noticed Mr. Gender as he slipped away into the dusk. Miss Jeacock looked round angrily as the loudness of the door bell startled her. But upon seeing O'Flattery her scowl diminished but did not entirely go when she saw by whom he was accompanied.

"Good evening, Mr. O'Flattery," she simpered, remembering at once their tea-break confrontation over the broken cup, but at the same time the sweetness of the memory being marred by the presence of the grinning Jennifer and the recollection of her morning's prank with its nasty implications.

"Hullo, Miss Jeacock," said the Irishman shyly, "what are you after?" Realising he was being rather inquisitive O'Flattery quickly added with an abortive movement towards Jennifer, "we've come to ask Mr. Nale about tortoises."

"Oh indeed," said Miss Jeacock puzzled as to why this ill-assorted pair should be seeking such information.

"Mr. Flattery give me 'Orny fer me birfday," sniggered Jennifer, perfectly well aware of the ambiguity of her statement.

"He did what?" said Miss Jeacock, her pupils dilated with amazement.

O'Flattery, flushing girlishly in some confusion made Miss Jeacock more suspicious than ever as he stammered:

"She means I gave her a tortoise for her birthday. Which she has christened . . ." then he stopped unable to go on.

"'Orny," bellowed Jennifer prodding home her point loud enough for even Mr. Nale to hear.

"Horny, because of its coriaceous shell," shouted O'Flattery at once.

"Like leather," Mr. Nale threw in quickly as if they were playing some parlour game, at which Miss Jeacock as quickly said: "Yes I see," thereby finishing the round, easing the tension and setting them all off into a pointless explosion of laughter.

Mr. Nale as suddenly deflated this bubble of hysterical mirth by banging fiercely on the red and black monkey's cage as it too had joined in the fun and was in danger of injuring itself, so fast was it whirling round in its confined world.

"We wondered if you would explain about tortoises to Jennifer, please Mr. Nale?" bawled the Irishman lamely.

"Explain, why yes indeed," said Mr. Nale smiling round and adjusting his hearing aid; then, launching out into a dissonant lecturer's voice, he began to deliver himself of stored up tortoise-knowledge.

"Although imprisoned in a suit of ponderous armour which they cannot lay aside, they are not precluded as one would suppose from activity and enterprise. On the contrary: only observe their nimble gait, see how they go on tiptoe," here he flung out a hand towards the pen of tortoises in which direction his listeners looked to verify his words.

This deaf ruminant man had a curiously eighteenth century mode of speech when speaking of his animals. A delicacy of phrase which accorded ill with his rough appearance and at other times coarse language.

Miss Jeacock looked into O'Flattery's eyes frowning slightly with bewilderment. He gazed back at her mesmerised by the tone of Mr. Nale's voice and the curiousness of the whole situation. Jennifer gaped.

The fly skated over the laminated backs of the tortoises alighting now on the trodden vegetable pulp which they had discarded and then returning to clean up on the top of one of their heads, which, like so many dried river beds, provided it with a cracked and parched landing ground.

Mr. Nale continued: "Their manner of going forward is by moving their legs one after the other, the claws with which the toes are furnished sink into the ground like the nails of an iron-shod wheel and thus assist their progression. Observe these nails are blunt and worn with use."

By now he had bent down and had picked up one of the creatures which he was so gravely describing; as he held it its legs hung down, helplessly pawing the ground that was not there, while its blunt nose pushed in and out on a weak neck which resembled a wrinkled kid-glove finger.

"Coo," squeaked Jennifer, "look at its back legs they're just like our Brenda when you 'old 'er out."

Even Miss Jeacock could not disguise her amusement at this and although actually ignoring Jennifer she allowed a smile to flicker round her lips for O'Flattery's benefit.

Mr. Nale proceeded oblivious of any interruption, holding his exhibit high in the air, referring to the poor reptile as if it was the only one of its kind in existence.

"Though peaceable in itself, it is formed for war in another respect, for it seems almost endowed with immortality. Nothing can kill it, the depriving it of one of its members is but a slight injury. It will live, though deprived of the brain; it will live though deprived of the head."

This his listeners clearly didn't believe, it being altogether too much of a tall story even for Jennifer who was tiring of this dissertation and was looking round to see what mischief she could do among the other pets. Mr. O'Flattery and Miss Jeacock were content to smile benignly at one another.

She was appraising the young man, running the stethoscope of her imagination as it were up and down his body. Letting her thoughts run wild in a way which surprised even herself and would have amazed her companions had they been privileged to see into the obscurity of her brain.

While he was abandoning himself to a condition which on rare occasions throughout his life had overtaken him when he listened for any length of time to the steady, monotonous droning of a human voice, discoursing on a subject which held his attention and obscured with its fog of words all other attendant noises. This condition, which rendered him almost in a state of unconsciousness, of suspended animation when he became practically mesmerised had been known to cause him great embarrassment as in some way quite unfathomed by himself, it must

have had some deep sexual significance which had sometimes resulted in his having a quite involuntary but nevertheless pleasurable emission. It was towards this event
that he was rapidly approaching and which result he as
quickly realised he must prevent. Had he been aware of the
trend of Miss Jeacock's thoughts he would have been quite
unable to jerk himself back to the more stark reality of the
Pet Shop, Mr. Nale and the goggling Jennifer. He was,
however, despite the searching quality of Miss Jeacock's
smiles, still some way from interpreting them completely
and therefore managed to stave off the coming about of
this self-induced trance.

On went Mr. Nale; nothing would stop him: "We are
told by an Italian philosopher that while making experiments upon vital motion he removed the entire brain of a
land-tortoise even going so far as to wash out the cavity.
Not the smallest part remained, but the tortoise appeared
to be unaffected, in fact marched about as before except
that it closed its eyes and never opened them more. After
three days a new skin had grown over the wound and in
this manner the animal lived without a brain for six months
walking about unconcernedly and moving its limbs as
before."

"That's rather fantastic surely?" said the Irishman.

"I can scarcely believe that," smirked Miss Jeacock, like
an inaccurate echo.

Mr. Nale looked hurt.

Jennifer prodded two frenetically copulating rabbits.

"Come away Jennifer," said Miss Jeacock distastefully,
barely looking round, "leave those bunnies alone," she
went on smiling once more at the blushing O'Flattery.

Mr. Nale returned to his discourse with renewed vigour:

"But not satisfied with this experiment he carried it still
further. This time he cut off the head altogether which
continued to rattle its jaws like castanets for above a quar-

84

ter of an hour and, notwithstanding, the decapitated animal lived for a further twenty-three days."

Triumphantly Mr. Nale took a deep breath and proggled at his ear with his hearing aid. O'Flattery taking advantage of this pause shouted:

"Very interesting indeed, Mr. Nale I am sure, but what is this child to feed her tortoise on?"

"Yare," squawked Jennifer, "'e 'ont eat nuffink I give 'im."

Mr. Nale swallowed hard obviously reluctant to go into such mundane matters but also prepared to do so if only to hear the sound of his own voice.

"Well now the Bishop of Peterborough's tortoise," he said in a pious voice, "if I might remind you, had both antipathies and predilections."

Miss Jeacock rolled up her eyes and looked at her watch, reluctant to leave the Irishman but eager to get to her television. Jennifer goggled once more; the fly spiralled round the excrement-encrusted perch of a mynah bird. O'Flattery noticed that the second button of Miss Jeacock's blouse was undone and became transfixed by it.

"It would eat endive, green peas and even the leek; while it positively rejected asparagus, parsley and spinach."

"That won't get no sparrow-grass in our 'ouse," whooped Jennifer.

"Its favourite pabulum, however, being the flowers of the dandelion and lettuce. It would also eat currants, raspberries, pears, apples, peaches, nectarines, the riper the better, but would not touch cherries."

"Bloody fruit salad," muttered Jennifer under her breath, "it won't get that neither. 'Ere Mr. Flattery," she squeaked so that Mr. Nale couldn't hear, "come on this 'ain't no good 'e's daft."

Then with uncanny timing as if he had in fact heard what she said Mr. Nale gave forth again in a less pedantic

85

way.

"If I were you, young lady, I should try him on a bit of lettuce, a half a tomato, an end of cucumber whatever you happened to have."

Jennifer made a wry face as if to say that all those foods were quite unobtainable, and shrugged her shoulders, already sick of the whole business and wishing she had been given something more exciting than a tortoise, all covered up, not like the monkey "without his trousers".

At this moment Miss Jeacock noticed that O'Flattery's attention had been caught by something in front of her; looking downwards she found to her shame that all this time she had been exposing a stretch of brassiere. So potent was her embarrassment that both Mr. Nale and Jennifer noticed the gaping pink fondant filled space at the same moment.

Mr. Nale turned away to his animals which interested him more than humans.

Jennifer gnawed her knuckles.

O'Flattery in confusion began stuttering out his thanks to Mr. Nale as Miss Jeacock fumbled desperately with her bag in front of her trying to think of something to say to get them all back to tortoises. Finally all she could muster was: "Poor tortoises, I always feel so sorry for them, they look so depressed."

How odd, thought O'Flattery, that is just what Mrs. Dymark said this morning. To which Mr. Nale added aloud, "Pitiable seems the condition of these poor embarrassed reptiles," as if closing the session.

Miss Jeacock then found herself able to scuttle towards the door, from which she bade them all a hurried goodnight, relieved at last to escape the burning eyes of the Irishman and disappointed that she would now miss the first part of her programme.

O'Flattery then took Jennifer to the greengrocers where

he bought her a lettuce and a half a pound of tomatoes.

"Mind you give them to Horny," he adjured, as he handed them to her.

"Ta," said Jennifer, "when are we goin' to the circus?"

O'Flattery already regretting his promise hid his face from this perspicacious child as he turned towards home.

"I'll let you know which day I can manage later."

But Jennifer hardly heard him, ungrateful to the last, she was already hop, skipping and jumping back to the Office, a tomato between finger and thumb as she loudly sucked the pips and pulp from within.

The fly remained behind to enjoy the foetid warmth of animal corruption with Mr. Nale and his pets; while Miss Jeacock on her way home thought tenderly of the young Irishman who, she realised, had been so affected by her blouse button.

"What hidden possibilities lay beneath the boy's sensible tweed exterior? I shall miss the telly but I have made a conquest."

7

MISS JEACOCK waited in the lounge of an hotel near the office, for her luncheon companion, Miss Seal. They had been friends from girlhood, and although they worked in the same building they saw little of one another during office hours. So that when they could, they lunched together, exchanging confidences and enlarging the comradeship which already existed between them. They told each other most of their secrets but, not being sisters, like Miss Betty and Miss Gladys Lynch, their confidences had more mutual interest than the inanities which shuttled back and forth constantly between those two withering maidens.

Miss Seal, for instance, knew that Miss Jeacock's father had been an epileptic; that she was still a virgin and that she had fears about the strength of her heart; today she was to learn even more fascinating truths, she hoped.

Miss Jeacock knew less about Miss Seal, for there was little of a spectacular nature to know. She knew that as a girl she had adored her music teacher; that she had never really recovered from the damage done by this fervent passion to her frail adolescent feelings, when the music teacher married a commercial traveller. She also knew the place of Miss Seal's birth; that her hobby was collecting wild flowers; that she still always looked under the bed at night in case there should be a man concealed there. But what exactly she would have done, if there had been, she was not quite clear. She suspected, and rightly, that Miss

Seal was still hopefully looking for her music instructress.

Miss Jeacock waited with tender anticipation for her friend, watching the other diners as they entered the revolving doors to meet their friends or to wait as she was waiting. She was much struck by the blurred appearance of each arrival, for like goldfish suspended in a bowl, they, as it were, swam into her focus as they negotiated, each with more or less efficiency according to their characters, the heaviness and complexity of these revolving doors. She attempted to sum up the depth of feeling expressed in each cry of welcome, each outstretched hand. She criticised the women's clothes and ignored the men.

The behaviour of one of the waiting crowd struck her as worthy of further study, so she stared unashamedly at her. This elderly woman entered with the erect carriage of a brigadier. She was dressed entirely in brown. As accoutrements to her costume she had, attached to her person, a veritable gamekeeper's larder. Feathers and an overwhelming amount of fur were humped about her shoulders. She wore a three-tiered choker of over-ripe pearls and long narrow court shoes. She stalked to an upright armchair, fluffed out her furs, eased herself carefully between the arms of the chair, settling herself, ruffling her furs now and again, as if unable to roost comfortably. Her face was as forbidding as a totem pole; its natural detail was almost obliterated by the white powder which nestled in the ridges of her wrinkles. A boldly stencilled mouth covered her real lips, the turned down corners of which were accentuated, rather than obscured, by their unsuitable lipstick coating. Once settled, she too glared round the room brooding, and for some minutes Miss Jeacock was out-stared into a pretence of reading a fashionable illustrated paper. While she was thus engaged, she heard a sudden dry noise, like that made by a young bird opening its beak from sleep. Looking up she saw that the old lady was holding her lips very tightly compressed together, sitting bolt upright with one long shoe swinging. Carefully she drew off her brown kid gloves; with her bony be-ringed hands she searched frantically in the recesses of her bag; a diamond ring flashed, a hairpin dropped unnoticed to the floor. At last she found what she was looking for . . . a letter apparently. Withdrawing it delicately from its envelope she read both sides of the sheet of writing paper, solemnly considered what she read with her mouth poked forward and her lips pursed.

Having read the letter twice she tore it, very deliberately, into small regular pieces and dropped them into the ash tray on the table at her side. Then, raising the empty envelope to her mouth she spat very loudly into it. With great care she folded over the flap of the envelope, over and over again until it made one long strip; this she then folded twice the other way and finally stowed the object away at the bottom of her bag. Snap shut went the clasp, on went her gloves, criss-cross went her legs, as she changed one over on to the other and once more she resumed her unflinching perusal of the room and its contents.

After this it was with relief that Miss Jeacock saw the shapeless mass of Miss Seal come rolling towards her. She looked as if a half filled sack of potatoes had been used for her body and by the movements of her walk she was, all the time, trying to jolt the vegetables into a better position.

"Hullo, Seal."

"Hullo, Jeacock."

Followed by peals of girlish hockey-playing laughter. The two friends embraced one another, kissing each other on both cheeks with whispered endearments.

"Hullo, Sealy, dear."

"Hullo, Cocky, pet."

They strode into lunch arm-in-arm. Two old-school

90

amazons with eager appetites.

A Cypriot waiter, whose obvious natural gifts of physical attraction were worn with consummate arrogance, ushered them obsequiously to their table in a corner near the orchestra, overlooked by a group of palms in brass pots.

On a raised platform above them, a quartet was getting through an obscure saraband. Three women and a man, aided by a short youth with a lugubrious pimply face who turned over the pianist's music in between sucking his fingers and fingering his spots. A thin-lipped woman, with a peaked face and two unlikely chins, stood firmly planted on large black feet playing the violin, wearing a blue dress with an imitation yellow lace collar. A fat bald man, with heavy hands which played much too loudly, banged on the 'cello. A girl, with a great deal of errant hair flopping round her face like a brown tam-o-shanter, scraped the viola. Her eyes were like two darts thrown aslant on either side of an elongated bulbous nose, she wore horn-rimmed spectacles, played with a rapt expression and swayed from side to side. The pianist was a woman with a face as white as alabaster, a prominent upper lip and a stonily beaky nose; she too performed more with gusto than with talent, her hair was arranged in fussy sheaves on either side of her face and on her powdered forehead there bobbed the remnant of a fringe. The light played up and down the musicians' bows, shooting joyful flashes from their silver-covered tips. The pianist banged down the pedals, the fat man humped himself feverishly over his 'cello. The saraband became hoarse and rusty, like a consumptive getting ready to spit, as this ill-assorted quartet ground on unaware of the diners who munched and gossiped before them.

Waiters moved in and out, pressing their way between the tables; their thighs, on a level with the food, tight in soiled black cloth. Their hands busily arranged and

91

removed dish after dish, with all the solemn ritual of a religious service.

Mesdemoiselles Jeacock and Seal enjoyed their food. They were accustomed when lunching together to exchange a few pleasantries and then they would in comparative silence eat until satisfied; later, over cigarettes and coffee, they discussed their problems at leisure and at length. Today they ate tinned grapefruit, in the centre of which swam one crystallized cherry; over-cooked sole meuniere; and hot boiled mutton, served with caper sauce which looked like a rolled-up blanket with bed-bugs in it. This was accompanied by a white china bowl of boiled cauliflower. All of which the waiter had plumped arrogantly before them. It was not properly cooked and must have lacked any vestige of nourishment. Having instead a sickening aroma, which made Miss Seal catch her breath and wrinkle up her nose into a sneeze. Neither of them cared to complain, the waiter being so handsome it did not seem right to grumble. But they finished up with fresh fruit salad and ice-cream, which they both pronounced delicious, although Miss Seal protested that she ought not to eat it because it was bad for her.

With the coffee Miss Seal unexpectedly donned her spectacles and with them assumed a profound look of mystery. As Miss Jeacock watched her, eagerly sensing something unusual, she drew out of her bag Mr. Gender's missive, which she had removed for her friend from the letter-board as she left the office on her way to their assignation.

"What's this, dear?" said Miss Jeacock, turning it over and over provocatively.

"I don't know, pet, open it and see. I saw it on the board so I thought I would bring it along." She gave a comfortable wriggle in her chair, anticipating some exciting new confidence.

Miss Jeacock slowly withdrew the paper, unfolded it and with a puzzled expression read over to herself Mr. Gender's protestation of love.

"My passion for you is a discontented jealousy,
concealed and hidden when your presence
satisfies the avid hunger of my unwanted love.
But drowning, overwhelming when I am left to
introspection and the delights of recent reminiscence."

She handed it across the table to Miss Seal, starry-eyed with wonder. Miss Seal read it through, half aloud, in a sing-song voice, brushing a fly away which did not seem to have been there before. Miss Jeacock played with the envelope as her friend read.

"Whatever is it?" she said, rather annoyed at her own ignorance.

"Why, poetry of course, Sealy dear," said Miss Jeacock, her voice choked with conflicting emotions. Miss Seal made a clucking noise of disapproval in her throat, to indicate that she thought it nonsense and didn't like her friend being affected by it.

"I think it's beautiful," said Miss Jeacock, in a far away dreamy voice. "Don't you, dear?"

"Of course it is, pet," said Miss Seal quickly altering her tactics. "But who wrote it?"

"Ah-ah! now that's telling," simpered Miss Jeacock. A shade of irritation swept across Miss Seal's face. What was the dear girl getting at? She had never known her like this before.

"Do you know, who wrote it?" she said rather sharply. "Because I think you might tell me as I was your Mercury," she went on jocularly.

"I think I do."

"Well, who then?"

"O'Flattery."

"O'Flattery!" said Miss Seal in amazement, surprised

by the look of pleasure on her friend's face while putting more expression into her voice than she meant to. "That boy?"

"Oh, but he's hardly a 'boy'," answered Miss Jeacock, at once protecting him and justifying herself. "He has to shave and he gives one such looks."

"Well I don't know about 'one'," said Miss Seal sarcastically. "He doesn't give me looks, he may you though; but then you notice these things," she ended acidly.

"Well, who else then?" said Miss Jeacock, who was too lost in preening herself to pay attention to her friend's tone of voice.

The quartet were now playing a waltz, very quietly, so that her sentimental mood was heightened. It would have taken more than Miss Seal to dampen her spirits.

"What about Gender? I should have thought it was him. He's obviously mad about you," bridled Miss Seal, as she saw that her previous remarks were making no impression on her companion.

Miss Jeacock, with all the unawareness of a loved-one, the admiration for whom is already known to everyone but herself, said:

"Oh no. It couldn't be him, he hasn't got it in him. Besides he just stares rudely at me as if I had two heads. Why, only yesterday evening he gaped at me like an imbecile when I took his files in to him. No, it must be O'Flattery. You should have seen the look he gave me when I broke that cup yesterday."

"Ye-es?" said Miss Seal expectantly.

"He's been looking at me like that for a long time. I'm sure he's too shy to say anything, but this is his way of telling me. Isn't that sweet?"

"I think it's daft," insisted Miss Seal solidly, "in any case I don't think it is O'Flattery at all. I am sure it's

94

Gender."

Miss Jeacock was too fond of Miss Seal to be annoyed with her, instead she conceived an instant dislike for Mr. Gender as a scapegoat for the anger she really felt with Miss Seal for trying to baulk her. Why did this stupid man, with his short sight and staring eyes, have to look so hard at her that it made other people talk? She would show him. The old subconscious Eve in her began to outline a plot. I'll show him. I'll lead him on and then let him see what kind of a woman I am. In any case, it would be good for O'Flattery to think he had a rival, it would "bring him on" all the sooner; make him all the more ardent.

As she sat formulating her plan of campaign she twined her coffee spoon in her fingers, looking across at Miss Seal with such an expression of innocence that Miss Seal began to forget her irritation. It was upon her that Miss Jeacock should have been venting her spleen to pay her back for her sarcasm, not upon the unwary Gender and the naïve O'Flattery; it would have been safer had she done so, but the Fates had been summoned up and in the confines of her mind had begun their dangerous machinations. Poor unsuspecting Gender; what a holocaust he had let loose upon himself and the inexperienced Irishman, who between them meant less harm to their fellow men than even Brenda.

Unaware of what was in store for them, these two were, separately, finishing their mid-day meal. Mr. Gender sat cramped at a table in a help-yourself restaurant of a large commercial combine. He had just partaken of beans and bacon which had given him indigestion, for which he was at that moment sucking a patent tablet, while staring helplessly at the crowd of sweating eaters who milled around him.

When he had arrived that morning at the Office his note for Miss Jeacock was still stuck where he had left it, but he was unable to remove it while under the eagle eyes of Mrs. Macklin. When he passed the board on his way out for lunch to his surprise his envelope was nowhere to be seen. He knew that Miss Jeacock was not at the Office and was troubled in his mind as to who could have taken it. Helplessly, he sat, weighed down by the thought of other eyes than those of his beloved reading his poem, sadly sucking his pill.

The Irishman, more spaciously, was eating his sandwiches in the park, lying on the grass among the trees. A wing of ilex arched across his vision, fringed with sunshine. The diamond leaves dazzling in the sun; each separate, defined, crystalline, edging the shadow alive with the creaks of starlings. Intensely deep, the confused shadow was blue black, its depths more dazzling than the light. Beneath this branch hung, as it were, a protected vignette of light cut off from the band of sunlight which framed the distant view. Within this framework of ilex arch moved miniature wooden wedges, horses gently cropping the grass; they moved, yet invisibly; their legs bent and unbent, their ears flicked, their heads made scooping movements through the grass. In detail all was movement, yet *en masse* all seemed immoveable. He listened to the plaintive cool-rool of the paired pigeons among the leaves above him. The quiet peace seemed unbreakable.

Miss Seal was put out. Miss Jeacock had withdrawn so far into herself and was not being at all confidential. The quartet had packed up their music and departed. The waiters slumped, idly admiring themselves in the mirrored walls, waiting for the late comers to go. The ubiquitous fly teased at some crumbs of wafer dropped on the cloth. Miss Seal was impatient either to go or to hear more.

Miss Jeacock was musing almost to herself. Not given to committing herself with positive statements she was carrying on an uninterrupted monologue of platitudes.

96

"Of course to say I love him," she mumbled, "would be an overstatement, but to say that I was fond of him would be an understatement."

Miss Seal looked black.

"I think I should always want to see him. However intimate we became, I mean. I don't believe in the old saying that 'familiarity breeds contempt,'" went on Miss Jeacock fatuously, an idiotic grin haunting her face. Miss Seal looked blacker. These negative statements annoyed a woman of her temperament. Miss Jeacock pulled herself together; seeing her friend's rising irritation, she sat up from her relaxed position and put down her teaspoon.

"Thank you dear," she suddenly began, "it was thoughtful of you to bring this note. Shall I tell you what I am going to do?"

"Yes, pet," whispered Miss Seal hardly daring to breathe lest she might change her mind, "do."

"I'll lead them both on!"

Miss Seal had no experience of this kind of thing and wanted none, so she couldn't quite see why Miss Jeacock looked so triumphant, but sensing some excitement, possibly ending in unpleasantness for the men, she brightened up.

"I should think that's a very good idea. Then you will be able to see which one really wants you. I still think it's Gender, though."

"Bet you a bob you're wrong, Sealy dear."

"I'll take you on, Cocky pet," said Miss Seal as they both rose smiling; at peace again, friends in complicity they left the restaurant arm in arm as they had entered it.

The waiters lounged to attention, proudly bowed Miss Jeacock and Miss Seal out, to return at once to the contemplation of their own charms. The fly, poised on Miss Seal's dowdy hat, rode in state unobserved back to the Office.

97

Miss Jeacock teetered off in the opposite direction on heels too high for her arches. She hadn't mentioned it to Miss Seal but when she had got up from lunch she had felt decidedly queer. Swimmy in the head and faint, with a constriction in her chest. "I expect it's indigestion and excitement," she thought, "but you never know, it's just as well to be careful. I think I won't go shopping after all, I'll go to a matinée instead, but perhaps first I'd better buy some *sal volatile*." This old-fashioned remedy was recalled as she saw a row of huge glass bottles, filled with coloured liquid, dominating the chemist's shop window with which she was now abreast.

As she entered the shop, a very pretty girl in a pink overall stepped forward to serve her, watched by a contrastingly old and wrinkled man.

Miss Jeacock asked for and obtained her specific. She was then attracted by a display of scent, the thick glass flacons of which were displayed in sawdust-filled, lace-edged boxes, further adorned by its name, "Entrée des Artistes", in embossed gold letters. Pointing rudely she asked if she could try this, resenting the petal-fresh prettiness of the girl and the lurking vulture presence of the old man. Smiling pleasantly the girl pulled a glass stopper elongated into a rod from a sample bottle and offered it to the inside of Miss Jeacock's outstretched wrist. The scent curdled upwards from her skin, it was thick and heavy, something between a tea-rose and a lily, a tuber rose and a jonquil; but underlying it there lurked the pungency of stale urine, the tawny odour of tigers, the smell of soiled sawdust in the circus ring. The shock of its strength jostled Miss Jeacock's flagging spirits and helped her to regain her composure.

"I'll take it," she said, with a whisper of a smile, then turned her back on the girl who wrapped up the small parcel and sealed it with red wax at a gas jet behind the counter.

"No string to carry it by?" Miss Jeacock snapped as she took the scent and stowed it away in her handbag, unable to keep pleasant-tempered under the limpid gaze of this girl with eyes like dark rain-washed pansies.

Outside, she bought a newspaper and scanned the entertainments column, deciding on a light modern comedy which had been running for some time and about which all the critics had been non-committal.

When she got to her seat the lonely pianist in the orchestra pit had just finished playing his selections from out-of-date musical comedies, the lights were down, the theatre was silent in a hush of expectancy. The curtain rose, slowly disclosing a comfortable fashionably decorated drawing room, in which sat the hero and heroine of the piece. A theatrical partnership of long standing and unquestioned popularity. Their appearance was greeted by a burst of applause out of which the play commenced with a flood of flatulent trivialities. Miss Jeacock could pay little attention to what was going on upon the stage, for with the rise of the curtain it was as if all her good spirits had been gently lifted from her, to be replaced by a feeling of imminent disaster. She sat at the end of a row and was disturbed by a programme seller who fidgeted in the shadows of an exit close by her. This woman had shown her to her seat. She was scrawny, middle-aged, with a bitter metallic smile which clicked on and off mechanically. Her black dress with its white front, accentuated the unnatural pallor of her complexion. Her vivid riot of hennaed hair was surmounted by a large black satin bow giving her the appearance of a half-starved, lop-sided fowl in the moulting season. Miss Jeacock resented her lurking presence near her. Each time she glared round the woman was smiling at her equivocally from the darkness. When the lights went up for the interval she was gone, as completely

99

as if she had never been there, and with her the feeling of foreboding.

Miss Jeacock was entertained and her spirits lifted once more by the conversation of the two women in front of her. Their words absorbed her far more than the performance on the stage had done. They were taut, spade-like women without sparkle and their conversation over their matinée tea-tray was ill-suited to their appearance.

"I love him and he loves me; no I won't have a piece of cake, dear, thanks."

"Yes, of course."

"She begged and implored me not to have Peter."

"No—"

"Ye-es, she says he can tell me things he can tell no one else."

"No?"

"Thank you. You have the éclair dear, no? Well, I will then. I think it's such a pity to have brought four beautiful children like that into the world and then to treat them like that."

"Yes."

"Peter says his father thinks of nothing but himself. But of course Isabel told me that before."

"Oh yes. Tea?"

"No thanks, dear. Now he's trying to persuade her not to go back to school, but to stop and keep house for him. Did you ever hear such a thing?"

"No."

"I let him say anything he likes. I know the state he's in."

"Yes. Of course you do."

"To think how his mother's been treated. You know Elsie's been told things that a girl of her age shouldn't know."

"No—?"

"Yes, and I am going to get hold of her and try to undo

100

the harm that's been done to her young life."

Half way through this last pronouncement the curtain had gone up but the speaker went on to finish her threat, regardless of the progress of the play and despite the hisses of her neighbours.

Like a cold draught Miss Jeacock felt again the slight pain in her side; like a gnat buzzing outside a shuttered window, it teased at her with an accompanying feeling of ill-fate. She half turned, only to see the programme seller back at her post again. She could have sworn too that the mask of tragedy in the proscenium arch had its sightless eyes trained upon her.

For the rest of the performance her mood was below par. She left the theatre wishing she had gone to the park or even out into the country. Returning home she felt middle-aged and had lost the zest for her plan to ensnare a lover. But alas, this enthusiasm was to return relentlessly with the next day's sunshine.

8

WHEN MISS SEAL got back to the Office, the fly, unbeknown to her, left her hat and flew off to doze on the top of the letter board in the vestibule. Inside the door Mrs. Macklin sat knitting where she could keep an eye on Leslie and Jennifer, who were parading, ostentatiously, up and down with Brenda on her legs staggering between them. She was far too young to walk and her legs were bowed already by the weight of her body, but her brother and sister were bored by the push-chair routine and wanted more action. Mrs. Macklin breathed heavily after a gross lunch and sucked a peppermint as she knitted.

"Where's Mr. Gender?" enquired Miss Seal nonchalantly.

"Oh, 'e's in 'is office," said Mrs. Macklin between sucks at her sweet.

"Where's Mr. O'Flattery?"

"Oh 'im. 'E's goin' to be late back. I 'eard 'im give the weeze to Dr. Booker."

Miss Seal was bursting to tell someone the news which Miss Jeacock had told her. She had not been sworn to secrecy, so why shouldn't she? Mrs. Macklin was not her usual familiar but it might be a lark to see what she had got to say about it.

"What do you think, Mrs. Macklin, Mr. Gender is in love with Miss Jeacock?" exploded Miss Seal, unable to contain it any longer.

"No-ow?" said Mrs. Macklin with mock incredulity.

"Yes, and so is Mr. O'Flattery," continued Miss Seal not being able to bear Mrs. Macklin's ridicule and determined to make her story more impressive.

She had no proof of either of these statements but merely relied on what she would have described, if called to task, as her "woman's intuition".

"What about 'er?" said Mrs. Macklin slyly, changing her peppermint from one side of her mouth to the other, so that it rattled against her false teeth.

"Oh, she's mad about the Irishman, of course, as he's the youngest," answered Miss Seal unkindly. Already wishing she had never spoken to Mrs. Macklin in this way, knowing that she had allowed herself to get carried away and had said too much.

"Well," said Mrs. Macklin thinking of Miss Jeacock's physiognomy, "what I always says is, you don't look at the mantelshelf when you pokes the fire, do you? Beggin' your pardon Miss, I'm sure, since she's your friend," she sneered sarcastically.

"You've been eating needle-pie and no mistake, haven't you?" rejoined Miss Seal sharply, furious with herself for talking to this low creature.

"Godfrey, Daniel, Isaac, cast-iron foundry, you're a fine one to talk I must say Miss Vinegar," snapped back Mrs. Macklin, trigger-happy to take offence. But Miss Seal was in too good a mood to retaliate further or even take umbrage. She considered Mrs. Macklin so far beneath her anyhow that she preferred to forget at once her social lapse in making a confidante of her. On her way back from lunch she had been thinking, with pleasure, of the future. Of Miss Jeacock and her two men and what a welcome change anything would be to alleviate the boredom of her monotonous office life.

"Oh well," she said, ignoring Mrs. Macklin's jibe, "you wait and see; between now and the Outing, for instance, a

103

lot of water can flow under a good many bridges; I reckon we shall see something happen by then, at any rate. You wait!"

With that she stomped off to the Ladies' Cloakroom. She had chosen the outing as a time by which something would happen, because she felt that on that day of relaxation one of them would be sure to show his hand, if he hadn't shown it already.

Leslie and Jennifer were making Brenda walk too fast and much to their amusement she had lost her balance and was flailing her legs on the ground, impotently, as she was dragged between them.

"Don't you walk that child so bloody fast, you little bugger," screamed Mrs. Macklin, tapping on the glass of the door with her knitting needles. They stopped dead as if they had taken root and Jennifer began to brush Brenda down theatrically with motherly clucking sounds.

"What are you doing to that bloody kid? You leave 'er alone or I'll tan the arse 'oles off of yer," yelled their Mother. Leslie and Jennifer put Brenda tenderly back into her push-chair-straight-jacket and strapped her carefully in. Jennifer wheeled while Leslie lent solicitously over his little sister, as they ambled off to meet Wendy whom they had seen approaching sucking an enormous toffee apple on a stick. Mrs. Macklin had got to a difficult part in her pattern, so she took no more notice of them.

She fell to thinking of what Miss Seal had said. Also of another little tit-bit she had gleaned through Mr. Gender's imprudent carelessness the night before. The letter to Miss Jeacock, which he had written to purge his feelings, had been retrieved from the waste-paper basket by the searching fingers of Jennifer, as she had followed her mother on her cursory cleaning round. Jennifer, fascinated by the tightly screwed up ball of white paper, was half way towards flattening and piecing it together, when Mrs.

Macklin snatched it from her. She had not been slow in spying the crumpled endearments with which the letter began. Pushing her daughter aside, she stuffed the fragments into the pocket of her apron until such a time as she would be able to re-assemble it and peruse it at her leisure over a late cup of tea.

What with Mr. Gender's letter and Miss Seal's confidence she was well armed with information, to use as and when she thought fit. But at present she merely ruminated, chewing the tasty cud of scandal, deciding how best it could be turned to her own advantage.

She had not actually seen any signs of the Irishman's interest in Miss Jeacock. "I should think not indeed," she said to herself. "Proper baby snatching it would be if she tried anything on with him. But that Mr. Gender, he was a hot one for all his quiet ways. You never know what's going on behind them thick glasses." She must keep her eye on that Irishman too, for a sign of any goings on; have a nice rummage round in his room as well, in all the wastepaper baskets and some of the desk drawers too if necessary, "wouldn't do no 'arm." For in her capacity as caretaker she couldn't have things going on that she didn't know about. "You can't be too careful," was what she said, profoundly.

Phlegmatically, she went on with her knitting, the brown coil lengthening into shape beneath her busy fingers. To outward appearances she remained calm. To the Office staff she was the usual not very good tempered Mrs. Macklin, engaged in rather an absorbing domestic task. But inwardly a forest fire of impatience consumed the dry tinder of her curiosity. She could scarcely endure the afternoon hours as they dragged ponderously by. The moment when she could commence her private investigations seemed as if it would never come. Impassively she knitted, venting her feelings every now and again on the children if they ever made the mistake of playing within her vision. Jennifer, alone among the people who came in contact with Mrs. Macklin, divined that something was brewing. Second sight, woman's intuition, the strange traces of similarity of temperament which went with shared blood, all or one of these told her as surely as a geiger counter that her Mother was plotting, planning courses of action far more fiendish than any harridan whose knitting was splashed by the gore spilt by the incisive blade of the guillotine. Jennifer, in her turn, resolved that she too would know what was going on; and thus was born the grotesque twin of their monstrous dual espionage.

Eventually, it was with ill-concealed bad-tempered relief that Mrs. Macklin slammed the Office door on the heels of the last staff member to finish over-time. Hurrying the children through their high-tea, pushing Leslie and Brenda peremptorily into bed, without even the suspicion of a wash, she went out to the cleaning closet to fetch her brooms and dustpans. Jennifer, curious to see what potent force was at work within her mother to make her in such a preoccupied hurry, followed unnoticed like a mongrel in this massive woman's wake. Outside the door of O'Flattery's office, the first and only one to be cleaned that night, Mrs. Macklin looked about her suspiciously, like a wild beast returning to its lair, and observed for the first time her silent companion.

"Bugger off, you," she yelled, "oo asked you to foller?" Driving Jennifer back to their quarters and ordering her to get on with the washing up, she closed the door of O'Flattery's office behind her and went to work. Jennifer however, a true daughter of such a Mother, crept fearlessly back and placed her eye against the draughty key hole, observing from a distance, but quite clearly, what went on within.

Systematically Mrs. Macklin went through the papers in

106

O'Flattery's waste-paper basket. Nothing but screwed up envelopes and old cigarette packets, torn paper and an old apple core which imparted to the contents of the basket a curious sweet autumnal smell of decay. This attracted the attention of the ever watchful fly but not of Mrs. Macklin or Jennifer. Scrupulously, she turned over the neat piles of paper on his desk; nothing there. She even attempted to decipher the writing on the blotter, by means of a little pocket looking-glass which she always carried in her apron; for vanity still lingered in this battered hulk of femininity. But to no avail, too much had been blotted and the superimpositions made it quite illegible.

Next she started on the drawers of the desk. They yielded nothing of interest either, only paper, envelopes, old carbon copies of forgotten lists, all the boring impediments of an office desk, pen nibs, fresh blotting paper, even unused rulers. But just as she was giving up hope the last drawer refused her repeated tugs to open it. What to do? Adept with a bent hair pin she could make no impression on the lock.

"Coo," said Jennifer under her breath, "she 'ain't 'arf a corker, she must be 'arter suffink good," as she changed over eyes and rubbed the cold circle made by the key-hole round her eye socket.

Mrs. Macklin was not to be outdone. She had seen films, she had read detective novels. She knew the answers. Pulling the drawer above the locked one right out, and placing it cautiously on the floor, she felt with her hand to see if the thin wooden lining between the two drawers was loose. She was in luck. It answered to her hand and slid out easily, revealing the contents of the locked drawer. One red-covered school exercise book. Greedily she drew it forth and opened it at the first page. There, in the Irishman's round childish writing she read:

"O'Flattery's Private Journal."

Of course that artless plea had no effect on her and only served to whet her already insatiable appetite. Jennifer, who could only see that her mother held a book in her hand, was choked with curiosity. She saw Mrs. Macklin settle herself down in O'Flattery's chair and start to read.

"As I write the opening words of this journal, write them and rewrite them, I know that I shall prune and change, dissect and fillet my sentences from one form into another in an effort to express the more clearly that exact shade of meaning which is presented to my pen by the changing visions in my mind.

"My nostrils are filled with the intoxicatingly romantic lemon fragrance of a magnolia blossom. This peerless beauty has been cut from its parent tree, to save it from the destruction of the late summer rains. I cut it also to preserve its sweetness for my enjoyment and possible spiritual edification. It is poised in a heavy stemmed drinking glass, the flaws in the sides of which are repeated by the crystal bubbles in the water surrounding the flower's stalk. The white sublimity of the flower reclines in an enfolding bed of polished green leaves, which twist and bend to catch the light revealing a rusty mealiness dusted over their under surfaces. From the centre of the flower rises a pistil in the shape of a hooked pineapple. Each beak is bent downwards, having down the centre a thin russet stripe following the curve of its own shape. Round its purple base, the neck upon which it stands and to which the petals and sepals are also attached, cluster the pale peeled-banana coloured stamens. Most of these have fallen and lie in the cup of one of the petals. The tips which have been attached to the pistil are dipped in Tyrean purple as if they have imbibed their colour from its surface. They are supported now in drifts like miniature logs caught as they have fallen among the petals and sepals of the flower. The corolla of six subtile white petals is encupped by the calyx of

108

three similar sepals. The whole perianth is of a texture and colour to defy the milky whiteness of the most pure virginal flesh. Its shadows are tinged with an olive haze and are both crisp and at the same time soft, inviting the teeth to bite and sully such purity. The light shining through one upraised petal reveals a complex system of interwoven veins. The petals are ladle shaped, the handles of three being narrower than the other three; three curve upwards and three recline backwards supported by the concave arms of the sepals which vary only ever so slightly in colour from their six fair companions. These handles have a brittle waxy appearance which does not spread upwards into the curves of the corolla. In this particular flower one petal has a small tear in it and curls over caressing its own surface; the edges of this wound are rusty red, accentuating the glowing pallor of the whole blossom. Over all this white starred beauty, in its collar of shining green leaves, there hangs the all-pervading aroma which stings my nostrils. Which drugs my senses with romance not untinged with depravity. . . ."

"What silly muck," said Mrs. Macklin out loud. She was just about to put the book down without ravishing its pages further when, as she flicked through it, her eye was caught by a stray word, the meaning of which appealed more than the foregoing to her coarse taste. Alas for O'Flattery, she resumed her reading, as the fly brushed its legs frantically, poised on the vantage point of her shoulder.

What she proceeded to read now and later made even *her* hair stand on end. Confessions, admissions, desires had streamed in one uninhibited flow from the young Irishman's heart in the form of a literary adolescent purge. Like Mr. Gender writing to Miss Jeacock, the action of putting words onto paper, had obviously been a great relief to this otherwise shy boy.

Mrs. Macklin of course had no notion of the artistic merits or demerits of what she was reading. Nor had this

109

woman of wart-hog sensibility any idea of the sources from which O'Flattery had either consciously or unconsciously imbibed his influences. In fact many of the paragraphs were his attempts at pastiche composed in the style of whichever author he most admired at the time. Destined for no other eyes but his own there had been no reason to keep anything back. This little notebook had become his homuncle confidant, his father confessor. Passages of descriptive writing with blots and deletions all obviously written in white hot haste, made Mrs. Macklin lick her lips salaciously; the one on which she had now begun had a naïvety, a penny-novelettish quality, which spoke directly to her low character. With the first words she was off to a good start in her search for excitement.

"They lay together, naked, on the headland. He with his hands fondling her hair, his lips devouring hers; honey and roses were under her tongue. He could feel the soft swell of her breasts against his chest and the tautening of her nipples as he crushed her closer to him. She felt the crisp hair of his belly and the short tugging feelings as they, at last, became one. She felt a stirring in her womb as he mingled with her; life throbbed between them, pushing, thrilling through every nerve. His loins were one with hers but yet still frustratingly apart. He felt a wild, animal dissatisfaction. He longed for more as he felt his strength flowing into her. She was possessed completely. In this moment all her senses seemed tuned up, everything was experienced more acutely. She felt the short curling hairs of his armpits against her arms and the heavy power of his thighs. She felt defeated, suffocated, but delirious with pleasure; then suddenly it was all over; almost as if life had been withdrawn. She felt an infinite tenderness and knew what it was to feel utterly fulfilled, utterly happy. She still clung to him and felt she could lie beneath him for ever. The sun shone down upon their bare flesh as the breeze moved the shadows of the grass over the

*muscles of his sleeping back, making them look as if they
rippled with . . ."*

Mrs. Macklin put down the book and wiped the moisture from her lips with her duster. "Well I must say," she
thought, "this is blue-pencil stuff all right. It was never
like that with Sergeant Macklin, and 'e was a man wot
knew 'is onions and no mistake."

The words which followed were deleted, furiously, with
red ink and a note in the same colour said: *"This is
terrible, I have used the word 'felt' at least ten times."*
This meant nothing to Mrs. Macklin whose own "feelings" at this moment were more aware of the tightness of
her corsets which pressed into her body and made her
sweat; she plucked at them trying to relieve their pressure
as she went on with her reading, goggle-eyed with interest.
There followed some short sentences in French which she
couldn't understand and then she read:

*"Thy lids are rimmed with silver; they have even bands of
bright silver lain upon them. Yea thy lids are like slices of
glowing light cut from off the moon."*
and then:

"Your kisses are like ripe figs, for they are soft and cool."

Jennifer shifted her feet out in the passage, making her
mother start and hesitate in her reading. But knowing that
the outer office doors were locked she went on, confident
that she could not possibly be observed. The fly moved
silently among the papers on the desk.

"Here," she thought, "is a peculiar one!"

"Idea for a story," it said, *"the central character is
speaking:*

*"Yes, she's going to have a baby. She thinks it's going to
be awful and dreads the pain. She's got a nurse already for
when the baby comes. She sits all day eating chocolates and
listening to sentimental mother-and-son songs on the gramo-
phone. She eats her breakfast to the tune of 'Sonny Boy',*

111

and throbs through the rest of the day with 'Little Man you've had a busy day', and old favourites like 'Don't tell Mother'. She sits staring in front of her watching masses of pink fluff in the hands of the nurse and whimpers when she looks at diminutive socks and woollen caps. I can't do anything with her. She won't let me make love to her, she just clings to me and sobs pathetically into my shoulder. I can't make her out at all. I think she'll go off her head soon, if she doesn't pull herself together."

"Bloody barmy," thought Mrs. Macklin, "what can a single feller like 'im know about 'avin' kids? I've never read such tripe, fine sort of story that would have been."

"Come on now," she said to herself, "let's 'ave some more dirt. 'Ere's another . . . *'Idea for a story'*, perhaps this one will be as juicy as the second bit. 'Ere goes."

"He raised the tankard to his lips and, as he did so, he saw out of the window a girl go by. He put down his drink, drew his hairy hand across his lips and left the inn with a determined look on his face. She passed him going across the yard. She was carrying a large yellow bowl from the dairy, clutching it with one hand by the rim. It was empty and swung against her leg as she walked. He couldn't look at her face. His eyes were hard, his mouth sullen and she saw his glance drop to the points of her breasts as they swelled beneath her thin dress. She knew by that glance what he felt for her. Her knuckles went white as she gripped the rim of the creamy yellow bowl. If only, she thought, she had been carrying a slim violet from the frame by the pig-sty, she would have whisked it in front of his nose and all would have been the way she wanted it. But she walked defiantly past, knowing the only way was his way, and that she had thrown away an opportunity never to be offered a second time. For this unknown drover would not come this way again."

Mrs. Macklin began to be bored. As bored as Jennifer who had, from squatting on her haunches, slid to her knees and then to the floor; where she lay like a watch dog, but fast asleep. The fly crept through the keyhole and searched Jennifer's recumbent body. Mrs. Macklin turned over several pages until she saw a word which took her fancy. It was followed by a numbered list:

"*DEBAUCHEE*"

(1) *Slightly hunched shoulders.*
(2) *Thighs thrust forward, hands in pockets.*
(3) *Rims of eyelids inflamed.*
(4) *Blue shadows beneath eyes.*
(5) *Tight white skin over well arched nose.*
(6) *Mouth damp, lips full.*
(7) *Eyes half closed.*
(8) *Finely curved nostrils.*
(9) *Cosmetics? Scent?*
(10) *Calves projecting backwards like cavalry boots.*

"Well I don't know," she thought, "that's not my cup of tea. What's 'e gettin' at?" Then she went on to read what seemed to be the reverse of the picture:

"*He was a desirable young man with supple narrow hips and a clear translucent skin. The hair on the back of his neck, which was straight and firm, was crisp and electric to the touch. His nails were well shaped and his hands were long and hairless. Everything about him was well finished and untarnished. His teeth were white as nuts and unstained by tobacco juice. His feet were finely arched and he walked like some wild animal, springy and lusty, each foot placed firmly but with a certain carelessness, his calves and thighs taut with energy.*"

Mrs. Macklin scratched her head. "He don't seem to know what 'e do like; sounds like a pansy to me. But 'ullo what's this?"

"*No one hides themselves unless they want to be watched.*"

"Well," she thought smugly, settling herself down to read again as if this sentence gave her enough licence to read further; nodding her head in agreement, she read on:

*"Those are the sort of men I like to have sleep with me,"
said Lady Celia, as she waved an elegantly gloved hand
towards a group of young workmen, who in the full sun were
breaking up the pavement, stripped to their waists, their
muscles rippling in the warm light as they laboured at their
work. "I like youth and virile male flesh," she continued,
pouting her perfect lips and tapping impatiently with the
point of her parasol. Leaving one in no doubt as to whether
or not she was able to achieve her ideal."*

As Mrs. Macklin read, the cast in her eye became more
malign than ever. She began to see possibilities in this
young man whose secrets she was violating. "I'm not sure
as I don't agree with Lady Celia," she thought as she
remembered Sergeant Macklin's truss and his long apple-
sauce-coloured combinations. She began to read again.
The writing was becoming neater. The pages were now
dated and were getting nearer and nearer to the present
day. The extracts were becoming longer too. "Here was
another which looked like being one of those spicy ones":

*"Suddenly one of his hands withdrew from their clasp,
fluttering like a bird and began to search out the secret
sensitive places of the other's body, feeling its way, searching
the shadows and hollows of receptive flesh, sending quick
shivers dancing involuntarily up and down his spine, delicious
ecstasy visiting every corner of his vulnerable being. With
each caress they plunged deeper into an agony of hopeless
frustrated involvement, an involvement from which could
only grow a love strangled at the very outset by the voice of
convention, censured by society. Love at the same time as
fierce in its masculine power as it was tender in its feminine
sincerity. Their mouths met at last in a deep warm kiss and
he felt the other's tongue against his teeth. They were as near
each other now in sympathy as they could ever be, as if they
trod cloudless paths united as one, towards a brilliant painful*

114

light which dazzled their eyes and made their heads sing.
At first he could not comprehend this strange feeling of unity.
At one moment they had been two people lying together in a
tight embrace, now they were no longer separate but moved
upward as a single entity, complete with two mingled sets of
sensations which vibrated to capacity in the highest key. No
longer were they hand in hand, cheek by cheek, but it seemed
as though each of their bodies and their spirits had become
overlapped; everything fitted together with the precision of
the pieces of a puzzle which slip together, one piece fitting
inside another to complete the whole; so perfectly suited and
so evenly shaped, that without difficulty they traversed
diversity without defeat. For a short space everything seemed
transfigured. Then, slowly, this feeling of unity began to fade
and there floated upon them a soothing tenderness; a heavy
drowning cloud which separated them once more until they
felt again the reality of their bodies touching, firm and moist
with the sweat of activity. They knew then that perhaps for
the last time they had experienced the depth of each other's
giving. It was terrible, this feeling that they were incapable
of giving more, that they were empty of the power which had
so recently infused them with such delight. Life seemed not
only complete, but ended; it seemed impossible, so exhausted
were they by each other's strength, that they could gather,
ever again, the energy and desire to repeat what had taken
place between them a moment ago."

When she got to the end of this one her mind was made
up. This untried virgin man, who had, so it appeared, his
sexual experience only on paper, was too good for such
as Miss Jeacock. What he needed was something more
mature, more motherly, a woman like herself for instance,
with some experience of life. Not a frustrated spinster who
didn't know her way about, as you might say. The fly left
its exploration of Jennifer and returned through the key-
hole to Mrs. Macklin. She continued to read avidly and

as she did so was unconsciously preening herself for conflict.

"He had the face of a smiling faun, the thick proud lips curled back from strong sharp teeth. His eyes slanted and were accentuated by the upward curve of his eyebrows, which lost themselves in the overhanging tangle of his fair hair. The sun had come to rest in his hair and lay tousled there asleep. A little moonlight had crept into his warm dark eyes. Troubled slightly, they peered out nimble-witted through his lacquered lashes. His deft brown hands parted the leaves, breaking the pattern of sun-flecked green with two quick darting curves of brown arm. He stepped into the clearing bathed in sunlight and hot shadow which caressed his lithe body, glancing along the mounds of his muscles. He walked silently to the pool, with the soft unheard tread of a wild beast. Without a sound he slipped into the water, leaving only a trail of silver bubbles rising and spreading unsteadily to the surface of the pool. He didn't appear again for some time. When he did he was panting heavily for breath. He held a glistening fish in one hand. The water fell out of his curls, dropping down the mounts and hollows of his face. Like the sunlight it licked him as if it loved him, not wishing to leave the familiarity of his body again for the wet cold comfort of the pool. Leaning forward to catch a better glimpse of him, my foot crushed a dry twig with a loud snap; in one leap he was out of the water and away into the trees."

This one was a bit too lyrical for Mrs. Macklin to stomach. "High-falootin-lardy-bloody-dar," she called it, "Fauns and such!"

It didn't matter to her that she was privileged to read the record of the gradual awakening of this adolescent Irish youth. Whether it was fact or fiction she was unable to discriminate, and cared even less. She was trampling through his most hidden feelings with cloven hooves of iron. However trite and ill-expressed these meanderings

116

were, they were the genuine outpourings of a lad lost in a world threatening him with the dangers and pleasures of love. A boy whose imagination and religious upbringing kept him from experimenting with life, but which turned him inwards upon himself so that his feelings found expression in such written passages as those she had already raped. Imaginary sins dragged painfully from him, so personal and private that he could not even utter them in the sanctuary of the confessional. Indeed, there had been little enough actual wrong-doing in his life to confess.

A pocket calendar stuck on the next page, covering a whole year, puzzled her. Certain days were crossed out, some once, some twice, others even more times. Certain others were ringed round and starred; this was beyond her comprehension.

After a good scratch in her back hair and a flick with her duster at the omnipresent fly which had started bothering her, she began on a much longer episode:

"It was quite by chance that I got on to that particular bus. I had every intention of going in the opposite direction, but the usual 'something', which figures so frequently in stories of the supernatural and accounts of queer happenings, seemed to propel me to that bus. When I got to the theatre towards which I found the bus was progressing, I alighted and took a ticket at the box-office for a seat in the Pit. Where, behind a lecherous old gentleman with a ginger moustache and an eyeglass fixed into a very prominent watery-blue eye, I settled myself.

"I was wearing my old tweed suit, a made-up tartan bow tie, and had the aftermath of a bad stye in my right eye. I must have been anything but prepossessing. Just before the curtain rose, a tall slim girl carrying an umbrella, fashionably dressed in a blue dress and a dark coat, came up the gangway. She had the clear fresh look of a thoroughbred, curly hair and a wide attractive mouth. I noticed her with

117

interest but as she sat behind me thought little more about her.

"In the second interval I was standing at the back of the Pit, idly watching the audience returning for the last ballet, when the girl with the attractive mouth came towards me. I suppose I must have looked at her rather too closely. Anyhow she looked back and stopped by the end of her row, hesitated and then came round behind me to have a look at me at all angles. Then she went back to her own row again. I went back to my seat glancing at her as I passed. I sat down, half turning to see if she was still looking. She was. Finally, just before the rise of the curtain, she got up and came asking, in the most musical of voices, if the seat next to mine was taken. I replied that it wasn't. She gathered up her umbrella and coat and sat down; the curtain rose once more; I asked her if my macintosh, which hung over the seats in front was in her way. She said it wasn't. The lecherous old man had also moved several seats nearer and was desperately trying to pick up this girl with the engaging smile, before she became too friendly with me.

"The ballet was invisible to me. All that I knew was that a pageant of vivid colour was moving before my eyes, the last act of 'Swan Lake' was unfolding, to the haunting strains of Tchaikovsky's music, the drama of Odette and Odile was reaching its climax. But I was blind to it, all I heard was the music and felt the presence of this girl, which was making me shiver all over, close beside me. I couldn't control myself, I was so sure that she wanted to make love as much as I that my whole body quivered from head to foot, in an ecstasy of anticipation. I could scarcely bear it. I must get out or the people near me would think that I had the ague. Quite suddenly she took my hand, so gently, so timidly and we knew that we both agreed. She touched it with such sensitivity, so sweetly; she knew every hollow from the wrist to the finger tips. Once, when I glanced into her eyes, I knew how easy it

118

would be to fall in love with her. Our legs leaned against each other. One side of each of our bodies was infused with a warmth far greater than the warmth of an old established friendship. I sought in my mind for a way of insuring that I should see more of her that night. Every way seemed impossible. Suddenly the ballet was over and we were hurrying to the exit, outside which we found that it was teeming with rain.

"We walked, our bodies close together, under her umbrella to the bus stop, stopping at a coffee stall to prolong the time of being in one another's company. She had to go back to her Mother's flat and I to my boarding house. I had never wanted a flat of my own more than at that moment. She told me how she had been to the country the week before, and how the weather had been 'lousy'. We spoke of unimportant things, with all the time an undercurrent of suggestion that we both avoided with laughter trembling on our lips. We finished our coffee. I explained again that I could not ask her to my room, she explained why it was impossible for her to ask me to go home with her; she asked me if she was going to see me again, and of course it is obvious what I said. We arranged to meet the next day. I rode home in a frenzy of apprehension."

Next Mrs. Macklin's prying eyes read a short sentence, obviously written the following day. It was simply:

"She didn't turn up."

"Whatever is this boy doing wasting his time with bits of girls like that," she thought, "I'll soon cure him of that." But the next long episode, which was far too detailed for her liking, rather dismayed her:

"The week before I came to work at the Office was really the most eventful week of my life. On the Tuesday evening of that week I was outside a café with N. We had just had a coffee and didn't know where to go next. We crossed the road and then together we saw the American. He was tall

119

and had good shoulders. This and the cut of his clothes was eloquent of both his attraction and the fact of his nationality.

"N. said didn't you want to go and phone and I said didn't you want to go and buy some matches. Then we both laughed nastily, but neither of us budged. We both stayed looking in the shop window, but really looking sideways at the American who was looking into the shop window further up, but was really looking sideways.

"Then it all happened quickly. We wanted to light cigarettes and the American gave us both lights, then we all stood saying nothing. But he was awfully nice and I felt glad. A bus came along and we all got on to it. N. nearly pushed me off trying to get up the stairs next to the American but I got up first and sat beside him. Our legs touched and his felt hard and muscular. I can't remember what we talked about but we talked. Then we got off and stood about aimlessly, N. and I trying to get rid of one another, while the American chuckled. He was cute. He was so cute that he didn't care which of us won, because we meant nothing to him. Nothing at all. So then he hailed a taxi and we all got in. In the musty darkness he kissed us both in turn. He tasted of cigarettes. His hand strayed about my legs and his own. His movements left no doubt about what his intentions were. I suddenly hated it, I felt horrid and hoped he was doing the same to N. as I knew he would hate it too and would probably make a fuss. It made me feel debased and ashamed. But he didn't do it to N. All the time the taxi driver's head was very upright and blind looking. I wondered how much he could really see and what vices the inside of this taxi had in the past enclosed.

"Then we got out at the address the American had given the driver. He paid the taxi, laughed as he said goodbye and in a moment disappeared into a house. I felt kind of dirty and wanted to cry. N. was silent, hard and somehow defiant. Perhaps he felt the same as I did, I never knew. Because from

120

that day onwards we grew steadily further and further apart."

"Well," said Mrs. Macklin, aloud. Jennifer stirred in her comfortless sleep. Her Mother continued with her reading:

"The next day was extraordinary. So extraordinary that I can hardly ever believe that it happened the way it did. I was standing outside the same café again, alone this time, something, a pretty obvious something, had drawn me to it, when I saw the negro. He was so very dark and handsome with broad shoulders and narrow hips, that it made me go all strange inside to look at his back, it was so big and strong. The night before I had not known clearly what it was that I wanted, but now it was as if I had been initiated. I knew, instinctively and at once that I wanted him to make love to me. So I followed him as he walked off up the street. He saw me and looked, I looked, in the same way, back. I could see that we understood one another's message. We walked on, stopping in turn, overtaking and re-passing, looking in shop windows. Until at last we looked into the same shop window or rather at the glass in the same shop window, so that we could see each other's reflexion. This window, I remember had in it some awful lampshades, but I could only really see him. My heart was beating very fast, I was watching the glossy purplish-black of his skin and the strange yellowness of the whites of his eyes. Then he said 'hullo' and at once I felt that I had known him for ever and that I loved him. His voice was so soft and southern that I wanted him desperately to want me as much as I wanted him.

"We walked on explaining that we had nowhere to go together, always nowhere to go, and I was very sad. All the time he twirled a bunch of keys round and round his finger at the end of a chain. It had close interwoven links and looked like a snake. He was wearing a light summer suit, blue, and a mauve tie. The shadows on his face were lit with strange translucent reflections from these colours, accentuating the

121

almost bruised black of his lips and skin. I remember that the pavement outside a shuttered shop near where we first spoke, was all wet and that there was a strong smell of fish. Then he suggested that we went to a hotel for a drink, as it was getting late and pubs were shutting. So we did. But it was already too late for them also and they wouldn't serve us with anything because we were not residents. Perhaps it was a good thing as I don't drink really and I had only enough money for my fare home. He also only had seven and sixpence, so together we hadn't enough money to take a room.

"We went on sitting. I wanted something from him terribly badly and he seemed to need me too. He said his name was Tommie. After we had sat there some time and the waiter wouldn't serve us, we were so intimidated by the stares of the other people that we got up and left, only to walk the streets again.

"The dry streets had been watered and we walked down a side street into a mews, where suddenly he said in a hard voice, 'This is where I must leave you', and at the same time put his arm round me. I remember that over his shoulder I saw a cat run across in the light of a street lamp and that he had a curious smell of vanilla, which was at the same time both attractive and repellent. All the time that we kissed he was whirling his keys behind my back. He felt good. Then, 'goodnight' he said, turned on his heel and walked away fast swinging his keys; not looking back, into the darkness, out of my life. I never saw him again."

Mrs. Macklin sat feeling very puzzled. This was something she didn't know about at all. This was something Sergeant Macklin had never told her about. Was this O'Flattery a man, or a woman in disguise? She knew dimly that people with such tastes existed, they were in fact nothing more to her than a half-comprehensible music hall joke. She preferred not to think about them, they were of no consequence to her. All that concerned her at the

122

moment was this boy with his unfulfilled but clearly expressed pent-up sexual desire. A desire which she intended to satisfy; an intention, which to her had nothing unreasonable or unnatural about it.

As she finished reading the last paragraph her eye wandered to the top of the next page. She realised that with this item she had reached the present day. She had now devoured the unfolding sensuality of this odd character up until the time when she herself might come into the picture. She read on with renewed appetite, greedily, but could not to her surprise find her own name anywhere. All at once she caught sight of, among a lot of French words, the name of Miss Jeacock, "There now the sly wretch, using that frog lingo." Now she really was flummoxed. But her eye ran on and at last beneath a very recent date, she came upon another reference to Miss Jeacock. This time, one that she could understand:

"I find Miss Jeacock, curious looking though she is, a woman who intrigues me."

"Coo-er, the young reprobate," sighed Mrs. Macklin aloud again, "I wish it was me." The more she read the more stimulated by the private vision of this young man did she become. By the time that the extracts had become up-to-date she had made her decision. She would get this lusty boy for herself. She managed to convince herself that the discrepancy in their ages was of no importance. Throughout history young men had been initiated by older women and why shouldn't she assume this role. As she read she began to imagine that O'Flattery could conceivably like her. She allowed the delusion to grow that he had in fact payed her compliments. Hadn't he given her daughter Jennifer a tortoise for her birthday, and hadn't Leslie burbled something about a promise to take them all to the circus? Surely this was a shy young man's way of paying court to the woman of his choice. The saucy rascal.

123

He seemed to know what was what all right, although he was a bit muddled up between men and women. But she would soon be able to sort him out and set all that right. The sexy young so-an'-so and no mistake.

She had read now to the end of what was written in the exercise book. So with a deep sigh of enjoyment, as of one who had eaten a large and satisfying meal, she carefully replaced the book in the drawer, the drawer lid in the desk and finally the upper drawer above it. Collecting the waste-paper basket and her brooms she marched off, with a hearty appetite for her supper.

Stumbling over the sleeping body of her daughter, she roused her by a spiteful blow with her broom and driving Jennifer before her down the passage she shouted:

"Get out, you bloody little spy. I thought I told you to get on with the sodding washing up?"

That impudent young Irishman, the more she thought about him the more determined she became. She would be the one to have him. She wasn't the one to let a scrawny old bitch like Miss Jeacock get the better of her. Oh, no, not she!

9

A NEW and complicated phase of this quadripartite chase can now be said to have begun. Mr. Gender—Miss Jeacock—O'Flattery—Mrs. Macklin, their lives were becoming inextricably intertwined. Slowly, like lumps of food in a giant digestive tract, they were being assimilated together but not without frequent twinges of dyspeptic pain. Weaving and writhing like maggots in a dead dog the feelings they felt for one another became daily more involved. Like the intricate and invisible path traced through the air by the Argus-eyed fly the intangible thoughts, the unuttered utterances of this quartet made a strange fabric which bound them together like a shroud.

The fact that Mr. Gender was besotted by Miss Jeacock had not entirely escaped the notice of their colleagues. The younger ones among them, while regarding his situation with bored indifference, found it inconceivable that he felt the way he did, but at the same time wondered why he did nothing to advance his position. All except the Irishman, who felt deeply for him but was wracked by conflicting doubts and indecision.

The two men were hopelessly inactive and could make no positive open display of their feelings. The women on the other hand did not share their reticence.

Mrs. Macklin, from the day after her discovery in his desk of O'Flattery's private drawer, began a campaign of ogling and smiling which was as incomprehensible to the bewildered Irishman as it was unwelcome.

Each day that he encountered her she wrapped him in kittenish leers or deluged him with fulsome compliments, inappropriate enough from the mouth of this incredible beldame.

She, who to him would have been more at home doing her knitting in a Goya etching rather than at the Office doorway, made herself increasingly ridiculous to her chosen paramour, the more she strove to woo him.

As her behaviour became more and more pressing so did O'Flattery's disquiet increase, until he fled at her approach in an endeavour to avoid as much as possible any contact with this amorous huntress. Miss Jeacock on the other hand was more subtle. Ever since the incident in Mr. Nale's shop when the Irishman had stared at her blouse button she had become more and more conscious of him as a man. Not being armed as was Mrs. Macklin with the information from the journal she was not aware of the hidden fires beneath O'Flattery's milk-white exterior. Her overtures, therefore, were more tentative and only perceptible to the Irishman and herself. Shy glances across the cups in the tea break, special smiles when they exchanged papers connected with their work, long deep-throated good-nights with blazingly direct looks, all of these spoke volumes and by their very restraint were more powerful than all Mrs. Macklin's ham-fisted attempts at seduction.

O'Flattery reacted like litmus paper. He wrote of Miss Jeacock almost daily in the red exercise book. Unbeknown to him, the scheming Mrs. Macklin was keeping abreast of his entries; every day by the same means as before she investigated the contents of the drawer to see what he had written. As each entry about her rival got more fervid she redoubled her efforts to attract the young man, while he in his turn was hard put to think of ways to avoid her.

In quick sequence her treacherous eyes read:

"*Miss Jeacock has been making cow-eyes at me for several*

126

months. *She fascinates me. I cannot say I am attracted in any ordinary physical sense but I feel a terrible desire to degrade her. But Mr. Gender is in love with her. I feel sure I recognise the signs. I like and respect him. I am at a loss to know what to do.*"

Then a week or two later:

"*She has started using a perfume which attracts me. It is very erotic, half disgusting, half intoxicating. Gender or no Gender, I shall not be able to hold out against this powerful feeling much longer.*"

Then a few days before that on which she was reading:

"*It is obvious now that she is pursuing me. I can help myself no longer. I have given myself up to the delicious abandon of being hunted. I no longer see her as I know she is, but as my predatory prey, although in reality it is she who acts the part of Diana.*"

Never once did she read the kind of reference to herself that she wished to see. Was there something wrong with the boy? Could he not see her or had he only eyes for Miss Bloody Jeacock? Or could this last entry, about Diana, be meant to refer to her? She'd made herself pretty obvious, which was more than she could say for Miss Jeacock, perhaps after all it was intended for her. So eager was she to read that O'Flattery found her an object of attraction, so distorted had her reason become through the debilitating growth of her depression, that even the most unlikely hint would have served to convince her completely that she was the loved one, however the present doubt was enough to foment her already putrid frustration. In truth, of course, he found Mrs. Macklin so repellent, the thought of what her looks meant so disgusting, that in his complicated simplicity he could not bring himself to defile his precious journal with any words about her.

Mrs. Macklin searched the journal in vain, driving herself to distraction with a volcanic jealousy which she

127

revealed to no one, except indirectly to her unfortunate children, to whom she meted out more violence than usual. She was storing up a battery of spite fit to shame the wildest jackal.

It was unfortunate for O'Flattery that the day after that on which Mrs. Macklin had formulated her hideous plan to pursue him was the very day that he had chosen to honour his promise to her children and take them to the circus. Mrs. Macklin, all too ready to misconstrue his intentions, had interpreted his action as a friendly overture towards herself, thus throwing combustible encouragement on the fluctuating fires of her obsession.

After persistent hints from Leslie and open demands from Jennifer, O'Flattery had capitulated and to his surprise found himself on his weekly afternoon off seated inside a stuffy tent among a howling mob of children. Wendy on one side clutched his arm, while on the other sat Jennifer with Brenda enthroned upon her lap and Leslie next to them. All the children gnawed toffee apples bought by Jennifer with some money unexpectedly provided by Mrs. Macklin.

O'Flattery's embarrassment at being in this strange company conflicted with his amusement at being in this situation at all.

Lothario's Circus was indeed a family affair, everyone took part in everything, their versatility was amazing. In fact the Irishman found it impossible to decide how many members of the family there were, so many times did they change their costumes and their functions. The overall feeling of hectic despair at the paucity of their resources seemed only increased by their astonishing ambidexterity. The music for the performance was supplied by a one-man-band who was strung about with bells, drums and other instruments fixed to home-made contrivances so that they were readily playable. He had cymbals on leather straps between his knees and a hat hung with bells like a Burmese temple, so that a shower of tinkling sound streamed round his head whenever he shook it. His nose had been eaten away by the depredations of some disease. This fascinated Wendy, who was continually staring at him and missing the turns which went on in the little sawdust strewn ring.

"Where's 'is nose Mr. Flattery?" she kept whispering, plunging her toffee apple in and out of her mouth as if she was working at unblocking a drain, while at the same time plucking at the Irishman's arm.

"Its dropped off," finally muttered O'Flattery.

"Where's it gorn to?" said Wendy looking at the man's feet, expecting to see the nose lying on the ground among the trampled sawdust.

"Shurrup cow," bellowed Jennifer, leaning forward so that Brenda's toffee apple dragged across the hat of the woman in the row below them, "hold yer row, can't cher!"

"Shit 'em," said Wendy slobbering over her toffee apple and only finally silenced by a rending Flamenco blast from a trumpet.

Some very rickety flights of steps and wooden trestles were being set up and a very old white she-goat was being led round the ring by a spare-ribbed boy. Between its horns it wore a rakish diamanté crown surmounted by nodding ostrich feathers, one pink, one blue, one bent and all dingy. A monkey, wearing a pink skirt dragged at the end of a long thin chain; when the group had made its tour of the ring it leapt upon the goat's back and crouched there jibbering as its attendant boy fixed the chain to a ring in the goat's harness. Then very laboriously, to a rising crescendo of sound from the one-man-band, the battered old goat began to ascend the lowest flight of steps. Very painfully, its rider snickering with fear, stage by stage it heaved its way to the top of the ladders where there was a

129

small table from the centre of which rose a blunt-topped pinnacle; reaching this it paused and then delicately as if the topmost knob was red hot it raised itself up until all four feet were balanced precariously on this tiny area. Solemnly it began to rotate, its swollen udders quivering pathetically, the monkey by this time flattened against its back blinking in the spot light which was trained upon it. The drums banged, the cymbals clashed, the trumpet blared forth as the bandsman went through a paroxysm of epileptic movement, throughout which Wendy muttered, "Shit 'em, where's 'is nose, shit 'em, where's 'is nose?"

This was the final turn before the interval. Suddenly the music ceased, leaving the goat to descend in the pool of gloom made by the equally sudden dimming of the spotlight. Chaos ensued with children elbowing and shoving one another to get outside the tent or to buy ices and sweets. Jennifer, who had been wriggling throughout the performance, hoisted Brenda unexpectedly on to O'Flattery's lap and before she could protest was scuttling off with Wendy and Leslie shouting urgently, "Got to go to the toilet". Brenda who had been unnaturally quiet throughout the performance immediately began grizzling, impotently floundering in the direction in which Jennifer had disappeared. O'Flattery, reminded of the Ugly Duchess and the Pig Baby, soon realised from the cold dampness spreading on his knee why it had not been necessary for Jennifer to take Brenda out with them. " 'Too late,' said the White Rabbit," thought the Irishman, smiling despite his discomfort.

The picture-book-gypsy sold balloons and as O'Flattery caught her eye he heard the steady droning of the fly, trapped somehow between the meshes of Brenda's hair and her pixy cap.

Leslie, Jennifer and Wendy soon came elbowing back to the relief of everyone in earshot, for Brenda's suffocating

130

yells had become impossible, but they stopped as quickly as they had begun as soon as she saw her elder sister and realised that she had not been totally abandoned. Nor did she appear to mind being dumped from lap to lap like a parcel in a party game, as Jennifer attempted to persuade Wendy to nurse her for the second part of the performance, but she would not oblige and let out such a tirade of "Shit 'ems" that Jennifer had to put up with the chilly moisture of her sister again in order to quieten her friend.

The second half began with a performing bear act. There were two bears, one was a real brown one and the other, it was easy to see, was a man dressed in a polar bear's skin. O'Flattery wondered how many of the children were taken in. It was very obvious to him but it was not clear from his companions' faces whether or not they were convinced by the travesty. Whether it was economy or whether it was supposed to add to the comedy of the act the Irishman found it difficult to decide. The spectacle of this false bear certainly was funny and reminded him of an old lady he had seen one winter day shopping in the intense cold. She had come staggering through the swing doors of a shop clad, it seemed from head to foot, in grey fur looking for all the world like a dirty polar bear walking on its hind legs. She wore a grey fur hat, a long shaggy grey fur coat, an even longer grey woollen skirt and finally her extremities were covered by fur gloves and fur boots. Her arms were stuck out before her from manoeuvring the door and the flushed pinkness of her face framed in so much fur heightened the illusion of ursine reality reminding the Irishman of those artificially pink tongues of the taxidermist's art. In fact he had to glance back over his shoulder to make certain that this was not one of those bears which sometimes stand outside tobacconists and was quite relieved when he saw the apparition stagger forward through the traffic to proceed with its shopping.

131

The sharp barking of a team of football-playing performing dogs brought him back to the circus from which his thoughts had temporarily wandered.

The dogs were followed by two graceful boys on a trapeze who showed off their young muscles, briefly touched with sequins, way up in the smoky heights of the tent. Wendy hid her eyes in her hands and Brenda became far more interested in the closer spectacle of a frightened Wendy than the more-difficult-to-focus-on contortions of the acrobats. While this was going forward the other members of the Lothario troupe were setting up a tight-rope in the un-netted ring beneath the brave boys; finally, to Wendy's relief, these heroes descended. Clad in little more than their firm moist flesh they had drawn from the breathless crowd strangled cries of terrified admiration as, like Icarus, they soared time and again towards the earth. But, unlike him, catching one another's hands or the glistening bars of the trapeze, when each time it looked as if they must be dropping to certain mutilation.

"Cor, ain't they smashin'," breathed Jennifer as the justifiably peacock-proud boys strutted to the applause which brought their act to an end.

As the clapping died away a spot light was hesitatingly trained on a frail figure in a ballet tutu who skipped youthfully into the ring and with an experienced performer's gestures bowed her way to the steps which led up to the tight rope. She was quickly followed by a somersaulting clown and an inappropriate granny-figure as rustily black as the other two were tinsely gay.

The tight-rope walker launched herself onto the slack wire and with out-turned feet ran deftly across her knife-edge path. As she ran through the brighter shafts of light O'Flattery could see that she was not as young as her youthful carriage had at first suggested. The low-cut bodice of her old-fashioned dress of pink and yellow net revealed

132

a lot of heavily powdered coarse flesh, tired and slack as the wire. Two paper chrysanthemums bobbed at the nape of her neck and as she performed to Tchaikovsky's music for the Sugar Plum Fairy, balancing with the aid of a Japanese parasol, the Irishman could see that she got through the performance with difficulty and that under her powder she was erupting with copious beads of sweat. So poignant was she that he hardly noticed the antics of the clown who was capering about below his partner and mocking the behaviour of the strange black granny-figure who was going through a pantomime act of either genuine or simulated alarm as anxiously she watched the middle-aged figure on the tight-rope. O'Flattery's attention was riveted to this vulnerable little figure spot-lighted in its loneliness in the middle of the ring and he suffered the complexities of what she was trying to do; he found himself very close to tears as he watched this brave battle with infirmity. The old lady too was clearly suffering, genuinely, afraid lest her daughter should fall. This beshawled crone was the butt of all the clown's senseless patter and made with her daughter a desperately tragic duet. The Irishman could bear it no longer when, for some reason which he had not heard, the clown, unbeknown to the old woman, filled his mouth with water. Then, attracting her close attention by pretending that he had something in his eye, he discharged the whole mouthful directly into her face. The indignity of it appalled O'Flattery and he could hardly believe that it was rehearsed and performed twice daily, so amazed and broken did the old lady look. Queen Lear to the Circus Fool.

It was a relief when all three left the ring and amidst ear-splitting yells the traditional finale of covered wagons being attacked by Red Indians got under way. The stink of gunpowder and horse manure choked those members of the audience who had ring-side seats; soiled sawdust was flung from the horses' hooves into their laps, so that children and the more timorous adults drew back in horror and were secretly glad that the show was nearly over. The whole troupe, male and female, ring hands, ice-cream sellers, all had been roped in to this final scene and were got up as Indians in full war paint or prospectors and their poke-bonneted wives. The whole thing was quite meaningless and silly to the Irishman who, worn out with conflicting emotions, only wished to get out of the tent and away from his companions as quickly as possible. They were all delighted by the final cacophony and added their own yells to swell the din.

"Shit 'em," cried Wendy.

"Scalp 'em," screamed Leslie.

"Glar, Glarge, Glar," gobbled Brenda in a paroxysm of delight as she was bounced up and down on her sister's knee to an unprintable chorus of imprecations, the meaning of which could hardly have been clear to her childish ears, for indeed they were obscure enough to the half innocent O'Flattery.

At last it was all over and the Irishman was able to drag his unwilling tribe out of the reeking tent. Now that they had experienced the magic world of the circus, they resented having to go back to the reality of their lives. They hung back, gazing about them, longing for more. As he pushed their way through the crowd, his nostrils filled with the smell of crushed grass, the children suddenly ceased in O'Flattery's eyes to be the troupe of little monstrosities that their previous behaviour had led him to believe they were. For this smell had taken him back to when he too had been their age, when as a solitary child he had lain in the grass, crying to ease a nameless heartache, sobbing desperately to himself among the broken stems of grass and buttercups, as through his tears he watched the painful progress of a brightly enamelled beetle which struggled vainly through the complex haze of bent stalks. A heartache which had been always with him made worse by the sparkling cries of happy children near by whose games he wanted to join but, by some feat of his own unique reasoning, he had proved to himself he was unfit to join and now cried because he had prevented himself from being happy and could blame no one else for doing so.

So that now when he smelt the grass crushed by the feet of the circus people, their animals and their audience, he could only see his little band of children as an extension of himself and thus was able to extend his own feeling of self-pity to cover them also. Jennifer was pushing Brenda in the push-chair which they had retrieved from somewhere, Leslie was walking in front of it balancing precariously on an imaginary tight rope in constant danger of having the backs of his legs attacked by vicious stabs from the front of the push-chair. Wendy had unaccountably slipped a sticky hand into that of O'Flattery and was walking along by his side, taking unnaturally long and solemn strides to keep up with him, while she peered up into his face with an expression of such sympathetic understanding that he felt suddenly very close to her. Without thinking of the consequences he gave her hand an earnest squeeze. The result was startling; Wendy's grip tightened and she began to drag on the young man's arm as if she wanted him to reduce his pace in order that the others should outdistance them and they should be left alone together, but it had the reverse of the desired effect and O'Flattery increased his pace and at the same time began talking very fast.

"Which of the acts did you like the best Wendy?"

"Them two big boys wiv no clothes on what swung abaht," breathed Wendy.

"Yes, they were very good, very graceful," conceded the Irishman.

"Cor, I should fink they wos too. They didn't 'alf

135

glitter."

O'Flattery was surprised that she had noticed that they glittered.

"Cor, they wasn't 'alf big and strong. Are you big and strong like that Mr. Flattery?" coaxed Wendy.

The Irishman thought of the well defined musculation of these two young men glistening with sweat and then thought of his own body as he frequently contemplated it spread out before him in his bath.

"No not really, Wendy," he felt bound to confess. Reluctant to admit, even to himself, that he could not really compare himself to these two virile boys who had swooped and dived like fearless swallows for their afternoon's entertainment.

"Coo, I bet you are really," fawned Wendy unctuously looking up at him with her great gooseberry eyes.

"Did you like the dogs?" hurriedly continued O'Flattery wanting to get round this dangerous corner of comparison.

"Yare," said Wendy rather unconvincingly, "however do they do it? All that runnin' about on their 'ind legs an all?"

"I don't know exactly," said O'Flattery eagerly, "but I remember once being given a pamphlet as I was leaving a circus . . ."

"Wots a pamflit?" interrupted Wendy.

"A leaflet, a piece of paper with a printed message on it, from a Society which tried to protect captive and performing animals."

"Why?"

"Because they believed that in order to train animals to do tricks people were very cruel to them."

"What did they do?" said Wendy salaciously.

"Well in this pamphlet there were a set of six drawings showing how a dog was trained to stand on one front leg."

"How?" said Wendy disbelievingly.

"Well," said O'Flattery wishing he had never started the conversation, "there had to be two men, one to be nasty to the dog and one to be nice."

"Why?"

"Well, the nasty one was supposed to whip the dog and then tie it up by one leg from the ceiling so that it hung upside down without support, until it was howling with pain."

"Yare," said Wendy slobbering with delight.

"And then after a while when they decided it had had enough the other one came in and put his hand up so that the dog could support itself by one leg on it. The dog soon found that if it kept still its hind leg was less painful, so that when the man gave it lumps of sugar and patted it, the poor animal learnt to regard this man as its deliverer and consequently tried always to please him. So that after much repetition of the torture by one man and the rescue by his colleague the dog is enslaved and will obey the master who has deceived it."

Wendy was bored by this time and wasn't listening. When the Irishman finished speaking she frowned up at him and said:

"Your hand's all sweaty," at the same time letting go of it and darting on to join Leslie and Jennifer who were just approaching the Office.

O'Flattery, whose momentary tenderness towards the children had been dissipated, now saw them as heartless little beasts and was about to turn on his heel and leave them without saying goodbye, when unexpectedly, almost as if they sensed his displeasure, the three turned back leaving Brenda's push-chair hooked on to the railings and surrounded him with linked hands bellowing, "For he's a jolly good fellow, for he's a jolly good fellow," until the passers-by turned their heads in amazement at this strange demonstration.

137

"Thank you, thank you," cried the embarrassed young man trying to break out of this terrible circle, only being released when Leslie espied Mrs. Macklin standing in the glow of light which streamed from the Office doorway and in it waving a monumental arm indicating, he knew, that they were to go in to their tea.

Wendy melted away into the darkness flapping her arms like a great bat. The Macklin children screaming "Ta, ever so much," obeyed their Mother's summons as she still stood, her arm raised reminding the Irishman of the statue of Liberty, for the light was refracted by this arm making long bars of diminishing light spread out into the gathering fog. He turned away with a feeling of sickening regret that he had involved himself with the children of this woman who had begun to menace him with her overpowering attentions.

10

THE EVENING before the day of the Office Outing was wet, cold and unpromising. O'Flattery had stayed late to finish some letters, knowing that the next day he would not be at the Office and that such a gap in his work would break all continuity.

Unbeknown to him Mrs. Macklin had decided to carry her weird pursuit one stage further. The strange wooing of the tadpole by the toad had begun.

She had laid her plans carefully and with a dedicated thoroughness. Arthur had been ordered to "sit in" with the children; Wendy had been allowed to stay for high tea; Mrs. Macklin had adorned herself with her Sunday finery and, concealing herself in the vestibule, had proceeded to wait patiently until the Irishman chose to leave.

The fly was in attendance, missing nothing.

Mrs. Macklin's timing was impeccable; for after ten minutes vigil O'Flattery came whisking lightheartedly towards the door and his evening's freedom. That was what he thought; he wasn't aware of the lurking presence whose intention it was to follow him wherever he went, like the ball chained to the foot of a convict, and if possible to present herself casually, unexpectedly, before him in some compromising situation.

When she judged that he had got well away from the building Mrs. Macklin gave chase, keeping in the shadows out of sight, should he for any reason turn around.

Back in the caretaker's quarters a scene of great festivity was being staged. Arthur sat enthroned in an armchair, his feet on the fender, enjoying a luxury he had scarcely ever before been allowed. His moronic face was garlanded with smiles. Surmounting it he wore a bright paper hat which had been further adorned by the tinsel band from some bygone Christmas cake. Jennifer and Leslie had dragged out a treasured box of old Christmas decorations and had, with Wendy's help, bedecked poor Arthur. He allowed himself to be subjected to this treatment with the patience of a child, amazed at his usual evening loneliness being so unexpectedly suffused with such warm well-being.

Brenda sat in her high-chair. With her was the tortoise who had somehow acquired a necklace of interlaced dandelions. Between chews on a dirty handful of crust, upon which she was cutting her teeth, she belaboured the tray in front of her with a wooden spoon, letting out a chorus of cries intending to express delight but which sounded to anyone unacquainted with her vocabulary more like agonised complaints. No one took a scrap of notice of her and for once she was able to bawl herself into a coma without being frustrated by her elder sister.

Eventually, when Arthur was entwined with paper chains and Brenda was asleep, Jennifer went off upstairs with Wendy and Leslie to "dress-up". Jennifer insisted, accompanied by pinches and slaps, that they should all be Eastern Princesses. Leslie, determined to stick to his manhood, was obstinate, but finally Jennifer's protracted threats of fearful future violence had routed him and he too allowed himself to be arrayed in a semblance of exotic raiment.

His short knickers were rolled up by the sniggering Wendy and then concealed under a length of old red curtain as a skirt. His shirt had been unceremoniously stripped off him; where his bust would have been, had he been the genuine odalisque he was to impersonate, a length of old chocolate box ribbon made a band of colour across his fish-belly-white flesh. A bath towel turban trapped some wisps of frayed raffia round his turnip head, making it look even more insecure as it wobbled unsteadily on his frail neck.

With one dancing girl complete, Jennifer started on Wendy whose costume took the same lines but the choice of materials being more suitable. Wendy, after much giggling, had consented to take off her dress and stood pigeon-toed in her knickers, before the wondering Leslie, open-mouthed with curiosity. Net curtain this time made the skirt, two oranges were shoved into an empty brassiere of Mrs. Macklin's which was strapped across the patient's chest like a surgical support. An old antimacassar, lashed on to her head with Leslie's dressing gown cord, completed her bewitching ensemble.

Then it was Jennifer's turn. She of course had saved the best bits of rubbish for her own costume. As carefully as her Mother had donned her Sunday best she attired herself. Old pyjama trousers, two lace curtains and a quantity of brass curtain rings, out of these she contrived the basis of her creation. Her evil little face was partly concealed by the folds of an old silk table centre which, anchored firmly to her head by the tinsel crown saved from some long forgotten Christmas tree Fairy Queen, hung in dusty folds to her shoulders.

The dancing girls being ready, downstairs they trouped. Leslie still complaining, Wendy doubled up with suppressed giggles and Jennifer serene in the delusion that she was a seductive enchantress from the East. To their surprise they were not received by the delighted audience they expected but discovered them to be boringly asleep. Brenda had worn herself out with banging and the heat of the fire had set Arthur off snoring. Like a satiated Bacchus he lay

141

stretched in the easy-chair, the room vibrating round him with gargantuan snores.

Their sleep was soon interrupted. Jennifer had instructed her minions on how to reproduce Eastern music with the help of two saucepans and an old kitchen funnel, while Leslie got rid of some of his spleen by clashing the saucepan lids together. Jennifer began to perform her interpretation of the dance of the seven veils, as learnt from lush-coloured Hollywood spectacles of obscure Biblical origin.

Brenda awoke and was transfixed. Arthur awoke to drool with delight, for he mistook the sight before him to be an erotic dream of his own imagination.

Concurrently, the Irishman was being trailed by Mrs. Macklin. He had decided to go to a cinema, but before doing so had his appetite to appease. Passing an Espresso bar and feeling drawn by its specious gaiety he retraced his steps and entered. The faithful Mrs. Macklin took up a position opposite the café in a doorway, shielded from the glow of a nearby street lamp.

O'Flattery found himself in a misty room hung with fish nets, Chianti bottles and green, evil trailing foliage. It was misty, because of the chain smoking of the clientele and the low power of the illumination, which came from candles stuck into bottles dripping with old wax. The customers consisted in the main of adolescents of both sexes, whose intention, it appeared, was to achieve an impression of complete sexual ambiguity. Some of them might, indeed, have been hermaphrodites; for the boys wore their hair in thick curls to the nape of the neck, and the girls wore theirs cropped short as if by the persistent attacks of many hungry rodents; but at least a few girls wore pony-tails, so that O'Flattery was certain of their sex. Amongst the throng there was not one skirt, but confusingly nearly all had piping sibilant voices and

142

gestures which are generally accepted as being feminine. The attendant Ganymedes who wore sailor trousers, striped singlets and brass ear-rings, either treated the customers to excessive familiarity or utter neglect. The Irishman was one whom they neglected. After sitting at a table for some minutes, he noticed a free stool at a high counter near the steaming coffee machine, to which he pushed his way. Once there, he managed to attract the attention of a proud slim youth, who regarded him as if he was something which had crawled out from under a stone and ought to go back there, but who did eventually condescend to give him coffee and a length of French bread containing a minuscule shred of ham. The whole room shook with the thunder of a juke-box, the front of which was illuminated by slowly changing lights, now pink, now green, now blue, now yellow; a never ending stream of rainbow hues each more crude than the last. This, and the hostile stares he received from the vacuous gum-chewing faces into which he looked with detached good fellowship, lowered his spirits while a sensation of heavy gloom began to spread through his whole physical system.

Outside, Mrs. Macklin was having trouble with a policeman. He had pounded up and down in front of her hidey-hole three times; each time he passed adding to her indignation which grew until she could contain herself no longer and burst out:

"Don't you stare at me like that. I 'aint doin' no 'arm. H'i'm a respectable woman h'I h'am," with such vehemence that she quite startled the policeman, who actually had not suspected her of loitering with intent but was just about to alleviate the boredom of his beat by starting a friendly conversation about the weather.

"Orl right, Mother, orl right," he soothed, trying to placate the irate woman.

"And don't you call me Mother, neither," said Mrs.

143

Macklin, furious at the suggestion that she was old enough to be the policeman's Mother, especially considering the self-imposed mission she was on.

Fortunately at this moment the Irishman came out of the Espresso bar and went off down the road, hesitating to buy an evening paper as he went; so that Mrs. Macklin brushed past the blushing policeman, thus relieving him of the responsibility of further complications.

As he hurried along O'Flattery studied the list of cinemas in the newspaper, glancing up now and again to see where he was going. When he came level with a public lavatory he went inside and to Mrs. Macklin's annoyance remained there for some time. Men and boys passed in and out until Mrs. Macklin was beside herself with impatience. An overgrown spotty schoolboy, with a dark down on his upper lip, had returned three times and she was just about to tell him sarcastically that he ought to see a doctor about his bladder, when the Irishman came out.

On entering he had disturbed a fly which was using the polished seat as a roller skating rink and which now left with him disguising itself as a button-hole on the lapel of his jacket.

He had now made up his mind which cinema to go to and so boarded a bus, mounting at once to the seats above. Nearly breaking her ankle in doing so, and earning the tut-tuts of the conductress, Mrs. Macklin succeeded in hurling herself on to the platform in hot pursuit just as the bus drew away. There were no seats near that end of the bus so she was forced to sit further up behind the driver, and had to keep turning round to make sure her quarry did not escape her. She did this so much that a woman sitting two seats behind her took it personally and began to look very belligerent. It was fortunate that just as she was about to protest Mrs. Macklin saw O'Flattery getting off and with difficulty held her tongue. As she passed the woman whom she had annoyed they both blew themselves out with such indignation that she almost became wedged in the gangway of the bus.

O'Flattery was going straight for his objective, quite unaware of the bloodhound behind him. While it was still moving he jumped off the bus as it drew level with the cinema, so that by the time Mrs. Macklin had walked back from the bus stop he was already standing in a queue, and enough people had joined it behind him for her to be concealed from him.

Meanwhile, chez Macklin, the cabaret for Arthur's benefit was reaching a climax. Jennifer had produced from somewhere a bottle of home-made wine and all of them, even Brenda, had been drinking it. Arthur now had firm hold of it and kept gulping back great draughts from the neck of the bottle itself. His eyes had begun to glisten warily and his saliva ran so that he was continually having to either lick his lips like a slavering dog or pass his hairy paw across them. As a result of the wine Jennifer and Wendy's dancing had become positively bacchanalian. Leslie crashed his instruments more furiously than ever, while amazingly Brenda had slumped once more to sleep, and was in imminent danger of being throttled by the reins which held her in place. Horny had been put by Wendy, when the dancing began, in a place of safety inside the fender.

In one of her turns round the room Jennifer had switched off the light leaving the scene to be lit by the flickering light of the fire. To Arthur these hideous maenads were nymphs who tantalised him with their captivating arts. The more home-made wine he drank, the more lascivious became his thoughts. Jennifer was beginning to tire of the game. Capriciously, she decided suddenly that it was time to send Wendy home and put the two smaller ones to bed. At the

145

back of her nasty little mind was the crumb of an idea, that alone with Arthur she might be able to force the moment to some half understood forbidden crisis. She yanked Brenda, who awoke with a frightened squeal, out of her high-chair and with her under one arm she shepherded the others upstairs.

"Yer can 'elp, Wend, if yer like," she said, "let's barf Brenda."

"Shit 'em," said Wendy not unexpectedly.

They all repaired to the antiquated bathroom, where a tomb-like stained bath on iron eagle's feet stood gaunt and forbidding, threatened by a vast obsolete geyser which roosted upon a bracket on the cracked wall above. This they somehow got to work and in clouds of steam began their ceremonious bathing of Brenda. Like two midget witches, about to practise the arts of Hydromancy, they moved to and fro in clouds of steam, shouting directions at one another. Leslie was forgotten, as he stood squirting jets of water at his own reflection from the taps of the wash basin.

"Take 'er jumper orf," yelled Jennifer above the rumbles of the geyser.

"Yare?" answered Wendy.

"Now 'er vest," went on Jennifer, as she swilled the water round and round.

"Yare?"

"Now 'er drawers," Leslie turned round to watch, stepping nearer out of the puddle he had made on the floor.

"Yare?"

"Now 'er nappies," screeched Jennifer.

Brenda was being whirled round and round like a demonstration dummy at a clinic, but appeared to like it.

"Phew they don't 'arf pong!" exclaimed Leslie, unwittingly drawing attention to his presence in the room.

"'Ere you, 'op it," menaced Jennifer, quickly smothering Brenda's eskimo nakedness by a counterfeit gesture of gentility with a towel.

"This is the 'Ladies'; you can buzz orf; nar then!"

"Well I'm supposed to be a 'lydy', ain't I?" taunted Leslie, mincing and lifting up the towel from the struggling Brenda.

"No you ain't now, that was before; and you wasn't too keen neither wos yer, but now there's suffink to 'ave a dekko at you've soon changed; bugger orf, go on." With her last imprecation she flicked the snivelling bogus slave girl to flight with triumphant shouts of "Shit 'em," from Wendy.

With much slapping and pinching Brenda's ablutions were completed, to the satisfaction of her two dishevelled attendants. Wendy then changed and was despatched home. When Jennifer went to look for Leslie she found that he had already put himself to bed and was snoring with a contented rhythm, no doubt helped by the wine which he had drunk at the party. She returned to the kitchen, musing that at last she had Arthur alone to torment how she pleased.

Outside the cinema things were on the move. O'Flattery had gone in, and by leaning forward Mrs. Macklin was able to hear the price of the seat he had asked for; fortunately for her he had to repeat it twice, louder the second time as the girl in the ticket kiosk was talking to her chum, the ice-cream sales girl, and hadn't heard the first time.

Mrs. Macklin champed outside in the queue, eager to get into the anonymous darkness within. When it came to her turn she pushed rudely past the last customer whose change got mixed with her admittance money, causing mutual annoyance and more delay. Eventually she was shown into a seat in the middle of a row by a shadowy girl

147

behind a small torch, which gave insufficient light to prevent her from stumbling across people's knees and barking her shins on protruding feet. With muttered oaths against everyone, she flumped down into her seat and searched around in the gloom for the Irishman's profile. Nowhere could she find it, and was at last forced to pay attention, out of boredom, to what was happening in front of her on the screen. The end of a Western romance was drawing near. The good men, obvious by their blonde suavity, were chasing the bad men, equally obvious by their demoniac swarthiness. They tore through a scrubby landscape interminably, passing the same clump of rocks a dozen times. Mrs. Macklin got more bored and started looking round again. She could distinguish O'Flattery's young head nowhere among the many similar which surrounded her. Her eyes strayed idly back to the screen where part of the picture was momentarily obliterated by a large fly which pirouetted on the lens of the projector. A finger quickly appeared monstrously enlarged, brushing it away towards the left of the screen.

It was towards the left of the screen that Mrs. Macklin's eyes were instinctively drawn when the chase of the outlaws was over, and it was there that she spied the Irishman, leaning forward in his seat, trying to attract the attention of the ice-cream girl. The house lights had increased to half strength and in the dim auditorium, fitfully lit by slides advertising local enterprises, uncouth figures flitted to and fro; moving in and out of the cloakrooms, plying backwards and forwards for ices, nuts and other confectionery rubbish. The girls minced and giggled. The young men held their coats tight against their flanks and moved from the hips with a rolling provocative gait. Staring about freely, inviting admiration, displaying blatantly for a brief moment in the cold spotlight which bathed the attendant in brightness, they sought to make contacts with suggestive

148

expressions of obvious meaning, brave in their adolescent brashness.

Mrs. Macklin found the whole sinister atmosphere of the place very sympathetic, very conducive to the chase with its hot smoky air and stale human smell. A smell which clung to one's clothes, infecting them with old odours of other people's presence. These smells had been collecting in the vast hall for years, as it was never properly ventilated they were never completely driven out. They hung there as the souls of the wicked are said to lurk, visible only to those who believe they have contact with the dead, in the precinct of an abattoir. Faces took on an evil, voluptuous beauty which they did not possess in full daylight. At a brutish level geese were transformed into the kind of swans which appealed strongly to Mrs. Macklin's nature.

In this light O'Flattery's head had an air of great vulnerability, like a green hazel nut in the metal jaws of a nutcracker. The angle at which it was inclined, as he licked a pineapple lolly, was infinitely articulate of his youth and inexperience. Mrs. Macklin kept her gaze riveted to the back of his head as if its hammer blows would stun him into awareness of her proximity. When the lights went down and the main feature started she was able to watch nothing but the action of the film. This was French with English sub-titles, a film of suspense, about men's bravery in carrying explosives over an arduous route, in order to bring relief to the fighters of a fire at an oil well. It had moments of great drama, and a tension which infected the whole cinema, straining Mrs. Macklin's already taut nerves, feeding her anxiety as if she were a battery being re-charged at a generator.

At an especially gripping moment in the film, when in order to prevent a spontaneous explosion the speeds of the lorries had to be very minutely gauged to accommodate

149

the bad surface of a part of the road, she noticed that the person who had been sitting next to O'Flattery had got up and was moving out along the row. Instantly, with more energy than the confined space would allow, she leapt to her feet and rushed headlong down the laps of the people in her way, making a commotion which brought angry hisses and shouts of "Shurrup!" Colliding with the vacating viewer she brushed rudely past him and heaved her way down into the seat he had just left. The tension was broken and all about her the darkness was punctuated by scowling faces. When Mrs. Macklin eased herself into the warm seat beside him O'Flattery scarcely turned his head. So taken up by the film was he that he had been oblivious even of the disturbance she had made and was quite unaware of her arrival. Her other neighbour, already made furious by her commotion, deliberately stubbed out his cigarette on the edge of her coat, which had further annoyed him by overflowing on to his knee.

Suddenly the whole row was again galvanized into a tirade of hushes, for one of the bored attendants had appeared and was remonstrating officiously with Mrs. Macklin who she said, had moved from the cheaper seats into the more expensive. Furious at such injustice and what she called "her sauce", Mrs. Macklin let the callow girl "have it", whereupon she very quickly departed amidst the jeers of all around her. Simmering down, the bovine audience turned, once more, their moons to the sun's rays of the cinema screen. O'Flattery glanced for a second at his neighbour, the altercation with the attendant having at last broken in on his concentration. He found to his horrified amazement that he was looking into the uneasy orbs of the Office caretaker, which gazed back into his with the sloppy devotion of a pet dog. Not knowing what to do, he smiled involuntarily and was more than surprised to feel a gentle pressure against his leg from the hot thigh next to his. So disgusted was he that he instantly dismissed such a thought, telling himself as he looked fixedly at the screen that he must have been mistaken.

O'Flattery was once more lost in the complexities of the film's action, caught up in the tension of suspense which permeated the black and white shadow drama which continued to unweave. He moved his legs, as far as he dared, towards the other side of his seat, until the man on that side in his turn gave him a suspicious look. Then he concentrated again wholeheartedly on the film. Mrs. Macklin oozed seduction, putting all her femininity into her glowing looks, her artful nudges and the sly squeezings of her person against her reluctant neighbour, whose attention, despite the gripping nature of the film, was soon forced to switch once more to flesh and blood human movement, rather than flat photographic images.

Emboldened by the dark, the furtive harpy laid a fat hand upon O'Flattery's knee. Its effect could not have been more electrifying if she had placed a red hot branding iron upon her prey. He leapt from his seat and careered with flailing limbs down the row, up the aisle and out of the cinema as if a fiend was after him. Nothing daunted, Mrs. Macklin grabbed up his forgotten macintosh and followed in a more subdued manner. Reaching the cinema foyer she caught sight of O'Flattery's back disappearing through the glass swing doors which led to the busy street outside. Her blood was up and follow she would, despite the obvious fact that her victim was trying to avoid her. Her rising passion had dulled her already half atrophied powers of judgement, and it was inconceivable to her that her attentions might not only be unwelcome, but actually nauseating to the fleeing figure whom she managed to keep in view amongst the crowd.

O'Flattery's intention was to make for home, to go to earth in the familiar protective surroundings of his lodgings. His way took him through a maze of streets and finally along the river bank. He felt sure he could manage to give this nightmare the slip, but he was ignorant of the awful persistence which drew her towards him. No matter how skilful he was at doubling back up dark alleys and hiding in pools of shadow she sniffed him out and bore relentlessly down upon him. The streets were empty and horribly quiet. Each could hear the other's foot-steps, the one with dread, the other with triumphant elation. When he plunged from the brightly lit streets into the contrasting gloom of the lonely river path, even the stalwart Mrs. Macklin's insensitive heart quailed. Somewhere down in the depths of her complicated nature there lurked the remnants of feminine fear, and she drew back despite herself when the chase led her to the cold shadows into which the Irishman had disappeared. O'Flattery looked back. The night curdled and thickened a little as Mrs. Macklin's figure approached hesitatingly. He flew on, taking advantage of her hesitancy. Wisps of river mist obscured him as she again moved forward, but the cries of strange birds above her in the darkness sent chills down her spine. A curlew whipped across the sky, adding its derisive laughing call to the eeriness of the night. The soft beating of wings in the darkness, the smooth stealth of the river as it crept by, finally made her halt and reconsider what she was doing. Already her hesitation had lost her any ground she had gained since leaving the cinema, and the bobbing light of a fast disappearing torch told her that the Irishman had gone too far along the river for her to catch him up. She did not know the difficult windings of the path. She could see by the frequent changes of direction of the weak gleam that it would not be an easy route to follow. Furious with fate, she retreated, sullenly admitting temporary defeat.

Hot and thirsty from this wild goose chase she entered

152

the first public house she came upon. With her first bitter gulp of stout creeping down to solace her disappointment, she took stock of her surroundings. The bar she had chosen was decorated in Scottish Baronial style and was populated by what were obviously regulars, who attended this temple of alcohol as devotees of boredom. A group of nondescript commercials soaked whisky at the bar, chaffing the good-looking Irish barmaid while the landlord argued with two men who stood by the beer pumps. One of these had a black miniature poodle on a lead, which he had tied to the handle of a door panelled with mock Tudor latticed glass. On this the whereabouts of the "Toilets" were indicated in almost unintelligible Gothic lettering. The silly animal was restless and persistently got itself entangled in its own lead. Its master was inattentive, being in heated discussion with his companion, whose large nose was so brilliantly inflamed through years of excessive drinking, that it drew one's attention like a lighthouse.

"Been orf work for six weeks," he announced proudly. "Never 'ad the doctor, don't believe in 'em, 'ad a cold thas 'orl."

"Can't make out why they don't concentrate on curing the common cold and leave atoms alone," said the licencee tactfully, trying to deflect the dog owner from continuing with an argument which had been proceeding, about some trivial incident in a popular radio programme. The landlady, a hennaed woman with vestigial good looks, hovered in the background polishing glasses. She was undecided whether or not to intervene, the cigarette which balanced in her vivid carmine mouth punctuated her tentative smile, revealing disastrous teeth, the horror of which was only accentuated by her excessive use of lipstick.

Between Mrs. Macklin and the fire sat a couple whom she took at first to be husband and wife. They sat in silence.

He was a heavy grey man bent over a stick, his hands one upon the other on the crook of it. He had a half-empty glass beside him. He was wearing a dingy black overcoat which had once been good, but his black shoes lacked all lustre and obviously had not been polished for a long time. She had a glass of stout, and was attired in a moth-eaten reprobate of a fur coat. Belted in with an ordinary leather strap it covered her like a shabby winter shroud. Her carpet-baggy face was a uniform drab colour, topped by a very unsuitable, old but jaunty hand-knitted hat. She wore a necklace and a brooch of tawdry mosaic. Mrs. Macklin decided that they might equally well be man and wife, or brother and sister. Impecunious they certainly were, but beyond that it was difficult to reach any conclusion.

Beside them, sitting in the embrasure of an imitation stained glass window, were three weird sisters, muffled in a collection of jumble sale garments. When Mrs. Macklin's tour of inspection finally discovered them, she found that they were returning her glares of undismayed enmity. They sat merrily guzzling their brown ales and grumbling about the weather, resenting heartily the intrusion of this large female stranger. It appeared from their conversation that one of them had a daughter who enjoyed bad health, and who was expected to arrive at any minute. This one, the Mother, wore gaiters and had her hat tied on with a long pale mauve scarf. Her turnip-lantern face peered out at the world through strong pebble lenses. With a mouthful of teeth like the clay pipes at a shooting gallery, Mrs. Macklin heard her say.

"I told 'er she'd better stay in bed. She looked that bad. But she wouldn't yer know. She would go to work."

"Oh, she's a nice girl," croaked another of the old beldames.

The fur-clad woman by the fireplace suddenly creaked

into life, and in a voice of the utmost despondency addressed her male counterpart.

"I'm tryin' to make up me mind if I should 'ave a pie."

A crinkle passed over her companion's dejected face, but he uttered no sound. After five minutes of silent communion accompanied by intense facial twitching, she rose to her feet and tottered to the bar, where she was given a dismal meat pie on a plate, beside which was balanced an outsize knife. Returning to her seat she sat down and contemplated her triumph for some minutes, still steadfastly watched by the old man. After a time she rose again to fetch salt and mustard before she started upon the pie. Some minutes were then taken up with furious, toothless mastication, followed by a vigorous sweeping down of her fur coat with a hard ball of handkerchief to get rid of the crumbs, and an even more vigorous sweeping of the tongue round the gums to clear away any lurking fragments.

"I enjoyed that," she said, in a flat humourless voice, "it was very tasty. Better than a pasty."

Her companion uttered never a word, but went on staring straight ahead.

"The worst of eating, it makes yer so sleepy," she continued funereally. "I nearly always dozes off after I've 'ad a bite, but then yer feels so doleful when yer wakes up, but there it passes the time." A long pause ensued, during which the old man took a small bird-sip of beer. Mrs. Macklin had been sluicing stouts into her, in an attempt to deaden the poultice of annoyance and disappointment which burnt her, but it was having the opposite effect. The more she drank the angrier and more depressed she became, the more her accustomed misogyny was increased.

"I 'ad two small ports last night," said the old woman, becoming loquacious again. "Don't like the taste yer know." She made an ugly grimace of disgust, as if she had just tasted gall. Her partner nodded as if he fully under-

155

stood this apparently disconnected pronouncement.

Suddenly the door burst open and in shot a very jolly looking girl, a better looking and younger version of turnip-lantern-in-the-mauve-muffler.

"Evenin' all," she sang out gaily to the three fates, who rustled expectantly in the window.

"Oh, you do look bad," said one.

"Nice girl," said the second.

"Ought to be in bed," said the Mother.

"Aint it cold?" said the girl, going straight to the fire and warming the backs of her stockings.

"How are yer?" said the fur-coated pie-eater, as if she hoped for bad news.

"Oh, I'm not so bad thanks," replied the girl, "I 'ave to go to 'ospital every day yer know. It's me ear."

"Yer can't tell me nothink about ears," said the pie-eater, "what I 'aven't suffered with my ears." Her male companion raised his eyebrows, but otherwise remained as lifeless as an Egyptian mummy.

"It was more of an itch," said the girl, fitting the action to the word and scratching behind her ear, "but I didn't seem as if I could get at it, yer know."

"Inflamed," said the pie-woman, delivering herself of the word as if it was some painful stone of which she was glad to be rid. "It's a good thing yer went to the 'ospital, it might 'a turned to meningitis."

"Ye-e-es," said the girl quite unmoved; "they are nice there, yer know, the sisters an all too. I went at 'arp-'arst eight afore anyone was there. But it didn't 'alf itch."

"That's on account of the air not being able to get to it," said the pie-woman with the knowledgeable air of a central-European specialist.

"It's better now though," said the girl cheerfully.

"Yer can't be too careful," pronounced the pie-eater gloomily, again gently exploring the cavities of her gums

156

with her tongue, while at the same time mopping at her eyes.

The old man shifted his feet and cleared his throat noisily, everyone looked at him expectantly as the door flew open and a dark French-looking woman rushed in. She was wearing a very short coat trimmed with artificial leopard skin and brought with her gusts of cold night air.

"Ain't it cold not arf?" she said going straight to the fire also. Lifting the back of her skirt to the blaze she faced the room.

"Cold," said one weird sister.

"She do look bad," responded the other.

"Ought to be in bed," replied mauve-muffler.

"Can't be too careful," said the pie-eater.

Ignoring them, the new arrival spied the poodle upon whom she immediately darted, showering it with a torrent of meaningless doggy language, at which all the old ladies winked and giggled, placing their withered fore-fingers against their noses in silent significant gesture. The lady in the leopard-trimmed coat finished her communion with the poodle, and left the bar with smiles and cheerful words all round, not having had a drink. The daughter of mauve-muffler also left soon after, amidst a chorus of "nice girl", and "ought to be in bed", from the choir of old women, she having drunk nothing also. Such a blanket of depression then settled down on this flotsam covered beach that Mrs. Macklin was glad to hear the familiar call.

"Time, Ladies and Gentlemen, please." Followed by, "Ain't none of you' erbs got no 'omes?" delivered by the landlady in a strident shriek, answered by cries of "Ain't she a caution?" from those left in the bar.

Out went Mrs. Macklin into the starlit street where the cold, damp air hit her rudely in the face, bringing out the maximum effect of the large number of stouts which she had managed to consume in the past hour.

Jennifer . . . "the chip off the old block", was at this moment returning to pester the sleeping Arthur. Not for long was he allowed to snore peacefully. With a spill of paper she tickled his nostrils, until with a loud sneeze she was awake. His first thought was for the home-made wine of which he took a long swig while Jennifer pirouetted round him aggravatingly. A long belch from Arthur reminded Jennifer of her mother at meal times, which further reminded her that she was hungry. Mrs. Macklin had locked up all the food, but her artful daughter recalled some sweets she had once hidden from Leslie on the top of a cupboard above Arthur's chair. Climbing by means of the chair rungs and arms she stretched upwards balancing against Arthur, her knees on a level with his face, as she fumbled for the hidden sweets among the cobwebs. The nearness of her hot legs, in their curious net-curtain skirt, stirred in Arthur a dangerous depth which would have been better left unplumbed. Uncanalised currents of desire, exacerbated by alcohol, flowed through him; putting out a hand to steady Jennifer he gripped her leg in a libidinous clutch, the peril of which even she with her limited experience understood.

"You smell," she sneered down into Arthur's face, bending over him. An expression of wounded vanity furrowed the Caliban mask into which she peered.

"You smell of scented stuff."

This was surprisingly true; for Arthur, when he had been summoned to "sit in", had in an effort to achieve refinement smeared his hair with the remains of a tin of solid brilliantine which he had previously filched from the waste-paper basket where O'Flattery had discarded it. He moved the position of his hand on Jennifer's leg and tightened his hold.

"Lego 'a me; you smell," repeated Jennifer fearlessly. "'Ere 'ave a sweet," she went on, as if she thought herself invulnerable. Arthur's greed for food overcame him, and he released her leg to take the proffered sweet.

"Myaing," howled Jennifer in derision, leaping down from the chair, whisking the sweets away at the same time. Arthur let out a whinny of enraged disappointment and staggered to his feet. This drunken silenus presented a pitiful sight, his Christmas garlands ill-according with his lumpy stature and gross features. He stood trembling with indecision; as he did so, Jennifer began hopping up and down before him, her strange costume rising and falling to reveal her limbs glistening in the fire-light.

"Can't catch me-he! Can't catch me-he!" she chanted spinning round just out of arms' reach. Arthur finished what was left in his bottle, flung it with a sickening crash into the fender and floundered forward, his hands outstretched to clutch his tormentor. Jennifer, younger, lighter and sober, evaded him with a quick side step. Losing his balance, he went crashing across the room. His whirling arms clutched at the window curtains, which in breaking his fall split and covered him like a shroud.

Horny drew in his head involuntarily as he lay protected by the fender.

As Mrs. Macklin wove her way home unsteadily, she clutched O'Flattery's macintosh as if it had been the Golden Fleece.

She now felt hungry. She began searching about for a coffee stall where she could satisfy her thirst with sweet tea and her hunger with a cheese roll. This she was soon able to do, for she came upon an oasis of dim light in the emptying streets, at a spot where several thoroughfares joined. A surly bruiser banged down the tea before her, sploshing it into the saucer. In return she flung her coppers into a pool of cold tea which lay on the rough counter, disturbing a fly which sipped at its edge.

159

She was finding it difficult to see straight. The cold, the drink and her normal squint made her screw up her eyes and peer too closely at the objects upon which she was trying to focus. The other clients of this night-haunt emanated an ill-feeling and secretiveness which was almost tangible. It was not until Mrs. Macklin had chewed stolidly through her stale cheese roll and gulped two cups of acrid tea, that she was aware of being the only woman at the coffee stall. A group of dog-eared labourers, Irish, she could hear from their talk, stood and leant against the railings, laughing at a story the youngest and dirtiest was telling. Their lilting voices reminded her of O'Flattery and so she did not find it difficult to return the unfriendly stares of a quartet of guardsmen who began elbowing their way to the counter. Big raw-boned men who filled their well pressed uniforms as if they had been poured molten into them. From under the low peaks of their caps they darted penetrating looks from eyes cold with unspoken vice. Coarse featured and coarse spoken, they cursed the cold and their lack of money. A drunk sailor, his square necked vest showing the top of a blue tattoo among crisp black hair, was being supported by an effete young man whose trousers were even tighter and more revealing than those of the brutish guardsmen. The washed-out blue of his jeans clung so intimately to his legs that they might have been painted on them. Like a handbag, he carried the sailor's hat as a trophy, and as an angry hen pecks at its neighbours he swung the hat on its ribbon, as if to keep the other customers at a distance, trying to prevent his sailor from even talking to any of them. Clandestine men, guiltily frowning, walked past staring hard at these lounging men with Mrs. Macklin in their midst; with unconvincing glances at their watches they passed and re-passed, sometimes stopping to light cigarettes with one of the wooden faced smokers by the stall, sometimes after a few

160

words going off in company with one of them.

The pavement surrounding the coffee stall and the stall itself had an indescribable effect on Mrs. Macklin's blunted senses. Something in her memory evaded her. The fly, as it buzzed from cup to cup, was like a nagging insistent memory trying to break through. Somewhere in the background of her insensitive fuddled subconscious there hovered the memory of a smell, the trace of some past experience, of corruption. She could not completely drag it forth. The struggle was altogether too much effort for her. It was in fact the similarity between a certain suspect butcher's shop where she used to buy slightly tainted meat for a pet cat she had once kept but which was long since run over and forgotten. The same evil aura hung over both places, strongly enough to affect Mrs. Macklin but not strong enough to break through the wireless telegraphy of her senses, so that she could tune into the two wavelengths and thus co-ordinate her impressions into a complete recollection.

The place both attracted and frightened Mrs. Macklin, who lingered over her empty cup unable to make a positive move. Finally, for the second time in one evening, fear got the upper hand. The tension around her was so strong that she could bear it no longer. As she pushed her way towards the curb the fair boy in the tight trousers blew a raspberry, raising two fingers triumphantly at her departing back. A guardsman sneered contemptuously and spat, while the Irish workmen stopped talking and laughed raucously at the sight of this large woman who minced unsteadily away into the darkness, swearing fiercely to herself.

Her temper fanned to white heat, by the derisive laughter of the men at the coffee stall, Mrs. Macklin entered her kitchen at the precise moment when Arthur, in his prolonged pursuit of Jennifer, had fallen stretched upon the hearthrug, his hand grasping her ankle.

In their ungainly flight round the room furniture had been overturned, rugs had slipped and a vase of paper roses had been scattered onto the floor, where they now lay squashed under the recumbent form of the half-clothed Jennifer, who, hysterical with laughter at the novelty of this wild game of tag, had not heard the entry of her Mother. She realised she was there only when Mrs. Macklin switched on the cold glare of the electric light, disclosing also the metronomic fly who conducted, so to speak, the overture of her wrath. Back and forth like the end of a baton it swung in the breathless quiet which suddenly stuffed the room.

"Wot the bloody 'ell's goin' on 'ere?" Mrs. Macklin yelled in a voice which would have astonished a sergeant major, sending the fly swooping for shelter.

"We wos 'avin' fun," answered Jennifer, in a voice as small as a moth, "we wos only 'avin' fun."

She scrambled to her feet to cower away in a corner, her arms protecting her face, not daring to look at the towering monster who loomed above her.

"Fun, do you call it? I'll give you fun you young bitch," screamed Mrs. Macklin, grabbing a large frying pan, which she brought down with such force on the table that a long sliver of wood splintered off it.

"Fun," she repeated again beating blindly at Arthur, who still lay silently across the hearth.

"Get up you filthy old bugger an' get out of 'ere 'afore I kill yer," she screeched, kicking him in the armpit and throwing over a tray full of crockery upon him, which bounced rattling across the floor, breaking when it hit anything stronger than itself. Arthur heaved himself up and sobbing like a child allowed himself to be insulted and belaboured out of the room, back to the safety of his stoke-hole domain. Jennifer could hear her Mother crashing home the bolts of the back door, and grasping her

162

opportunity she scuttled under the table which miraculously was still covered by its long cloth.

Mrs. Macklin returned, swiping about her with the frying pan, wild eyed, her hair fallen down and her shoes kicked off. Jennifer heard her beating at everything she could see and trembled for her life. Foul curses accompanied her blows, which to Jennifer's surprise contained the name of O'Flattery more often than those of Arthur or herself.

Gradually the tide of Mrs. Macklin's rage ebbed, the hurricane had spent itself and with one last sledge-hammer blow she bent the handle of the frying pan double on the anvil of the grate and hurled it into the corner which had been so lately vacated by Jennifer, where it lay unrecognisably mangled, its enamel clicking and ticking off in fragments like a live thing, as it would if it had been left empty upon a flame.

All was now silence except for the drip of cold tea which ran from the spout of the overturned tea-pot upon the table, and the hoarse breathing of Mrs. Macklin, who in her exhaustion had collapsed into the armchair by the now dead fire. Gently a pool of dark tea stained the carpet with tannin as Jennifer watched and waited, hardly daring to sigh.

Simultaneously, she and the fly decided that the coast was clear. Jennifer, on naked feet, padded softly to the bed from which she could now hear the strangled wailing of an alarmed Brenda. The fly swung guard over the besotted form of Mrs. Macklin; she lay asleep, dead to the world, among the havoc she had wrought, clasping in a tight bundle the forgotten macintosh of her imaginary paramour. The tortoise still lay in the fender, peacefully unaware, deeply asleep in the unaccustomed warmth, its forelegs slightly protruding, entwined with the wilting dandelions, its head withdrawn. Undisturbed, it lay forgotten by everyone, even Brenda.

163

11

It was a brilliant blue morning, a morning which invited one to break with routine and do something special, something long anticipated. A morning when to be in a city would be a lifetime wasted, when the wet-cold of the night before seemed aeons ago.

It was fortunate that the weather was so kind, for it was the day of the annual Staff Outing from the Office. They were going out into the country to a small zoo, their destination having been chosen, after long discussion, over many eleven o'clock tea breaks.

They were all assembled by the bridge, as had been agreed upon. All except the Irishman, who characteristically was going to be late. An azure veil threaded with pearls hung over the river. At least that is how the sunlit mist appeared to Miss Seal, who was in high spirits. But she did not remark upon it to anyone, not even to Miss Jeacock or the Postage Clerk, preferring to keep it a poetic secret beneath her own wide breast, festively covered this morning by a loose blouse of flowered cretonne.

They waited in groups asking each other, first what had become of the bus which had been hired by Dr. Booker to transport them, and second, where was O'Flattery? As if in answer to these questions, both prodigals appeared in the distance simultaneously. Parting the curtain of mist the bus creaked down upon them, a snorting juggernaut bearing the word "Private" upon its brow. While from the opposite direction a figure, with his coat flapping open,

164

hurried towards them at surprising speed.

With excited cries everyone sorted themselves out and settled down to enjoy the drive. A struggling engine and a set of hysterical brakes made of their journey through the dingy suburbs an adventure instead of a bore. The stops at traffic lights were legion. At each one, the shriek of the brakes tore at the Postage Clerk's head, for already she had neuralgia; but no one else appeared to notice, for they continued to chatter at the tops of their voices, as if, thought she, they were getting into training to compete with the parrot house.

Leslie and Jennifer, to their utter amazement had as a special treat, been allowed to accompany their Mother. The Postage Clerk was not the only one who was relieved that Brenda at least had been left at home in the tender care of Arthur and Wendy. To the rest of the staff the journey seemed rapid, and it was with surprise that they all turned in their seats, to follow the pointing fingers of the sisters Lynch, who in chorus were screeching:

"Oh how jolly, how jolly, do look," while they gesticulated towards a moth-eaten looking llama, which stood cropping the grass in an enclosure next to the main entrance of the zoo. They all stared wonderingly at this first animal as the bus drove through a crude rustic gateway and laboured to a stop.

This zoo was in the grounds of a large gothic-style country house which had now been converted into a restaurant. Notices, which one of the clerks read out to Mrs. Macklin and the children with studied carefulness, announced seasonal opening times and prices of admission, amongst other dull facts. The arms of a Shiva-like signpost pointed in all directions. Here the party split up, agreeing that they would reassemble at a quarter to one for lunch at the restaurant. Miss Betty and Miss Gladys Lynch ran off giggling, hand-in-hand, in search of the "Ladies". The pool-typists trundled off in pairs, arm-in-arm, to take cups of much needed tea, followed by Mrs. Macklin, Jennifer and Leslie, all of whom looked as dazed as minnows in a jam-jar. Dr. Booker, his Assistant and the Senior Clerk ambled in earnest conversation, ignoring their surroundings, towards the first of the green huts which evidently housed the exhibits.

The Postage Clerk, Miss Seal and O'Flattery found themselves left behind by Mr. Gender and Miss Jeacock. They had hurried on ahead, across a wasteland of cinder-filled puddles and mud-rutted paths, towards a delicately poised grey tea cosy which stood silhouetted against the sky. When they came up to it they found it to be an ostrich, which with Agag-walk was picking her way between a fallow deer and a motionless bundle of kangaroo. It seemed hardly possible that the soot-stained feathers, which framed her naked pink hams, could ever adorn anything as elegant as sloping feminine shoulders.

"Fancy having those dirty things on one's head," cried the Postage Clerk to Miss Jeacock, as the two groups caught up with one another at the wire barrier.

"Well, they would clean them first," answered Miss Jeacock, somewhat shortly, angered at being followed by the other three, when she thought she had escaped with Mr. Gender, upon whom she had decided to turn her vulpine wits today. He stood awkwardly, watching the kangaroo as it rummaged in the most intimate parts of its grimy hair. Torn between loyalty to Miss Jeacock and tact towards the Postage Clerk, he added rather shame-facedly, "At least one need not choose a feathered hat."

"Or a feather boa," proffered Miss Seal dreamily. The thought of bulky Miss Seal in a feather boa brought smiles to all of them; as they moved on the ostrich wandered off also, towards the middle of its compound.

"Can this remnant of English parkland really contain a

166

zoo?" shouted Mr. Gender to the others as if he were declaiming a prepared speech. "It is with surprise that one beholds the animals at all," he concluded, in a slightly more restrained tone.

The illusion of emptiness in these wind-swept paddocks, lit on this unseasonably warm day by bright sunshine, was so complete that Miss Jeacock startled them all when she cried out, "Oh look, do look." From one of the huts a sharply barred zebra had stepped, accentuating for the moment the brilliance of the sunbeams. Her mate stamped angrily from the green gloom of their hut, and with a toss of her mane she retreated once more inside, leaving them all wondering if they really had seen a sudden vision of the African veldt and not a captive zoo inmate.

"One almost expects to see a troupe of hartebeest accompanying it," said Mr. Gender. Miss Seal and her new friend looked at each other, ignorant of what he meant, shrugging their shoulders, thinking he was trying to be clever. The Irishman had not heard. But Miss Jeacock turning to Mr. Gender, treated him to a dazzling smile, for she knew her South African fauna, and was grateful to him for this remark which excluded the others from their conversation. It made her feel superior to the other two women. Her smile made Mr. Gender swell with pride; he too felt that they were now in a secret alliance against the others. But he was rapidly brought down to earth by the angry belching of the sun-dazed kangaroo in the enclosure behind them.

Miss Seal and her companion wandered on ahead gossiping together in low voices. Miss Seal could see that, as she had predicted to Mrs. Macklin, her friend Miss Jeacock was busy at her work and had no time for her old girl-friends today. O'Flattery lingered behind alone, watching reflectively a white pigeon which clapped from tree to ground and after pecking over a heap of manure back again from ground to tree. Miss Jeacock and Mr. Gender, with what seemed like pre-arranged duplicity, gave the others the slip; for they could see Mrs. Macklin and the children approaching from the end of a vista. The children were both armed with sticks, with which they were making a concerted effort to prod a very comatose wart-hog into action. Mrs. Macklin, who carried a macintosh on one arm, was hung-over and already bad tempered; she handed out continual reproaches, as she dragged Leslie away from his sister who, as usual, was the ringleader. Before they could see Mr. Gender, he managed to steer his companion down a side alley as far away as possible from the three fiendish Macklins, towards another group of wooden sheds. Peering into several of these they could find no animals except a tortoise-shell cat, which cowered unaccountably behind the broken wire netting of a disused grass-grown pen. Through the cobwebbed window panes of the next hut, they saw the lemon crest of a white cockatoo.

"Let's go in here," said Miss Jeacock, grabbing Mr. Gender's hand and pulling him over the threshold.

"Oh wonder!" he thought at the unexpectedness of her gesture, "she has guessed who sent the poem." He was so elated that he hardly noticed his surroundings. Once inside they were almost choked by the rank breath, strong enough to shock a skunk, which hung over the place. Along the wall of windows hung cages of cockatoos and macaws, who at the sight of the human pair set up a maniac choir of "hullos" and "pretty polls". Beaks rattled bars, claws chafed perches, while stunted black tongues cleaved against trim beaks, producing a frightening semblance of reedy human voices. To the strains of this foreboding threnody Mr. Gender's courtship of Miss Jeacock had its birth.

"Isn't it silly, I keep expecting to see Mr. Nale?" laughed Miss Jeacock nervously.

168

An indignant "hullo" came from a posturing scraggy bird, ridiculous in the midst of its moult, so naked that it was more fitted to grace the hooks of a poulterer's shop than the cages of a zoo. Another with solemn bows chanted a monotony of "hullos" with the serious aspect of a judge pronouncing his verdict. A slender streak of a bird clothed in tight-fitting yellow and scarlet plumage, threatened a sore finger with its rapacious fruit-devouring beak, as Miss Jeacock tried to coax it into a good humour.

On the opposite side of the hut, away from the windows, they beheld when their eyes became accustomed to the weak light, what Mr. Gender at first took to be a human being. A female chimpanzee enveloped in a sack was watching them with deep-sunk inscrutable beady eyes. Next door, her neighbour, an ape, hung callous-handed from the wires of the top of the cage. His protruding lips were drawn back over yellow teeth in a dumb inane grin, while her other neighbour, a mandrill, with eyes of lunatic intensity and a posterior hot as the summer dawn, passed restlessly back and forth from dirty well to broken wire, its head brushing impotently against the confines of its narrow prison.

Suddenly, as Miss Jeacock and Mr. Gender stood watching, a flicker crossed the cretinous mask of the chimpanzee as she flung herself upwards to hang from the roof of her cage; while her neighbour the ape, as if to counterbalance her, dropped with a harsh grunt to the floor. She hung from one hand in the front of her cage gently massaging her hind quarters which, red-ripe, exuded moisture like the split sides of some monstrous tropical fruit. She scuffed her hands across her mottled scurfy tortoiseshell skin, passing them characteristically from bottom to face in a gesture of tired ablution, then from face to bottom again. All at once, with the silent intensity of the mentally defective, she was having a tug of war with

169

her neighbour the ape, gripping one end of her sack with one hand and the bars of the cage with the other. While her would-be suitor the mandrill, quivered in an agony of excitement. With a phallic thread like a sliver of raw meat standing erect from the dirty horror of his loins, he emitted sad yearning sighs which would have melted the stony heart of even the virtuous Senior Clerk.

To his surprise and confusion, Mr. Gender found that he was still clasping Miss Jeacock's hand in his. Turning to her, he found she was not watching the antics of the ape but was gazing into his eyes with the most appealing expression. To his utmost amazement he found himself sufficiently emboldened to stammer out:

"Er, Miss Jeacock, I was, er, wondering maybe, perhaps, you would give me great pleasure and have dinner with me tomorrow night in my rooms?" In his embarrassment he had said "rooms", thinking back carelessly to his college days. He did in fact live in one room only. No doubt his unintentional slip had been a subconscious desire to impress Miss Jeacock.

"Rather unconventional of me I suppose, but—er, much more, —er, cosy than a restaurant, don't you think, perhaps?" he added almost appalled at his own temerity. Out of a cloud he heard the voice of his beloved raised above the shrieks of the parrots, whose cries had become louder when the activity between the chimpanzee and the ape began.

A fly, hitherto unseen, concealed in the interstices of the wire moved stealthily, attracting no more attention than the quick flicker of the mandrill's eyes.

"Of course, dear Mr. Gender, I should be delighted to come; in your rooms too, how nice."

He could not believe his ears. Not only must she have guessed the authorship of the poem, but she must also reciprocate his feelings; or she would never, surely, have

170

accepted his invitation to a *tête-à-tête* dinner. Flushed hot with excitement he dropped her hand, and fled with her out into the open air, where the sky had lost its brilliance and was beginning to cloud over and become sadly threatening.

Once outside, he could hardly realise that he had at last asked her, still less that she had accepted; it was with a heart brim-full of a *mélange* of agitation and pleasant anticipation, that he walked beside her towards the restaurant where they were all to meet for lunch. They had not gone far when they caught up with the poor unfortunate Irishman, who had unwittingly got himself into the toils of the Macklin gang.

Jennifer and Leslie had turned the heat off their mother and were concentrating on O'Flattery, as one on each side of him they hung on to his hands. Mrs. Macklin, her face in shadow from her uncustomary hat, had said nothing to the Irishman. But he had seen what she carried and saw with a stab of fear that she was beaming as if she bore a coveted prize.

"What's that animal doing?" said Leslie, indicating a bear which moved backwards away from the bars and then forwards again, with monotonous regularity.

"Shut up you, it's dancing," said Jennifer.

"Why's that monkey all red?" she went on plucking at O'Flattery's sleeve, in coy imitation of an innocent child.

"Cos it's got a sore bum, a course," shouted Leslie, furious with her for trying to draw the Irishman's attention away from him.

"Now then you children, you leave the gentleman alone," leered Mrs. Macklin, with a look of unconcealed adoration at the blushing O'Flattery. Then in honeyed tones to the uncomfortable young man she continued:

"We understand them, don't we Mr. O'Flattery?" wriggling herself with delight inside the armour of her

171

corsets, as if he had just paid her a compliment instead of looking as if he wished a crevasse would open and devour her.

Jennifer looked up with dawning intelligence from her mother's smiling face to O'Flattery's blushing one, remembering in a flash the frequency of the Irishman's name in the oaths which she had heard her mother utter the night before. She felt she was beginning to understand why no reference had been made to that awe-inspiring storm and why no punishment had been inflicted. She had come down to breakfast terrified at what she might find, but instead of a roaring lion she had found, not quite a cooing dove but at least a pacified Amazon, who went about preparing the breakfast in a straightened room which showed surprisingly few scars from the eruption of the previous night. It was then like a drowning man that O'Flattery welcomed the approach of Miss Jeacock and Mr. Gender, as they came up alongside them.

Miss Seal and the Postage Clerk were, a little further on, contemplating a stale looking muff which lay curled up in what appeared to be an old bread oven. A painted ticket said that it was "*Meles taxus*"; a badger, as Mr. Gender, all smiles, translated to the whole group. Miss Seal, and her companion laughed and rattled the wire, while Miss Jeacock looked inscrutable but faintly contemptuous of the rest of her sex. Nothing would call the animal out, not even the raw carrion lying in a puddle on the concrete floor, which Leslie titivated with his stick. The now fitful sun made the beast shrink even further into itself, as the sunbeams painted an all too clear scene of domestic squalor within the recesses of its cage.

The members of the Office staff were gradually converging upon the restaurant, with hungry looks and expectant smiles, ready to enjoy their food and to exchange pleasantries about the animals they had seen.

"Sealy dear, Gender has asked me to dinner tomorrow night," hissed Miss Jeacock, unheard by the rest of the bunch.

"Has he?" replied Miss Seal, her tongue vibrating in her mouth like an adder's, "You look out or you'll be losing your job," she went on, also in a sibilant whisper.

Miss Betty and Miss Gladys Lynch were added to the slowly moving party, as they both caught up with the others at the spot where they were eyeing a huddle of tigresses sleeping in a parcelled sapphic embrace, their tight-wrapped somnolence giving off a peculiarly rancid smell.

They all moved on together to the next cage, where they were joined by a bevy of clerks and typists, who precipitated themselves round a corner of the cage as if in full flight towards their next bite of sustenance.

Here they were all awed to silence by the beauty of a newly painted cage, framing, as it were, a primitive picture of more normal domestic leonine bliss. A dignified lion and lioness were confined in a small brick box, indifferent and passive. The female, resplendent in her tawny beauty, was eating, with the utmost delicacy, a scrap of meat which adhered to one of the bars of their cage; with shell-pink tongue she licked the bars before the impenetrable, unblinking ease of her sculptured mate.

The whole party stood silently watching, even the Macklins, until they were recalled from their individual reveries by Dr. Booker coming upon the scene and calling out: "So you are all looking at the lionscape are you?" which made them all laugh, even Miss Seal, who had practically no sense of humour.

"Isn't it extraordinary," went on Dr. Booker ponderously from behind his Assistant, "how like one's human friends the animals contrive to be?"

It appeared that he could not bear to let his first joke go,

173

without trying to improve on it with another. The Senior Clerk smiled wanly. Nobody else laughed. Dr. Booker cleared his throat. It was as if until this moment the party had been intruders, as though they had stumbled unexpectedly upon a forgotten collection of creatures at the bottom of somebody's garden. The animals had, as it were, been unable to make the effort to show off their graces. Instead, they smelt of winter vices and stale air. But here, before the lion house, was rare beauty indeed. The hand of the cleaner had started here and had touched the cage with new paint, which appropriately framed the untouchable beauty of the lions. The whole picture vibrated in the sunlight, redolent with slumbering strength. A whiskered yawn, revealing the rough arched tongue of the lion, showed them to be alive and not merely superb specimens of the taxidermist's art.

With the lion's yawn a spell was broken; all the human beings began talking at once as they trooped through a provincial rockery unsuitably decorated with a plaster bust of Saint Veronica. With eyes cast down demurely into the leaves garlanding her bosom she smirked at a host of curious Nuremberg dwarfs, who squatted archly among untidy evergreens. They found Dr. Booker, who had gone on before with his Assistant and the Senior Clerk, chatting amiably with the manageress, waving his hands in welcome to them all as if he was meeting them for the first time that day. At the sight of them arriving the manageress clapped her hands and commanded two ageing girls in youthful aprons to serve them with their food. Amid much laughter and the perennial jokes of Dr. Booker, they seated themselves at a long table set in the middle of a verandah, away from the rest of the restaurant which was empty, chairs piled bleakly on the other tables, for no one else was lunching there.

The Irishman came in last and took a seat next to Miss

Jeacock, on whose other side Mr. Gender was sitting.

As they all began to talk about how they had spent the morning the two waitresses pushed plates of tinned tomato soup before them. The Postage Clerk who was sitting opposite Miss Seal glanced surreptitiously at Dr. Booker who had arranged the menu, and silently mouthed the word "tinned". Miss Seal nodded and looked down at her plate; wrinkling up her nose in agreement she deftly took a spoonful of the hectic red liquid into her mouth, as noiselessly as an elephant emptying a bucket of water. Next came a slice of corned beef with a dismal salad of cooked beetroot and tired lettuce accompanied by hot boiled potatoes. Bottles of bought salad cream were handed up and down the table, with the appropriate questions and replies. But these were disdainfully refused by Miss Seal and the Postage Clerk who, although she would have liked some, was afraid not to follow the example of her over-bearing neighbour. Miss Seal ate stolidly, her denture champing its way through large mouthfuls of food. She ate as if it was a duty and not a pleasure, rather in the way in which she performed her work at the Office.

The Misses Lynch pecked like birds; flicking away a fly, which settled on her corned beef, Miss Betty was mindful of the one she had seen on the dung in the lion's cage.

"You never know where they have been," she shouted across the table to her sister as she waved it frantically away, and fastidiously cut off the corner of the meat where the fly had been, pushing it to the edge of her plate.

The typists held up their little fingers in genteel crooks. The Senior Clerk chewed with his mouth open, obviously having tooth trouble. Dr. Booker swallowed with hearty indifference, his Assistant with an assumed air of assurance. Miss Jeacock and the Irishman were laughingly engaged in a conversation about monkeys and gobbled their food between sentences. While Mr. Gender, too excited to eat, cut up his food into dice, pushing it round and round in patterns on his plate, which no one was interested enough to notice.

After a plateful of tinned peaches and condensed milk they were served with bottled coffee, very weak, with two coffee-stained lumps of sugar nestling in each saucer. While they were drinking this unappetising beverage, Dr. Booker rose to his feet and launched himself into the speech which he made with few alterations at each yearly outing.

Mrs. Macklin and the children had been put for company with one of the less important executives, who it was thought, mistakenly, would not mind, at a smaller table slightly removed from the main party. As the Macklins had been added to the party as an afterthought there had not been provision made for them at the main table. But this woman sat with an aggrieved air and Mrs. Macklin wore an expression like thunder. Leslie and Jennifer squabbled over their food and whined until their mother struck them, threatening them alternately with the lions or Dr. Booker's wrath. The Irishman caught her eye as she did this and was puzzled by the complete change which came over her countenance. Could she possibly be signing to him? It was difficult to tell with those eyes.

Dr. Booker thanked everybody for their hard work and co-operation throughout the previous year; from a plethora of clichés it was gathered that he was satisfied with the work that they had all done, and was at the same time urging them on to start a new year with ever increasing ardour, as if the lunch which they had just consumed was supposed to instil in them a positive mania for work, until the next Office Outing came round. While he was talking storm clouds had closed in outside and the darkened sky started to pelt with rain. It drummed on the iron roof so that his words were lost. Everyone began to get restless and started to think about going home. Miss

Betty and Miss Gladys, who were both wearing new white sandals, looked very crestfallen at the thought of getting them sullied by the unexpected rain.

At last Dr. Booker wound up the relaxed spring of his boring speech; with thumps and admiring cries the staff applauded him. Then with a scraping of chairs they got up and separated into two groups, the women being shepherded out ostentatiously by the older of the two waitresses. The men lit pipes or cigarettes and the Irishman disappeared into the rain, reappearing a minute or two later with one of his fly-buttons unfastened, which caught the eye of the manageress, who frowned and spoke unnecessarily sharply to the younger of the two waitresses as she cleared away the debris of the meal.

When they had all forgathered again and the rain had ceased for what was obviously only a short time, Dr. Booker, after consulting with his Assistant and the Senior Clerk, suggested to the others that they should call it a day and make for the bus while it was dry. As no one wanted to trudge about for the afternoon in search of rain soaked animals, it was soon agreed that they should set off home. So with exaggerated thanks to the manageress they left the restaurant and in a straggling crocodile made their way to the bus.

They passed a prancing pelican with a split beak and a mouldy olive green pouch. They hurried past the seal's pond, bleak now under a leaden sky of fast gathering clouds. Its two inmates in a continuous forlorn ballet dived and floated in the solid green filth of their water. One stilled as in death lay suddenly recumbent, half submerged in the clutches of the water. One flipper gently waved, the other clasping its wind-dried tail in an endless whiting-arabesque. Its companion sank and dived in monotonous Jack-in-the-box rhythm, blowing trails of bubbles, like pea-green marbles below. Both, strangely, had opaque unseeing wall-

177

eyes which gazed into the grey and threatening sky. Dr. Booker's Assistant unexpectedly nudged Miss Betty Lynch and said archly, "Look Seals." She and her sister giggled hysterically and hid their smiles from Miss Seal, who seemed quite oblivious of the joke, although she must have heard as she stood close by, still with the Postage Clerk beside her.

A wind-swept dromedary was almost invisible against the dun-coloured landscape, but for the blowing straws in its second-hand coat. An ageless eccentric, with bags and cartons stuffed with scraps for her animal friends, was washing tins at a tap amidst blowing newspaper. She glared at the other visitors suspecting them of usurping her self-appointed privilege. Her wild hair matched the fur of a snarling polar bear, which also seemed irritated as much by the visitors as the rising wind. The mood of the day was completely broken.

Dr. Booker came to a halt beside the fabulous bulk of a great rhinoceros and, in order to show his authority, motioned the others to stop and admire. The great creature stood motionless but for the twitching of its lower lip. Its warty armour was gathered about its limbs like ill-fitting loose covers. A fly buzzed round its mean eyes, the only vulnerable part it could find.

"Oh look how jolly," chirped Miss Gladys Lynch inappropriately. She had no sooner said this than an embarrassing plop, plop, plopping began as the huge beast voided a pile of steaming excrement upon the beaten ground. Miss Betty gasped. Miss Gladys said: "Oh Betty," reprovingly. Miss Seal just stared in enigmatic amazement. Mrs. Macklin knocked Leslie and Jennifer's heads together fiercely, as they began to snigger, smiling to herself at the crestfallen Irishman who was looking at his macintosh which she had not returned to him. The pool-typists looked at each other and frowned, clicking their tongues against their teeth. The Postage Clerk said: "Well, really, I must say," as if speaking for them all.

Dr. Booker, his Assistant and the Senior Clerk all cleared their throats, looked distractedly round and began to move towards the bus, as the Irishman laughed suddenly, openly and unashamed. The Macklin children looked from one adult to another stuffing their fists into their mouths, purple in the face from suppressed laughter.

Miss Jeacock looked at Mr. Gender and smirked. Mr. Gender blushed so deeply that the whites of his eyes and the grey hairs at his temples stood out unnaturally. He felt he could stand no more of the uncontrolled behaviour of this barbarous collection of animals, nor of the unpredictable effect it was having on their human counterparts on this side of the barrier.

Hastily everyone turned, following the lead of Dr. Booker down the slope towards the bus. Mr. Gender glanced uneasily at Miss Jeacock and the Irishman who had hesitated to look at the last cage by the exit. They appeared to be talking, but he could not hear what they were saying; as the sky began to spit rain he broke into a run behind the retreating figures of the rest of the staff.

"Mr. Gender has asked me to dinner tomorrow night," said Miss Jeacock to O'Flattery. "In his rooms," she added with assumed carelessness. "I think I shall go."

"Of course. Why not?" smiled the Irishman. His face betrayed no hint of his feeling but an icy hand had gripped his heart; for the first time in his life he knew what it was to feel jealousy. This woman who he had come to believe was pursuing him, was attracted by someone else after all. For Miss Jeacock had made it quite clear by her expression, and the wayward look in her eyes, what she wanted him to think her feelings for Mr. Gender were.

They looked one another directly in the face. Miss Jeacock knew then that her dart had hit the bull's eye and had drawn blood. She smiled to herself and tossed her hair.

179

A large fly was worrying a heap of offal at the bottom of the cage in front of which they were standing. Behind the slim wires two scarlet-pated turkey vultures faced each other on a dead branch. They inclined their heads and stretched their necks, gaping for all the world like two notaries entangled in an eternal legal argument. Their raw wrinkled heads, like the freshly skinned bloody necks of two rabbits, rose aggressively from neat black feathers, rusty green with age. Bone-white treacherous beaks searched frowsty armpits and calcined claws fumbled against the rotting windpipe of some dead animal which protruded from the flesh of their last meal. Miss Jeacock shuddered. All the thrill of her recent triumph over O'Flattery's virgin heart seemed to drain from her as she turned away and followed the others, who were already settling themselves down amidst jolly chatter in the awaiting bus.

As she hurried towards it, the rain began to teem down and, with a vicious stab, that pain was back beneath her heart.

12

NEXT DAY, as Mr. Gender left the Office early, his mood of elation had so far lifted him from his usual rut, that he took Leslie and Jennifer, who were wheeling the bundle that was Brenda, along to the corner for an ice-cream. He was about to have one himself but was prevented by the thought of Dr. Booker "catching him". They made an incongruous quartet on the busy corner. Leslie licking stolidly through his wafer, Brenda plastering her tear-stained face with her cornet, and Jennifer looking up at Mr. Gender impertinently, out of the corners of her eyes, as she licked the chocolate off her bar.

"Go on Mr. Gender, you 'ave one," she encouraged. Managing to look as if she was suggesting some much more serious break in decorum. Mr. Gender laughed gaily and said "No Jennifer, not today, I'm in a hurry and must be getting along."

"Go on, I would, you can lick it goin' along," said Leslie. But Mr. Gender would not be persuaded.

"Where you goin'?" inquired Jennifer, writing on the pavement with her toe.

"Ah! hah!" said Mr. Gender mysteriously, keen now to get away. "Goodbye, see you tomorrow."

"Goodbye," chimed Leslie and Jennifer together.

"Ood-i," grunted Brenda out of her Aunt-Sally face.

With an ineffectual wave at them with the tips of his fingers he was gone.

"What's 'e doin' leavin' early? An' buyin' us ice-creams

181

too. Cranky old tool!" said Jennifer.

"Don't know and don't care, smack 'im till 'is bum's bare," chanted Leslie as they ambled back to the Office again. Here they found Wendy with her bicycle, who made an ill-aimed lunge at Brenda's ice and said:

"Where'd yer get 'em?"

"Old Gender bought 'em for us. An' you can't 'ave a lick. For if yer did yer taste 'ud make me sick," teased Leslie.

"Shit 'em!" said Wendy and scooted off rapidly on her iron steed.

Mr. Gender had left early to prepare his room for the dinner party with Miss Jeacock-the-Fair, to buy food for the dinner and meat for his cat. At last after waiting so long she had consented to enter his territory. It was, he thought, the beginning of victory. He had for a long time been under the impression that his intentions towards her were quite clear, and it must be no mystery to her now why he had asked her to his room. The fact that she had accepted meant, he was certain, that her feelings for him had undergone a change. It must mean in fact that she would spend the night there with him. It meant that she would become his wife in due course, that all the drudgery and loneliness of his bachelor life would be at an end. He was precipitate in planning his future.

He had left the Office feeling more light-hearted than he thought it possible to feel; his smile and his cheerful "goodnight" to Mrs. Macklin, at the main door, had made that knowing old Jezebel scratch her head in perplexed surprise.

After he had left the Macklin children he went straight to Mr. Nale's shop for the cat's meat. Mr. Nale was unfortunately in a very talkative mood. After several abortive attempts Mr. Gender managed to get hold of the cat's meat parcel and, frantically explaining at the top of

182

his voice that he was in a hurry, he succeeded in backing out of the shop, leaving Mr. Nale still in the full flood of his reminiscences.

He bought some anemones from an old man on the corner by the Tube station, but was now in such a hurry that he couldn't even bother to stop when he realised the old man had given him short change.

He called in at the delicatessen where, mercifully, he was the only customer to buy some hors-d'oeuvre, for he meant this to be a proper dinner rather than his usual meagre supper. Inside the doors of this clean, savoury smelling shop he was surrounded by a bewildering crowd of tubs, jars and dishes with the most appetising-looking contents. Black olives he chose, because they were exotic; white onions, no he thought not, with a wry smile to himself; Russian salad, yes, a portion of that, enough for two in a neat waxed carton; smoked herring he thought was harmless enough and a better choice than rollmops because it contained no onion; and finally sweet corn, taken off the cob and nestling in a clot of mayonnaise, would go well with his other purchases. A Camembert cheese he could not resist. Finally two packets of potato crisps, these he planned as part of the second course to be eaten with an omelette, which he felt sure he could soon knock up and cook on his single gas burner.

In the grocer's he bought some freshly ground coffee and a bottle of what he considered was quite expensive sherry. Over this he had hesitated as he was not a drinking man himself, but then he decided to get it as he wanted to make a good impression on Miss Jeacock, in order that she might get some idea of the standard of living, which he planned she was soon to share.

At the baker's he was held up and forced to listen to a conversation much against his will. A woman in a white coat, obviously from some neighbouring factory, was buying cakes.

"How you feelin' this evenin' Jos?" the shop assistant said with exaggerated feeling in her voice.

"Bad, dear."

"Bin't the doctor?"

"Not till Friday."

"I reckon it's them tablets."

"Yare, ha you bin takin' 'em?"

"Yare, little white ones."

"Two night an' mornin'. They make me feel that bad. Didn't nearly come ter work yest'day."

"Noooo, you don't want to take two. One, I used to take, then I used to feel bad till ten o'clock, didn't know what I was doin' when I come down 'ere first thing."

"Oh, two I always take."

"No, one dear, quite enough."

"Yesterday the pain was 'orrible at work, every now and again I 'ave a dance and joke."

"Ye-es, one night and mornin'."

"I'll 'ave four Banburys, six cream slices and three japs."

All this was carried on with feminine conspiratorial intensity, completely ignoring the presence of Mr. Gender. When he finally attracted the assistant's attention he bought a cut-loaf and a hectic-looking sponge sandwich, filled with jam and covered with artificial cream, dyed in three colours and laced in a garish tracery over the surface of the cake.

He began to think there really was a conspiracy to delay him when at the greengrocer's a woman began to talk just as she was about to leave the shop. The two women started like birds pecking at one another.

"I think they're more apples about this year than there were last."

"Yes. But they're eaters as a rule aren't they, Worcesters?"

184

"I don't know. I don't like 'em. Don't like any fruit. Only buy it for my 'usband."

"Ohow, I like a nice apple if that's nice. Fruit's good for you."

"Can't bear 'em. I like anything sweet like a cake or something."

"Well, I don't like 'em, tart or anything like that but a nice apple's always nice."

"Couldn't touch a grape. Ugh!"

"Oh well, it wouldn't be no good bringin' you a nice bunch a grapes then?"

"No grapes, or anything like that, can't bear 'em."

"Well that's what I was brought when I was in hospital, a nice bunch a grapes."

"Oh well, my Father used to grow them you see, great big bunches."

"I didn't know if they disagreed with you or anything, you know."

"No, just can't bear 'em."

Mr. Gender danced from foot to foot, trying to interrupt this flood of irritating small talk, until his request for half a pound of mixed nuts seemed hardly important enough to wait for. But just as he was going he got served and then as he left the shop he became lost, as he hurried homewards, in a reverie of himself and Miss Jeacock sitting, their heads together over the fire, cracking nuts and exchanging confidences until the inevitable intimacy to which his dinner preparations were leading, finally occurred.

Struggling with his purchases stowed in two carrier bags, he managed to unlock the front door. Collecting his milk bottle on the way, he toiled up the dark stairs to his room. Perhaps it was just as well, he thought, that they were dark as then Miss Jeacock would not see the cracks in the plaster or the places under each landing window where the distemper was peeling off in ugly scabrous flakes.

Once inside his room he began to create the necessary festive background for the conquest of his guest. His short sight made his efforts at cleaning very imperfect. His onslaughts with a dustpan and brush made little effect upon the drifts of blanket fluff, which had collected along the edges of the floor boards. However, being unable to see this it did not bother him. Humming gently to himself he made his bed, patting the counterpane solicitously, as if his beloved was already beneath it; he drew the curtains very carefully so that, even if it had been possible for anyone but a very long sighted aeronaut to look through his window, no human eye would spy out a thing.

With the anemones arranged in two Benares brass vases on a folding card table covered with an orange and blue chequered cloth and the fire lit, the room, to Mr. Gender's eyes, took on a look of gaiety and promise. His optimism succeeded in blinding him to the real appearance of the fireplace which on less propitious occasions resembled pink marzipan and pastry, overbaked to a brown vomit colour.

Two glasses and the sherry on the mantelpiece; coffee percolator already filled and standing in the hearth; the various hors-d'oeuvres in saucers on the table, which was set with all the battered cutlery he could muster; the bizarre cake standing with the cheese, in company with his hair-brush and brilliantine on the chest of drawers; all this made up the party scene.

He broke four eggs into a bowl, beat them vigorously with a fork and stood them beside the cake. He wiped his one and only frying pan round with some salt and a piece of paper from the wastepaper basket, then putting in a knob of margarine he set it, with the coffee percolator, in the hearth. Looking round for more jobs to do to pass the time, he noticed the nuts and the potato crisps, lying together unopened on the draining board by the sink. He had never wished more fervently that this eye-sore could be hidden out of sight. He must, he decided, contrive some kind of curtain before Miss Jeacock came to live with him; for he felt certain that, for one with such tender suscepti-bilities, the constant sight of a white porcelain sink would be more than depressing. He could find no nutcrackers but smiled to himself as he added the pliers from his tool drawer to the bowl of nuts. How amused and touched he thought Miss Jeacock would be at this sign of inept bache-lordom. He emptied the packets of crisps into a pie dish; the little blue twists of salt which fell out reminded him that the salt in his salt cellar was damp. He threw its contents onto the fire, which made a hiss and a momentary blue glow. Then he refilled it from a canister. This un-accustomed sound awoke his cat, which had been lying forgotten and asleep in a dark corner of the room. As she was expecting a family of kittens her sleep was so lethargic and deep that she had not stirred when Mr. Gender entered the room, but now that she was awake she came forward into the fire light and stretched awkwardly in the warmth.

"Poor Pussy," said Mr. Gender out loud as he scratched behind her ears with his fore-finger, "Poor Pussy, didums master forget oo?"

Then, blushing with shyness at his own unusual tender-ness, he hastily cleared his throat and offered the cat its meat which he had been at such pains to get from Mr. Nale. But drawing back her whiskers she refused it as if insulted. Repeating the process a second time as he offered her a piece of smoked herring from the dinner table. Absently he replaced the piece of herring on the saucer. Frisking her tail in disgust, and shaking each of her back legs, the cat stalked to the door and gratingly demanded to be let out, disappearing in a scurry down the now pitch dark stairway to go about some business of her own in the untenanted basement of the house.

With her departure Mr. Gender felt suddenly lonely, which was inconsistent of him as he had, up till now, ignored her presence in his bustle to prepare for his visitor; but now that all was ready, sitting waiting before the fire, he felt uncertain and not a little afraid of what he was planning to do. As he was a man of no experience with women, he was tormented now with powerful misgivings.

The room seemed to Mr. Gender to smell uncommonly stuffy. So many conflicting food smells pressed against one another that the atmosphere was as tight and unbreathable as the florets of a cauliflower. He remembered some joss sticks that a smiling Indian had once inveigled him into buying at the door. "Take away bad smell," he had chanted continuously in a persuasive voice until, to get rid of him, he had been forced to buy a packet of "mixed Agarbathi." So far he had only used a few, but they had all smelled alike to him. He lit one now at the fire and stuck its sharp wooden end into the intricacies of a brass bell. A twisting, coiling ribbon of grey smoke rose from its glowing tip. The white edges of this ribbon spread outwards writhing in fantastic arabesques, as the invisible air currents of the room caught this perfumed conflagration spreading its sweetness about the room, warring instantly with the more acid odours of the food. Grey coils of burnt out ash dropped to the table cloth in a broken line as the length of the joss stick diminished as it burnt.

A fly appeared from somewhere near the sink, buzzing its unwelcome flight over each of the saucers of food. It flew into one of the empty sherry glasses and its angry whining, magnified by the enclosing glass, drew Mr. Gender's attention to the bottle beside it. Perhaps, he thought, a small glass might help to steady his nerves. It would be better to start the bottle or Miss Jeacock might think it was a special treat and not the customary thing.

So, gingerly, with the greatest care, he extracted the cork and poured himself a glass of the dark amber fluid, which for him symbolised all the intoxicants he had held in such awe for the whole of his life. To him it represented evil, pure and simply. Drink was the gate through which one entered the region where control could no longer be called to one's aid, a control which he needed in order to curb those passions which arose, even without the help of stimulants, and which he felt certain would assail him with greater fury while under their mysterious influence.

His love for Miss Jeacock could never have been described as purely spiritual, but it was to this aim that he aspired. To be able to put down the lust of his flesh and give rein to those sweeter, more enduring, less destructive elements of his love was his constant wish. Yet the conflict which ensued between his better self and his carnal self, at times almost completely annihilated his peace of mind. He felt himself at this moment of waiting, on the brink of a precipice, the perils of which he could not escape. He felt as though he had climbed so far and now faced a leap into oblivion, or alternatively the continuation of a darker, more difficult, struggle ahead. The steep path below him had crumbled away and mists obscured the way back. There was in fact no going back. There was only going forward with Miss Jeacock, over the brink into an unknown territory. But Miss Jeacock was not there to take his hand and help him onward. It looked as if she had failed him before their climb had begun. Where was she? What could be keeping her? How could she do this to him?

He raised the glass of sherry to his lips and held it for a moment away from his mouth. His lips protruded. The little finger of his hand was crooked, his whole arm trembled with fear. He was about to break a habit of years. The principle, to which he had unquestioningly adhered throughout his youth and middle-age, was to be denied.

He was St. Peter waiting for the cock to crow; he was a bride upon the threshold, so intense were his palpitations; a schoolboy on the eve of puberty. The sherry touched his tongue and surprised him with its pleasant flavour. He sipped again, then with a thrill of daring he drained the glass. A warm glow began to infuse the chill fear beneath his solar plexus. A diffusion of ease and indifference. He was hungry for he had not eaten since midday. The food invited him, the bottle lured him. All too easily his will conceded to the demands of his body. He poured himself another glass. With half of it drunk in one gulp he picked up the piece of herring shunned by the cat and savoured it on his tongue. The herring was very salty, so it was not long before the other half of the second glass of sherry followed the first. Neither was it long before the third glass followed the second, nor the fourth the third. The glow in his inside had now seeped into his legs, even behind his eyes and it was with unsure fingers that he picked at the olives and pieces of herring. To his surprise, he had almost forgotten Miss Jeacock.

It was not until the telephone began its clamour, recalling him to his vigil, that he remembered her and that she was now an hour late for dinner. As he stretched out his hand for the receiver he decided that this must be her, telephoning to explain her tardiness. But it was a man's voice asking if it was a cinema; when Mr. Gender replied that it was not, incredulity in the voice gave way to irritation and finally an angry click as he rang off. Now that Mr. Gender's mind had been jerked back so rudely to reality, perplexity, caused by the continued absence of Miss Jeacock, was added to his loneliness which became more painful than ever. This time, as if from long established habit, his hand went out to the sherry bottle and poured himself two more glasses in quick succession. He realised now that his vision was becoming obscured, that the fly which buzzed angrily round the food and before his spectacles, left a vapour trail which remained as a blur on his retina after it had passed out of view. His speech, when he had answered the telephone, had been distinctly blurred. His step was not straight when he walked over to the sink. His head felt very hot and there were tight iron bands round his brow. His tongue cleaved to the roof of his mouth and, strangely, he was outrageously thirsty. He turned on the tap and ran himself a cup of water. Drinking it down it had the instant effect of making him feel much worse. It seemed to mingle in his stomach with the sherry curdling the very fumes which rose to his brain.

Miss Jeacock was not coming. Miss Jeacock was not coming. Miss Jeacock was not coming. It was like the mocking voice of an arrival and departure clerk, amplified in the wastes of an empty railway station. The full impact of his disappointment now hit him. He staggered back to the bottle and this time raised the neck to his lips, taking a long smooth gurgling draught. More than half was gone and its cheap potency was making him feel drowsy; she obviously was not coming. Damn the bitch, an expression which at normal times would not have been further from his thoughts. He would go to bed. Best place. If she comes now, best place. I'll show the bitch! Best place, where she belongs! With each angry exclamation spat out like owls pellets, he threw off first his shoes and socks, then his trousers, his coat and shirt, until he stood naked. I'll show her, he thought. He had an intense desire to be methodical. He felt that he must put on his pyjamas. Floundering unsteadily, he dragged them from a drawer and somehow pulled them on to his trembling limbs. Once more grabbing the sherry bottle, and in a frenzy of agony hurling the vases of anemones into the grate, he tottered to the bed. One more long swig; oblivion and the end of the bottle were closer together; another and they had been introduced.

191

With his head in a whirl and his stomach revelling he fell onto the bed; with a last desperate clutch at the clothes he heaved them up over his head, as the bed careered under him like a run-away horse. He lay in increasing insensibility. Leaving the wreckage of his nuptial feast to be enjoyed by the single fly which buzzed dejectedly from herrings to cream cake and back again; from beaten egg to the corners of Mr. Gender's mouth, from which there trickled a thin stream of acid froth, soaking the pillow beside his ear.

13

THIS WAS an evening presaging such horror that the Fates could have been heard, by the discerning, beating their foetid wings through a sky thick with portent. The moon was indeed veiled in blood. The astrological position of the heavens was one of great complexity, professing misfortune and disaster.

The shutters were already up, the working day over, the Office blinds drawn, when Miss Jeacock and the Irishman eventually came face to face in the vestibule, on this evening of the day after the Outing.

He stood, his back pressed against one of the radiators, his feet stuck out before him side by side, the soles of his shoes grating against the flagstones of the passage. His hands were in his pockets, so that nothing supported him except the weight of his body against the radiator and his sliding feet. He was acutely aware of the dry unreasonable heat. As he stood there, beads of sweat began to collect in his armpits and in the small of his back. Contrasting with the unpleasant heat of the radiator he had two centres of extreme chill as the drops of sweat dropped cold from his armpits down his body. Although fully clothed, in his normal clothing for that time of year, with most of his body feeling over-heated, these two centres of damp cold gave him a sensation of being naked, clothed only in his own hair, his own flesh, his own particular body odour. As he stood thus, his thoughts were completely taken up with this feeling of nakedness within the carapace of his

193

clothes. So that, when Miss Jeacock appeared at the head of the stairs, he was surprised that she showed no sign of astonishment. He, on the other hand, was taken somewhat unawares, as if he had been disturbed in his bath or at some more personal occupation. She hesitated on the bottom tread of the stairs. The light on the staircase was not switched on so that she stood, a shadowed figure, looking out of a pool of darkness at the Irishman, who leant against his radiator in a pool of light, beneath the uncovered electric light bulb of the vestibule. She stood kicking the lead which covered the edges of the treads, with the iron shod toe of her shoe. The Irishman was impaled against the radiator, like an insect on an entomological pin. He was intimidated by the obscurity of her features and fascinated by the gentle tapping of her foot.

Although their meeting at the foot of these stairs was not a pre-arranged assignation, they both knew that each had a purpose in remaining there together, that a moment of crisis had arrived. During the last weeks Miss Jeacock's feminine predatorial instinct had vanquished the remaining shreds of the young man's inherent prejudices. Her inquisitorial leer from the shadows of the staircase had finally ensnared him.

He waited and watched; she watched, tapping with her foot and waited. His hands fidgeted with the coins in his pocket, inside which his fingers picked up a handful of coins, dropping them one by one until he was left holding one only, round the milling of which he ran his thumb nail. This one he dropped and withdrew his hands, pushing back his hair with both of them. His mouth was dry and his tongue failed to moisten his lips.

To Miss Jeacock his eyes were dull unpolished black, without a trace of light in them. She stood saying nothing, simply looking at him, out of the shadows into the light. To say that she was the spider and he the fly would be to make too simple an analogy. The juxtaposition of these two individuals, in this particular setting, at that particular moment, was far more subtle than a conventional spider-fly relationship. The Irishman was certainly entangled in a web from which he now realised there was no escape. It was, however, a web partly of his own spinning. The relationship between Miss Jeacock and O'Flattery was that of two far more compatible creatures than the spider and the fly. Rather was it spider confronted by spider. The female spider figuratively circling round her prospective partner; the victim of an avid conflict between the desire to satisfy the demands made by her digestion and her obsessional sexual hunger. Each human arachne felt the strands of, and was in danger of being overcome by, the web of their own and each other's spinning.

As the Irishman stood suspended before Miss Jeacock, he studied in detail each object upon which his eyes rested. He saw the observant fly which buzzed round the flex of the electric light bulb. In the bright light its flight seemed to leave a visible trail behind it, a complex interwoven thread of pattern. He was dazzled and Miss Jeacock became for a moment even less visible, became an insistent tapping merely, doubly obscured by darkness and his inability to focus.

Neither of them saw that Mrs. Macklin had slipped out of a door halfway up the stairs, and was also the silent observer of this dramatic meeting. Not even the fly was aware of her as she glided, strangely quiet for a woman of her graceless bulk, across the landing and away upstairs.

O'Flattery's eye was fixed by the slowly crawling arm of the barograph, tracing a violet path over its ruled squares. In the second during which his eye rested upon it, it covered continents. He focused upon the intersections made by the black tapes on the letter board. His thoughts fled backwards into the past, to a conjurer's contrivance

195

he had possessed as a child, a trick which could make a visiting card disappear and appear again, appear and disappear again, depending on how you opened the two halves. Back in a deluge he came to the present, as the wagging pendulum of the clock took his eyes once more to the impatient tapping foot of Miss Jeacock. Her square toe dented the lead and in it he counted six copper nails before his eye travelled the length of her leg, upwards to her face.

She was wearing a green knitted dress. A posy of orange woollen flowers at the throat flamed against the vivid skin of her flushed neck. His nostrils were filled with the strong aroma of the scent which she had affected of late. She had shaken a generous sprinkling into the palm of her hand, then rubbing her hands together she had spread this sickly bait up and down her arms, like scented bird-lime. Such a concentrated perfume was incongruous emanating from the person of Miss Jeacock.

Penetrating the silent thunder in his ears he could hear the steps of Mrs. Macklin as she moved about upstairs, cleaning, he supposed. He heard no one else, nothing but the dull tom-tom of Miss Jeacock's toe; still no word was spoken. Miss Jeacock's right foot suddenly stopped tapping and with her left one, carried her off speedily down the passage. The hydra-headed animal of Sex was off through the Office corridors on the prowl. Past Dr. Booker's room, past Mr. Gender's office, past the Irishman's own office and down into the Ladies' Cloakroom. O'Flattery followed the lead of Miss Jeacock's feet. Incongruously she held the door open for him as they passed into the tiled room.

Once protected by a covering of darkness the Irishman wasted no time.

An unexpected voice suddenly shrilled along the corridor, its shrillness increasing by the addition of

196

another. Betty and Gladys Lynch had not yet gone home, they were coming to wash.

Without speaking, O'Flattery and Miss Jeacock stepped through the nearest door into the narrow confines of one of the compartments. The absurd juxtaposition of Miss Jeacock's disarranged dress and the yawning white porcelain emptiness, kept him from losing his head. The banality of the drama forced a smile which he hid from Miss Jeacock's bowed head. They both held their breath. Outside the unlocked door the two Miss Lynches had flicked on the electric light; they were apparently noisily washing their hands and combing their hair. He could hear the jerk and splash of the water in one of the basins followed by the harsh scrapes of a metal comb through coarse hair.

"She wouldn't speak to me, Betty."

"Who wouldn't?"

"Why, Jeacock wouldn't."

"Well who does she think she is anyway?"

"I don't know. She had that black stuff on her eyes."

"Yes and lipstick right down to the edges of her mouth too."

"Yes, I know, and that perfume she's started to use. Phew!"

"Do you remember me putting black stuff on my eyes once?"

"Yes I do, Dad nearly turned you out."

"It's terrible, they say, if you go to the pictures with it on and it's a crying picture. Oo it does smart so. So Beryl said."

"Yes. I know."

"I shan't get up on Sunday. I shall lie in bed all day."

"Isn't it awful?"

"I shall get up if there's some sun. But I shan't if it's raining."

"No, nor shall I."

"What's the good of getting up if it's cold?"

"Sun's the only thing that'll get me up."

"Well you'll have to get up on Monday, girl, sun or no sun, to come to work."

"Oh well, that's different."

All this time the sounds of gurgling water and the revolutions of the roller towel indicated what they were doing.

"Going in there, Gladys?"

"Yes . . . no . . . I don't think I will. I'll wait till we get home."

"Come on then."

The need for such tense self-control had weakened the remnant of the Irishman's opposition and despite the absurdity of their situation he once more fell upon the unreluctant Miss Jeacock.

Miss Jeacock had that painful heaviness in her chest again, accompanied by an overpowering feeling of foreboding. This was not the pleasure she had long anticipated. Not the thing at all. The pain reached a crescendo and she began to fall. They were cramped for space and as she slumped so heavily before O'Flattery, he did not suffer the intense enjoyment he had expected. It puzzled him. Was it their mutual avidity or their mutual inexperience? He soon knew the reason. Miss Jeacock had not enjoyed herself either. Although the ensnarement of this young man had been for some time both life and death to her, the capture had proved her death.

At first the Irishman was panic-stricken. He could hear Arthur stoking up the furnace outside the Office building. Except for the bodies of drowned animals by the river bank he had never experienced death before. It had all happened so quickly, but he found that he was surprisingly calm. Hemmed in by the walls of the compartment, he went over

198

in the darkness the alternatives before him.

Should he slip out, fetch his coat and hat and leave the building quietly?

Should he fetch Mrs. Macklin and tell her the whole story?

Should he pretend to Mrs. Macklin that as he was passing he heard a cry and the noise of someone falling, but had not liked to enter the Ladies' Cloakroom, so that he had fetched her and now returned to find with her what he knew to be there?

Should he leave the cloakroom and continue with his work, waiting for Mrs. Macklin to come and find Miss Jeacock?

Of these four plans the first seemed the one least likely to direct suspicion towards him. Something in the looks which Mrs. Macklin had been giving him all day since the Outing, combined with her strange manifestation in the cinema, made him afraid to pursue either the second or the third alternative. As to the fourth, he did not know the usual procedure taken by Mrs. Macklin in her cleaning and for all he knew she might not come near the cloakroom at all that evening. No, it was best to get clear away, fast, and leave Miss Jeacock's body to be found by the first comer, grizzly as it would be.

Having made his decision, he wasted no time before acting upon it. He succeeded in leaving the Office unseen by anyone inside it. Mrs. Macklin was bumping about cleaning on one of the upper floors.

No one saw him as he left the building, except Brenda.

Leslie and Jennifer were still patrolling their beat up and down outside the Office with their sister. But they had left her in her push-chair, nursing Horny the tortoise, while their attention was taken up trying to overhear the conversation of a caller in the telephone box. The shadow of the phone booth played across Brenda's great white head, as

199

it lolled over sideways from the push-chair. The eyes, as they rolled over towards the Irishman, looked as if they were about to spill out down her face. The whole child had the appearance of soiled porridge boiling over the edge of an old saucepan. O'Flattery was a favourite of hers and always when she caught sight of him her porridge appearance was heightened by an even fiercer show of agitated, boiling-over movement. Fortunately for the Irishman, Leslie and Jennifer paid no attention to her. She might choke for all they cared.

Brenda could hardly count as a witness; with a shudder he crossed himself as he sped away into the evening.

14

O'FLATTERY FELT very confused. The events of the last hours were entirely beyond his comprehension. His mind refused to face the actuality of either Miss Jeacock's present whereabouts or her condition. His immediate thought was to get as far away as possible from her. He felt that he could neither face the solitude of his lodgings nor the dark loneliness of the cinema. He wanted to go where there was more life than mere celluloid images, where there were lights and music. He wanted to shut out from his mind all recollection of the extraordinary thing which had just happened to him. He particularly didn't want to remember the way Miss Jeacock's body had slumped away from him; the awful slowness of her crumpling limbs; the heat of her body against his, and then its sudden stillness; nor his furtive gestures as he left the lavatory morgue. His reason shied away from the reality of what must happen on the following morning. Mrs. Macklin would most likely be the first to find her. His feet hurried him on towards diversion, but his thoughts raced backwards despite himself to the very things from which he wanted to escape.

A brightly coloured poster, outside the tube station, advertised evening excursions from a main line terminus to a Mecca of pleasure on the coast. It caught his eye, bringing his wayward reason to the apex of making another decision. The place was within easy reach of the metropolis, it would be crowded and noisy. Once there he could lose himself in the innominate pleasure-seeking crowds. He might even forget enough to collect and prepare himself for what must happen next day. Joining the throng of late returning workers he was engulfed and spewed into a train.

Without being fully aware of the sequence of events, or of the people around him, he was soon sitting in a second class carriage of a train leaving the main line station. An excursion ticket was in his trouser pocket and an empty feeling in his stomach. With a bemused sense of forgetfulness blanketing down upon him, what had happened gradually became dim. He scarcely knew where he was, nor exactly what he was doing, where he was going or why. As the train sped through the suburbs he began to take note of his travelling companions.

A workman sat opposite him, thickset, his body generously covered with flesh under his work-stained blue suit. It was tight almost to the point of bursting the seams. His thighs particularly drew the Irishman's attention. Firm and strong they were thrust forward as the man balanced on the edge of his seat. The front of his trousers, up to the fly buttons, round the pockets and across the waistline, were thick with grease. The Irishman decided that either his work entailed leaning that part of his body against something, or else that he must continually be hitching at his trousers with dirty hands. He was altogether a soiled and dirty man, smelling of the factory, a sordid mediocre man. He coughed, a continual harsh smoker's cough. When he did so his whole torso moved with the cough, like a piston rod moving in a cylinder, an ill-fitting piston rod making a grating noise despite its well oiled action. The grease on his clothes, his cough and his likeness to a piston, provoked in the Irishman's mind the thought that this man was not a human being at all but a metal robot, a component part of the mechanism of a machine.

202

Between coughs he was talking to his neighbour, a younger cleaner man who was not paying much attention to him. Instead he was looking at the backside of a girl who stood with her giggling companions in the corridor.

The Irishman's eyes turned away from the men to the countryside which was pouring by. The train was leaving a cutting where knots of flowers were buttoned into the ground and then emerged into open fields, upon which a collection of four-legged worn out hearth rugs moved erratically. These he saw when he looked more carefully were sheep. They must, he thought, have something wrong with them, no normal sheep surely had such matted tufts of wool hanging from them. Before he had time to consider the matter properly the whole vista had changed. He lay back in his corner and closed his eyes.

He felt overcome with a creeping lethargy which attacked his body from the soles of his feet, climbing upwards, sapping the strength from his knees as it rose, so that if he had been standing he would have sunk to the ground. He felt so weak that he was sure he must look weak, that the other occupants of the compartment would notice it and perhaps ask him what was the matter. But when he opened his eyes no one was looking at him; the piston rod man and his companion had left the carriage, the other people in it were so nondescript that they made no impression on him whatsoever.

The train swept towards the sea as the landscape folded and unfolded, muted in the waning light.

They passed a large stretch of pallid grey water, out of which stuck the decaying arm of a dead tree, fringed by a ring of half submerged bushes. A dreary waste of still flat water over which floated a solitary bird lay there calmly among the fields as if it had welled up from the ground over night, choking the existing grass and trees, drowning their roots in a briny black darkness. It was so unusual

203

that it made him sit up, leaning forward to see it better.

It was then that he realised that he had been asleep. He had been dreaming and could not distinguish between reality and fantasy. He felt terribly tired. Wave after wave of sleep lapped him, a succession of images took shape in his mind . . . a hanging electric light bulb dimly shining, a weak low powered light. Round it a fly was flying in an unnaturally regular circle; now it dipped up and down so that its flight, always round the bulb faster and faster, made the pattern of a coiled spring; now it was he who was imprisoned inside the bulb and instead of a glowing element his naked white body was providing a faint tepid light; round and round flew the fly. Its eyes, huge waxen blobs, veered in and out of his vision as it swung past him. The size and shape of the eyes was altering as the fly flew. Two gigantic lenses now obscured the pale gaze of Mr. Gender. The fly's eyes were changing. Now each one was the tiny replica of the whole of Mr. Gender's head. They swelled, stared and swelled as the fly went round; Mr. Gender's face was undergoing a transformation. The fly now bore in its eyes the white pulpy face of Brenda. Then as a slide changes in a magic lantern, it was the dead face of Miss Jeacock. Now it was Mrs. Macklin nodding and beckoning; in the fly's eye the image dilated and receded, within the image another fly flew with the same distorted eyes; within which the image of another fly flew, within which the image of another fly flew and so on; as if through an interminable hall of mirrors another fly flew. O'Flattery struggled to escape from the bulb; in so doing he shattered the glass and began falling, falling, falling. Instantly, the fly swooped upon him as a falcon and he cried out, an agonised tormented cry, waking himself as he did so. Fortunately the carriage was empty, all the other travellers having left at stations unnoticed by the sleeping Irishman.

The night sky was closing in as the train sped on; on

each side of it tender green fields fled away bearing crests of cardboard-cut-out cows. Long shadows deformed them into ugliness. O'Flattery's vision had become a distorting glass and it was with a feeling of the utmost relief that he saw the fields were gradually giving way to strips and ribbons of bungalows heralding the outskirts of the seaside town. The engine let out a great shriek as the houses unravelled on each side like an unrolling carpet, then dived hysterically into a tunnel. Inside the blackness of the tunnel he at last felt safe, calm but at the same time suspended in a horrible temporary release. He had returned to a madly rushing womb. Then with another birth-giving shriek the train tore out of the tunnel and down a slope into the town. As it slowed down O'Flattery watched the glittering panorama of lights which fought with the declining light of day. An ever deepening indigo sky merged into the placid sea, which mirrored the first pin-pricks of stars.

The main thoroughfares of the town were thronged with people. Tired families; plimsoled fathers, mothers with wind reddened faces, irritable wailing children trudged upwards from the beach, while a fresh intake of pleasure-seekers, less dog-eared, moved towards their evening's destiny. Two interweaving ceaselessly moving tides of people mingling and separating, filling the town with a noise of feet and voices, producing an atmosphere of expectant, disquieting tension.

In a huge almost empty pub in a side street, the Irishman started drinking. The barmaid was listless and hardly appeared to understand his order. So noteless did she seem that it was with surprise that he saw her bringing him what he had asked for. Her face floated above her body, a soft rubbery unhealthy mask. Her black-pinafored figure scuffled to and fro on bedroom-slippered feet, silently extending a claw to receive and return money for the drinks which she placed on the long counter before her. Unlike most barmaids she never spoke. She made grunts to indicate that she had heard the orders, or else interrogatory moans to show that they must be repeated. Her silence unnerved the Irishman and after two drinks he left.

From this stagnant bywater he once more thrashed out into mid-stream. The daylight had lost its losing battle with the invading night. Everywhere, coloured artificial light outdid the departed sun. Lights sprouted in clusters from the branches of the very trees. Festoons of multicoloured bulbs joined the trees to the lamp standards, so that an endless ribbon of light stretched as far as could be seen in both directions along the sea front.

O'Flattery realised that he was hungry. Descending from the dignified heights of a terrace of old houses, all that was left of the original watering place, from which he had been overlooking the pier, he went in search of what he hoped would be an appetising meal in one of the huge luxury hotels of the town. He felt he needed the soft carpeting, the potted plants, the comforting palm court strains of a provincial orchestra, all the vulgar ostentation which surrounds the eating of expensive but indifferent food.

His aimless wandering about the town's bars idly gazing at the lights, had taken up more time than he realised. His request for food at each hotel was met by stony glares from irritable cashiers busy totting up the day's takings. Received as though he were a foreign traveller from some outlandish spot, rebuked for his extraordinary ignorance at making such a request at such an hour, he resolved to make one last attempt at the largest of these palaces. Here he was met by the head waiter and the chef who had emerged from his kitchen to gossip with the cashier at her desk by the entrance. Such amazement greeted him, so

206

many upturned noses snuffed at his effrontery, that he felt he must appear to be rancid with all the dirt and stains of a nomad's wonderings. As he turned to leave them in search of a more humble café or fish and chip shop, he heard the chef say with the greatest disdain: "Who does he think he is? You'd think I cooked for the love of it." The head waiter scornfully turned away muttering something about "the catering wages Act". At which the cashier in a mocking stage whisper added: "Of course, if he made it worth your while?"

Shortly after nine o'clock the poor Irishman, still hungry, and made by these three flinty-hearted servants of the public to feel that he had somehow overstepped the bounds of social behaviour outrageously, wandered disconsolate and lonely into a dirty but friendly Italian-owned café. Here he got through a very tough, very over-grilled horse steak, some greasy twice fried potato chips and a melting zinc-ointment-textured ice-cream, with a cup of tea to round off this ill-starred and inedible meal.

His hunger appeased at last, but his loneliness still gnawing at him, he once more sallied forth upon the thronged streets in quest of human warmth, understanding, forgetfulness of this terrible day. He began to stroll the length of the promenade towards a Fun Fair, radiant with light and resonant with canned music. His progress was slow for people crowded in dense groups round each shop or stall; these either opened straight onto the pavement on one side or stood actually half on it and half in the gutter on the other. There were barrows selling shell fish; large glistening piles of shrimps; heaps of oversized grey encrusted oysters; little thick white saucers of picked winkles and whelks, but most unappetising of all, chunks of eel, suspended like pieces of hewn off limb, motionless in truncated movement, swam in a sinister trembling jelly, pale green as solid sea water. Hot-pie stalls on which balanced primitive braziers over which piles of slowly charring pies were stacked; the fumes of glowing coke imparting to them, no doubt, a singularly original but disgusting flavour. Ice-cream bins from whose depths were drawn dreadful coloured concoctions on sticks, in wafers, cones and tubs in a never-ending stream.

As he passed along, a chromium-plated object caught his eye. A round container the size and shape of a dustbin from which was scooped on long light sticks a whole flambeau of pink spun sugar, which stuck in wisps to the lips and cheeks of those who tried to eat it, giving them pink Father Christmas beards or cavalry moustaches. Next door was a large open fronted shop dispensing funny hats to be worn by the most inappropriate people, Kate Greenaway bonnets with coloured crêpe paper ribbons and transparent plastic brims, on which were pasted mottoes of indescribable incongruity. One hippopotamus-hipped matron wearing spectacles and a dazzling over-white *ratelier*, sported a bonnet on which he read the strange invitation to "Roll me over".

The welcoming glow and the noise from a pub next to the Fun Fair enticed him into the midst of a scene of unbridled gaiety. The floor of the bar was slippery with spilt beer but nothing daunted old crones were footing it, singly and in pairs, to the accompaniment of a piano accordion. Their teeth rattling in their heads, their glasses slopping beer down their wrists, they sang and let out primitive whoops of delight at their own pepped-up vitality. A "Roll me over" bonnet executed a complicated *pas de deux* with a "Kiss me quick" fez; while a serious fat woman in a blue fur panniered coat and a red hat with a feather danced a delicate *pas seul*, avoiding all the beer puddles as if they were holes in the floor. On the highest heeled shoes laced round her ankles with thin leather straps, she wove in and out of the company, alone on the floor

208

of a deserted ballroom.

O'Flattery bought a drink and stood watching this extraordinary mêlée. The people all appeared to be either half dazed with age or drink-sodden into noteless weariness, or so alive and full of spirits that their incontinent feelings had to come out in full throated bursts of song. A changing crowd of young men, coarsely handsome, oiled hair, padded shoulders, blunt tobacco-stained fingers, jostled one another at the door looking over the heads of the crowd searching for something or someone; while a frieze of old age pensioners lined the walls of the bar, holding their cigarettes between thumb and forefinger in that protective secret way, half covered by the cupped palm of the hand, as some men cover themselves when making water.

The piano accordionist began to play a popular sentimental tune to which everyone began to sway, singing their own versions, regardless of their neighbours. An antiquated old tart began to sing in a throaty unmelodic voice. With its rasping persistence it gradually conquered the noise made by the other singers until it rose and fell by itself, reminding O'Flattery of Flamenca singers. The woman walked in and out of the groups of drinkers with long lingering steps; black hat, black coat, suspiciously black raven hair; gold crescent ear-rings, barbaric, gypsy, swung against her lined cheeks daubed with rust-coloured rouge. Her teeth were false and her breasts hung low in her dress, too low for the tight high waistband intended to be swelled by the firm figure of a young girl. She sang into the faces of the virile young men as she turned coquettishly on one heel, but they moved away lifting one shoulder and drawing down the corners of their mouths. She came at last, in her cork screw path, to the corner where O'Flattery was standing and with her face pushed up into his she regaled him with the final chorus of the song. When her song ended and her voice no longer dominated the attention of the crowd, the accordionist once more struck up a wild melody to which everyone resumed their yelling and furious drinking. O'Flattery found himself isolated in his corner with this strange companion who still ogled him with the brazen eyes of her trade. Encouraged by the alcohol he leant towards her and handed her a drink.

"Thank you ducks, I don't mind if I do," she said eagerly, insinuating her hand on his arm and coming so close that she almost rubbed the thick impasto of her make-up off against his cheek. The heavy odour of woman mingled with cheap scent made him feel as if he would puke. His head was beginning to reel with the unusual amount of alcohol which he had drunk.

In a confused way this wreck of femininity pushing against him reminded him of some painful, very unpleasant, recent occurrence, but already, mercifully, his befuddled brain could not encompass it. Something terrible had happened, he knew that. At the sight of a fly which skated nimbly round the beer stains on the counter, he was near to recalling what this "something" was from which he was retreating. But an interruption in glucose tones from his companion cut short his enfeebled recollections. He came back to the present to find the old whore's tired eyes, red rimmed between mascara-ed lids, earnestly questioning his own.

"What is it dear?" she said as he swept the fly away from the counter with a viciousness which excited her.

"Well, what about another drink then ducks," she went on, leering into his confused face as she got no reply to her first question.

"Port and Lemon's my drink, reely," she added as he still did not answer her. O'Flattery attracted the attention of the barman and ordered two large Port and Lemons. With another drink in his hands and with the sticky sweetness of it trickling down his throat, he felt once more reassured. He managed to smile at his companion, who reacted immediately like an old actress responding to her cue, with the forced spirits of a long run; she nudged him saying:

"That's right dear, you cheer up, Edna'll look after you," and when he didn't answer her again she went on:

"That's right, Edna's me; go on, don't be funny," but nothing she could say would rouse him from his puzzled lethargy.

"Come on you buy Edna another drink, dear, and then we'll go to the Fun Fair, eh?" she wheedled as a nurse does a sulky child, but he only looked increasingly hunted and uncertain.

But eventually her harsh forwardness and the drink broke down the last vestige of caution which he might have had left. After gulping down a double gin he meekly followed her to the door and out onto the pavement. Once outside, away from the accusing eyes of the onlookers, who had unconcernedly watched the progress of her pick-up, she took the Irishman's arm and clamped herself firmly to his side. It was she who took the initiative and paid the entrance money for the Fun Fair.

The noise of the streets and of the pub were as whispers compared to the cacophony of sound which hit them as they entered through a triumphal arch, shaped like the open jaws of a fabulous monster. Its drawn back open lips revealed evil rows of teeth, each outlined by vile coloured neon light, while the illumination from its goggling eyes revolved as it winked on and off. Puffs of smoke and flames were all that was lacking to make it like the very entrance to Hell. They passed through a pretentious foyer from which led a dance hall, cloakrooms and the Fun Fair. Once inside she let go of his arm, holding him by the hand; like a child she led him along a corridor made by the two

211

rows of sideshows.

A woman dressed in white with a long wart on her lip tried to sell them ice-cream; they passed by stopping at another to watch a woman stacking, very gingerly, gold and crimson swans alternately with vases wreathed in roses and swallows, who sang in a breathless creaking voice as she worked.

Further on, a hump-backed woman, dressed as a Red Indian squaw in a fringed leather tunic, thrust a rifle into O'Flattery's hands. Before he knew what he was doing he had shot, the target was in Edna's hand and she was congratulating him, thumping him on the back and shouting: "Well done ducks, three on the target and all through the bull. Your aims not 'arf bad, love yer."

"'E knows where to bloody put it," screeched the Red Indian squaw, looking fiercely at Edna.

"I'll look after 'im, don't you fucking worry," snapped Edna, drawing him roughly away.

A large coloured man was packing up a suitcase. From a black velvet board held on a pole he unhooked celluloid kewpie dolls that wore blue sashes and pompoms made of real ribbon. With infinite tenderness he laid each one beside the next in a sad slow manner as if he was laying out dead children after some appalling disaster.

Outside a dismal caravan in which sat a dark Romany suckling a child, hung a notice in crude red letters which Edna read out with such difficulty that one would have thought the effort actually hurt her physically: "MADAME POLA IN FOUR DARING ACTS."

Below the notice was an indistinct print of Madame Pola, a flaccid lady in tights with ostrich plumes round her head, riding, it appeared, on a white cart-horse over tramlines and cobble sets.

"My gord!" commented Edna as she dragged O'Flattery on.

212

Outside a tent hung a hand-written notice: "Only a 1d. Almost Human"; a swarthy man with grey hair sat outside paring his nails in an aura of garlic. As they passed he gave Edna the glad-eye, but she tossed her head and hurried the unresistant Irishman on to a switchback which was roaring round beside them. Twice round they went, down the sickening slopes and racketing up again, only to hurtle down with everyone but the Irishman screaming their heads off. Edna was paying all the time. The Irishman behaved as if he was in a trance.

"Snap out of it, come on ducks, do," Edna persuaded as she pressed his knee with hers. In answer he smiled wanly and got up to get off the switch back. Edna followed, then pulled him towards a blaring merry-go-round. Twice round this and Edna saw that her man was looking green. They were riding on the same dragon and she didn't want him being sick all down her best dress so off she heaved him encouraging him with: "Keep up ducks. Edna's at the helm. Edna's looking after you."

She tried, unsuccessfully, to get him to dance with her in the ballroom. But it was no good. His legs moved as if they were weighted with lead and he clung so close to her she could scarcely breathe.

"This is a funny customer and no mistake," she thought, "one of those deep studious ones out on a binge, I'll be bound; they're always the most passionate."

"Come on duck," she said, less aggressively than before, "let's be goin'," as she glued herself to him more insinuatingly than ever.

"I wonder what that was that was almost human, wish we'd 'ad a butchers. I shall always wonder." They were out in the street now and Edna was bravely gossiping.

"Rum one," she said under her breath, then out loud: "You remind me of someone. 'Ow do you get your kicks dear?" she asked, giving his arm one of her vice-like

213

squeezes. Getting no answer as usual she went on as if they had known each other for years.

"Did I ever tell you about the feller I used to 'ave regular every Tuesday? Jewish feller 'e was. Years ago it was mind you. Used to pay me seven quid a week regular 'e did. Six pound for meself before we started and a pound to get me macintosh cleaned. It was like this yer see . . . it was the time when them belted raincoats was all the go and I used to 'ave a fawn one, yer see. Always had to wear this fawn raincoat for 'im. He used to pick me up in 'is car and we'd go to 'is place just round the corner from my beat. 'E was a furrier you see and 'e 'ad a room behind the shop through where all these furs were. There wasn't nothing in it except a coffin and a kind of altar thing with candles on it. You'd 'a laughed. I used to 'ave to get in this coffin in me raincoat and then he walked round the room mumblin' to 'is self and did some kind of mumbo-jumbo at the altar, gave 'imself a wank and then it was all over, see. Then 'e'd say all right Edna, 'ere's a quid to get yer raincoat cleaned and I'd get out and we'd go an' 'ave a drink together."

As she was speaking they walked slowly along the street. O'Flattery said nothing but gazed appealingly at the sheepish policemen who marched in pairs through the crowd.

Edna's voice continued, terrifying O'Flattery more and more:

"One night 'e 'ad a drop too much so I said to 'im, I said, 'Ere 'ow did you get like that, 'ow did you ever start to get your kicks like that? 'Ee was a bit tight 'n' 'e told me 'is wife 'ad run away an' left 'im see, gone off with another man. 'E 'ad all 'er clothes back there at the shop. She used to wear a fawn raincoat too yer see. It's a good thing you're skinny Edna 'e said to me. My wife was a bigger girl than you, if ever I find anyone with a bit more

214

flesh on them they'll be in that coffin with the lid on. I've got the lid back there, yes an' the screws an all. Coo was I scared? You can say that again. I never saw 'im no more I can tell yer. I didn't 'alf miss that regular six pound and the pound extra for cleaning the raincoat. Paid my rent that did and plenty over. Funny 'ain't it 'ow some of them get their kicks?"

The Irishman propelled himself along beside her desperate now to escape. Suddenly, by a cockle stall, the flow of her conversation ceased and she released his arm and said:

"Just a minute dear, I've got to go and you-know-what," and winking artfully she scuttled off. Now was the moment to escape, but all he could see were policemen and he was afraid to run. Besides, the cockle stall keeper was soliciting him to buy and she looked as if she wouldn't take no for an answer. She was in league with Edna, he felt sure. A fly left the cockles and settled on O'Flattery's ear. Before he could start to run, Edna was back again. Her make-up refurbished, her eyes bright. She wanted to eat whelks and eat them she did, with loud smacking noises of delight as the Irishman looked first this way and then that through the thinning crowd. Then, clasping his arm again they started to walk. Now she wanted some of the pink spun sugar, which stuck to her lips and made her snigger like a little girl. At last her stomach seemed satiated, but it was all too clear that hunger for food was not the only appetite that was aroused in her. The crowds were substantially thinner now and it was darker, less garishly illuminated, and fewer policemen seemed to be about.

Spotting a deep recessed doorway she pulled O'Flattery into its shadows and pressed her ghastly lips against his, open mouthed and abandoned. Her breath smelled of whelks and vinegar, her tongue tasted of the sweetness of

215

spun sugar and port. Her whole face smelled of stale vomit and cheap cosmetics. O'Flattery was nauseated by this troll, this travesty of a woman. The memory of the other kiss swelled in upon him and, pushing her violently from him, so that she staggered and fell, he began running, running, running. Shouting faces and blurred lamp-posts shot past him. The brutal peak of a guardsman's cap suddenly thrust itself into his face, then reeled backwards; people scattered and away in the distance he could hear Edna screaming maledictions, pouring out filthy curses like the open sluice of a sewage farm. He ran until he was on pavements where there were no people. He ran still. He ran until his chest felt as if it would burst and his tongue as if it had swollen to fill his mouth. Some unknown sense of self-preservation had taken him in the direction of the railway station; some guardian spirit still hung over him as he wrenched open the door of the final carriage of the last train of the evening. He stumbled in as it began to move. Too exhausted to look around him, he lay back panting, struggling for breath and gulping his own dry tongue.

Gradually he came round. The train had stopped and started several times before he had opened his eyes to observe his companions. It was a non-corridor train. Everyone in the compartment slept the dead sleep of either the drunk or the exhausted. All except one boy who, when O'Flattery awoke, was staring candidly into his eyes with the innocent look of a child. He was well made but girlishly pretty with a short retroussé nose and full-bowed mouth. His eyes slanted slightly upwards at the corners and had an expression the exact quality of which the Irishman had never seen before. This, together with a mole below the left hand corner of his mouth, unmistakably invited kisses. His hair was cut very close to his head and he wore suede shoes with a light check suit. A signet ring gleamed on his little finger and peeping from his sleeve hung a gold wrist chain. He sat like a poised humming bird, incongruously holding the hand of a large but spotty American service-man, who slept, his uniform tunic unbuttoned, his head on the window, his breath shuddering heavily through his open mouth.

Round the lips of this wide-awake boy a smile flickered as he stared at O'Flattery, who turned away trying to sleep. The train stopped and started, stopped and started. With each stop the compartment emptied, the travellers waking like automatons in time to alight, until O'Flattery was left alone with the serviceman and the nubile boy. O'Flattery tried again to sleep. But the boy's eyes invited him even through closed lids. When he opened them again the boy had left the sleeping G.I. and was sitting beside him. Softly, gently, caressingly, he took the Irishman's hand and said: "Hullo." O'Flattery was bewitched, he found he could not withdraw his hand. The boy started talking quietly, quietly in a mesmeric monotone.

"I like you. I've taken a fancy to you," he edged nearer, squeezing O'Flattery's unanswering fingers. The sleeping soldier snored. The lights were very bad in the compart-ment. It was as if the electric power was too weak to struggle to this final coach. In the semi-darkness the boy looked like a marmoset, his eyes were dark holes above his sunken cheeks. The Irishman and the boy stared for a long time, mutely into each other's eyes. The G.I. stirred in his sleep, cleared his throat and eased his crutch. He still slept. The countryside slowly rumbled past, dotted with lights. The boy's lips were wet and parted invitingly. O'Flattery's eyes were moist with unshed tears. The boy put his hand on O'Flattery's knee who flinched and glanced at the G.I.

"Get her," said the boy in a changed voice, "get her on a Sunday afternoon with her teeth out. She's a dead loss. Only interested in the drink." Then in a soft wheedling

217

voice he said:

"My name's Roy. But you can call me Rowena if you like."

Amazed, the Irishman retreated further into his corner, deeper into the shadow where his tears began to flow unchecked. The boy started to speak again:

"She's so fat. Get the swing on her back porch," he flipped his unoccupied hand at the G.I. in a dislocated gesture from the wrist, his fore-arm raised stiffly, his hand loose like a dummy.

"But I took a fancy to you the moment I saw you. I'd do anything for you for £3. I'd stay all night and do anything, if you've somewhere to go?"

Transfixed, like a wraith the Irishman flattened himself into his corner, the tears flowing unnoticed. As he talked, the boy's hands crept, exploring further and further. Feeling cold the Irishman heard the boy's voice saying with a note of surprise as if it were a long way off:

"Oh, I'd do anything for you, darling, for nothing."

Sobs of exhaustion burst from the Irishman, sighs of incomprehension shuddered his whole frame. Scared, the boy returned to his still sleeping companion and without speaking again began pounding him into wakefulness.

Brief lights flashed by, illuminating the carriage, then by their comparative brightness plunged it into deeper gloom when they were gone. As the train staggered to a halt the boy jumped up, grabbed the G.I.'s hand again and with him left the carriage before the train had finished easing itself against the buffers.

In the unexpected light of the station the Irishman looked down at his body. Finding the buttons of his trousers undone he doubled up in a tempest of weeping, blind to the fly which nestled, bivouacked for the night, in a fold of his suit. Heartbroken he surrendered himself to grief. This day had seen his disillusionment complete.

218

15

Mr. Gender was asleep, he was dreaming. It was early morning just becoming light, soon he would awake. He lay on his back. The fly took an early morning reconnaissance flight in the air above his open mouth. It lost control each time it flew through the awful exhalation which arose from the humours of his stomach. Each time, out of range of these breaths, it righted itself and returned for more. Mr. Gender was being woken on this unfriendly morning by five different influences. Through his dreams his senses were penetrating, sending him messages which he could not much longer ignore. His whole body was chilled, for during his wild night some of the blankets had fallen upon the floor. His neck and chin were being chafed by the rough hairs of the remaining blanket. His ears could dimly detect the persistent buzzing of the fly. His bladder was making more and more insistent demands to be relieved of its over-taut load; this, combined with the position in which he was lying and the substance of his dream was about to cause him to ejaculate. The consequent dampness in his tepid bed would be the final cause of his awakening. For a moment longer he continued to dream...

Mr. Gender stood alone, clutching in his arms the body of an ensnared animal. It exuded a foxy taint. He strained his eyes in the increasing darkness and saw that it was a long-legged, slender-bodied cavey. It was neither dead nor alive; he felt its semi-warmth pressed into his body with an unspeakable feeling of horror. His fingers felt the taut

219

tendons of its furry legs. It lay motionless in his arms, the still conserved energy which seemed to be concealed in its sleek body gave him the most intense feeling of dread. Suddenly it sprang into life and bounded from his arms, leaping away, nimbly avoiding his involuntary convulsive movement towards recapture. He felt horribly alone . . .

It was at the moment of the animal's escape that Mr. Gender awoke; he awoke to despair. In this moment of waking he knew fully the moment of the most secret private despair. The weight of the bed clothes strained against his tumescence. The spreading clamminess from the damp patch on his pyjamas made his whole body feel colder than ever. He drew up his legs so that his knees came level with his chin and his skinny thighs were pressed against the hollow of his chest. In this back-to-the-womb position he hoped he could generate enough body heat to dry the wetness caused by his disquieting dream.

Mr. Gender was awake. That is, his eyes opened and he became conscious once more of the world of reality. The electric light was still on, the food still lay untouched upon the table. He awoke to the warm smell of his own body between the crumpled sheets, to the stale atmosphere of his ill-ventilated room, a smell which took him back to his childhood, to the servants' bedrooms in his mother's house, the bedrooms to which he had sometimes been sent to fetch something from a drawer or a yellow trunk, in particular the housemaid's bedroom, which he had visited on the night of his eighteenth birthday . . . but no, that was too painful to think about. Shut out the smell; shut out the thoughts. He would not think of that, he simply would not. It reminded him of the more immediate past, of last night. No, no, no, he must not think of that either. Once more the despondency of his dream returned, bringing with it again that agonising moment of private despair. The intimate agony when he met despair face to face;

220

despair, hollow, empty-ringing despair; echoing-back despair. He felt a desperate kinship with uncontrollable, unutterable despair. His mind was clogged and stoppered with misery, so that nothing, nothing squeezed through to become an articulate thought. His whole past life appeared as nothing more than a confused but intended preparation for his present desperation. The inevitable result of his own laziness, his own inability to be attentive to the demands of his body, to be vigilant, to encompass and grasp the meaning of his real needs. During his life at the Office, the cries of his body had become muffled. Miss Jeacock's continual diffidence had muted them into a suffocated silence. Nevertheless, they still existed, although stifled, making their inroads in more subtle less recognisable ways. He was no longer capable of understanding them, constantly disturbed, ridden by the jockey of his own bulimia. Crouched thus in bed he knew too the moment of self-disgust at his own filthy stupidity of despair; he knew the hatred of his own tears.

The past months were choked with disappointments which now obliterated all his thoughts. The painful disappointment when the expected word is left unsaid; the hoped-for letter does not drop onto the mat; the anticipated telephone call does not shatter the lonely silence with its bell. He had known all these, they were his most intimate fellow-travellers. He was on close terms with those disappointments which are so personal that they feel like the flaying-off of a layer of skin from the tenderest part of one's body. Each and every memory of past happiness was obscured; the expectation of future joy no longer operated as an incentive to hope. His wave of misery had crashed right up the beach beyond flood level, and was now tearing backwards dragging every pebble of feeling into itself, ready for the next and more awful breaker to smash down upon him as he struggled to escape. In this moment his

221

hands were too small to obliterate his tears, his body was too large to curl up into the protection of his thighs.

He opened his eyes. Slowly he unbent his legs and thrust them down into the cold corners of the bed. With one hand he fumbled to push the blanket away from his neck, trying to cover it with the sheet to stop the coarse chafing of the cheap wool. Clearly now he heard the zooming of the fly. His efforts to make himself comfortable in the bed, instead of encouraging sleep, were speedily awakening him. The urgent desire to urinate, which tormented his half conscious body, was centred behind his pudenda like a rod of red-hot metal. The exertion of trying to make himself comfortable and the draughts of cold air, which his battle with the sheet had let into the bed, now made him fully awake.

The fly landed within an inch of his eye, upon a fold in the sheet. Its impudence infuriated him; with an avalanche of sudden movement beneath the bed clothes he dislodged it in the middle of its wash-and-brush-up performance. He must get up. His myopic eyes did not allow him to see his watch, which lay with his spectacles on a table beside the bed.

He sat up and fumbled among the assortment of objects which cluttered the table, his wandering fingers strayed from aspirin bottle to half eaten apple; from vaseline pot to glass of water containing his denture, which he had somnambulantly removed in the middle of the night. With each object his irritation mounted until with a gesture of annoyance he swept the surface of the table, hoping at last to feel his spectacles. Instead, over went the tumbler of teeth carrying with it the undiscovered spectacles; a miniature Niagara bearing upon its bosom the flotsam of Mr. Gender's most necessary personal impedimenta. Beside the bed the carpet slowly absorbed the pool of liquid, leaving stranded a forlorn set of artificially pink gums biting, without appetite, the carpet's sodden pile.

Furious, Mr. Gender heaved his legs over the side of the bed and stood up. His head throbbed until he thought it must crack open. The ball of his foot came at once into uncomfortable contact with his denture, too late to draw back his foot for they lay now in two halves; brokenly yawning at the spectacles which he was still unable to find. At last after a frantic search on his knees, dizzy among the wreckage, his hand alighted upon the truants. Hitching them upon his nose he surveyed the damage. His broken teeth presented to him a problem of great importance; for although by no means handsome, he had his vanity and did not like people to know that his baby-round cheeks contained not their second but their third set of teeth. But first he must know the time. If Mr. Gender was awake he must at once know the exact time, for him that was most important. His dependence upon his watch had become a mania. Holding it close to his face he read in the dim light that it said a quarter to seven.

Finally out of bed and now made fully conscious by the cold and his exertions over the spectacles, he began to take stock of the room, to hear the first early morning sounds and to face once more his own death's-head of depression. Looking down at his rumpled bed and noticing with distaste the brown impression of his body upon the sheets, the hardening outline like a map painted in white of egg and the greasy hollow where his head rested upon the pillow, he made a mental note that he must change the linen, knowing at the same moment that he would be sure to forget.

The fly was settling upon the damp stain on the upper sheet, making an angry buzzing; with a movement disproportionately fierce he aimed a savage blow at it and felt the damp chill of his own frustration.

The cat was mewing plaintively outside the door. The

223

tap in his sink was dripping into the washing-up basin already full of water. Remembering again the urge which had awoken him, temporarily forgotten during the denture drama, he groped feebly under the bed. His pyjama cord had come undone and his trousers were slipping down his legs. Stumbling out of them he bent to pick up his chamber-pot. He was unable to direct the jet which he expelled without aim into the pot. Hot splashes fell on to his naked feet and yellow droplets splashed back and hung suspended in his pubic hair. The fly zoomed past, once round the pot and away again. Bending to replace the pot a spasm of liverish nausea struck him, so that bright sparks lit the leaden darkness behind his closed lids and a flood of deep depression consumed his whole body.

This sensation of somatic pain was centred in his chest. For a long time past, before the disasters of the evening before had overtaken him, Mr. Gender had thought long and carefully about his own despair. He had analysed this pain for himself, he had formed a mental picture of it, which recurred to him each time he felt overwhelmed by this corporeal misery. It was as if behind and across his breastbone, within the barrel of his chest, there was fitted a diaphram of some thin flexible material. This was suspended from his shoulders on delicate threads, two of which were rigid and the rest elastic. The rigid pair formed the spine or fulcrum of his misery. As the pain of despair grew stronger, the thin sheet began to bend. Like the covers of a book it started to fold inwards, along a line between the two rigid suspension threads. It was drawn down by the compelling power of small triangular weights which were hooked on wire below it. First the corners began to curl, then gradually the strength of the weights became more powerful, and the two halves of the sheet began to sag, stretching the elastic strings, filling the inside of his body with a consuming pain of disembowelment.

His entrails were being dragged from him and he felt that it was only by the greatest physical effort that he prevented the two sides of the diaphragm from flapping hopelessly together, so that each collection of weights became inextricably entangled and he was in danger of finding himself in what unknown new depths of unplumbed despair.

He knew that when in the grip of this malaise he must force himself to pin his mind down to something else; to distract himself from himself, yet this morning he lacked even the desire to do so. Without energy, clad only in his pyjama jacket he stumbled towards the window to shut it, only to find that contrary to custom he had not opened it the night before, and that the wisps of acrid smell which he thought was fog were actually the odours of ripe Camembert, which nestled among his hair brushes, where he had put it during his dinner preparations.

Mist hung low over the view of dismal back gardens and high up above it was a strip of pale clear sky. Across it, too high for the drone of its engines to be heard, Mr. Gender perceived an aeroplane travelling very slowly, trailing in its wake an advertising streamer, too distant to be legible but so high up and far away that its lonely isolation made tears come to his eyes; in the way that for some people the sound of martial music is the certain catalyst to a deluge of weeping.

The fly buzzed angrily against the window. Earlier, it had been content to fly back and forth in the confines of the room, now it wanted to get out. Mr. Gender made one or two ineffectual attempts to squash it, then gave up, going to the door to let in the cat, whose mews had become more and more demanding since she had heard him moving about in his room.

The cat stalked round the jamb of the door, heavily pregnant, rubbing the sides of her swollen body against his bare legs. Pirouetting on her paws while looking

225

pathetically upwards, like an ageing ballerina, whose figure has gone but whose feet still insist that she should perform; she was hungry. Going to a perforated zinc meat safe hanging above the sink he took out the bottle of milk; he eased the nail of his index finger carefully into the centre hole of the cardboard cap to lift it out, but his usual caution had failed him. Before he could stop himself he had pressed too hard and the bent disc had gone into the neck of the bottle, sending a spurt of cream all over his hands, down onto his legs and feet and round them on to the floor. The cat began to purr and to lick the cream from her master's feet; the fly settled for a moment on the hairs of his stomach and then darted away to the cat's back. Infuriated by his own carelessness, he pushed the cat away roughly, then stricken by the thought of her condition he poured her out a generous soup plate of milk. In that infuriating way known only to domestic pets, the beast seemed satisfied by the drops she had scavenged from his feet. After breaking the pure circle of milk gingerly with her nose, she stalked off to wash herself by the fireless grate, leaving the milk to the fly which immediately descended to the edge and did a series of advancing and retreating movements, crossing and recrossing her legs as if it was worshipping the white moon-like expanse of liquid. The cat stared with huge eyes expressing nearly human astonishment, then with a nonchalant wave of her tail continued to wash herself in the most inaccessible places, her distended shape making her usually elegant movements uncomfortably awkward.

Mr. Gender struggled into some clothes. His collar stud was missing. The soles of his feet were spotted with the fluff from his blankets which he had failed to sweep up properly the night before. He brushed it off and dragged on his socks, tearing one of them as he forced it too energetically over his instep.

226

The cat had stopped washing and now lay flattened on the floor, moving the skin along her back in convulsive twitches. Rolling over uncomfortably she began to mew again. Wriggling first on one side, then on the other she abandoned the hearth rug and wandered about the room mewing. Her labour was about to begin. She tried several places in the room and finally came to rest furtively in Mr. Gender's ill-kempt bed. Fascinated, he watched her, horrified yet unable to shoo her off. Twisting and turning among the sheets and blankets to make a rough nest the cat squatted in the lowest hollows of the bed. She reclined scowling, the weight of her shoulders supported on one forepaw, the other raised as if in defiance of the pain to come, her back legs straddled open. Mr. Gender felt like a voyeur. Her vagina opened to emit a greenish oily bubble, containing a kitten's back legs. The claws were clearly visible. She strained; she mewed in protest; the bubble became more inflated, darker in colour, until Mr. Gender saw that the whole trunk of the first kitten had emerged inside it; the head remained inside the mother. For a moment her bedraggled belly steamed. A pulse beat beside one of her swollen teats. She began to lick furiously. The kitten's head emerged. The new shining black body added its steam to that of its mother; she washed herself and the kitten frantically. The kitten's mouth, obscured by mucus, began to move and out of it came a feeble plaint. The mother continued her vigorous ablutions and in so doing somehow disconnected the umbilical cord. After several minutes of washing her own legs and the body of the kitten, the afterbirth was expelled. This she neatly consumed. Mr. Gender heard the squelsh of her teeth as she bit through the congealed mass of tissue.

He rushed to the sink and retched helplessly over the unwashed plates. When at last he returned to watch this strange delivery in his bed, five kittens squirmed like maggots between the protecting confines of the mother's legs. She purred, proud and pleased that her work was over, looked up at him once, then continued to lick her writhing family.

Mr. Gender's nausea had left him but he felt cold. He began to lay and light the fire. Automatically he went through the accustomed routine. After he had struck six matches the paper began to smoulder and he left it to make himself some coffee. Methodically, he peered into the coffee percolator. With a pang he recalled his previous preparations and realised it was already filled with water and coffee from the night before. He set it on the gas ring. The power of the gas was discouragingly weak. Once more back at the fire he found that nearly all the paper had smouldered away without making enough flame to ignite the wood. Hastily he stuffed the evening paper beneath the debris of what had already been consumed, once more rekindling it. He knelt beside it and blew, getting choking breaths of smoke into his lungs and particles of burnt paper in his hair. Once more he abandoned it and glancing at the coffee, which had not yet started to boil, he walked over to the window, where he lost himself in a sightless reverie, his forehead pressed to the cold clammy surface of the window pane. His teeth . . . what should he do about his teeth? He must mend them, but he remembered that he had no sticking plaster and could for the moment think of no other way. His brain felt unfertile, costive, a hard-boiled egg in the cup of his skull.

He sought to elucidate the defeatism which suffocated each impulse, which strangled the neck of each embryo thought with a thin membrane of abortive albumen. Recently, tears had always been just around the corner. The pain centred beneath his breastbone was directly connected with his tear ducts. This pain, what could he call it? Perhaps after all it was not depression? But what

228

should he call it? What? Call it Envy? Call it Jealousy? It was still a pain, it was still there, it knew no assuagement under any name. When the acme of control could be forced to operate it diminished to a small glow perhaps the size of a pea. But then, should he for a moment lose hold, it swelled, enlarged, germinated, shot, branched, budded, flowered in profusion and bore fruit on every twig of the tree of his senses. But the fruit of destruction not construction. It was an agony which knew no end, it was an agony composed of facets and angles of a hundred agonies.

Among the agonies was the tyranny by telephone. The torments were many, the doubts legion.

"Will the loved one telephone today? Does the loved one in fact want to telephone but does not do so because she thinks to disturb? Oh no of course not, she does not want to telephone at all. How could she? It isn't she who is in love. Besides she telephoned only two days ago." Respite for a second, then it starts again.

"If I go out will the loved one telephone?" or "I have been out for a few snatched essentials . . . has the loved one telephoned?" or "if I have remembered to take the receiver off before I went out will she ring again when she finds the number engaged? I can never know. There is no way of finding out." Indeed once this despotism gets hold it ramps like an insidious weed, it respects no boundaries, it gives no quarter. The appearance of this Moloch spells end to peace of mind, dislodgement to balance, finish to anything creative. Paralysis to movement outside the confined circle of one's own lair, it dictates one's reduction to the state of dumb beast, one can only defeat it by a superhuman effort of will.

Mr. Gender's greed, his jealousy, his envy now took possession. Angry, destructive, domineering voices whispered for attention, insisting that they should be heard . . .

"Those hands which you want to hold, they won't hold

229

yours, they will hold perhaps another's. Those lips which you want to caress, they won't caress yours, they will caress perhaps another's. That tongue, those teeth; those eyes are not brimming with love for you. You satiate none of those senses. She will find another who is more satisfying than you, younger; more attractive, gayer; more seductive, more virile; wittier, more intelligent; richer, socially more desirable. He will steal her away from you for longer and longer periods, so that you are left stranded with nothing.

"Nothing but tormenting voices to mock you, tantalising visions to make you more and more desperate.

"You will never possess peace of mind with this woman. Always your greed for her will overwhelm your understanding of her needs. Your tenderness towards her will be vanquished by your passion to possess her. But she doesn't want you anyhow, she doesn't want you. *She does not want you . . .*"

Some early riser in the building was practising a Chopin nocturne, the limpid notes dropped like reverberating pellets of ice-cold lead into his brain.

Depression now really enveloped him. Those little weights, which he had described to himself as hanging behind his breastbone, had now become inextricably entangled. They danced and jangled together in a very ecstasy of depression.

The coffee still did not boil. The fire showed no glimmer of flame, the smell of the Camembert was thicker than ever in the room, it coagulated against the window panes. His toothless gums were uncomfortable, they made him feel interminably old. His head was splitting, the room was filled with a stale feline smell, it echoed with the shrill mewling of the kittens. The fly's insistently tedious buzzing round his spectacles was intolerable. It was all intolerable. His whole life was intolerable. He couldn't think how he stood it for so long, it was a matter of amazement to him

230

that he had not come to a decision before. It was only a matter of moments to make the actual decision now . . .

Down the stairs, out into the street, along the usually busy thoroughfare, no one noticing his bedroom slippers, to the station. As he entered the booking hall he saw only a puddle of water in which lay a soggy blood-stained piece of paper, no doubt blown from some butcher's tray.

What price ticket should he take? It was almost funny, a macabre joke: a sixpenny ticket to Kingdom Come?

A train was just thundering down the slope into the station, a juggernaut on an electric rail, or a merciful rescuing Salvationist? A moment later, and he would have had the chance to change his mind; but now there was no going back, this time an unalterable decision had been made. In two seconds the decision had become an implacable fact.

A crowd had collected from nowhere and an official was running, pale faced, to the driver's cabin.

Back down the road in Mr. Gender's room, life still ebbed and flowed. Nothing there was as yet so shattered as Mr. Gender's body. His watch ticked on the table by his bed where he had replaced it. The flames licked over the coals in the grate. Shreds of scorched paper and fragments of burnt wood dropped silently from the gathering embers. The last match struck by Mr. Gender had eventually caught the damp paper and infused a little life into the dead fireplace. But it would be of short duration, unless other hands came to put on the coals.

The cat rose from feeding her kittens, yawned, arching her back. The kittens complained at having their christening feast disturbed. With a look of uncanny sagacity round the room the cat jumped down from the bed and walked delicately to the fire. Her very walk seemed to say: "Now I am mistress here," it was so arrogant. Was she gifted with second sight? Did she know that the coffee percolator

231

would go on with the bubbling that it had just started, spitting coffee out to dribble down its side, making the gas sizzle, until the water boiled dry? Did she know that the room would gradually be pervaded by the sharp odours of burnt coffee and hot metal, until the shilling in the meter was exhausted and the blue flames ebbed and went out, one by one, in company with the dying fire, whose feeble glow burnt away its impotent warmth? Did she know that the telephone would begin to ring with the irritating efficiency of a living organism, echoing through the empty room?

One would have thought she did know as she leapt on to the window sill to watch the sparrows which swung on the plane tree so near her glazed inscrutable eyes, leaving her pitifully mewing family plaintively crying and weaving in and out of one another in search of warmth.

The fly buzzed against the window pane, between the cat and the sparrows, making her revolve her head slowly. The ash from last night's dead joss stick fell noiselessly in a grey disintegrating coil, moving in the draught.

The fly settled among the kittens going round and round their bellies like an acrobat balancing on a turning ball.

A second fly joined the first in its gyrations round the kittens. Their paths coincided. Instead of flying off they leapt upon one another commencing, frenziedly, to copulate.

To see the brute's seraphic smile one would have thought that the cat did know everything; every detail, understood it all, but cared not a pin.

The damned insensate beast.

16

THE MORNING of Mr. Gender's suicide. The morning on which the Irishman too woke with a heavy dread gnawing behind his breast bone.

A misty morning of strange bangs, and unexplained echoes where there have been no echoes before.

A morning when Mrs. Macklin overslept and woke to the hungry bawling of Brenda, her last born. Hustling herself into her vast corsets and guzzling her tea she hacked chunks of bread off a stale loaf for the children, smeared them with margarine and marmalade, doling them out like playing cards to her sleepy brood. They sat huddled round the kitchen table watching the flame, which Jennifer had put at her mother's command to the paper in the grate, lick upwards to the kindling. Each snatched their breakfast and devoured it like beasts, in great gobbets washed down with gulps of tea. When they had finished, Mrs. Macklin threw the key of the door, which divided their quarters from the Office, at Jennifer and told her to go to work.

Her regular morning job was to tidy the Ladies' Cloakroom, to pick up the wisps of powder-stained cotton wool, the match sticks and the cleansing tissues. If necessary she had to mop over the tiled floor, wipe round the seats of the lavatories and always count the towels which hung on named hooks, with a roller towel for visitors; then report back to her Mother that the correct number of towels were present and the rest of the work done.

Jennifer trudged, gummy eyed down the long corridors, trailing her mop in one hand and a floor cloth in the other, jealous of the immunity from work of her younger brother and sister. Grumbling she pushed open the frosted-glass panelled door marked "Ladies" and went in. Sleepily she started to count the towels, first on one side, then on the other. As she looked across the opening which led from one half of the cloakroom where the wash basins were, to the further section which contained the lavatories, her attention was drawn to something most unusual.

Two feet protruded from the first compartment, the door of which was wedged half open.

Slowly she went towards them, curiosity battling with fear. Gingerly stepping over them she edged round the door, pushing it back against the wall. In the confined space Miss Jeacock lay in fearful intimacy cheek by jowl with the porcelain pan. Her eyes looked out at the floor with a peaceful faraway look; her no longer florid face was the colour and smooth texture of candle wax; her lips were parted and a slight relaxing of the facial muscles made her look as if she was smiling. The smudged lipstick on her mouth stood out starkly in contrast with the pallor of her face; the two spots of rouge on her cheek bones were like the dotted complexion of a dutch doll. A faint plum-coloured contusion had arisen on her neck. A fly had settled on the corner of her mouth where a tiny trickle of saliva had dried. She clutched a handkerchief in one clenched fist while the other arm was folded under the weight of her body. One shoe was half off her foot and Jennifer noticed that she had a hole in her stocking. Her hair lay spread out round her face, pressed to one side of her head by the pedestal. The fly had moved and was skating on her eyeball, blotting out the pupil. Suddenly Jennifer realised that she was not dreaming, nor was Miss Jeacock asleep, for her eyes would have been shut. Something was

234

wrong or she would have brushed the fly away.

Jennifer's scream in the confined space sounded loud and unnatural, echoing back to terrify her all the more. Arthur, stoking the furnace, lifted his head, like some forest animal as he heard it, snuffing the air. Dropping her mop and floor cloth Jennifer rushed, scream following upon scream, down the corridors until she ran full tilt into her mother, who still in her petticoat and mules had come panting to meet her.

Fetching her a cuff to quieten her Mrs. Macklin said:

"Come on now, what's all this row about? You little bitch you, frightening me like that. Shut yer trap."

"Oh Mum, Oh Mum!" sobbed Jennifer, scared to tell and scared not to tell.

"Put your tongue between your teeth and pack it up," snarled Mrs. Macklin who couldn't bear any show of emotion. "What's the matter with yer?"

"Oh Mum, it's Miss Jeacock, Mum. Down there in the lav."

"Wot about 'er she's early, ain't she?"

"No Mum, somethinks 'appened to 'er. She's all funny on the floor. She's 'ad a as-ci-dent."

Dragging the unwilling child behind her by the upper arm Mrs. Macklin stormed down the corridor.

"You wait, my girl, if this is a trick I'll pay yer."

Jennifer's sobs were continuous, punctuated by gusty hiccoughs. Reluctant to pass through the glass door again she clung to the door frame so that her mother had to release her, letting the door swing back on to her as she commanded in her Sergeant Major voice: "Stay there and don't 'cher move a bloody step."

Jennifer obeyed, too scared of this terrible half clothed figure to cry, let alone move. Her sobs stopped and round the door she watched her mother's back, transfixed and dumb. Mrs. Macklin's back revealed no outward sign of surprise at what she saw. She saw what Jennifer had seen but realised its implications sooner. Unlike her daughter she made no sound, a devilish expression unseen by the child passed across her face. She stood for a full five minutes in reflection; one hand up to her face, the forefinger along her cheek, the next beneath her nose, the others crooked below her lower lip, her lips pouting against them. Then she bent and took up Miss Jeacock's shoes and with them in one hand she came towards Jennifer, a menacing finger pointed in accusation.

"You tell a living soul of what you've seen or what yer goin' to see 'ere today and I'll smash every bloody bone in yer body, so help me," she threatened, articulating every word and smashing each one home with a warning shake of Miss Jeacock's shoes in her daughter's face. Jennifer, too paralysed with fear to speak, nodded her head until her teeth shattered. Was this awful giantess *really* her mother?

"You stay there and don't let anyone come in or I'll kill yer," said Mrs. Macklin and strode off out of sight before Jennifer could protest, leaving the terrified child to keep vigil over the corpse of Miss Jeacock.

After what seemed hours but what in reality was only minutes, Mrs. Macklin returned, still in her petticoat and slippers. She was followed by Arthur who loped behind, head drawn in and eyes piercing the shadows like a savage in an unknown country. They brushed past Jennifer without speaking and entered the cloakroom.

Mrs. Macklin squeezed into the cubicle and lifting Miss Jeacock's skirt, with a look of unutterable contempt muttered under her breath: "Just as I thought. This is O'Flattery's handiwork," her voice too low for either Arthur or Jennifer to hear. She grasped Miss Jeacock's shoulders and ordered Arthur to take her feet, which he did as if they were the two handles of his wheel barrow.

With a complicated manoeuvre Mrs. Macklin unwedged herself and her load from the narrow space. They proceeded past Jennifer, grunting and sweating under their burden, for Miss Jeacock had been a well built woman. Jennifer stayed where she was, noteless, completely cowed, unable to utter a sound. The ghastly *cortège* disappeared out of sight, the back of Miss Jeacock's hands scraping unnoticed on the floor.

The fly went wild and darted ahead of them, back to Miss Jeacock, behind them, ahead of them again, never letting them out of its sight.

Jennifer saw no more but heard a great deal of banging in the stoke-hole.

When she had gone out to fetch him Mrs. Macklin had ordered Arthur to open all the dampers and roar up the furnace. By the time they returned there was a raging inferno within this great iron monster. Arthur stood grinning, still holding Miss Jeacock's feet. Mrs. Macklin dropped her end and heaved open the heavy furnace doors with the poker. The heat which came out made them recoil and a tongue of flame leapt out singeing Miss Jeacock's hair. Quickly, with instructions to Arthur which he followed in a trance, Mrs. Macklin and her minion heaved the corpse of Miss Jeacock into the waiting embers. As they crammed the unresistant body into the gaping mouth of the furnace they were hampered by the beginnings of rigor mortis, and were choked by a smell like the breath of some carrion-eating animals which filled their nostrils and brought crocodile tears to their eyes. Their work done, Mrs. Macklin turned to Arthur with flushed and sweating face. Threatening him with the poker she said:

"Never a word to a soul . . . or else!"

Arthur with animal devotion nodded and smiled his obedience to this awe-inspiring ogress, going back unmoved to his breakfast of bread and onion which stood half eaten on a soap-box by the door.

Mrs. Macklin returned to Jennifer. Suddenly and surprisingly she was all sweetness and light.

"Come along dear," she cooed, throwing open the window of the lavatory, "I'm going to give you a sweety."

They left the cloakroom where faint but unmistakable traces of Miss Jeacock's scent wasted themselves on the empty air. Open-mouthed, Jennifer followed her Mother back to their kitchen, where the breakfast table stood still stacked with last night's supper things. On the entry of Mrs. Macklin, Leslie and Brenda who, with the intensity of the very young, were playing trains with Horny and pieces of coal on the hearth rug, got up off the floor and stood in the case of Leslie, and staggered, in the case of Brenda, to attention. They had either not heard Jennifer's scream because of concentrating on their game or else they were crafty enough to keep silent.

Jennifer's eyes were drawn as if by magnets to Miss Jeacock's shoes, a better pair than she had habitually worn at work and with higher heels, where they stood among the riot of junk upon the dresser where they had not been before breakfast. Mrs. Macklin, seeing the direction her eyes had taken, hastily grabbed the shoes, ramming them into an already overflowing cupboard beneath the dresser.

"Now, did yer clean the basins proper?" she began interrogating Jennifer, glancing warningly at Leslie.

"Yes, Mum."

"Did yer count the towels?"

"Yes, Mum."

"Was there the right number?"

"Yes, Mum."

Jennifer's head was nodding like a mandarin.

"And did yer wipe round the lavs proper?"

"Yes, Mum," whimpered Jennifer, in hardly a voice at all, thinking that because of what she had seen this morn-

ing she would never be able to go to the lavatory again
without a shudder.

"And did yer mop the floor?"

"Yes Mum," lied Jennifer playing her part for Leslie
and Brenda's benefit.

"There's a good girl then," said Mrs. Macklin beaming
with pleasure at finding that Jennifer had passed the test
of her first cross-examination without giving anything
away.

"Here's a stick of toffee for yer and off yer all go to
play. Go on. And mind," she raised a warning finger to
Jennifer, as she darted out followed by Leslie lugging
Brenda behind him.

Once outside Leslie became vocal:

"Wot's all that in aid of mine-head?" he said cheeking
his sister with an old insult referring to the curlers she
sometimes wore in her hair.

"You mind yer business," snapped Jennifer and kicked
his shins when he wasn't looking. "And you shut up too,"
she stormed at the amazed Brenda as she landed her one
across the face before she had time to utter a syllable.

Leslie shut up; Brenda made not a moan; this figure
was a tigress compared to the usual spiteful Jennifer. In
silence they crossed the quadrangle and stood grouped
closely together beneath the plane trees where there still
hung the tattered condom.

Here they waited as Jennifer sucked her toffee to herald
the arrival, as they did each morning, of the Office staff.

First came Betty and Gladys Lynch.

"Gassing as usual," said Leslie. Then followed in quick
succession Miss Seal in single strictness; the Postage
Clerk and one of the Computer Programmers; Dr. Booker
and his Assistant plodding side by side; the Senior Clerk
alone as usual; and then a motley assortment of clerks and
stenographers, in more or less of a hurry according to

239

whether or not they cared about punctuality.

Lastly, dragging his feet as if they bore heavy chains, struggled the exhausted O'Flattery.

As he went through the Office doorway, Mrs. Macklin, stationed by the letter board, was the first member of the staff he had encountered since the night before. His eyes, haggard with animal pathos were trapped by her twisted gaze, as he heard Leslie pipe up outside:

"Where's Mr. Gender 'e ain't come yet?"

"'Ow should I know dope?" Jennifer replied caustically.

"Where's Miss Jeacock then? She's late this morning too." Then O'Flattery heard a resounding smack followed by a prolonged wail. The fly practised aeronautics in the cube of air between the door and the notice board.

Mrs. Macklin looked at him with her irregular eyes as if she saw through him and beyond him. A look which was supposed to convey sympathetic understanding and which seemed to say: "We Macklin women know, but don't you worry we won't let on."

Bewildered, the Irishman stumbled on through the hall and to the blessed quietude of his office, vaguely concerned as to why Gender's usual punctilious arrival had not that morning occurred.

Jennifer and Leslie began to play at milk bars with Wendy, who had ridden up on her outsize bicycle. Two or three mornings before they had hidden some milk in a medicine bottle under the leaves in a corner by the telephone box. Jennifer had told them, and they had believed her, that it would go thick and then it would be cream. This morning they were going to open it and find out. Wendy fumbled beneath the leaves and brought out the bottle, the unsuspecting Brenda followed every move from the fastness of her push-chair clutching Horny in her lap. Leslie took out the cork.

"Coo!" he shouted, "it ain't 'arf fick. 'oo's goin' to

240

try first, bags I last?"

"Bags I next to last," said Jennifer quickly.

"Bags I next to that," squawked Wendy feebly.

"That's first, ass. Go on fool, taste," shouted Leslie.

"Shit 'em," said Wendy succinctly.

"No it 'ain't," continued Jennifer, "Brenda's first. She 'ain't bagged at all."

Tickled by this original piece of justice, Leslie held the bottle upside down near Brenda. The whey ran out and down the cover of the push-chair and dribbled down Horny's shell, the white curd fell into the neck of the bottle with a sickening suck.

"Ere, lovely, lovely," crowed Leslie, proffering the bottle's neck to the open-mouthed Brenda. All unsuspecting she slug, glug, glugged some of the sour curd down, and as she tasted it as quickly spat it out again all over herself and Wendy who was bending down close beside her to watch this phenomenon. Roars of laughter followed this and howls from Brenda, which reached the ears of the Irishman as he sat in the backwater of his office, his head sunk in his hands.

"Ugh, you dirty girl," cried Jennifer smacking down her defenceless sister, smartly.

"Shit 'em," said Wendy.

"Aing, aing, aing," screeched Leslie in hideous mockery of the two girls and their plight, his laughter trailing off on the cold wind which had blown up, scattering the dead leaves in angry flurries against the Office windows, making the Irishman start and shiver more guiltily than ever, despite the heat which all over the Office building was unbearable that morning.

241

17

AFTER SUMMARY ablutions with dirty pocket handkerchiefs and the front flaps of Jennifer's coat, Brenda once more regained a semblance of humanity. Horny had been put, while this was going on, down on the pavement where he looked extremely incongruous. He had the appearance of an animal accident, as if some almost immovable, ungainly weight had been dropped on to two pairs of odd, unmatching, reptilian legs and one reptilian head. His moving parts had an air of not belonging to his shell, as if the weight of it was a crushing burden and as if furthermore his slow gait was caused by this painful weight. Jennifer had, from some deep recess of Brenda's push-chair, found a tomato which she flung in front of Horny where he was bound to find it. Slowly his front legs spooned their way along like a penguin's flippers through water, his head swinging from side to side until, like a blind man, it hit up against the tomato causing him to stop and retract his head and neck, pushing it out again almost at once with a strange compressed squeak of air as the folds of his skin grated against one another. He then began to eat the tomato avidly in big snatching bites, the juice and green-jellied seeds pouring down his beak-like jaws on to the pavement. He steadied the remains of the tomato with his front feet and went on eating, revealing with each mouthful his unexpectedly pink tongue, until there was nothing left but a damp mark on the concrete and a few seeds.

Peace had been restored between the four children and

they played at suspiciously quiet games in and out of the telephone box. These involved peals of suppressed giggles and a great many guilty side-long glances down the road to see if anyone was coming. Horny wandered aimlessly about watched by Brenda, who whenever he strayed too far attracted the attention of one of the others by frantic contortions and loud glug-glugs, as a result of which he was retrieved and put close by the push-chair again.

Mrs. Macklin was, with an ill-grace, managing the telephone switchboard in the absence of the regular girl who was away sick.

This extra task always annoyed her for with her passion for knowing everything about everybody she found it very tantalising. Each time she got interested while listening in to a conversation somebody else would come on the line, down would go the indicator and buzz would go the buzzer until she was forced to pay attention to its noisy insistence which prevented her from hearing anything else.

This morning was not very busy and she was able to carry on her usual occupations of knitting and watching her children. Just as she was in the middle of a particularly complicated piece of pattern, where she always had to count, the switchboard announced an incoming call. Reluctantly she answered it, to hear from a gruff male voice that he wished to speak to whoever was in charge of the Office.

"Dr. Booker is the boss 'ere," replied Mrs. Macklin without subtlety, "'oo wants 'im?" The voice with some authority continued to speak.

"Be so good as to put me through to Dr. Booker, please."

"I ain't allowed to do that," lied Mrs. Macklin, "unless I can tell 'im 'oo you are first, 'es very partickler about that in case 'es busy."

There was a long pause during which Mrs. Macklin could scarcely contain her curiosity as she could hear the

243

voice consulting with another at the end of the line. When it spoke again it nearly deafened her, as she was forcing the earphones so close to her ears in an effort to catch the muffled conversation. The voice roared with more than authority this time:

"Inform Dr. Booker that the Police wish to have a word with him!"

Fascinated, and almost stifled with curiosity, she put the call through to Dr. Booker's office hardly able to breathe out:

"Dr. Booker, sir, the Police wants yer."

Silently she waited, holding her breath, for the conversation to begin; just as Dr. Booker and the voice made contact another call came through and their voices were obscured by the racket of the damnable buzzer. Cursing her luck, Mrs. Macklin answered the inside caller, obtained the number and returned as quickly as possible to the mysterious Police conversation only to find that it was just finishing and that she had missed the whole reason for it. Mrs. Macklin made up a hundred reasons why Dr. Booker should be wanted by the Police and was on the verge of apoplexy from controlling her curiosity over this strange call when she realised it was time to ring the bell for the tea-break.

As the last peals of the tea-bell died away Betty Lynch came out of Dr. Booker's office where she had been taking letters when the Police call came through. She held her handkerchief up to her mouth and in her disengaged hand she fluttered a piece of paper. This she pinned to the notice board with reverent care, then fled, gulping back hysterical sobs.

"Poor man, poor man," the hidden Mrs. Macklin heard her whimper as she went in search of her sister Gladys with whom to share the misery.

"What does she mean, the silly bitch?" thought Mrs.

244

Macklin, "poor man; poor woman she means surely? And yet how could the Police know about Miss Jeacock already? Surely O'Flattery can't have been such a fool as to report her death?"

Conjecture nearly choked her as she crossed the vestibule and read the notice which made a white scar on the empty green of the board's surface. To her great relief and surprise she read:

"It is with deep regret that I have to announce the suicide of G. A. Gender, B.A. The funeral will take place at St. Leofric's Parish Church on Thursday at 2.15 p.m. The staff will send a wreath. Miss Betty Lynch has volunteered to collect contributions to defray the cost of this."

signed R. Quentin Booker (Dr.)

Miss Lynch, displaying her love of ostentation, had drawn round this strange notice in heavy pencil, making a thick black line to intersect at the corners in rough crosses.

"Hullo, here's a lark. Old Gender out of the way too. Who's been up to what?" she thought as she hurried away to brew the staff tea, leaving the telephone switchboard to click and buzz as much as it liked.

The other members of the Office staff on their various ways to their eleven o'clock tea-break all had to run the gauntlet of the notice board.

First Miss Seal, who read the announcement and let out a distressed cry as she fumbled in her bag:

"What will Miss Jeacock say?"

The Senior Clerk was next, he read the notice, turned on his heel without a sound and went on his way out into the street for a breath of fresh air, instead of the elevenses of which he did not approve.

The Postage Clerk and her friend the Computer Programmer came down the stairs together, read the notice

245

and said:

"Oh my dear how awful, why did he do it?"

A fly swung like a pendulum to and fro across the notice board, settled on the expanse of white paper and was brushed away by Gladys Lynch who had just come up with her sister. They both read it as if neither had seen it before and then turned, blinded by their tears, only to bump into Mrs. Macklin who had come back to say waspishly:

"Your tea's poured out. I shall be back in a minute."

She put her head round Dr. Booker's door and in a voice smooth as molasses said:

"Your tea's spoiling, sir. I've just poured it out." So eager was she to hear more of what had happened to Mr. Gender.

"Thank you, Mrs. Macklin," the muffled voice of Dr. Booker called and followed it up by appearing himself with his Assistant, nodding his head and saying: "Bad job, bad job."

Mrs. Macklin let them pass bowing with mock humility, for she had heard dragging footsteps approaching which she recognised as those of the Irishman and she wanted to observe what effect this typewritten announcement would have on him.

This was the moment for which Mrs. Macklin had been impatiently waiting. O'Flattery came slowly down the stairs. The blue stains under his eyes made his face whiter and more pathetic than a sick child's. He read the notice listlessly as Mrs. Macklin watched him unobserved.

He stood long enough to read it ten times, then looking wildly from side to side he hurried away in the direction of the Gentlemen's Cloakroom. The fly appeared again, settled once more on the white paper of the notice tracing a meaningless black maze across the typewritten letters, almost as though it was trying to decipher what was

246

written there. Mrs. Macklin tip-toed stealthily after the Irishman. She heard him belching as he spilt the contents of his stomach into the first basin he had time to reach. When he came out she put up a strong arm to help him. His shoulder was pressed into her great bosom and he could smell her sweat. His head was lowered and his eyes were shut but he opened them to behold this female apparition, who was saying to him:

"Come along now dearie, a cup of tea will do you good. Come along, the others are all having theirs."

Without staying to hear more O'Flattery fled down the passage towards the protection afforded by the rest of the staff in the tea-room. He had heard enough of her cajoling voice; and seen more than enough also. On Mrs. Macklin's swollen feet he had seen the shoes; those iron shod shoes of Miss Jeacock's which had beaten such a tattoo that their appearance had burnt indelibly into his brain.The fat of Mrs. Macklin's ankles spilled over the edges of the shoes and the heels looked as if they must break under her excessive weight.

The appearance of this phantom with her dreadful eyes, where the Irishman read the unflinching look of an accomplice, was the first fanfare of trumpets to herald the apocryphal partnership in guilt between this ill-assorted pair. He knew in one moment that she knew his secret and that despite himself he had been drawn into a web of conspiracy and deceit, escape from which would be impossible.

In the Recreation room to which O'Flattery retreated the rest of the staff awaited Mrs. Macklin's return to dispense second cups. So powerful was her unpleasant dictatorship over the tea-pot that no one dared to help themselves; there was a sigh of relief when she followed the Irishman into the room, and quickly stationed herself at her usual post, slopping the dark brown steaming liquid into the proffered mugs.

Dr. Booker cleared his throat and with the air of one who was about to thank the assembled company for attending a charity bazaar said:

"I should like to take this opportunity, now that we are all gathered together, of expressing my deep regret at having to make the announcement which you have all, no doubt, read upon the notice board." Here he stopped to clear his throat and draw breath, whereupon the Misses Lynch filled in the silence with a tempest of snivels, gulps and half suppressed exclamations of "Oh dear!"

Dr. Booker ignored them and continued:

"As I am sure you will agree we do not want any unpleasant publicity. Any more than we are bound, I dare say, to get, and so I would ask you, out of deference to the deceased, not to speak of this tragedy outside this building. If you have any information which you feel would assist the coroner in his unfortunate duties perhaps you would be kind enough to mention it now as briefly as possible, so that I can pass it on to the proper authorities."

At this point Dr. Booker who had been standing, sat down and buried his nose in his tea.

Everyone began whispering at once, except O'Flattery and Dr. Booker.

Out of the confusion of questions and statements which buzzed like hungry hornets through the room, one desideratum was insistent, demanding solution:

"Where is Miss Jeacock?"

No one admitted to having seen her since they had returned home the night before and no one had ever known her to be late or miss a day in the whole of her previous office career.

Miss Seal was aware of her friend's assignation with Mr. Gender, in his "rooms", and so was the Irishman. But Miss Seal had no intention of communicating this fact

248

to Dr. Booker in front of the whole staff so that they could all jump to conclusions which might sully the reputation of her friend. Nor did she think that Miss Jeacock would be very pleased with her when she returned, if she let out this little secret now.

O'Flattery was too confused to speak and could not trust the sound of his own voice to come out normally. Mrs. Macklin had him completely mesmerised with her overwhelming unspoken sympathy.

No one had any real light to throw on the problem of why Mr. Gender should want to destroy himself. The Senior Clerk even had come into the room curious to see why the break had been prolonged, and was heard to say:

"Pity, pleasant enough fellow, poor chap, seemed rather too quiet to me." Which coming from him was considered strange as he scarcely ever spoke himself.

Nobody wanted to become implicated, nobody wished to speak and draw down suspicion upon themselves, so that they were all relieved when Dr. Booker rose and said: "Very well. Thank you. I think we must return to work now, but before doing so I propose that we stand in silence in token of respect for our late lamented colleague."

Everyone scraped to their feet at this preposterous suggestion and no sound was heard save the heavy embarrassed breathing of the men, the sniffs of the women and the angry buzzing of the omniscient fly.

The Irishman dared not raise his head as he stared at the floor boards, for he felt Mrs. Macklin's look upon him like a blowlamp seeking to penetrate the thin armour of his deception.

Clattering respectfully, as people do when they leave church, the staff returned to their morning tasks. Miss Seal burning white-hot with theories, O'Flattery more dead than alive with apprehension, Mrs. Macklin triumphant in depravity. The rest of the staff, more or less affected by the

249

tragedy according to their glandular construction or temperament, went back to their offices either to brood over or to forget the circumstances of Mr. Gender's death.

When Mrs. Macklin went back to attend to the clamour of the impatient switchboard, her children were nowhere to be seen. Jennifer had noticed that the parental eye was no longer upon them and had considered that out of sight they were out of mind and had therefore taken her little band for what she called a 'nature walk' by the river. Jennifer's knowledge of natural history or botany was limited to the names of about two birds, rats, buttercups and of course daisies. However, what she didn't know she made up with astonishing ribaldry and so if the walk was not elevating it was at least informative and occupied them until hunger drove them home again.

18

As DAY folded and unfolded into day O'Flattery became more and more persecuted by his own guilt and the dumb conniving blandishments he constantly received from Mrs. Macklin. He couldn't work; he couldn't sleep; he couldn't eat. He took to leaving the Office early and arriving late, adding to his load of misery by the expectation of dismissal for unpunctuality. However, unbeknown to him, his hell-hag aide was covering up for him.

He formed the habit of walking all the way to and from the Office. Partly to take up more time, partly to try and give himself an appetite but mostly in the vain hope of tiring himself for the healing balm of sleep which stubbornly evaded him.

The evening before the final *dénouement*, which was to end the ugly drama into the cast of which events had cruelly thrown him, O'Flattery left the Office particularly early unseen by even Mrs. Macklin. The evenings were getting longer and an indescribable lightness in the air proclaimed the advance of spring, increasing his already intolerable burden of frustration. He longed for freedom from the Office and the chafing yoke of his guilt. He had listened to endless conversations between his colleagues about the suicide of Mr. Gender and the so far unexplained disappearance of Miss Jeacock, until he felt he must throttle the speakers, lash out blindly at them, obliterate them and their words completely from his beleaguered memory.

The coincidence of the two events concerning Miss

Jeacock and Mr. Gender were naturally connected unofficially in the minds of their colleagues, if not officially in the labyrinthine police mind.

The usual verdict had been returned at the inquest on Mr. Gender. Namely, that the balance of his mind had been disturbed. Nobody except Miss Seal understood why and nobody was interested enough to find out. She had her theories but except for one hysterical visit to the police station, after a wet Sunday afternoon's reading of too many sensational newspapers, she held her peace.

Detective Inspector Litover, whom she had seen and to whom she made a statement, gave scant attention to what he obviously dismissed as an old maid's fancies. She poured out a story of Mr. Gender's love for Miss Jeacock, his frustration at not being able to win her culminating in a *crime passionel* and his ultimate self-destruction. How a man of Mr. Gender's temperament could murder the woman whom she said he loved and then dispose of the body, with such expertise that not a single clue remained, she could not explain so carefully. The police, however, did not overlook this fact and treated the whole statement with bare civility.

At the Office Mrs. Macklin had started a whispering campaign about "old lovers" and "suicide pacts". Until when Miss Jeacock failed to appear after some days Dr. Booker felt that he was forced, in the presence of his Assistant and Miss Betty Lynch, to search her desk and by so doing put a stop to these rumours.

The search revealed no evidence whatever. Miss Jeacock's desk was a model of order and contained no personal possessions beyond a packet of hair-grips, sixpennyworth of coppers and a half-full box of paper tissues.

After her lack of success with the police inspector Miss Seal gave no more information to anyone. She locked up in her breast the confidences of her supposedly dead friend.

252

She told no one that Miss Jeacock suspected that she had a weak heart, that her Father had been an epileptic or that she knew of the prospective dinner party on the night after the Outing. She was not going to be laughed at any more or sneered at by smug policemen who thought they were fooling her by their tact and kid glove treatment.

Mrs. Macklin was made of stone. The last shred of evidence had disappeared. O'Flattery no longer saw the shoes, those horrible reminders of what had happened. Jennifer knew they were not in the kitchen cupboard, for she had peeped. Her Mother's feet had been pinched enough by them and she was glad to send this last sign of Miss Jeacock's vanity after her into the furious maw of the central heating furnace.

The inarticulate Arthur could not, and in any case for reasons of his own did not wish to, communicate his knowledge to anyone.

Jennifer with the flexible memory of the young was quickly forgetting the whole scene, or rather covering it fairly successfully in her subconscious, where it remained glowing like molten lava to erupt at less and less frequent intervals until a hard crust of forgetfulness had formed and deadened the volcano.

She played at 'Bodies' with Leslie and Brenda, but they did not understand the significance of the game; and for their part, thought it was Mr. Gender's mangled remains they were making away with; for they had learnt every imaginable gory detail from Wendy, who had overheard people talking about it and who had added a good deal more besides, from the lurid fecundity of her imagination.

The Irishman was becoming haggard to the point of decimation. He was completely mystified by the disappearance of Miss Jeacock's body. He was tormented by memories of that evening. The reality of the events were becoming more and more obscured, the sequence disordered. He could no longer discriminate between fact and fiction.

He was appalled at the unexplained looks and intimate gestures made by the grotesque Mrs. Macklin. His nerves had become as brittle as dried grass under a tropic sun.

On this warm evening with spring in the air, when he left the Office extra early, he was very near breaking point. He left the building and made his way towards the house where he lived through mean and half-deserted streets. By the suffering of the past weeks the acuteness of his senses had become greatly intensified. Taking the longest way round he entered an alley which led eventually to the river and finally to his home. In this narrow retreat lived Mrs. Dymark, the swarthy, squat-faced charwoman from his lodgings. He saw that two sand-coloured motor-bicycles were parked blocking the way outside the Dymarks' cottage. He saw too at a glance that they must have stopped abruptly, after having been in a great hurry, as they had made clearly visible skid marks in the dirt road.

As he came abreast of the cottage, two doors before that of the Dymarks', he saw that the owner was painting the fall pipe from the roof guttering. All at the same moment, as these unimportant details were registering on his mind, an open Army truck, like an explosion, careered up and stopped at the entrance to the alley. Out of it jumped two military policemen, scarlet hatbands and grim jaws, who in the same movement of alighting from their vehicle buckled on immaculate white webbing belts. They came striding past him, for he had stopped ostensibly to pass the time of day with the man who was painting but in reality to prevaricate and see what was up. He longed for any excuse to think about something or someone else other than himself.

The soldiers looked very much as if they meant business. With one tenth of his faculties O'Flattery was talking to the painter and with the other nine-tenths he was sizing up the situation. In a few steps the two soldiers were at the Dymarks' door, knocking perfunctorily. They were like blood hounds on a strong scent, firm of purpose and inflexible, but their faces lacked the humanity of dogs. They knocked; one stood back, unbottoned a tunic pocket and withdrew a notebook, while scrutinising minutely the sand-coloured motor bicycles parked before the door. Almost at once the Dymarks' door opened and out came two shamefaced military dispatch riders. Quite young, stocky, dressed in khaki riding breeches and blouses, the buttons of which both were busily fastening. They shut the door tactfully behind them as the military policemen began their interrogation. One boy was unintelligent and uncouth; the other was fair, handsome and had lively blue eyes. Both were very flushed, very young, very well put together in their uniforms, muscular. The Irishman caught the words "corporal", "official", "permission", and it was easy to guess which way the questions were going. The embarrassment of the blushing truants was painful and O'Flattery felt he could spy no longer. Bidding good day to the painting man he hurried past the khaki group turning his head away.

As he went on he could not help letting his mind dwell on the incident he had just witnessed. Sympathy with the two boys who had been disturbed lay uppermost in his mind, alongside the dislike of authority, as represented by the dehumanised policemen. His imagination boggled at the scene inside the Dymarks' cottage, at the picture of the once pretty but now pregnant Dorothy and the hideous sow-like elder sister with her monkey-visaged baby. What delights had already been vouchsafed the two boys before the arrival of the policemen, what pleasures had been so rudely interrupted? The dejection of the house and the squalid appearance of the two girls, younger replicas of

255

Mrs. Dymark accorded ill with the blue-eyed vigour and well-turned out look of the better-looking of the two dispatch riders. O'Flattery wondered which was the father of Dorothy's unborn child and found himself hoping it was not the ill-favoured-looking boy. He wondered, also, if the corporal would lose his stripes over this episode. Where was Mrs. Dymark and what badly written notes must have passed between the boys and their girls to arrange this assignation? Who had peached on the boys or had they been followed? Was Mrs. Dymark out or was she perhaps at home unconcernedly getting on with her ironing? It was a subject for extensive conjecture.

Further along after more unfriendly streets one of these questions was answered, for he saw coming towards him the figure of Mrs. Dymark, walking between two of her cronies. They were dressed in their Sunday best and had obviously just come from chapel. O'Flattery remembered that it was the afternoon of the Mothers' Own Service, about which he had heard so much from Mrs. Dymark if he happened to be present when she cleaned his room. Part of his quandary was thus elucidated. Mrs. Dymark had been out and he was fairly certain that the soldiers' visit had been intended to be clandestine. Would Mrs. Dymark notice the wheel marks outside the cottage? How would Dorothy and her sister carry it off? Would they be able to counter their mother's suspicious questions or would there be "a good swear off", such as he had often heard while passing the cottage? For the Dymarks paid little concern to the opinions of others and hardly ever shut their front door, so that their life was almost public property. What Mrs. Dymark did not already tell everybody could be seen by anybody who was interested enough to look.

He might never know; his well-meaning but interfering interest would probably remain for ever unsatisfied, unless

Mrs. Dymark related the whole story to him when he next found himself the victim of her crude cleaning routine. At all events he had two companions in guilt now, however tenuous the connection.

Mrs. Dymark bowed to him as she passed, with the dignity afforded her by her best clothes and as she drew away from him he heard her say in a clear stage whisper:

"That's that young Irishman from where I work. Don't 'e look bad. Shouldn't wonder if 'e ain't bin crossed in love or suthink?"

He could positively feel her two companions turning round in unison to have a second look at this pale paragon of dejection.

His heart remained heavy until he reached the river bank where a high tide lapped against the edge of the footpath. The vision, lit by a shaft from the dying sun, of a brilliantly white swan rocking, bosomed on the water, temporarily raised his poor bruised spirits. With a desperate floundering of wings and feet clacking across the water the swan raised itself from the surface and went woosh-woosh-wooshing up into the clear air, leaving a diminishing trail of the sound of wing beats singing in O'Flattery's ears.

Looking up from the path after he had gone some way, he saw two figures in front of him walking as one, their arms round one another. Both were dressed in black jeans and dark green pullovers. One carried a long stick. They stopped every so often and the one with the stick pointed with it down the river. Now and again they appeared to embrace. But as these hesitations and O'Flattery's forward steps caused them to get closer together he saw, to his surprise, that they were two boys. At least he could scarcely believe they were until he caught up with them when they had stopped and turned about.

They were, indeed, two boys. One he estimated was about sixteen and the other possibly fifteen or nearly

257

sixteen; at any rate they were as close together in harmony as they were in age, but O'Flattery felt sure that one was slightly older than the other. The older one was more robust in figure and had already the build of a man, with grown muscles and a heaviness which the other boy lacked. The younger of the two was slighter in physique but in no way effeminate. They both possessed a youthful masculinity which made their easy amity so unbearably poignant. They had been walking in step; the taller of the two boys, who carried the stick, had his disengaged arm flung over the other's shoulder, not loosely but with a tension and a feeling of weight, which enclosed the other boy in a protective curve. The younger boy's arm was around his friend's waist and his hand rested in his companion's hip pocket. Their heads were close together and they walked, as it were, enclosed in a private bubble, unaware of the rest of the world or their effect upon it. They only drew apart from one another to step aside and enable the Irishman to pass.

He wanted desperately to talk to them. For some extraordinary reason he felt that to do so would be his only hope of salvation from the dreadful fate which he was beginning to feel must inevitably overtake him. But try as he would he could not summon up words with which to address them. His tongue seemed to fill his mouth like a mouthful of dry wheat, as he cudgelled his brains to form some sentence with which to accost them, but he could only keep silence and with the greatest effort conjured up the ghost of a smile for them which they both returned unstintingly.

Already, before O'Flattery had passed, their arms were once more about one another, enclosing one another in a womb of gentle masculine tenderness. He hurried on, turning later to see if they were coming towards him, but trying to pretend to himself that he really did not care.

The sun was going down, the mud was a shimmering mirror of neutral grey, the low line of the sky and the water accentuated the size of the two boys as they walked along the bank towards him. He had come now to the point where the path divided, one path went off and through a deep wood, while the other still followed the twisting course of the river. Further down, the paths joined again and soon after that O'Flattery had to turn off into the road where he lodged. At this first junction he turned again to look back up the river. There they were swinging along talking to one another, unconcerned, looking completely happy; engrossed in one another. He could not go on without speaking to them, his feet were as if fused to the ground and yet his tongue still could not form words. So greatly did he feel the necessity to make contact with them that he began to sweat with the effort of trying to speak. He hoped that if he could communicate with them some of their happiness would, as it were, rub off on to him like the pollen from a flower on to the legs of a bee; but he did not on any account want, by intruding upon them, to lessen the nectar of their happiness.

Finally they caught him up again, smiled shyly and were about to pass on into the wood. With a superhuman effort O'Flattery managed to break silence. Stuttering, and with an intensity which did not fit the meaning of his words, he told them that if they were going through the wood, there was a place in the path which was very wet and would surely go over their shoes.

"It would be better to go along the river path," he stammered. But in reality only saying it because he wanted to keep them in sight for as long as possible. Obviously it was a matter of no consequence to them, and when at last he saw this he managed to tear himself away; saying goodbye he once more trudged on towards home.

Again he looked back and saw they were not going to

take the river path but had turned off and were already entering the wood. Their green-clad figures were losing their outlines among the shadows of the sheltering trees. He turned his head away, his eyes scalded with tears, his throat stiff with sobs. He cried, mourning what he felt was the inevitable shattering of their innocence, the pricking of their bubble by the world's opinion which he knew the future held in store. He cried also with self-pity at his own predicament, all too aware of his own unhappiness, the intenseness of which rivalled their felicity.

He had been looking on the countenance of love. Love between two boys who so far had been uncorrupted by the world. Whether their love was physical or not did not matter; to him it was of such an exclusive character, had such a tangible quality, that it left him with a pungent grief; full of regrets for his own prematurely lost youth, lost innocence and his few wasted years. He had felt that he wanted to give the two boys something, some wisdom, some advice but he had, alas, none to give. He had learnt nothing in the course of his short life that they needed to know. There was no reason to break in upon their privacy to offer them some half-digested gobbet of philosophy. But he had wanted to give them his blessing, if such it could be called. To tell them that he was on their side against the world if necessary, that once not so very long ago he had felt that life held the promise for him that it held now for them.

But had it? He wondered now if his empty life had ever held any promise at all? If he had ever believed in any fundamental reason for continuing to live? Why should they be concerned with the quality of his despair? Why speak to them of the terrible pastime of love in which one of the protagonists must surely forfeit possession of himself?

What would have been the point of bothering them with

such thoughts, why risk awakening them to any ugliness which all too soon might be revealed to them?

If they had entered the wood in order that they might enjoy the more complete intimacy of each other's bodies in the gathering private dusk offered them by the trees, who was he to try and prevent them, with old-maidish advice about wet feet?

He envied them, but at the same time he wanted to encourage them with some kind of parental word. But he could see, all too clearly, that they were in no need of it. They were complete, inviolate.

He felt the loneliness of self-knowledge; the anguish of self pity; the remorse of lost boyhood. They were setting out, he was on the way back. What would they achieve? Where would they get to? How would they be treated by society? What stresses and strains would bear in upon them? He longed to be able to prolong for them their happiness; were they perhaps unconscious of its inestimable value? But they had gone out of his life as quickly as they had stridden through it, leaving behind them an impression of young love as real as the ground he walked on. But alas, thought O'Flattery how much, much less durable.

He trudged brokenly on, longing for release from his burden of cares. The complete disappearance of Miss Jeacock's body began once more to prey on his mind. Mrs. Macklin's ghastly leers were daily forcing him to believe that she knew all and was trying to use this knowledge in some way, hoping to receive his favours. The deformed notion had at last taken root, and was growing in his consciousness that this odious Hecate was physically attracted to him and was slowly using her hold over him to blackmail him into obtaining her will. Tarnished already as he was, bedaubed with his own lubricity, the thought of such a hideous business was sufficient to send the delicate balance of his reason tottering towards the brink of

261

insanity.

The more he dwelt upon this obscene idea, the more baldly it stuck out like an awful phallus from the recesses of his introspection. Some one had been tampering with his desk he felt sure; could it have been this ill-favoured female suitor? If so, she must have read his journal. In which case she was in possession of his most personal secrets, his passions, his most intimate frustrations.

In a flash, which made his entrails revolve with horror, he knew that this was the truth.

It could be the only explanation of Mrs. Macklin's weird behaviour over the last weeks. This incredible woman was as misshapen in mind as she was in body. He tried to think if he had ever given her the slightest encouragement. He had given Jennifer the tortoise; he had taken the children to the circus. He recollected occasions in the past when he had greeted her with a friendly smile or some jocular comment about the weather. But . . . No! a voice cried inside him in a panic-stricken scream, no! these crumbs could never have been re-mixed and baked into the monstrous cake of her deluded lust.

When he reached the comparative safety of his land-lady's house he fell, rather than walked, across the thresh-hold of his room. Fortunately she was out and no one had seen his wild progress from the river bank down this quite residential backwater. Nobody, that is, except the fly, which never left him.

With trembling hands he searched for some sleeping pills, which he had wheedled out of a sympathetic doctor to whom he had gone with a story about insomnia caused by the tension of worrying over an exam. Swallowing he knew not how many he collapsed insensible upon his bed, asleep with mental exhaustion, even before the medicine had time to affect his system.

His last decision, taken at the same time as the capsules,

had been that the next day he would search out a priest and, returning to the long abandoned beliefs of his upbringing, would confess the whole repulsive story.

Heavy, painful breaths tore his fragile body as he fell asleep guarded by the sinister presence of the resonant fly.

19

MR. GENDER was dead, and in accordance with the instructions left by him some time previously, and now produced by his solicitor, cremated.

Miss Jeacock was also reduced to ashes, but not in such an official manner.

The Irishman was sobbing in his sleep, lying fully clothed, in the chill embrace of misery, on the bed where he had fallen the evening before; his disillusion was drowning him even in sleep.

Mrs. Macklin lay snug in her feather bed; half awake and half asleep she scratched and explored contentedly the hollows of her recumbent body.

Jennifer lay in the room across the passage from her mother, ending a night of torture. Mrs. Macklin had allowed her to gorge herself on cheese and pickled onions for supper and, coupled with her conscience, such as it was, it had had a disastrous effect upon her rest.

The fly, still at last, slept upon the glazed tiles of the Ladies Cloakroom, at an intersection which harboured the dirt uncleaned by Jennifer's casual brush. That ubiquitous fly was everywhere at once.

Jennifer had gone to bed the evening before at the usual time, putting her brother Leslie and her sister Brenda to bed also, while Mrs. Macklin clattered below with stoves and washing up. But as soon as the light was out her tormented little brain became active and switched on a series of moving pictures, as in a cinema, memories of how

264

she had found Miss Jeacock and of how her body had been disposed of. She had lain sweating with terror listening to the barrage of snores which came from Leslie and Brenda, who occupied a bed in the same room. By the lurid light cast by the street lamp outside she could see their bodies rising and falling beneath the blankets like a miniature earth tremor. The more she watched and listened, the more like an animal about to spring out of the ground did this shapeless mass become, like some horrible mole which was tunnelling just below the surface of the earth. She heard heavy footsteps going towards her mother's room; she saw the light disappear under the door of her room as her mother's door was shut.

Usually she sank into flatulent somnolence the moment her head was laid upon the grey pillow, but on this night the memory of Miss Jeacock's distorted face and twisted body refused to leave her alone. With it came other remembered horrors from unsuitable films which her negligent parent had not prevented her from seeing. A stalking Frankenstein monster with pegged neck loomed over her, only to be replaced as this vision faded by the beating wings of Dracula, who plucked at the bedclothes, trying to get at her toes from which to quench his thirst for blood. Lunatics with goggling eyes walked the house, dragging dry hands across the door panels; werewolves bayed to the rising moon and mysterious presences scratched at the window asking to be let in. As cars passed and lit the room momentarily with flashes from their headlights they were to Jennifer's disordered imagination nothing so harmless, but became science-fiction sources of atomic power, attacking the world from outer space.

The rest of the house sank into sleep, leaving Jennifer to her imagined alarms until the early hours, when she too fell into a fitful doze from utter exhaustion. From this, just as the dawn broke in ribbons of rose-gold and scarlet, she

265

awoke with a blood-chilling shriek. Leslie and Brenda snored on, but Mrs. Macklin, lying dozing, heard it and swearing gently to herself swung her great legs reluctantly out of her warm bed, fumbling with bunioned feet for her downtrodden feathered mules.

Jennifer had been dreaming. *She was lying on her back and had imagined herself as being in a huge dark castle, the walls of which were so massive that to be inside them gave her a feeling of terrible oppression, as if at any moment they would fall and crush her. At the same time she knew that beneath this castle was a dungeon filled with innocent people in chains, who held her responsible for their unlawful incarceration. There was going to be a mass break-out and it was vital that Jennifer escaped first or she would surely be torn to pieces by the angry prisoners. The passages of the castle, dripping with damp and dank with the smell of smoky torches, were a maze without a solution. Doors refused to open and turned into walls without gaps in them, huge blocks of masonry blocked her progress at every turn; she fell down again and again. Stumbling forward with cut hands and knees she rounded a corner, before her silhouetted in a bright light was a figure, behind which, in the glow of this light, a turgid mass heaved and moaned like maggots. The figure was the first of the escaping prisoners, who was being encouraged from behind by a mob of a hundred others. Jennifer could not move, the creature staggered forward towards her and she saw that it was a man half-covered in funeral cerements, his arms outstretched from which hung tattered rags, one leg dragged behind the other and the whole of one side of him had begun to rot away oozing pus from which rose the smell of ghastly putrefaction.* It was then that Jennifer found the use of her lungs, setting this nightmare to flight and at the same time summoning her Mother with her penetrating scream.

266

Opening her eyes she saw Mrs. Macklin bending over her and exhausted by terror and lack of sleep was about to start her yells afresh. But recognising her parent, she swallowed her screams and began crying instead.

"Wot is it mate?" enquired Mrs. Macklin with a tenderness that amazed her daughter.

"I 'ad a dream Mum," gulped Jennifer, "a man was 'arter me."

"There ain't no man 'arter you luvy," crooned Mrs. Macklin sleepily easing her weight down onto the bed, "and if there was Mum 'ud look arter yer. You tell yer Mum if any man comes arter you."

"Yes, Mum," piped Jennifer solemnly.

"Don't you fret, there ain't nothin' to be afraid of anymore," yawned Mrs. Macklin. This vast protective form, grotesque as it was, still meant security to her child and rapidly all phantoms were dispelled.

Conventionally, a distant cock crew and a clock began to chime as the sky became palely lighter.

"We may as well get up now," said the mother as she made a rough maternal movement with her hand, half blow, half caress, towards her crouching daughter.

As she said this, Jennifer became aware of mountainous snores arising from the depths of her mother's room and could see from where she lay Arthur's boots flung down beside his mistress's bed. In the moment that she saw this, the realisation that she had done so dawned on Mrs. Macklin, who shifted herself off the bed and blocked the doorway with her uncorseted body. Her whole manner changed and it was as though the previous moment of tenderness had been a dream and the previous dream a reality.

"Get up then yer little sod and go down and put the kettle on; wakin' people up at this time of the morning. I never 'eard such nonsense," shouted Mrs. Macklin, her

267

old self again. Whereupon Jennifer shot out of bed and huddled into her clothes, eager to escape and be about her morning chores as quickly as possible. Her mother returned chuntering to her den, slamming the door so loudly behind her that it woke Brenda up; who began to grizzle instantly and as smartly received a smack in the face from Jennifer whose temper that day was going to be worse than usual.

20

It was another day of glittering sunshine, like the day of the Office Outing.

The Office staff had arrived, including O'Flattery whose sedative had not entirely worn off and who walked to and fro in his office like a somnambulist. Work was progressing when there appeared in the clear sky a cloud no bigger than a man's hand. At that moment Jennifer perceived the distant shape of a man coming towards the Office.

This was Detective Inspector Litover. As a result of Miss Seal's hysterical outburst, a grain of suspicion had been sown in the official mind about the disappearance of Miss Jeacock; it had been decided therefore that before the word "Unsolved" was stamped on the file which contained the details of her life up to when she vanished, a further investigation should be made. Miss Jeacock was now recorded merely as a "missing person" and as such it appeared she would sink into oblivion. But before doing so it had been felt by officialdom that they should close the case with some attempt at finality.

Therefore, Detective Inspector Litover was on his way to the Office, to see if there was anything his expert hands could uncover.

He was in appearance a very ordinary man. His ordinariness was in fact almost an affront to the intelligence of those from whom he sought to conceal that he was a policeman. No ordinary civilian citizen would ever have worn such boots, such a macintosh, such a bowler hat or would have taken such care of his fingernails, which he kept faultlessly manicured and covered most of the time with brown leather gloves.

He drew near to the Office, observed as were all visitors by the trio of Macklin children. At least by two of them, the unspeakable bundle being in a state of semi-inertia, broken only by intermittent gusts of internal wind.

Jennifer and Leslie stood agape. She was dressed in her Brownie uniform, ready for their meeting which she was to attend that afternoon. Leslie was his usual servile self. Jennifer whose embryonic "woman's intuition" was already astir, was on the alert. Her sleepless night had sharpened her wits as well as her temper. Perceiving the Inspector's nonchalant, but regular tread as he came towards them, her suspicions were aroused. Nudging Leslie she whispered:

"Look at 'im."

"Oo?" said Leslie adenoidally, obstinately squinting up his eyes in the opposite direction.

"Not that way ape," screeched his sister with an appropriately sharp elbow-attack, "this way. 'Im with the big plates of meat."

"Oh 'im," said Leslie, obviously seeing nothing unusual in the man.

"Yes 'im. Bet yer 'es a nark," said Jennifer mysteriously.

"Wots a nark?" queried Leslie vacant to the last.

"A copper, 'a course, when was you born?" angrily answered Jennifer. Blandly smiling and rocking Brenda for the benefit of the Inspector's observant eye, who she could see was already scrutinizing the Macklin group at a distance.

"Nar, corse 'e ain't," scorned Leslie, "'e ain't got no 'elmit."

"Betcher?"

"Wotcher bet?"

270

"Betcher yer 'afters' this dinner time."

"Orl right then," said Leslie suspecting that she would never be able to get his 'afters', even if she did win, as their mother would be watching out for any irregularities in their behaviour.

"Wait and see then," said Jennifer. "'Ere 'e is. Mornin' sir," she simpered sweetly to Inspector Litover as he stopped beside them. "Say good mornin' to the gentleman,' she chided Leslie with mock gentility.

"Mornin'," mouthed Leslie.

"Morning kiddies," said the Inspector, thinking here was easy material upon which to start his investigation.

Within Jennifer's agile head was reflected almost the identical judgement of him as presenting fair game for gulling. Not for nothing was Jennifer the eldest daughter of the Macklin harridan.

"You're brother and sister?" he went on amicably as he took out a packet of cigarettes and went through the time-honoured process of delayed action while lighting one, the ceremony which bridges so many gaps.

"Yes sir," smirked Jennifer. Leslie merely sniggered through his grey snotty nose.

"Who is this?" enquired the Inspector, keeping his enquiries on a strictly informal level, inclining his face downward towards the solid mass of clothes which parcelled up Brenda's inanimate bulk.

"That's Brenda," hollared Leslie loud enough to wake the dead, but making no effect upon Brenda's impassive mask.

"Say 'sir' to the gentleman, Leslie," reproved Jennifer with unctuous politeness.

"Sir, that's Brenda our Sis sir," said Leslie making the whole sentence absurdly sibilant.

The Inspector blew streaks of smoke out through the gaps in his widely spaced front teeth, as he looked with

271

misgiving at the mottled face which was all that was visibly human in the push-chair.

"Pretty little dear," he lied with utterly unconvincing fulsomeness. "Is she all right?" he added anxiously.

"Oh yes sir, she's always like that when she's asleep sir. Don't you worry," replied Jennifer confidentially, and at the same time reassuringly.

Relieved, the Inspector turned his attention to the façade of the Office; the children unseen by him also inspected his person with a minuteness surprising for their years. Behind him, Leslie capered silently like an animated gargoyle, while Jennifer unobserved raised two fingers in a famous gesture of scorn.

"I expect you know everyone who works here?" smiled the Inspector with heavy tact, in an obviously off-hand way.

"Oh yes," said Jennifer, "we knows 'em. When they comes and when they goes too we know," she added unexpectedly, eyeing the Inspector craftily from under her Brownie beret.

"Indeed," said the Inspector, put off his guard by having one of his next questions anticipated.

"I expect you do, I expect you notice a lot," he said hurriedly and as quickly regretted his hasty words, "a bright little girl like you," he finished lamely; chucking Jennifer playfully under the chin with a gesture about as gentle as a poulterer who is about to wring the neck of a chicken.

Jennifer who hated being touched, sidled away sensing in this man a menacing friendliness from which she must protect herself at all costs.

A fortunate diversion was created by Wendy who arrived like a bomb on her bicycle, clad also in Brownie uniform, looking more disordered than usual.

"And who is this?" asked the Inspector playing for time.

272

"That's Wendy my friend, she's dotty, she don't know nuffink, do yer Wend?" announced Jennifer firmly.

"Shit 'em," put in Wendy as her only contribution to the conversation.

"And the same to you," chimed in Leslie receiving a smack from both girls for his wit.

"There's our Mum," Jennifer suddenly shouted making the Inspector start, "lookin' art a the door."

Inspector Litover followed the direction of her pointing finger and could just descry the pallid floating face of Mrs. Macklin watching what was going on from behind the glass panes of the main door, like some vast immovable fish suspended in the water of an aquarium.

Aggressively, seeing she was observed, Mrs. Macklin opened the door and shouted:

"Oo d'yer want?" and at the same time making a gesture which seemed to both beckon the man forward and drive Leslie and Jennifer with the push-chair further away.

The Inspector moved towards the shapeless woman whom he now saw standing on the steps before him, pinching out his cigarette and dropping it on the asphalt as he came nearer.

"Good morning, madam. I am Detective Inspector Litover from Scotland Yard," he said giving his words the proper emphasis for this quiet revelation of his identity. "I wish to make some routine enquiries," he added in sepulchral tones, especially lowered out of respect for the children who were still at his heels, "into the disappearance of a Miss Jeacock, who I understand worked at this address for a number of years prior to her disappearance," he droned on in his evidence-giving police court voice.

"That's right," said Mrs. Macklin, instantly militant but showing no outward signs of her inward perturbation as she stood holding the open door.

"Wot did I tell yer?" hissed Jennifer into Leslie's black-

273

head-infested ear. "The old fool is a nark. I've won yer 'afters', garn yer."

"Perhaps you'd better start yer hinquiries on them then?" said Mrs. Macklin insolently, indicating the group of children.

Jennifer stepped forward, as demure as Joan of Arc, handing over Brenda's equipage to the wide-eyed Wendy, whose comment was as usual.

Ignoring Mrs. Macklin's manner the Inspector began:

"Did you see Miss Jeacock on the day of her disappearance?" he asked Jennifer kindly.

Mrs. Macklin stood without blinking an eyelash, her arms akimbo, her eyes concentrated painfully on Jennifer's, who gulped back a snivel under the double onslaught of Inspector Litover and her Mother.

"No she never," answered Mrs. Macklin.

"Let the child answer for herself, if you please," said the detective frowning at this female gorgon.

"Did you?" he repeated.

"No sir," replied Jennifer in a bold voice.

"Did you see Mr. Gender on the day after the Office Outing?" went on her interlocutor.

"That was Mr. Gender wot did 'er in, I know," blurted out Jennifer.

Mrs. Macklin's knuckles went white, unseen by the detective.

"Did you see him?" he repeated patiently.

"'E done it an pushed 'er in the river I reckon. We saw 'im come away late didn't we Les?" she continued lying.

"You saw 'im too, didn't yer?" she crowed at Brenda, pinching her savagely in the arm. "Nod yer 'ead at the gentleman. Go on," she commanded.

Everyone remained silently watching in a circle round Brenda's push-chair. She nodded solemnly like an eskimo baby, her hooded Mongolian eyes shrouded in fat, clutch-

274

ing, as always, the beady-eyed Horny.

Inspector Litover turned away shrugging his shoulders, realising that he was up against a brick wall. Mrs. Macklin twisted Jennifer round, patted her head, and with a shove launched her towards Wendy and the push-chair. Knowing quite well what this meant, they all chased off at breakneck speed as Jennifer carolled:

"I've won 'is 'afters', I've won 'is 'afters'," until they were out of hearing.

Mrs. Macklin wiped away false tears with a handkerchief smelling of "Entrée des Artistes", which she now inappositely used. From behind it she caught a glimpse of the Irishman, who had been listening from the shadows of the vestibule to the whole examination. To this crouched white sentinel she flashed an insinuating leer and even, he thought, waved her handkerchief provocatively.

With the departure of the gang of children Detective Inspector Litover removed his bowler hat preparatory to being invited to enter the Office building. Mrs. Macklin, seeing that he had done this, scrutinized his close cropped grey head and cold slate-coloured eyes, saying:

"Yer'd better see Dr. Booker then, 'e's the 'ead about 'ere," and led the way forthwith to Dr. Booker's office. As the Inspector entered the doorway, a fly whizzed past his face making him draw back and raise a finger to scratch his nose.

"Nice weather for the time of year," remarked Inspector Litover brightly, trying unsuccessfully to ease the tension of silence expressed by the massive shoulder-blades in front of him. But Mrs. Macklin appeared to be suddenly deaf as she offered no reply except:

"Wait there," indicating a wooden chair which stood against a radiator, a pace or two from Dr. Booker's door.

Knocking loudly and receiving the expected summons, Mrs. Macklin disappeared from view, only to reappear

275

after some minutes scowling more than ever at the Inspector and motioning him without a word to enter.

As the Inspector entered, Dr. Booker was in the act of dismissing Miss Betty Lynch with whom he had been going through his usual morning post. With a frightened dipping inclination of the head towards the detective, she scuttled out to spread the news at once to her sister and quickly to the other ladies of the Office.

Within ten minutes everyone in the building knew, from the least important typist to the Senior Clerk and, of course, including the Irishman, that Dr. Booker was interviewing or was being interviewed by an Inspector from Scotland Yard, who had come about "poor Miss Jeacock."

Dr. Booker rose from his desk and, not altogether affably, extended his hand. He was impatient at the waste of time indicated by this police visit when, in any case, he considered the matter closed and wished to cut the interview as short as possible.

"Pray be seated," he said, indicating a chair by the side of his desk.

"Thank you sir, I am much obliged," said the detective, recognising that respect was due to the age and learning represented by this venerable white-haired man before him.

Inspector Litover believed in coming straight to the point. As he fumbled in his pocket for some papers he said, once more in his court-room voice:

"I trust I am not intruding, sir, and I hope I shan't keep you long. But I am here to make certain enquiries concerning the disappearance of a Miss Jeacock, who has not been seen at her place of residence, nor at this, her place of employment since . . ." here Dr. Booker interrupted him:

"That is perfectly correct," he beamed absent-mindedly, for he respected accuracy more than anything, "perfectly

276

correct. Poor Miss Jeacock. Very sad. Very sad. We miss her lamentably. Such an able worker. So very able," he repeated ruminatively.

"Quite so, sir," said the Inspector patiently.

"I do hope that your department does not suspect foul play," trembled Dr. Booker as he leant across the desk, raising his eyebrows to this alien man from another world.

"Oh no, indeed, no," hastily replied the Inspector, seeing the old man's evident alarm and wishing at once to allay his fears, the more easily to open the way to further questioning.

"We were just wondering if anything in the way of a clue had turned up since her disappearance was reported, anything from which we could get a lead?" he went on, raising in his turn his eyebrows and cocking his head on one side.

"Absolutely nothing, Inspector, nothing," answered Dr. Booker. "The poor dear lady seems to have vanished into thin air, into thin air." He looked very old and frail. This double tragedy in his department had been altogether too much for him. He waved an ebony-white hand to demonstrate Miss Jeacock's illusionistic disappearance.

Inspector Litover could see that he was tiring the old man and also from his experience of people and situations that his questions were going to lead him nowhere. As Dr. Booker had nothing to hide he had nothing to reveal; he could shed no light whatever upon the problem which occupied the detective, who was very quickly coming to the conclusion that, as usual, it was a pointless waste of everyone's time to spend any more effort on an investigation, based on nothing more concrete than a hysterical spinster's suspicions.

He asked a few more questions but soon rounded off the interview, inwardly determined that Miss Jeacock's file would remain closed. As he took his departure he said:

"Perhaps if anything comes to light sir, you would be kind enough to contact me at the Yard," pushing his card at the same time towards Dr. Booker. But he could see that the old man's attention had already wandered, as he rummaged among the papers on his desk, burying the detective's card under a pile of official documents.

"Of course, of course, naturally," Dr. Booker replied already completely pre-occupied.

Mrs. Macklin was towering outside the door like an eastern genie waiting to speed the Inspector on his way. She hurried him out, swelling with pleasure, for she had been listening with her ear to the keyhole and had heard all that had passed between the two men. She felt secure now and sure of her quarry as she slammed the door on the detective without even wishing him good-day.

As he descended the steps of the Office, the Macklin children and Wendy stood in an aimless line opposite him, doing nothing.

Unable not to be authoriative and having failed so signally inside the Office, he could not resist saying in a pleasant, friendly voice:

"Why don't you children pick up some of this paper which is blowing about here and make the place a bit tidier?" A welter of old fish and chip paper and cigarette packets had eddied round the telephone box and now littered the surrounding pavement in a messy whirlpool.

"Why?" said Jennifer rudely.

"I thought Girl Guides did good deeds and helped people?" said the Inspector.

"We ain't Guides," said Jennifer flatly.

"Well what are you then?" asked the Inspector, his choler rising.

"We're Brownies, so boo sucks to you, and we don't do jobs unless we're paid for 'em," replied Jennifer impertinently.

278

The children about-turned as if at an order and ran off one by one in several directions, screaming with brazen laughter. Wendy yelling:

"Shit 'em, shit 'em, shit 'em," fit to burst her lungs.

Mrs. Macklin, watching again from the doorway, laughed until her stays cracked as the disgusted detective turned on his heel and hurried away. As she left the light of the doorway and advanced into the vestibule, the fly flew a halo of flight round her head, like a triumphant tiara.

O'Flattery who in his turn had been watching the course of events from a bend in the staircase, saw her look of exultation and quailed.

21

THE SMELL of death hung over the Irishman. The fly was now never absent from him. It was as if corruption had already started in his body and was perceived by this hungry harbinger.

Imperceptibly, delusions began to take hold of him. At last he knew that he was losing his reason. Gently but irrevocably it was slipping from him; as the petals of a rose drift to the ground at the end of its blooming, noiselessly loosing their hold from the scented entirety of the flower-head, so did his powers leave him as quickly and with as much finality. His ability to concentrate, his ability to make decisions, to choose one course of action rather than another, to distinguish between choice and compulsion, slowly, unrelentingly they ebbed away.

He became preoccupied with the number, the smallness and blackness of the printed word. Millions of words in thousands of books, papers, magazines, files weighed him down by their unseen presence around him; now they were words, now they were flies. At times he could not determine between them. He read voraciously every book he could lay his hands on about flies. Their names flowed through his head like the responses of the Mass. *Homalomyia brevis—Kyrie, eléison—Muscina stabulans—Kyrie, eléison—Lucilia caesar—Christe, eléison—Scatophaga furcata—Christe, eléison—Sepsis violacea—Et clamor meus ad te véniat.*

But no one heard his cry and there was no one to come

to his aid.

He was haunted by what he read of the diseases which he could catch from contact with flies. He imagined himself the prey of dysentery, tuberculosis, leprosy, syphilis, malaria, small pox, even the plague. There seemed no end to the lurid diseases disseminated by flies. But above all his fear of typhoid grew until it reached the point of mania. He washed his hands incessantly. In the course of his reading he had been particularly struck by the case of an Irish girl who in 1906 had been the cook with a family on Long Island, America. During that summer numerous cases of typhoid fever occurred and it was discovered after the proper examinations were made that Mary, the cook, was a chronic carrier. Upon further investigation into her past history it was found that in nearly every family with which she worked there had been cases of typhoid. The unfortunate woman was immediately apprehended and kept in isolated custody for three years, afterwards promising never to engage as a cook and to report for examination at frequent intervals. Upon finding she could secure no employment, she was placed by the authorities in one of the laundries of a public institution, where she disappeared into oblivion.

Mrs. Dymark, in the demented mind of the Irishman, became identified with this woman.

Imperceptibly, the delusions took hold. He read of a brown rat which had once been observed, between the lace curtain and the window of a storeroom, busily catching and eating flies. It was seen to become very expert, standing on its hind legs against the glass moving backwards and forwards across the window catching the flies between its paws and conveying them to its mouth. It even instructed one of its companions in this art and the two were frequently seen together pursuing this occupation. Each time he passed the larder window of his lodgings he looked for these rats and the slightest movement of the curtain by a breeze made him sure they were there.

At times his mind felt like a kaleidoscope, through which he had to look in order to be able to think. He saw events and objects clearly with his eyes but his judgment and faculties of conception were becoming distorted. It was as if some refraction of his senses was taking place, as if a whole section of the vision through this kaleidoscope was missing. Try as he would, he could not shift the pieces of his thought into place so that they made sense, so that they made a balanced pattern. He was not aware whether or not this was apparent to other people or whether it was evident exclusively to himself. He felt at all times that he was being watched. This sense of evil observation increased daily making him irritable with everyone with whom he came in contact. It seemed to him that each day began with the suspicious attentions of Mrs. Dymark, whose kind-hearted anxiety about his appearance he was quick to turn into malicious interference. Whenever she could she engaged him in conversation or rather indulged in one of her endless monologues, which to her were relevant but to the listener always difficult to follow and to O'Flattery at this time completely incomprehensible. Or if comprehensible at all he was quick to see in the complicated gist of her talk some attack on himself. She would come bustling into the room while he was at breakfast, ostensibly to dust or give him more hot water for his tea, and start straight off, as if they were in complete accord and were already in the middle of a long conversation.

"Course she give 'erself away by 'er face when he come into the room. I could see she loved 'im. Yes. 'E's a nice feller but I shouldn't want 'im for an 'usband. Yer know what I mean 'es got no fire in 'im. I remember once one Christmas we was foolin' about and 'e kissed me under the mistletoe, 'oo I wasn't 'arf disappointed."

"Why?" the Irishman to his own surprise heard himself say.

"Well," went on Mrs. Dymark delighted to get some reaction for a change, "it was more like a butterfly, you know what I mean. 'Es a nice chap orl right but 'es got no go in 'im. I can't see 'im as a married man yer know. No wonder they ain't got no children, shouldn't think 'e could make any. No go in 'im. But 'es a nice feller. Do anything for anybody. As I said to my girl Dorothy yer don't want to keep on about a thing like that. I mean I know she's 'ad 'er troubles and so on but wot I always says is yer can't marry the dead nor the departed and the best thing to do is to make the best of it."

The pieces in O'Flattery's kaleidoscopic mind clicked round, forming distorted images as Mrs. Dymark rattled on. Mrs. Dymark's Dorothy walking up the aisle in white carrying a sheaf of madonna lilies towards a black-suited skeleton, who turned its sightless eye sockets towards her as she approached, smiling a fleshless smile with its naked teeth. But a segment of the image is missing and as Dorothy moves her limbs melt and dissolve into the gap, seeming to flow towards the tottering skeleton on another plane, at a different angle. Mrs. Dymark is still talking, although the Irishman has said only one word to her and looks deathly pale.

"Well, I mean to say, I've 'ad an un'appy marriage, but I never mention 'im, never mention 'is name. I just lives me life decent and keeps cheerful."

Miss Jeacock has taken Dorothy's place. The edges of the Irishman's vision are scalloped with white flowers. A cobbled street plunges steeply away behind Miss Jeacock's over-life-size face, the eyes of which are glazed and ringed with flics, organ music swells, she begins to run down the street and as she does so she trips and falls sprawling across the cobbles, the lilies fall from her arms spilling pollen and yellow-dusted flies as if from a dozen white cornucopias. As she sprawls she disintegrates with a silent explosion leaving her empty wedding garments stretched like a scarecrow among the flowers.

"That's wot I say," goes on Mrs. Dymark indomitably, "it's the mystery of the world. You bring nuffink in wiv yer and yer takes nuffink art. As Ethel said when 'er Dad was dyin'. It don't make no difference 'ow 'eavy yer are. Yer gets lighter as yer grows older. Yer bones get 'oller. 'Er Dad was a big man. Well when 'e was dyin' 'e always used to go to the lavtry by 'iself. You leave me alone 'e used to say, I'll go by meself. Marvellous ain't it?"

"Marvellous," echoed the Irishman almost inaudibly, seeing Miss Jeacock's head obscenely close to the pedestal, the old man's feet astride her. The buzz of invisible flies penetrating the awful quiet.

"Well one day 'e sat up and said shouldn't 'arf fancy a glass of beer. I'll get cher one sez Ethel. So she sez I'll just make yer bed afore I go. Yer needn't get out, I'll move yer over. So she goes to 'eave 'im over and 'es as light as a fevver, bones gone 'oller yer see. Marvellous ain't it?"

"Marvellous," silently mouthed the Irishman, appalled at the thought of Mr. Gender and Miss Jeacock, boneless like filleted meat on a marble slab.

"Queer though ain't it? I don't 'arf fancy a glass a beer 'e said. Gone as light as a fevver 'e 'ad." Mrs. Dymark at last realised that O'Flattery was unwell for he was clutching at the table cloth, dragging it together into a handful and making everything upon it topple like a miniature earthquake, as his whole world had toppled about him since Miss Jeacock's death.

Mrs. Dymark, terrified at what she saw and quite unable to deal with this disintegrating human being, fled, frightened from the room.

284

He would awake in the night with raging tooth-ache and lay battling with the pain feeling as if his face was devoid of flesh. Conscious of each tooth in its socket in his skull, aware of his eyes looking out of his head into the darkness like loose floating marbles which would drop out if he dared to turn on the pillow.

He caught himself standing aimlessly lost in thought on one spot, not knowing how long he had been there, unaware of the passage of time, only conscious that he was cold and numb from standing on one leg on one spot. He had found himself standing thus on the river bank, staring fixedly at a seagull whose white almond shape opened and shut as it folded and unfolded its wings. He found himself with his arms bent and elbows up, moving them as if they were wings and he was trying to fly. He wondered what the sensation must be like of being able to fold one pair of limbs over onto one's back and longed to be able to wing away into the heliotrope distance away from all his cares.

He caught sight of Mrs. Dymark coming towards him, wheeling in front of her a pram which he soon saw contained her monstrous grandchild. Its head was enormous, its flesh had fallen away from its limbs so that its clothes no longer fitted. Whatever wits the poor thing had ever possessed had departed and with them its vitality. It lay dwindled, all but its head, and motionless without even the energy to brush away a fly, which played about its swollen lips, the only movement being the slow roll of its pathetic-ally penetrating eyes. He saw, manifest in this wretched child, the dying personification of all the diseases about which he had been reading.

Mrs. Dymark started to talk about Mr. Gender's suicide and Miss Jeacock's disappearance, having heard about the tragedies at the Office through the gossiping of shop assistants and the less discreet members of the Office staff. O'Flattery forced himself to look away from the baby and

285

to look into Mrs. Dymark's deep-set brown eyes where, instead of the kindness and concern which was clear to see, he saw only suspicion and mistrust. The more she enlarged upon her theories the more frantic the young man became, until this time it was he who fled from her as if she were Mrs. Macklin herself, leaving his startled interlocutor, with her deformed grandchild, puzzled and hurt by his apparent unfriendly reception of her sympathy.

That night his sleep was even more disturbed than usual. Time and again he wandered off into semi-consciousness, only to be woken each time by his own sobs. Finally, he fell into a deep trance, out of which only minutes afterwards he emerged with a terrible shriek, waking his fellow-lodgers, who turned in their beds humping the bedclothes about their ears. He switched on his bedside lamp and as he did so, out of the darkness there instantly flew a fly which made straight for the cone of light inside the lampshade. Round and round it flew, the noise it made being amplified by the confined space. Out it came for a wild dash round the room, then back again as if mesmerised by the light and resolved to destroy itself. O'Flattery determined to be free of it snatched up an open book and trapped it in the hot prison of the shade. The buzzing reached a crescendo and just as the Irishman, after a prolonged pause, thought he was rid of his tormentor it escaped from a crack between his thumb and the fold of the book. Its size in the restricted light was over-emphasised by the red halo shining through the flesh of O'Flattery's thumb and he dropped the book as if a monster was issuing forth from hell.

He lay now soaked in sweat and shivering with terror, face to face with thoughts of self-destruction. Cold-bloodedly he began to go over a catalogue of ways to end it all. Characteristically, even on the brink of this irrevocable step, he still retained his usual concern for the

286

feelings of others. This concern being the final factor which prevented him from destroying himself.

He could jump out of the window—but was his room high enough up the building for the jump to be fatal? Would he not, most likely, have to face a future made more hideous by a broken body or an even more twisted mind?

He could hang himself from one of the beams which crossed the attic ceiling of his room—but what a dreadful discovery for poor Mrs. Dymark to make. How could he inflict the sight of his swollen purple face and his limp stained body upon such a fundamentally homely little woman?

He could buy a revolver and shoot himself—but what an even more hideous discovery for whoever entered his blood-and-brain-bespattered room. Or if he did it at the Office, who there would make the terrible discovery?

He could drown himself—often during his life, when feeling more than usually morbid, he had planned a contrived, and what seemed painless, way of making away with himself. He would take out a boat and after rowing well out of sight of land would slip over the side, having first taken an overdose of sleeping pills so that his struggle against the water would be brief and final. He *could* take the sleeping pills in his bed or curled up in some secret place like a tramp in the country, but he hoped that by this complicated method there would be no sordid discovery of his body. In the next instant he saw his body washed up with the flotsam and jetsam which always fascinated him so much.

He could make no decision. He was afraid of death, more terrified of the unknown than by the horror of the life he was already facing. Complete physical exhaustion was his only release and it was only when this overcame him that his mind was able to snatch a brief respite from its torments.

The poor Irishman fared little better at the Office. There he was constantly reminded of both Miss Jeacock and Mr. Gender, and always under the sentinel eye of Mrs. Macklin.

Life had become completely sullied for him, a soiled farce without hope, without love, void of any gentleness or peace . . .

He was obsessed by the constant reappearance of one particular fly among the many which seemed to haunt him. It was a large blue-bottle, dusted with what looked like white powder. He could never get near enough to decide what it was, whether it had flown among some flour in a kitchen or at a bakery or whether it was afflicted with some kind of mildew and the disease-bearer was itself diseased. He found that the watching eyes of Mrs. Macklin, Mrs. Dymark and the flies hedged him round in a narrower and narrower area. His life was becoming as constricted as a coffin and the harder he struggled the more entombed he became. He was like a man in a bog, the more he floundered the deeper he sank. Mrs. Macklin, as blind to circumstances as a hibernating tortoise, drove on relentlessly.

His nights became worse and worse, until finally he no longer slept at all but lay cowering, his head protected in his hands as if warding off an expected blow. Pictures of such horror moved before his eyes, a constant reminder of those things he struggled to forget. Sometimes, in ghastly slow motion, then rushing with absurdly exaggerated speed, only to stop in *tableaux vivants* advancing nearer and nearer in gigantic close-up, engulfing him in a tide of panic.

His persecution mania was becoming acute. Everywhere he went he was being watched, in his lodgings, at the Office. Nor was he safe out-of-doors. The crowds he tried to lose himself in constantly threw up replicas of the gypsy, Edna, Roy, all seeming to look at him as if they were at that moment going to betray him, shouting some dreadful secret for all to hear. He would catch the eye of one of these phantoms and immediately they turned, whispering to their next door neighbour, pointing, half smiling, working out in mime his destruction.

But it was at the Office where it became intolerable. In the corridors he saw Mr. Gender or Miss Jeacock at every dark turn. He heard their voices murmuring, now a stifled, scarcely audible susurration, now gathering power until he was amazed that no one remarked upon the noise. Sometimes the buzzing of the fly merged into imagined conversations between his dead colleagues. He would hear them discussing their work, to begin with, then the tone of their voices would change and become distorted, as did the content of their conversation, until they were shrieking the kind of obscenities at one another which he would expect only from Edna. Then if he turned round to look for them, their voices ceased for a brief moment only to continue again as soon as he tried to concentrate on whatever it was he was trying to do. Wherever he fixed his eyes for any length of time flies seemed to appear. Oozing from the corners of windows in a dark trickle, seeping under doors, blackening the corners of ceilings, sizzling quietly, massing as if for attack. Constantly his hands were raised, beating off real or imaginary flies from his face.

On the morning of Detective Inspector Litover's visit the voices, and what they were saying, had become insupportable. He fled from his room, trying to escape but taking the voices with him. Everywhere he hid they became louder. The privacy of the cloakroom was already denied him, as it was here that the presence of Miss Jeacock completely overcame him, and where the obsessional flies were at their worst.

If he visited the lavatory to excrete he now dared not look behind him as he got up, for he knew what he would

289

see, not the faeces which one would expect, but a terrible bloody discharge of slithering flies, glutinously heaving up the sides of the bowl, the visual and certain evidence of the misgivings which hounded him that he was infected, and that his inside was thoroughly destroyed, by the depradations of a typhoid bacillary septicaemia.

He could find no resting place from his imaginary pursuers or the all too evident caretaker, whose mysterious parley with the obvious policeman sent his reason toppling.

His days at the Office could no longer be faced. Mrs. Macklin had become—diabolical.

It was ironic that it was she who should be the one to find her intended in the broom cupboard, where he had gone to earth at last, crouched in the attitude of a self-abusing monkey. He was pressed back into the depths of the cupboard, his bright eyes dulled, his once errant hair lank and dusted over with a film of cobwebs. His breath pumped out of his diminished body in urgent stricken sobs, unintelligible cries of anguish which kept time with the puppet movement of his hands. The persistent fly was there too, circling the spots on the Irishman's trousers.

Mr. Gender's death and the mystery of the disappearing body had been too much strain for O'Flattery. The conflict between his bewilderment and Mrs. Macklin's devilish purpose was at an end.

His exit from the stage was almost as complete as that of Miss Jeacock and Mr. Gender, his fellow mummers in this drama.

The martyrdom of the last weeks had finally unbalanced his reason. With the departure of Miss Jeacock from the scene, Clytemnestra Macklin may have thought that she was to wear the diadem of success. It was to be a crown of thorns. She had driven too hard and too fast. Not for her the sweets of mutually shared passion. Far from it. Bitter were to be the fruits of her reward. Asylum visits were all she could now look forward to. O'Flattery had gone over the edge into another world. He now inhabited the lonely continent of the insane. He had taken the vertiginous leap towards which his latent schizophrenia had always beckoned him.

As Mrs. Macklin staggered back from what she saw, the disturbed fly left its quarry and flew out of the cupboard. Its mission completed it left the Office, in search of new lives upon which to spy.